HI STRUNG

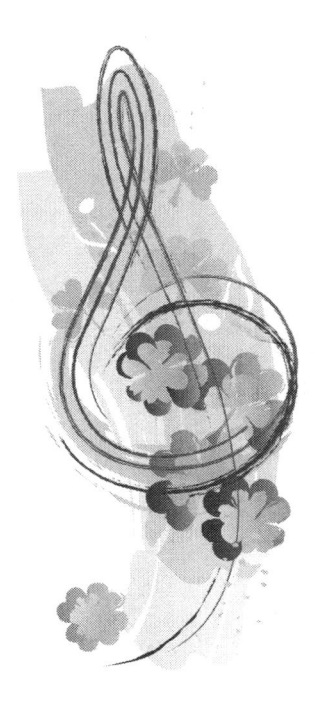

T GEPHART

HIGH STRUNG
Copyright 2014 T Gephart

ISBN-10: 0992518814
ISBN-13: 978-0-9925188-1-3

Discover other titles by T Gephart at Smashwords, or on Facebook, Twitter, Goodreads, or tgephart.com

This book is licensed for your personal enjoyment only. This book may not be re-sold or given away to other people. If you would like to share this book with another person, please purchase an additional copy for each recipient. If you're reading this book and did not purchase it or it was not purchased for your use only, then please return and purchase your own copy. Thank you for respecting the hard work of this author.

This book is a work of fiction. The names, characters, places and scenarios are products of the writer's imagination or have been used fictitiously and are not to be construed as real. Any resemblance to persons, living or dead, actual events, locales or organizations is entirely coincidental.

Edited by Marion Archer
Front Cover by Gianni Renda
Cover Image by Angelique Ehlers
Back Cover by Hang Lee
Formatted by Max Henry of Max Effect

To anyone
who has dared to dream
and been brave enough
to step out into the unknown.

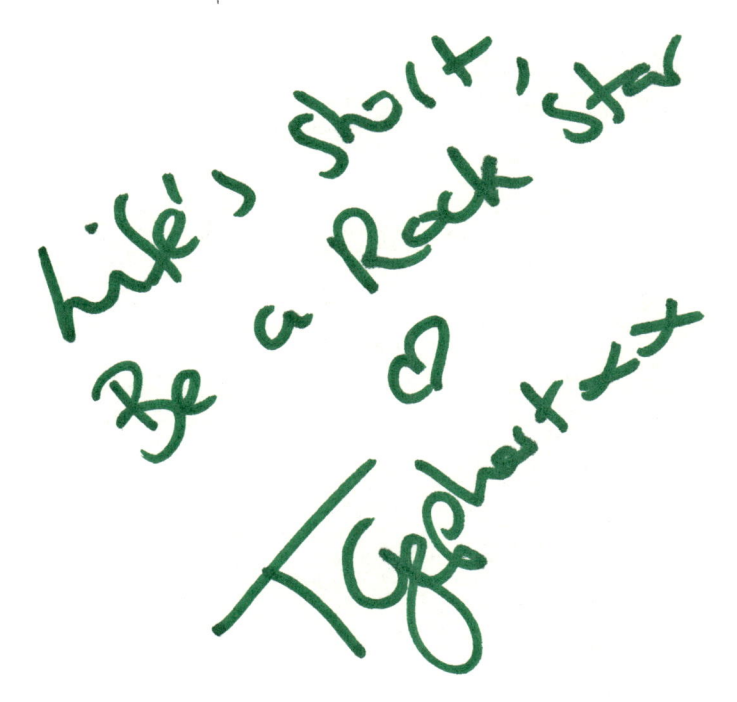

*Life's short,
Be a Rock Star
❤
Tephot xx*

1
Ashlyn

I FELT BEADS OF SWEAT STARTING TO FORM ON THE BACK OF MY neck as my fingers drummed restlessly on the arms of the chair. I needed this job in the worst way and I didn't think I could cope with another rejection. Despite being ridiculously overqualified for the position, I would do anything to get out of the hospitality industry. Sure, it was something I was good at, having parents that owned a small Irish pub meant I grew up in a bar, and being able to pull a perfect draft was a skill that provided no trouble landing a job back in the industry. However, I was getting really sick of being called "sweetheart" and if one more jerk grabbed my ass while I served him his beer, I was seriously going to lose it.

This had not been my dream when I moved to New York five years ago—making minimum wage and living in a shitty, cubby-hole apartment I was sure violated every safety code known to man. Still, it beat living on the streets, which is where I would find myself if I didn't start earning more than I was now. Of course, I hadn't always been so desperate. I couldn't believe my luck when I had landed an entry-level associate's role at a small brokerage firm straight out of college. I had stepped off the greyhound bus like a cliché in an '80's hair band video, leaving my nervous, conservative parents and six siblings back in Boston. I should have known it was too good to be true. Three years later, just as I was about to make the progression to junior broker, the company—like so many others—went bankrupt and closed its door. I found myself out of work and out of luck.

There weren't many opportunities for a commerce major during a global financial crisis. Any jobs there had been were snapped up by seasoned veterans, which is why I'd had no choice but to take a job at Garro's, a sports bar on the Lower East Side. My previous bar knowledge had made it a safe and familiar choice even if the money wasn't great. At least it was only a short commute from my Brooklyn apartment and it meant I had at least one hot meal a day.

I looked nervously at my watch. Two o'clock. Shit. I still had another thirty minutes to wait before my appointment, and my bravado had already started to wane. Desperation was a horrible thing, because I knew either way this whole experience was going to suck. If I got the job, I was going to hate it, as it would no doubt be mind-numbingly dull, and if I didn't, I should pack up my shit and reserve my park bench in Central Park. I was out of options and out of time. I took a deep breath as I tried to harness the nervous energy buzzing through my body. Rock stars. This is what it had come to.

The job I was so desperately vying for was personal assistant to Lexi Reed, the head of Reed Public Relations. She held the account for a massive local rock band, Power Station. I was not a fan. Of the band I mean. The five-piece New York natives were gritty and raw with their sound featuring torturous guitar riffs with an unrelenting rhythm section. It was in-your-face loud. Obnoxious. Sure they were blessed with good looks. Okay, each one of them was insanely handsome but that still didn't mean I would throw myself shamelessly at any of them and lose my self-respect. I never understood the allure of a rock band or why women with so much going for them would lower themselves to being

HIGH STRUNG

groupies.

Ms. Reed, on the other hand was, by all accounts, a fierce businesswoman. An import from the land Down Under, she had a reputation for being a hard-ass with an amazing sense of style, and a respected determination that led to her playing with the big dogs in the industry. Despite me loathing the assistant position I was hoping to land, I did have an amazing amount of respect for her. She not only held Power Station's PR account, which was huge, but she was also successfully building her own company by bringing in lots of new business. Smart move. The growth projections in the industry were huge if she could land the right clients - a statistic I was hoping to wow her with when I finally got into the interview. It wasn't my style to go in unprepared and my late night research had been fruitful.

"Ms. Murphy?" A slender and attractive blonde with a strong English accent approached me.

"Yes. Ashlyn." I stood up and offered her my hand hoping it wasn't too clammy.

"Ashlyn, I'm Sydney. I'm Ms. Reed's current assistant." Her bright blue eyes sparkled as she accepted my hand graciously. "Lexi is just finishing up with another interview and then you are up next. Is there anything I can get you while you wait?"

"No, I'm fine, thank you." I was relieved the wait was almost over.

Sydney nodded and disappeared back through the doorway from which she had emerged, her cute bob haircut bouncing with each step.

I sank back down into my seat, rubbing my palms nervously against the fabric of my skirt. I hated job interviews. They were the intellectual version of a beauty pageant. Here are my qualifications. Smile. Judge me. Smile. I hope I'm good enough. It was enough to make me want to vomit. My stomach churned in solidarity with my train of thought.

The previous candidate stepped out from Ms. Reed's office and into the reception area, signaling the end of her appointed interview. She used her sly glance and cocky grin, I assumed, to unnerve me further. So that's how we're going to play? I'm one of seven children, honey. I am the master of the mental psyche-out.

I stood, in preparation for my turn, when I felt a shadow cast over me blocking out the midday sun. It was just my luck to finally get an interview with a halfway decent job and some crazy-ass Armageddon took over New York. I slowly turned—might as well get a good view of whatever fate was about to befall me—and I almost smacked directly into Alex Stone.

crickets

Alex Stone was the lead guitarist of the band, Power Station, and while I had not been a fan of the band, I was definitely an appreciator of this fine specimen in front of me. Standing six four, with an amazingly toned body, ice-blue eyes, and magnificent blond hair, he had been engineered to be a sex symbol. Rivaling Michelangelo's David, he was chiseled to perfection. The fact I didn't care for his music did not detract from my fascination. In fact he could probably give up his music career, stand in the Met Museum and allow us mortals to glare longingly at him all day. What? Living art is a legitimate gig.

"Hello," Alex purred, dazzling me with his amazing devilish grin. "Are you waiting to see Lexi?"

Of course I knew Lexi Reed was not only the band's publicist but also married to the guitarist, aka the guy in front of me, but man, Lexi was like Barbie. The bitch had everything.

I blinked, allowing my eyes to float down his sexy muscular chest and noticed he had a Baby Bjorn carrier with a sleeping infant inside strapped across it, hindering my view. I think my ovaries just exploded. It was too much. Because when Alex wasn't sending the panty-wearing population into overdrive by being a rock god, he was a new dad to his baby daughter, Grace. I mean, seriously, how could a woman not swoon over that deadly combination?

"Um," I mumbled like a moron, all my years of education flashing before my eyes, unable to make my mouth function. He was talking to me?

"I'm just going to need a moment of her time, mind if I step in ahead of you?" His smooth voice curled around every word, making love to it.

I nodded wordlessly, feeling compelled to continue the moronic theme I had running. It was better than throwing myself at his feet and worshiping him, a very real danger the longer he stood there. He was more than just good-looking, he was obscenely attractive, and I had this unbelievable urge to lick him, slowly, like a cat.

Taking my wide-eyed, enthusiastic nod as a yes and seeing he wasn't going to get anything more intelligible out of me, Alex strode into Lexi Reed's office. I watched as his ridiculously hot body disappeared through the doorway, my eyes straining to catch the last glimpse of his incredibly toned ass before it slipped from view.

"He's married and a douchebag," an uninvited voice said, pulling me from my happy place.

"Huh?" I twisted around, ready to disembowel the owner of said voice for ruining my Alex Stone fantasy.

"He," the owner of the voice pointed to the door Alex had just walked through, "Is. A. Douchebag." He enunciated slowly before continuing, "Alex. Is. Also. Mar-ried." He paused before each syllable for effect.

Standing in front of me, marring my memory of Alex, was the owner of the voice – an annoying man. Shorter than Alex, at what I assumed to be roughly six foot, he eyed me with more interest than I was comfortable with. He had a mess of dark hair, smoldering dark brown eyes, and was covered in tattoos, the evidence poking out from the sleeves of his T-shirt. Next to the word badass in the dictionary, I'm sure there was a picture of this guy. Dressed in torn, dark blue jeans, and a Misfits T-shirt, he was the epitome of a rock star, without the finesse Alex possessed. Despite his unkempt look he was strangely sexy, although his smug smile made me want to add ripping out his tongue to the disembowelment I already had planned.

"I heard what you said," I snapped. "There is nothing wrong with my hearing. I just don't know why you cared to volunteer that information." Despite his good looks, I think if either of those two men was a douchebag it would be the one who was still talking to me.

"Oh cool, you talk." He laughed. "I just wasn't sure if you were just a star-struck fan or you had a disability. I was trying to be polite." He moved closer, stretching out his hand. "I'm Dan. Dan Evans."

"I'm not a star-struck anything. And I don't have a disability. I don't know what you are talking about." I purposely rejected his handshake and instead adjusted my jacket, annoyed he had assumed I was just another one of *those* girls. Who was this guy anyway? Judging by his appearance, I guessed him to be another member of the band, possibly the drummer? He probably needed to compensate about not getting enough attention being holed up behind a drum kit.

"Look, it's fine, babe. We're used to it. Girls get crazy over us all the time. You don't need to be embarrassed." He pulled back his hand and shrugged, seemingly unfazed by my lack of civility.

"I'm not embarrassed. And I'm not your babe. Whatever you think you saw, you were mistaken. I don't get crazy." I was slightly embarrassed, but more irritated I'd been caught staring...*and* called on it.

"Sure. Okay. You don't want to admit it, that's fine but I know what I saw, and you were throwing so much heat in Stone's direction I'm surprised the paint didn't peel off the wall." He pulled out a stick of gum and popped it into his mouth, thoroughly enjoying the fact I was irate. Clearly not a gentleman.

"Oh my god. I was not throwing heat. Are you insane?" I hissed, my embarrassment manifested into full-blown anger as I tried my best to save face. No matter how gorgeous this man in front of me was, I was not going to let him get the better of me.

"You can keep denying it all you like, babe. Makes no difference to me. I just thought I'd be charitable and point out it's a waste of your time." He chewed on his gum, smirking. "You have a better chance of the Cleveland Indians winning a World Series than Stone sleeping around. Now me on the other hand, I don't have those kinds of restrictions."

My face flushed with anger, as I officially wanted to kill him. Yet stupidly, I couldn't deny how attractive he was as he smugly stood in front of me, his broad chest filling the material of the tee that did little to hide the toned flesh that lay beneath. What the hell was wrong with me? He was rude, arrogant and probably teeming with every STD known to man, and he'd called me babe... twice. I was not going there.

"Did you take some kind of class to learn how to be so offensive or is this a natural ability?" I leaned forward, refusing to allow him the pleasure of knowing he was getting under my skin.

"How did I offend you? I have been nothing but polite. I haven't even looked at your tits." Dan stared at me bewildered, actually confused.

"Wow. My *tits* and the rest of me thank you for your lack of interest." I gave him my best death stare, disappointed I didn't have some mutant ability that would render him incapacitated. I blamed my pre-teen fixation with comic books for giving me such unrealistic expectations.

"Don't mention it. They are a little on the small side, it makes things easier." He shrugged, talking about my breast size like it was no big deal. The edges of his mouth curved as his eyes dipped down to gaze at my aforementioned *tits,* which were thankfully contained by my conservative business shirt.

"Really? You're not even going to hide the fact you are now staring at my breasts?"

"Well now we are talking about them, I kinda can't help myself." He grinned, not even having the decency to be remorseful. "You know, now that I've looked at them, they don't seem so bad. You should maybe pop a button or two though, work with what you got."

"Dan!" Ms. Reed fired from the now opened doorway startling me from my seething rage. Alex Stone, aka sex god, was standing beside her, looking somewhat amused.

"Don't harass my candidates." Lexi turned to Alex, gently touching his arm. "Can you please remove him from my office? I'll call you later." She tenderly kissed the top of baby Grace's head and whispered a soft goodbye.

Alex nodded as he walked over to us. "My apologies for Dan, he has no impulse control." Alex gave me a blinding smile, grabbing Dan firmly around the arm. "Let's go."

"Don't apologize for me, numbnuts. We're just talking." Dan protested against Alex's grasp.

Lexi rolled her eyes at the commotion before addressing me. "Ashlyn, if you are ready I can see you now."

"Your name is Ashlyn? Unusual. It's pretty." Dan's eyes lit up with excitement at finally learning my name. Not that he'd asked, clearly he was too preoccupied with being an ass to worry about regular pleasantries.

"My life is a little more complete knowing you approve. Thanks for that. Have a wonderful day." I gave a forced smile as I pushed past him and strode purposely toward the open door of Lexi's office.

I needed to get my head in the game and flirty Dan was not aiding my cause. Instead I focused forward as I followed Lexi into her large and neatly maintained office, mentally evacuating thoughts of the tattooed, scruffy rock star I left in the foyer.

"I'm sorry about him. Dan really is a unique human being." Lexi gestured to the large plush chair opposite her desk. "Please, take a seat."

Lexi Reed was stunning; a petite brunette with feminine curves, she owned the fitted, bright green shift dress she was wearing. Finishing her look with an impressive black pair of heels and a fancy twisted up-do, her appearance had me feeling slightly underdressed in my Target-purchased jacket and skirt combo.

"He is harmless. Obnoxious, but harmless." I settled into the chair not willing to admit Dan Evans had unnerved me. After all, if I was going to be Lexi's assistant I was going to need to be able to handle the likes of Dan.

"Well, that is reassuring." Lexi smiled as she settled into her leather office chair. "So, Ashlyn. Tell me why someone has a commerce degree from University of Massachusetts, and who previously worked on Wall Street, wants to be an administrative assistant?"

I took a deep breath as I tried to determine the best way to rationalize my position. Damn. This was going to be a hard sell.

2. Dan

"DAN, DO YOU GO OUT OF YOUR WAY TO PISS OFF MY WIFE?" STONE chuckled as we walked back to the car.

"Dude, come on. You know she loves it, her day isn't complete until she has gotten her daily dose of Dan."

Lexi and I were cool; she knew the score as far as I was concerned. Granted our friendship had started with me trying to crawl into her panties; she's a solid ten. Who wouldn't try for that? But I totally respected she was now off the market and happily married to Stone. I never understood what the attraction was. Sure the man wasn't ugly but he got *way* more than his share of pussy. At some point when Lexi crossed our path, the two of them had started fucking and somehow managed to keep it from the rest of the band. I was absolutely appalled. If you're banging a girl like that, then it's your civic duty to share details with your brothers. Fuck, photos would have been better. Instead they kept that shit on the down low leaving us oblivious and not contributing any new material for my spank bank. Of course they eventually got it together enough to be a couple and did the whole walking down the aisle thing, and as much as I think marriage is for suckers, those two pretty much belong together. Not that I'm getting soft, 'cause Dan Evans does not get soft, but after the amount of shit those two have gone through, to see them happy with a kid was kind of fucking awesome. Oh and the kid, Grace, pretty much owned me. That little girl had me wrapped around her finger so tightly I'd move the world to please her. Between her and Noah, James and Han's little dude, I was happily playing Uncle to some of the coolest kids on the block. Not to mention the gaggle of nieces and nephews my sisters had given me. Being Uncle Dan was a pretty sweet gig.

"So what was up with the stare down with the redhead? Wasn't the whole reason you begged to come with us was so you could put the moves on Sydney, despite her telling you there was no chance?" Alex hit the keyless entry on his brand new, fully loaded Escalade. The bastard had caved and bought a family car, leaving his bitchin' Maserati parked in his garage whenever he had Grace in tow. I guess it could have been worse; at least the Escalade was still pimp. If he'd bought a Dodge Caravan then I'd have had to take him outside, kick his ass, and check his man card. I don't give a fuck he's got a kid, Power Station does not do minivans.

"Oh, Syd wants me. She's just being English." I watched as my former fellow skirt-hound loaded his daughter into the car seat. Man, times had changed. Back in the day the only time we were utilizing the back seat was to get lucky, now it was being used for its intended purpose. It was just all kinds of wrong.

"What do you mean she's being English? How is that even a thing?" Alex handed Grace her fluffy pink unicorn as he covered her with a baby blanket. I hoped my balls weren't going to suddenly shrivel up surrounded by all this pink.

"Really, Stone? Aren't you supposed to be smart? We totally told her

HIGH STRUNG

country to go fuck themselves, don't tell me the fact we're American isn't the reason she is blowing me off." I jumped into the passenger seat, no longer caring about why Sydney wasn't interested, as I tried to shake off the memory of the redhead who made my junk get tingly. Despite trying to keep her body under wraps in that lame-ass corporate get-up, there was no denying she was hot. She was rocking some killer curves. Granted she spoke way too much—I liked my girls with a different kind of mouth action—but other than that, I would totally be down with her playing naughty secretary.

"Dan, I seriously doubt the Declaration of Independence has anything to do with her disinterest in you." He slid into the driver's seat and hit the ignition.

"Don't kid yourself, Stone. Those bastards are still pissed. Anyway, her loss."

Sydney had been fun. Lexi had hooked up the date with her friend-assistant so I wouldn't have to brave a family wedding, stag. I knew she wasn't a hundred per cent cool with it, thinking I would be a total asswipe and try and hump her friend's leg or something, but I promised I'd keep my dick in my pants. Family celebrations when you are a thirty-three-year-old single dude were down right dangerous. Sure they accused me of acting like a teenager, but getting older didn't mean I had to change. It's who I was. They didn't care I was livin' large and didn't want to be saddled down with one girl. It was like talking to a fucking wall. So going solo into the lion's den with as many meddling aunts as I have would have been catastrophic. Fuck! They would have sent out the bat signal in the hopes of finding me a wife. Luckily with Syd on my arm, radiating professionalism and that cute English accent, they'd been appeased enough to stay off my ass. We both actually had a really good time, which was unexpected bonus. So when I took her home and she paused before stepping out of the car, I knew I had an in. She gave me this speech about it being one time and shit, and neither of us wanted anything more so what the hell. It had been good, real good, and I was all up for perhaps working her into a constant rotation but she hadn't been down with it. Giving me some bogus line about me being a bad investment. I didn't get it. Was I supposed to be showing her my investment portfolio? My 401K? I would have thought the only thing she would have been interested in was my ability to make her toes curl—which I did, no less than three times—not whether or not I had a retirement plan.

"Please tell me the redhead wasn't your attempt to make Sydney jealous? Lexi will have your balls if you're messing with her applicant pool." Stone continued to run his mouth as we pulled into Manhattan traffic. We weren't going anywhere, anytime soon. NYC in the afternoon was solid gridlock.

"Oh no, she was just some random groupie I was having fun with. Way too uptight but I thought I'd give her something to tell her friends about. You know me, always thinking about the fans." I omitted telling him she'd obviously had a thing for him. Despite the bastard being married and a walking advert for Babies-R-Us with all his diaper bags and shit, broads were still throwing themselves at him. I really needed to work on either him or James letting me borrow a kid for a few hours. Girls just seemed to eat that up

"She didn't look like a groupie. What she looked was a lot pissed off." He raised his eyebrow and gave me his usual cocky grin.

"Listen, brother, not to be an ass, but you're out of the game now so you don't know how it works. Trust me, I got this. Fifty bucks says as soon as she's done with her interview she is going to find the nearest bathroom and rub it out." I stretched out my legs hoping to ease some of the tightness in my crotch. Imagining Ashlyn scratching that itch had me thinking I was going to have to do the same. That tight little body, those fiery green eyes, those cute little freckles on the bridge of her nose. That's putting aside the fact I have a thing for redheads. It looked natural too; wonder if she had any hair down there? Yeah, a stroke was definitely on the cards.

Stone popped me in the arm, crashing through my triple-x fantasy just as it was starting to get good. "Dude, my daughter is in the car."

"She can't talk yet, so she has no idea what I'm saying." I turned around and checked on Grace who was oblivious to anything I was talking about. Her tired little eyes were fighting the rock of the Escalade that was bound to send her to sleep. Her lips curled into a precious little smile as her eyelids finally gave up the fight. "But if some piece of shit ever speaks to her that way, you need to call me and we're putting that asshole in the ground."

"Don't even go there, I'm already contemplating buying a gun." Stone gave me a sideways glance and I knew he wasn't kidding

"Fuck the gun, she looks like her mother. You're going to need a motherfucking arsenal, brother."

3
Ashlyn

TOO DEPRESSED TO GO BACK TO THE APARTMENT I WOULD PROBably be evicted from in the next few days, I took a bus to Megan's loft. Although we had only met about a year and a half ago, we had become incredibly tight in a remarkably short time. She was my best friend. We had both started working at Garro's around the same time, with me working behind the bar and Megan as a waitress. Her warm smile and easy personality were a welcome change from the cold world of the brokerage firm I had come from. The sports bar was meant to be a temporary job for both of us until we gained more meaningful employment.

Megan Winters had studied psychology at Georgetown and after completing her psych degree she had decided to take a year off before going into practice. She was a five-foot-four powerhouse with long blonde hair, bright turquoise eyes, and an obscene IQ. Her dad was a highly respected cardiothoracic surgeon and her mother a pediatrician, so it had been assumed she'd follow in their footsteps and go into the medical field. Megs had said that going into psychology was as rebellious as she dared to be. Her parents were both lovely people who, despite their high-geared careers, were supportive of their daughter slumming it for a year. In fact, they had encouraged her, as they considered it to be character building, and were proud they had raised a daughter who, despite her privileged life, wasn't afraid to get her hands dirty. My hiatus from the business sector hadn't been by choice. The forced redundancy and a slow economy sealed my fate. Eventually Megs's time at the bar came to an end and she was now a clinical psychologist at Mount Sinai while I, unfortunately, was still fending off drunkards and popping caps off pilsners.

"How did it go, Ash?" She welcomed me with a hug as I walked through her doorway. Her Greenwich Village pad, flooded by the midday sun, was as warm as her beautiful smile. Her surrounds reinforced she had money. It wasn't flaunted, but it stirred my desire to have nice things too.

"Terrible," I mumbled returning her hug. "Not only did I probably not get the job but I made a complete ass of myself in front of Power Station's drummer." I had officially hit a new low.

"You got to meet Troy Harris?" Megs's eyes opened wide with excitement. I must be the only person in the five boroughs who wasn't a fan. "Ash, he's all kinds of hot. Those hazel eyes, the Mohawk, that body. Wow, just wow."

"Hazel eyes? Mohawk? No, I met Dan Evans. Dark messy hair, dark brown eyes, bad attitude. Isn't he the drummer?" I collapsed onto her sofa not needing an invitation. The beautiful plush cushion that wrapped around me allowed my muscles to ease. Mismatched thought waves continued to turn in my head despite the meeting being over. While I really didn't want to relive my meeting with Dan, I needed to somehow expunge him from my mind and figured a debrief with Megs was the best way to do it.

"Ashlyn, seriously? Dan Evans is the bass player. I saw him at a nightclub once; he's really cute. Troy Harris is the drummer." The iPad that was never far from her grasp was commandeered for my education and thrust into my hands. The band was the background wallpaper. There he was, his smug sexy smile, taunting me from behind the glass.

"Well hopefully if there is a god, I will never see Dan again, so it doesn't matter which instrument he plays." I handed the iPad back to Megs and let my head fall back against the cushion of the sofa, closing my eyes in an effort to ward off the headache threatening to take up residence in my frontal lobe.

"Why? What happened?" The couch cushion beside me compressed as Megs obviously joined me on the two-seater.

"He caught me gawking at Alex Stone like I wanted to eat him." I cringed, squeezing my eyes tightly, stupidly believing that would shut out the embarrassment of my earlier activities.

"Alex Stone was there, too?" Megs's voice rose in excitement, taking my arm and shaking it vigorously.

"Yes, and he is every bit as impressive up close. I'm pretty sure my tongue was polishing the floor." I opened my eyes to Megs's beaming face.

"I just want you to know I hate you right now. It's not fair you got to meet Alex and Dan and you aren't even a fan." Megs folded her arms across her chest and pouted. "So...were they nice?"

"Trust me, I would have rather it had been you. No matter how cute Dan is, he is also an obnoxious pig." I can't believe I just called Dan Evans cute. Why couldn't I focus on the fact he was offensive rather than the fact he was attractive? When was the last time I had eaten? Maybe my blood sugar was low.

"Aw, you think Dan is cute?" Megs smiled, unfortunately not willing to let the tiny word that had unconsciously slipped from my mouth, go. "Wow. Your libido is still intact. I was sure it had taken a flight to Boca. When was the last time you went on a date?"

"There is nothing wrong with my libido. I'm just choosey about who I date. I don't see the point wasting time with someone who obviously doesn't have the potential for my long-term goal. I told you, I have criteria."

HIGH STRUNG

Sure, there had been guys that had caught my attention and I had dated sporadically in college, but I hadn't met anyone I'd really wanted to hold on to. I could count the number of guys I had slept with on one hand and still have a finger or two spare. It's not that I was saving myself or I had an aversion to sex, I just had found it a little underwhelming, usually having to take things into my own hands—literally—to climax.

"Ash, you know you are allowed to date just for fun right? You don't have to see every guy for his *long-term potential*. Maybe just go out and let your hair down. Screw your criteria."

"No. I refuse to be a woman who settles. I worked my ass off to get into a decent college, and even though things are tough right now, I'll eventually make it back onto Wall Street. I want to find a guy who's going be a good husband with a decent earning capacity. I'm not trying to sound conceited, but my parents have both been slaving away at that bar their whole lives. They'll be working till the day they die. I'm the first one of my family to go to college. I love them, but I don't want that life for me. If my future husband and I are smart, we can build up a sizeable nest egg and let our money work for us. I need someone who is disciplined and like-minded in order to do that."

"What about being in love, Ashlyn? It can't just be about money and security. Don't you want a guy who will give you butterflies? Someone who is more than just a financial partner but who will also love you back?" Megs was ever the romantic. Her ideas of love were twirled around a wonderful fantasy, tied with a fancy red bow, and while my heart craved it, it was luxury I would admire from a distance.

I winced, realizing how contrived it all sounded. "Well of course I have to like the guy, it's not like I'm going to marry someone I don't like. I'm not that shallow." *Is that how I came across?* Shallow? Conceited? Vocalized, the clinical plan for my future sounded so much worse than it was. I envied the freedom Megs had, to live without the fear of being broke. With that freedom, love stood a chance. How did the conversation turn from the interview from hell to my dating life?

"Okay. Here is what is going to happen." Megs's eyes gleamed with excitement. "The interview is done and we have no way of controlling the outcome. Right?"

"Sadly, you're right." I nodded. There was really nothing I could do. While I had answered Lexi Reed's questions competently, I could tell she wasn't convinced. She saw through my bullshit and knew it was a Hail-Mary move, an effort to reenter the corporate world in the hopes of getting something more suitable in the future.

"So why don't you take a night off from your grand plan and get crazy with me?"

"Um, no. My plans for this evening include being online, job hunting, while drowning my sorrow in three-cheese pie from Carmine's Pizzeria." The promise of cheesy goodness was guaranteed to make my night suck slightly less than my day had.

"Ashlyn, you can take one night off from being responsible. One night, come out with me. Get drunk. Act like a regular twenty-seven-year-old. Who knows, maybe find some totally inappropriate guy and make out with him on the dance floor." Megs lifted herself off the sofa; the conversation was far from over.

"Megs, you know that isn't me. Besides, I can't afford it and I have nothing to wear."

"So borrow something of mine. I have a whole closet full of clothes; pick anything you like. And it's my treat so you can't use money as an excuse."

"What do you think one night is going to achieve?" I couldn't see the point in her expedition, other than delaying the inevitable mind-numbing search through pages of dead-end employment opportunities. And possibly sparing myself an increase of calories that was probably going to land straight on my ass.

"Nothing. That's the whole point. Sometimes you don't need to achieve anything. You can just do it for fun. So come on. Be reckless, we can even pick up some pie on the way out. Angelo's is just as good as Carmine's." Megs wiggled her eyebrows enthusiastically.

I wanted to argue, to tell her no, but in all honestly, it was easier just

HIGH STRUNG

to give in. One night wasn't going to change anything and if it meant appeasing Megs and making her happy, then I could put off my pity party for twenty-four hours and hit it hard tomorrow. Besides I knew she wasn't going to let up until I agreed. She would probably blow up my phone until I eventually gave in, so I was probably just saving us both the time in between.

"Fine. I'll go," I conceded, raising my hands in defeat. "Tonight better not suck."

After a quick trip home to Brooklyn, I packed an overnight bag, ignored the final notice bills stuffed in my mailbox, and made my way back to the city. I had decided that while I was happy to raid Megs's wardrobe for our evening adventure, I wanted to get a few personal items to equip me to crash on Megs's sofa, rather than to try and navigate my way home later in the dark.

I had settled on a simple, fitted, little black dress that was way shorter than I was comfortable wearing, teamed with a pair of my own chunky black wedges. It was by far the most conservative outfit Megs had decreed acceptable, nixing most of my earlier choices. I made my peace with the fact I was going to be flashing a little more flesh than usual, applied some makeup, and left my long hair untethered to tumble down my back.

"You look great. Stop tugging at your hem," Megs whispered as we stepped out of the cab and onto the sidewalk.

I couldn't help it; the dress barely covered my ass and it had been a challenge not to flash anything as I navigated out of the cab.

"It's so short." I couldn't resist giving the dress one last tug as we made our way to the long line that stretched out in front of the doorway of *Panic*, the ironic name of the club Megs had taken us to.

"We are going to be out here forever. This line is so long." The girl in front of us complained. Her male counterpart simply shrugged and pushed his hands into his pockets. She was right; it was going to be a long wait.

"Let's see if there isn't a quicker way." I smiled, pulling Megs out of line and approached the giant who was guarding the entrance.

"You ladies on the list?" The large bouncer looked us over, his security number swinging from the chain around his thick neck.

"Sure," I smiled hoping we could wing it and get into the club sooner. While I wasn't thrilled about coming out in the first place, getting inside was going to be a hell of a lot more fun than standing outside on the street. Especially given the cheery disposition of our fellow waitees. Losing my nerve and hailing a cab was also another possibility the longer we stood outside.

"I'm Ash and this is Megs. We should be listed there somewhere," I bluffed, wondering if we got caught out whether he was going to make us go to the end of the line.

He consulted his clipboard before raising his eyebrow in question. "Ashley Brookes?"

"Yep. That's me and this is my plus one," I lied, silently hoping karma wasn't going to bite me on the ass and the real Ashley Brookes didn't arrive in the next five seconds.

"Says here your guest is supposed to be your husband, Keith Brookes."

"He's not feeling well tonight, so I decided to drag out my best friend instead. You know how men can be when they get the sniffles. I left him tucked up in bed." I smiled sweetly wondering where this new bravado had come from. I guess I had committed so it was best just to see it all the way through.

"Well okay then, show Mack your IDs on the way in. Have a nice night." He pointed to the other bouncer, sporting the number thirty-four, whose job it seemed was solely checking IDs. I guess there was a pecking order even with security guards.

Mack grunted as we held up our IDs for inspection, barely taking the time to check if they were authentic before waving us over to the line that required no payment of cover charge. Score.

"That was amazing, Ash. I can't believe we bypassed the line." Megs's face beamed with excitement as we walked into the belly of the club and were hit by a wall of flashing lights and deafening noise.

"So now what?" I screamed over the loud music pumping through the space. The wild strobes that were sweeping through the room seemed to have no sequence or rhythm.

"Drinks. Lots and lots of drinks. You, my friend, are going to have a good time tonight. Forget your grand plan, forget the interview, and forget everything else. For one night, you need to just *BE*," Megs screamed back, her voice barely audible over the thumping bass.

"Is that some new-aged therapy shit?" I laughed as we waded through the crowd toward the bar, feeling more comfortable taking my chances with the friendly bottles of alcohol rather than the dance floor.

"You don't need a therapist, Ash, you need to relax. Stop putting so much pressure on yourself." Megs put her arm around my shoulders and hugged me. She was right. One night wasn't going to kill me.

"I'm trying." I shrugged, wondering when was the last time I had honestly loosened the reins. While most kids had been partying through high school I had been studying my ass off for my SATs. When I hit college, I continued to keep my head down, not willing to throw away the opportunity to achieve my dreams for some keg beer and Sorority parties. Besides, when I wasn't studying I was helping out my parents, hiding out in the kitchen until I hit twenty-one, and then behind the bar.

"Well, try harder. We've been in this place for fifteen minutes and we haven't had our first drink yet." Megs squeezed her body close to mine. Her gorgeous face had started to bead with a thin sheen of perspiration.

"Okay, okay." We made our way to the bar in order to rectify the no-drink situation. Knowing how obnoxious it was when some jackass waved or hollered in your face, I waited until the bartender made his way over to our side of the bar before attempting to place our order.

"What can I get you?" The bartender leaned into us, grinning appreciatively at Megs's barely there dress. Out of the two of us she was the one who usually got the attention. She was not only extremely intelligent but she was also classically beautiful. Her blonde hair and blue-green eyes complemented her delicate features. Add to that her pint-sized figure, she was most men's dream girl. If she wasn't my best friend I would have had to hate her.

"I'll have a Long Island Iced Tea." Megs smiled, thankfully not ordering anything that required a cocktail umbrella and embarrassing us.

"And I'll have a Dirty Martini, but can you make it fifty-fifty Noilly Prat and Tanquary 10, lots of brine with three olives." I leaned over the bar in an effort to make myself heard.

"She'll have a Dirty Martini, make it how you want to make it." Megs waved me off. "You're not working tonight, remember? Let the man do his job. After a few of those suckers you aren't going to care how they are made."

"It's no problem, sweetheart. You're paying for it so I'll make it anyway you like." He smiled. I wasn't sure who *sweetheart* was directed at but either way I was happy to see he was making my drink as per my prescription.

"Thank you." I watched as he grabbed the liquor bottles off the shelves and started mixing the drinks. There was something poetic about watching the liquid spill from the measure pourer and into a Boston glass.

I tried not to stare as he shook my Martini, giving me a wink as he poured it into the chilled glass resting on the bar. He then turned his attention to building Megs's Long Island in the high ball in front of us, garnishing it with a lemon spiral. I had to hand it to him, he took pride in his craft.

"Keep them coming." Megs handed over her black Amex that he happily exchanged for a bar token.

"Megs, you don't really want to do that. Remember, I grew up in a bar." The delicious icy gin-vermouth sensation complemented by the saltiness of the brine exploded across my tongue as I took a sip.

"Yeah, I actually do. Last time you were drunk was New Years Eve when we were doing shots of Jose Cuervo in my apartment. I think you're due." Megs grinned, reminding me of the impromptu party we'd had after finishing our shift at Garro's. Having not being able to participate in the revelry until after the bar had closed, we'd made our way to her apartment and did shots of silver tequila until we both passed out. New Year's Day did not treat us kindly.

"Fine, it's your money." I took another sip from my glass.

Megs held her glass up with a mischievous grin. "I propose a toast. To great friends and great futures, and to wherever either of those takes us."

"And to the questionable decisions we're undoubtedly about to make," I added before clinking my glass against hers.

Megs shimmied with excitement, her grin splitting wildly across her face. "Now you're talking."

4
Dan

"I'M TELLING YOU, I THINK WE SHOULD HAVE SOME INPUT INTO who Lexi is hiring." I threw back the Jack and Coke the waitress delivered, wanting to get my buzz sooner than later.

This wasn't our usual hang out but I was in need of a change, bored with the same faces I'd been seeing at the other Manhattan clubs. The strobes flashed with an irregular cadence while the big-ass screens designed for our privacy shook under the thump of the bass. The gen pop part of the club was separated from us by a bunch of drapes and out-of-work linebackers.

I'd dragged Jase and Troy along for the ride with neither of them giving me much resistance. It's not like either of them had plans, and with Jase having recently broken up with his off-on, long-distance girl, Erin, I decided it was time to go on the prowl, and for me and my brothers to enjoy being single in the greatest city on earth.

HIGH STRUNG

"Why the fuck do you care who she hires? This isn't the whole Sydney thing again, is it?" Troy stood and grabbed the two beers off her tray and handed one to Jason.

"Thanks, Beth. Give us twenty and then bring another round." He slid a fifty onto her tray giving her the all clear to leave. She gave him a pretty smile before she turned to walk away. He didn't even look at her ass as he sat back down on the couch. Troy had always been so fucking smooth; why he wasn't banging a different broad every night still perplexed me.

"No, it's got nothing to with her." I put my tumbler onto the table in front of us. "Fuck, you boys gossip more than a bunch of old ladies. Who even told you about her and me?" Syd and I had only happened one time but everyone seemed to know about it. I assumed she must have talked; after all, it had probably been a while since anyone had made her come like I had. I wore the scratches she tore into my back for a fucking week. Who knew she was that wild in the sack.

"You did, numbnuts." Jason laughed, bumping my shoulder with his fist.

"Okay, so maybe I did. Who remembers?" I couldn't recall spilling but honestly it was months ago, it's probably for the best, I didn't like hiding shit from my brothers. "Anyway, it's got nothing to do with Sydney. Shit wouldn't have worked out with us. She's *English*."

"You make it sound like she has an extra head or something." Troy laughed as he nursed his beer. He and Jase hated clubs, preferring shit-hole bars with pool tables, dartboards, and draft beer. He didn't bitch about it though, which was cool, proving what a team player he was by tagging along.

"Not you, too. I explained it to Stone this morning." I failed to understand why this concept was so fucking hard. Didn't we all study this shit in school? No wonder there is an outcry over the state of the education system.

"Is this the Declaration of Independence thing or the zee versus zed thing?" Troy piped in giving me faith the bastard had been paying attention.

"It's the Declaration thing but seriously, who even says zed?" I shrugged.

"You do realize the language we speak is *English* so *they* are probably right," Jason added smugly, the fucker probably thinking that because he had a college degree he knew better.

"Screw zed. As far as I'm concerned, that fancy piece of paper our forefathers signed means *I* get to say zee." How this was even up for discussion was beyond me, Ben Franklin would be turning in his grave with this completely unpatriotic banter.

Troy placed his longneck on the table, stretching his hands behind his head. "I'm sure that's exactly what old Thomas Jefferson was thinking when he dipped his quill in ink."

"I assure you, Tom J would have definitely been a zee man." I'd have put my nuts on it.

"How did we get from talking about Lexi's new assistant to Thomas Jefferson?" Jason grinned as he took another swig of his beer.

"Who knows, but I now could totally go a Philly Cheese Steak." Troy laughed, scooping his beer back off the table and taking a mouthful.

Jason leaned back into the couch. "So, Dan…enlighten us as to why you are so passionate about this cause."

"I was just thinking, seeing as whoever it is will be working with us, we should probably get a say. Technically we're like the boss, aren't we?" I scratched my head wondering why I hadn't thought of it before.

Troy's face lit up with a big shit-eating grin. "Wow, can you please call Lexi and tell her we're the boss, that shit would make my week." Bastard knew there was no way I'd call Lexi and poke the bear. I'd rather keep my balls attached, thanks.

"Whatever, nutsack." I gave him a friendly punch in the arm. "I was there this morning while Lexi was interviewing and I saw some potential." I couldn't help but think of the smokin' redhead I'd caught staring at Stone's ass.

"So who's the girl?" Jason chimed in, guessing correctly it had been a

HIGH STRUNG

skirt that had got me interested.

"Here's the thing, she was totally into me. She didn't say she was but I could tell. You know when you can just tell?" I figured maybe if we did a recap I could work out what got her panties in a twist. All I had done was point out Alex was off the market, why she got all ate up was still a fucking mystery.

"So she shot you down, huh?" Troy cupped my neck, giving me a shake.

I shrugged him off not wanting his fucking sympathy. "She said I offended her."

"Go figure." Jason laughed, the wiseass not adding anything helpful to the conversation.

"I was just being myself but she got all defensive." I pushed my hands through my hair, honestly confused as to why she had been so pissed.

"Was this before or after you opened your mouth?" Jason chimed in.

"Shut up, asshole. I was just introducing myself 'cause she seemed like a fan, but then we started talking about her tits," I tried to explain, replaying the conversation in my head, unable to stop my grin at the thought of Ashlyn.

"Only you can go from *hello* to *tits* in zero point three seconds." Troy chuckled like a fucking schoolgirl, getting all up in my grill. It's not like *they* didn't think about tits all the time. I was just more honest about it. Girls should be thanking me.

"I'm choosing to ignore you right now 'cause you're shitting on my parade." I pushed my palm into Troy's face and shoved him out of the way. "She had some bullshit business shirt and jacket on, but hiding underneath there were these amazing perky tits. Now, you guys know I generally like porn-star big but seriously, all I could think about was licking them. I'm getting hard just thinking about it."

"So did *tits* have a name? Or did you scream out your own when you jerked off." Troy knew full well that an image like that would have sent even the strongest man to go have a stroke. I don't know why anyone fights the urge to masturbate; it's in our nature.

"Yeah, her name is Ashlyn." Just saying her name sent a shiver down the length of my cock, and I may or may not have screamed it out when I jacked off into my hand earlier. Granted it would sound even hotter if I was calling it out while I was balls deep inside her, but that was a whole other story.

"I need to get her out of my head or I'm going to need to jerk off again." I shifted in my seat as my pants started to get tight around my crotch, just thinking about her was giving me a wicked hard-on. "I'm going to go check out the talent. There are a couple of girls over in the corner who look keen."

"Maybe give them a few minutes before you talk about their tits." Troy snorted as he grabbed his beer off the table and took a swig.

I flipped him off as I walked over to the two gorgeous brunettes who were giggling nervously in the corner. While they might have been working the shy vibe, I was willing to bet there were a few Trojans tucked away in their tiny purses.

"Hi, are you Dan Evans?" The shorter one bit her cherry-red lip seductively, flicking her long hair over her shoulder.

"Sure am, sweetheart, and what would your name be?" I moved in closer, tilting my head to the side as I took them both in. They looked so similar they could be sisters, dark brown hair with large brown eyes. They looked like they'd had been poured into the tight, tiny dresses they were wearing, not that I was complaining. Both of them were sporting rather impressive racks.

"I'm Lili and this my friend Skyla." She nodded to the cutie on her right. "I thought it was you but was too nervous to come over. Is that the rest of the band?"

"You don't have to be shy, I don't bite. Well, not unless you want me to." I couldn't help but smile. It wouldn't be the first time a girl liked it rough and I would be happy to play it either way. "James and Alex aren't here but those two losers over there are Jason and Troy."

"Wow, we've never met famous people before." Skyla stepped

HIGH STRUNG

toward me, her pouty red mouth looked primed for a monumental blowjob.

"We're just regular folks, babe." I brushed some hair away from Skyla's face as Lili slid up beside me. "You wanna come over and say hello?"

"Yes," they chimed out enthusiastically in stereo. I was definitely getting lucky tonight and these two lovely ladies seemed more than willing to get onboard. Even if I struck out with one, I had the other ready to go. Like a boy scout, I was prepared.

I wrapped my arms around both of their waists, letting my hands drop down to skirt the top of their asses, and pulled them in close to my side. While I was happy to do intros, I wasn't planning on sharing. The other two would have to find their own tail tonight.

We walked over to where the douchebags were sitting; Troy was busy running his mouth about some bullshit while Jason deep-throated a beer.

"Ladies, meet Troy and Jason. While I can confirm I've had all my shots, I make no promises on these two."

"Ladies," Troy tipped his chin hello, standing up to offer them the couch, no doubt hoping to get lucky with whichever one I struck out with.

"Hi, girls," offered Jason, sizing them up as he drained the last of his beer. Both of them were sadly mistaken if they thought they were going to get in on this action.

The girls both giggled nervously and introduced themselves, hugging each of the boys before returning to my side - as it should be. I pulled them onto the couch that Troy had vacated. My ass had barely made contact with the chair when Lili forgot all about her shyness and slid her hand up my thigh, her long red nails squeezing as they neared my balls. My grin widened as I leaned back into the couch spreading my arms across the back of the chair and inviting more. If this fine piece of ass wanted to jerk me off with an audience, I wasn't about to stop her.

"Hey, I saw him first," protested Skyla as she grabbed my chin and whipped my head around to face her. "I'm a *big* fan," she breathed into my mouth. "I know you probably hear that all the time but I want the opportunity to show you."

"Relax, ladies, there is plenty of me to go around and it would be very rude of me to not show my appreciation for such huge fans." I tilted her chin and brought her lips closer to me. My cock jerked assuring me, in case there was any doubt that we were on the same page.

"You think you can handle us both?" Lili's lips hit the skin on my neck as her hand moved from my thigh to my crotch, making me slightly nervous as she squeezed the denim separating her fingers from my cock. "'Cause there is no way I'm going to let Skyla have all the fun without me."

If I wasn't hard before, that situation had well and truly rectified itself as my dick struggled not to be choked out by my jeans. "Babe, no one is missing out tonight." I moved from Skyla's mouth to Lili's, proving I wasn't about to let anyone feel like the consolation prize.

As the girls moved around me, taking turns with my mouth, I shot a glance over to Troy who rolled his eyes and shook his head. "Dude, do what you want, but if it hits the papers tomorrow, it's going to be a shit storm I want no part of. Keep it clean or find a room."

Jason nodded, siding with Captain Fucking Lame. "Take it to the bathroom at least, brother."

I didn't bother to answer, instead flipping them off as I continued the tongue action I had going on. Assholes were just jealous I had scored both of the hot girls while they were left with their dicks in their hands. Besides, if I wasn't seeing Ashlyn anytime soon, I needed something to tide me over. Jerking off wasn't exactly what my dick was after.

"Wanna grab another beer?" Jason pointed to the vacant couch on the other side of the VIP section, "I'll meet you over there."

"Yeah, I'm going to take a lap first. I'm getting bored." Troy shrugged as both of them walked off in different directions.

"Did we make your friends mad?" Skyla blinked as she ran her hands underneath my shirt, her nails against my skin making me shiver.

"They're just jealous, babe, pay them no mind." I wasn't about to have the fun police cockblock me, it had been a while since I'd last had a threesome.

"Good," Lili licked her lips, "because Skyla and I are about to blow your mind."

5
Ashlyn

THE ROWS OF LIQUOR BOTTLES CAUGHT THE LIGHT, SHINING DOWN on us like twinkling stars. It contrasted nicely with the dark red walls of the club. We had managed to secure two unoccupied bar stools and perched ourselves at the bar. This meant two things: the drinks were readily refreshed and replenished, and we didn't realize how much we'd drunk until we stood up.

"I need to pee." Megs giggled, pulling gently on my arm. "We need to find the bathroom."

"Okay." I giggled back like she had delivered the world's greatest punch line. "There's bound to be one around here somewhere."

"If you head upstairs, the one up there is bound to have a shorter line," Kirk, the bartender we'd become rather fond of, helpfully offered.

"Thanks, Kirk. We love you." Megs blew him kisses as I pulled her from the stool.

"You need to walk, Megs. I can't carry you," I protested, trying to right her back onto her own two feet.

"I feel like I'm wearing stilts. How high are these stupid heels?"

HIGH STRUNG

Megs lifted her foot in amusement, inadvertently flashing her crotch to the group of guys in front of us. Thankfully she was wearing underwear, though that didn't stop the whistles of encouragement from our makeshift audience.

"Just walk slowly," I encouraged, our swaying bodies making little progress as we moved to the edge of the stairs.

"But I'm going to pee my pants." Megs laughed as we slowly navigated one stair at time. The click-clack of our heels against the wooden steps could still be heard above the music. At this rate there was going to be a puddle on the floor before we'd even made it halfway. "Take your shoes off until we get to the bathroom."

"Ew. I'm not walking in bare feet. It's a club, Ash, lord knows what's down there." Megs scrunched her face in disgust.

"Well then, walk faster or your pee is going to be added to the list of unidentifiable things *down there*."

While our ascent up the stairs was painfully slow, we did make it to the top without any incidents, be it falls or further indecent exposure. The sacrifice of footwear was also avoided, Megs unwilling to let herself be defeated by a pair of Loubutins, despite their height.

"Salvation." Megs pushed opened the door of the bathroom, sending us almost spilling onto the tile floor, the shiny, white-tiled floor and chromed surfaces, pristine, and thankfully, vacant. "Kirk was right, there is no line. Remind me to give him a big tip." She hurried into the stall.

I shuffled into the stall beside her, using the walls to steady myself before allowing myself to feel the sweet relief.

"Ash, I heard this story of this girl who was drinking all night and didn't pee and then died the next day. Lucky we made it to the bathroom," she shouted despite there being only a few inches of wall separating us.

"That's just some bullshit urban legend, Megs. You have to stop reading Internet spam," I shouted back, having trouble regulating my voice. I blamed the booze or perhaps the onsets of deafness, probably escalated by prolonged exposure to DJ madness from downstairs.

33

"Hey, if you get this job with Lexi Reed you need to introduce me to the band." Megs giggled through the wall as she hit the flush. "I want to make out with Troy Harris."

"I thought we weren't talking about it." I tried to stand and pull up my panties, the seemingly easy task almost beyond me. "And you aren't just going to make out with someone you don't know, even if he is famous."

"Why not?" We both exited at the same time, Megs pulling at the fitted, glittery scrap of material she was passing off as a dress. Her effort to cover more of her breasts almost exposed her ass. "We can be bad girls. Why can't *I* kiss some random guy? Even if I sleep with him, who cares? Everyone is so judgmental. I say, it's my vagina, if I see fit to give it away then it should be no one's business."

"Megs, when you are throwing out the word *vagina*, I would say you have had too much to drink." I laughed and adjusted her glittery scrap so while she was showing a little more cleavage, the rest of the club wouldn't get a free *up-skirt* on our way out of the bathroom.

"Vagina, vagina, vagina," Megs gleefully sang as we washed our hands, her inhibitions long gone.

"You have issues, you know that?" I threw paper towels in Megs's direction, which she tried to deflect with uncoordinated karate-style moves.

"I wonder if there is a bar up here? I am not liking the idea of going down any stairs right now." I pushed open the door and we exited the bathroom, returning to the light and sound of the club. Had it gotten louder? Or had our bathroom visit just given us a reprieve?

"Surely there's a bar up here, the VIP section is down that hall. You should use your super powers to sneak us in there. I bet they have free snacks, those slices from Angelo's were hours ago."

"Yes. We should go to the VIP section." I raised my hands in agreement forgetting that it inadvertently raised my already too-short dress higher. "You're a genius."

"I'm a doctor, all that schooling has to count for something." Megs held onto my arm as we pushed through the throng of people assembled near the VIP area.

"Everyone who doesn't belong here, move along." Two security guards attempted to clear the area.

A large ornate chandelier peeked out from the top of the massive erected barriers, its shimmering gleam taunting us from the other side.

"Someone good must be in there," Megs complained. "Security is tight."

Pulling Megs with me, we squeezed back through the throng of people and circled to the opposite side of the club. "Let's go around to the other side, if we go over to the balcony, we can probably see through the screens."

On this side of the club there was a small balcony, which jutted out like an old school theater. The gilded railing and large velvet curtains fringed what I could only assume was the designated resting area, a chaise lounge and a couple of plush armchairs sat vacant in this forgotten corner.

"Can you see anything?" Megs happily fell onto the chaise, her toned, bare legs stretched out in front of her. "I'm just going to lay here, maybe take a nap."

"Oh you have got to be kidding me," I huffed, able to catch a glimpse through the thin gap between the barrier screens.

"What?" Megs sat up suddenly her quest for a nap forgotten.

I pointed wildly, wondering if the universe was somehow conspiring against me. "Dan Fucking Evans is right over there." Of all the gin joints in all the cities, he had walked into mine. Okay, we weren't in a gin joint and he hadn't walked in, but still, what were the chances?

"Are you sure? We've had a lot of drink. It could be some random who looks like him." Megs jumped off the chaise and moved to my side, squinting her eyes in an attempt to see.

"No, that's him. I'd know that smug grin anywhere. Seriously, twice in one day. Look at him, smirking his ass off with a couple of girls draped over him." My fever rose as I watched him through the gap. I despised him and yet, he looked downright edible in tight black jeans and a vintage Ramones tee. Clearly I was drunker than I thought.

"Wow, he's actually better looking in real life." Megs pushed me out of the way, able to see more clearly from my vantage point. "I know we are staring but I can't stop looking at him. I think his tattoos are hypnotizing me."

"I should go tell him what an ass he was," I stated, fuelled with a good dose of liquid courage and a case of I-no-longer-care-what-anyone-thinks.

"Ash, this is probably not a good idea." Megs swayed unsteadily on her feet, having as much trouble standing as she was trying to convince me of my bad idea.

"Didn't you say you wanted to meet him? Well, let's go over there." I turned and made for the VIP area, unsure exactly what I would say to him once I got there. Ass. How dare he? This was my night of irresponsibility. I didn't want him here.

"Is there anything I can say that is going to stop you?" Megs grabbed onto my arm, trying her best to keep up with my accelerated pace and not trip over her own feet.

"No, probably not." I smiled, knowing my mind was made up.

"Okay, fine. Let's go over there but don't get us thrown out, all right?"

I dragged a stumbling Megs by the hand as I wandered to the VIP area, trying not to make my forced grin look like something out of horror movie.

The large security guard put his arms out to hinder us moving forward. "Sorry, ladies, this area is reserved."

"But my friend is in there, I just need to tell him something." I sounded surprisingly calm despite my quickened heartbeat. I gave him another smile, not sure if I was going for seductive or meek. The twitching of my lips probably made me look more like a stroke victim than a femme fatale.

"Who is your friend?" I could tell he was skeptical, and had probably been fielding women all night.

HIGH STRUNG

"It's Dan Evans, he's just over there. If you let me through, I'll just talk to him and then we'll be on our way." I placed my hands on my hips, hoping the fact I was wearing very little clothes would work in my favor. If I'd been less inebriated I would have been horrified by my brazen attempt, but in my current altered state I was resisting the urge to give myself a high-five.

"Listen, babe. You aren't the first lady here tonight to tell me he's your *friend*. Either way, unless a VIP escorts you in, I can't let you through. It's nothing personal, I just have a job to do." While he wasn't rude, he wasn't sympathetic to my plight either, shooting down any further conversation. I narrowed my eyes, silently cursing his personal integrity.

"But I really do know him," I protested, wondering if my earlier conversation with Dan constituted *knowing* him. I'd met him; that had to count. Semantics.

"I'm sure you do but rules are still rules."

"Well your rules suck." I stuck out my tongue defiantly. Seriously, who was I and where was Ashlyn Murphy?

"Hey, Barney." A tattooed, guy with a Mohawk, and the most amazing hazel eyes tried to squeeze past. His large frame inadvertently brushed up against us. "Hi, ladies."

"Oh shit, that's Troy Harris. He's so hot. Did I say that out loud?" Megs panted as she smacked her hand across her mouth.

His lips spread into an amused grin. "Yes I am, and yeah you did." It made him look sweet actually, all tough guy exterior paired off with a really nice smile. I was either drunker than I thought or I had never noticed.

"So you are the drummer? Huh, I had totally thought that dickwad was." I pointed to where Dan was sitting, his duo of *skank sca*rves still draped around his neck. "My apologies to you. You are so much *nicer* than he is. He is a total jerk. You even said hello without being an ass."

Troy's face looked animated as he laughed. "I'll take that as a compliment. I assume you are talking from experience?"

37

"I met him this morning. He told me I had small tits. Look at them." I glanced at the swells of my breasts that peeked out above the tight black fabric. "They look adequate, don't they? Who even says that to a girl?" Did I just ask Troy Harris to inspect my breasts? The words coming out of my mouth were fuzzily entwined with my internal thoughts, so I couldn't be sure which was which. Not with any certainty anyway.

"Sure they look...um really nice." His grin widened as he briefly looked down, confirming I had in fact verbalized the request.

"Troy Harris. Hi, I'm a fan." Megs grabbed his hand and started shaking it wildly, his arm bouncing up and down as Megs continued to shake. "I just want to say that I told Ashlyn you were the drummer when she thought Dan Evans was the drummer. Tell him, Ashlyn. I totally said Troy Harris is the drummer."

"You don't have to say my whole name, you can just call me Troy." He smiled carefully using his other hand to free the one currently caught in Megs's death grip. He surely had to think we were insane; he was just too polite to say so, further proving what a nice guy he was. Not like Dan. Dan was un-nice. Huh? That's not a word. My eyes crossed as I tried to find the adjective I needed, *sexy* was what kept flashing repeatedly, unwelcome in my mind.

"Wait, did you say your name is Ashlyn?" Troy studied me curiously, must be my freaky crossed eyes that had him interested. I really am such a catch.

"Yes, I'm Ashlyn." I stood up a little straighter, pushing back my shoulders proudly. Seriously, who the hell was I right now?

"Oh this is perfect." He clapped his hands together as the smile hit his eyes. "You met Dan this morning when you had an interview with Lexi, right?"

"Yes, I had an interview this morning and Dan was there with Alex. Not that I even looked at Alex. I mean I looked at him but not in *that* way. I mean he's *married* with a *baby*. I was most definitely not throwing off heat of *any* kind." Abort! Abort! My mind shouted and my mouth refused to obey. It's as if the words spewed from my mouth like inmates in a jailbreak. Sound the alarm. It was anyone's guess what I would be saying next.

"Ashlyn, are you drunk?" His eyebrow rose as his smile widened, clearly enjoying this, whatever *this* was.

"I would say if we are talking probabilities, the chances are pretty high." I stepped closer in an attempt to whisper in his ear but ended up smacking my forehead against his cheek. "Are you going to get us thrown out?"

"This just keeps getting better and better." He threw his head back in a full-throated laugh. "Hell no, you ain't getting kicked out. I think you lovely ladies need to come back and be my guest. Barney, I'll take responsibility for these two."

He offered me his arm that, thankfully, I latched onto. Megs, bypassing formalities, hugged his chest, her grin threatening to split her face apart.

"Your call, man. Just get them to drink some water. Lay off the booze for a few, yeah?" Barney offered as he stepped aside, shaking his head.

"You cool, ladies?" Troy asked as he looked from his arm that I was holding like a life preserver, to Megs who was snaked around his waist like a human boa constrictor. Neither seemed to faze him.

"Hell yes, Troy Harris, we want to come back. I'm Megan Winters by the way but you can call me Meg or Megs or just call me Megan." Megs nodded, her head bouncing so violently it seemed she had lost all muscle control in her neck.

"I'll make you a deal, you just call *me* Troy and I'll call *you* Megs." He chuckled at Megs as his bright hazel eyes moved to me. "Ashlyn, you want to come back and hang?"

I tried to harness what control I still had over my mouth to smile, but as it had been spewing crazy talk, who knew if it actually had the ability to curl upward to form anything close resembling to a grin. I was going to enjoy this. "Lead the way." I smirked.

6

Dan

THINGS WERE JUST GETTING INTERESTING WHEN SKYLA AND LILI excused themselves to hit the bathroom. We'd been making out and playing touchy-feely for a while and both of them seemed eager for us to make tracks and head back to their place. They shared an apartment in the Chelsea area so I guessed sharing bodily fluids wasn't going to be a big deal. Who was I to argue? I wondered if they would let me film it? They seemed up for just about anything, so it couldn't hurt to suggest.

I pulled out my phone and scrolled through messages, nothing really interested me but it sure beat sitting on the couch by myself looking like a douche. How long does it take to go to the bathroom? Women take too fucking long. What do they do in there? I've been in a few ladies rooms and it's not like they have anything interesting going on in there. It's just toilets and sinks. I wondered if they were getting started without me? 'Cause straight up, that would *not* be fucking cool.

HIGH STRUNG

Out of the corner of my eye, I saw Troy saunter in with two babes wrapped around him. Well, fuck me. Looks like the big guy finally got some sack and was taking my lead. I immediately snapped my head around to get a better look; no harm in admiring the view. After all, I'd just given him *that* pleasure not half an hour ago.

Was that? I felt the blood drain straight from my head and into my cock as they got closer, confirming that the smoking babe holding onto Troy's arm was the same feisty redhead from this morning.

"Ashyln?" I rose to my feet like a marine called to attention. Holy shit, she was hot. She looked so different, her long wild hair probably covering more of her pale skin than the dress she was wearing, not that I was complaining.

"Hello, Dan." She breathed into my face as she leaned into me, swaying slightly on her feet.

She said my name with such distaste and venom, her breath smelling of gin and the possibility of bad decisions. I'm not sure why, but I fucking loved it. The outfit she was wearing made me instantly hard.

"I seemed to have stumbled onto some fans." Troy grinned, his arm still wrapped around the other girl. "I think they might be *friends* of yours."

I swallowed hard as my eyes raked up and down Ashlyn's body, my balls begging me to hurry up and get with the program. "Nice...very, very nice."

"Um, Dan?" Skyla appeared at my side like some wicked magic trick, looking all pissy.

"Yeah?" I responded not wanting to be distracted from my current view, completely forgetting I had already made plans to leave.

"We're ready to go," Lili snapped, tapping her foot impatiently.

Ashlyn continued to eyeball me, ignoring Skyla and Lili.

I waved them off. "Yeah, I think I'm going to hang for a while longer." Strangely no longer interested. "You girls go on without me, have a good time."

"Are you *fucking* kidding me?" Skyla or maybe it was Lili shot in my direction. "You are just going to ditch us?" Okay, that time, it was definitely Lili.

Ashlyn leaned closer and whispered into my ear, "Your pussy party seems angry." She paused before adding, "Tell me, Dan, are there any women who *aren't* pissed at you?"

"You think that getting girls is a problem for me?" I laughed. No really, the fact she thought I ever needed to spend a night alone when I didn't want to was seriously amusing.

"Listen, girls." I twisted back to face my *pussy party*. Pretty cool name actually, I should think about getting shirts printed. Like an unofficial Dan fan club or something. "This isn't going to happen tonight. Thanks for the hand job but I'm no longer feeling it." I shrugged deciding that should be enough of an explanation.

"You are such an ass," shouted Skyla, or was it Lili? I'd be lying if I said cared.

"I have to agree, he *is* an ass," Ashlyn slurred as she backhanded me across the chest. "Ass," she repeated.

"Come on, Skyla, let's go. No way is he getting laid tonight." Well that one was obviously Lili. She frowned at me before pulling her friend toward the doorway.

"Well done, you're all class, Dan," Jase said, chuckling. "I'm Jason, don't judge me by my association with this numbnuts." He bumped me out of the way and offered Ashlyn his hand, like he was negotiating a used car deal.

"Hi, Jason." Ashlyn grabbed his hand enthusiastically and pulled him in a little closer. Her body crashed against Jase's arm, the dickhead smiled smugly as it made contact. "I'm Ashlyn and this is my friend Megs. She's a big fan."

Ashlyn motioned roughly to the direction of the short, sexy blonde who had walked in with her and Troy. I must be losing my edge 'cause I hadn't even noticed the rocking curves she was working.

"Hi, Jason Irwin, I'm Megs. I'm a big fan." The blonde nodded, talking so fast she sounded like she might be high. Come to think of it,

HIGH STRUNG

they both were acting really strange. "He plays keyboard, Ash." Megs cupped her hand and attempted to whisper but it was actually louder than her regular volume. This was so fucking weird. "I'm so excited to meet you, Jason Irwin." She waved, not letting go of Troy. While she might be a fan, obviously she had a favorite.

"She has a tendency for saying our full names. I think it's easier if we just go with it." Troy grinned like a douchebag, giving Megs a squeeze. He clearly wasn't hating the attention. Not that I blamed him, the blonde who had the death grip on him was all kinds of hot. Troy glanced up at me, biting back his shit-eating grin. "Ashlyn apparently thought *you* were the drummer, Megs was kind enough to set her straight."

"I sure did, Troy Harris." The blonde bobble head chimed in.

"Are you girls loaded?" I asked, looking between them. They had to be. Their eyes were glassy and they could barely stand straight.

"My alcohol level is not relevant here." Ash strutted back over to me and I could feel the heat roll off her body as it stood inches from mine, her lips in my face were driving me insane. "What is relevant is that *you*, are a pig."

"Is this shit for real?" I wanted to laugh, I didn't care she was paying me out. She was drunk, and her pouty lips fumbling with words was fucking hot.

"It's pretty awesome if you ask me," Jase added from the peanut gallery.

"No one asked for your opinion," I shot back, not even attempting to take my eyes off Ash. I couldn't look away, hell, what I wanted to do was throw her over my shoulder and take her home. Let her work out some of that aggression.

"You were rude to me this morning." Ashlyn pushed her finger into my chest. "I need to set you straight."

"Babe, you were practically hyperventilating when you met me. You don't have to deny it now." I couldn't help myself as I pushed a little further. My dick screamed in agony straining against the fly of my jeans.

"I am not a fan." She breathed into my face. "I worked my ass off and graduated from college with honors. I was working fifteen-hour days and handling accounts worth hundreds of thousands of dollars. I wouldn't just hyperventilate over someone like *you*."

"What do you mean someone like me?"

"Someone like you. You play in a band. How is that even a real job? Did you even graduate?"

Well fuck me, she thought because I played in a band it somehow made me stupid? I didn't need to go to College. I'm doing what I love and making bank doing it. I've come across people who judge us 'cause we have tattoos and don't dress a certain way, but I couldn't give two fucks. I'd rather hang myself than have to wear a suit and tie all day and punch some fucking clock. I didn't care what anyone thought. I was living my dream and if anyone had a problem with my lifestyle, then it was just that – *their* problem. "Do you get lonely up in your ivory tower, sweetheart?" I tilted my head back and laughed.

Ash smacked me across the chest with her hand. "Why are you laughing at me?" It was just enough to sting.

"Jesus, woman. Why the fuck are you hitting me?" I laughed harder, seeing how aggravated she was that I hadn't been offended by her attitude. She was so fucking adorable.

"Don't laugh at me." She huffed, planting her hands on her hips, giving me a better look at that fine body of hers. If she was trying to turn me off, she was failing.

"Babe, you can think whatever *you* want about me and *I* get to laugh at whatever I want, that's how it works."

"I hate you."

I leaned in and whispered, "No, you don't. You're just mad 'cause I make your panties wet."

"You disgust me!" She pushed against my chest.

"And yet, you still want to sleep with me, don't you?"

"What? No. Are you insane? I don't want to sleep with you. Not *every* woman wants to sleep with you."

"Maybe that's true, but you do."

HIGH STRUNG

"You...you...ugh!" She opened her mouth and shut it, wordless.

"It's okay, sweetheart, don't fight it. I promise it will be good for you."

She slammed her lips onto mine, her tongue invading my mouth. It was hot and I could taste a hint of whatever she'd just been drinking as she swirled her tongue around mine. I pulled her head closer, ignoring our audience, as I fisted her crazy red hair. Her tits pushed up against me and I heard her moan as I pulled up her leg, hitting that sweet spot with the throbbing hard-on that was begging to climb out of my jeans. I didn't care she said she hated me, or that I disgusted her, her body was telling me she wanted me, wanted this and I wasn't about to deny her.

She leaned into me, her hands getting crazy as they moved down my back and squeezed my ass, pushing her hips harder into me. I could feel her grind against the friction of my jeans, using it to work herself up, the action making us both crazy. It felt so good, her mouth hungry for every little inch of tongue I gave her. I could only imagine how amazing those lips would feel wrapped around my cock. I needed to get inside of her before I blew my load in my pants. I couldn't remember a time I had been this worked up over a girl. It was like someone had flicked a switch in her and all that anal control shit just exploded into a big ball of want. Oh yeah, I said anal and I would be happy to work that out with her too, but right now, I need to get my dick suited up and buried into her pussy.

She pulled away in a rush, her face flushed and her lips puffy from making out. Her chest heaved up and down as she pushed her hair out of the way. She backed away steadily and gave me a fucking drop-dead gorgeous smile, her tongue tracing her perfect cock-sucking lips.

"There, I've made a questionable decision. Megs, I would say our night is done."

Smart! Seems like that fancy degree was worth something, despite getting hot and bothered. She was telling her girl to wrap it up so we could go get busy. I had to respect the fact she didn't want to fuck me right here in the club, it was a little skanky. I mean, I would have done it if she'd asked but I was looking forward to taking her home and fucking her properly, having her come so fucking hard around my cock she forgot her own name. Yeah, we needed to eject from this club ASAP.

Megs's bugged eyed expression matched that of Troy and Jase. "Uh Ash, you just made out with Dan Evans."

"Wrong, he just made out with me." She smirked and turned away from me. "Troy, Jason. Have a good night."

What the actual fuck? Is she leaving? No, she can't be leaving. Coming up for a breath I understand, but calling curtains is a whole other matter. One minute we're getting hot and heavy, going at it like a porno, and the next minute she is saying goodbye? Who does that? I've got the worst case of blue balls and she was just going to walk away?

"Wait, you are just going to leave me like this?" I pointed to the bulge in my pants thinking she must be kidding. Maybe this was like foreplay for her, we could get aggressive and then fuck hard.

"Kind of ironic, isn't it? Think of it as character building. Write a song about it. Either way, I am not sleeping with you. Megs, let's go."

Shit, she was serious. She stalked over to a bewildered Troy and unwrapped her friend from his body. Megs was not able to offer much more than a wave as Ashlyn pulled her out to the main area of the club.

"What the fuck was that?" I stared dumbfounded at Troy and Jase.

"I believe you just got owned, my friend." Troy patted me on the shoulder like some poor little puppy. "Looks like it's just you and your hand tonight."

Jase gave me a friendly punch in the arm. "I like her. I'm going to see if Lexi will give me her number. Maybe I'll ask her out, she seems like a fun time."

"Don't even play me right now, asshole." I ran my hands through my hair, five different shades of worked up.

"Oh come on, Dan, you've got to admit that was funny. You did the same thing to those other two girls not five minutes before." Troy crossed his arms in front of his chest. He was a big bastard too; all that cymbal crashing and drum bashing made him solid so I wasn't going to argue with him even if I didn't agree.

HIGH STRUNG

"She was totally hot for me, her leaving was to prove a point." I flagged over a waitress, needing a drink to calm me down. I should just tell her to bring the whole bottle.

Beth brought over our standard order and I snagged the tumbler of Jack and Coke I knew would barely make a dent. Troy grabbed his bottle of beer. "Well I guess she did that, didn't she?"

"Whatever man, that was fucking bullshit. Bullshit. Who gets a guy all fucking hard and then walks? Not even an offer of a blowjob or anything. It's not like I wouldn't have reciprocated." I swallowed the drink and slammed down the glass.

Jase tipped his bottle of beer and took a swig. "Don't be looking at me, dude, I'm not blowing you."

"Nice one, asswipe. Like I'd want to have my dick sucked by you." I've got nothing against dudes sucking other dude's cocks; I just don't subscribe to it for myself.

"You baited her dude, what were you expecting?" Troy took a seat on the couch and pointed at me to do the same.

Like I was going to chase after her like a loser. Dan Evans did not chase after a girl no matter what she looked like, even if she gave amazing head. Okay, if she gave amazing head, that would be grounds to break my rule but it was too late now. She had too big of a lead and I had no idea of her head-giving talents so therefore, by my own rules, I could not pursue.

"Just let it go, man. You've both had your fun, now move on." Jase sunk his ass into the chair beside me.

He was right. I should let it go. She was beautiful, there was no denying that, but she had a chip on her shoulder a mile fucking wide. A girl like that meant work, and she obviously thought she was too good for me, her and her fucked-up idea of who I am was too much trouble.

I clenched my fist, my body still all jazzed up from her little stunt. I should just go find a random girl and forget it even happened. Forget her and her delicious fucking mouth. Damn it, now I was thinking about her again.

"Dan." Troy snapped his fingers in front of my face, snapping me back to attention. "I can see your cogs turning, let it go."

I nodded, pretending to agree with him and he rolled his eyes, giving me *that* look. The look that told me, we both knew I wasn't letting it go. I don't know why but that girl had gotten under my skin and come hell or high water I was going to need to figure out why.

7

Ashlyn

WITH THE DAWNING OF THE NEW DAY ALSO CAME PANIC. PANIC induced by the foggy memories that slowly bubble to the surface, panic about the half-remembered words that float in your subconscious that you hoped never spilled from your lips, and panic from the body aches echoing through your muscles which point to an *active* night.

I was home in my Brooklyn apartment which gave me pause, as I had remembered deciding to spend the night at Megs's, but after leaving *Panic*—the club not the state of mind which was burning through my body today—I had very little recollection of what had transpired. Perhaps, I just caught a cab and came home? Maybe Megs had found someone she wanted to share her vagina with; she'd been pretty intent on it earlier. That would have definitely prompted me to hightail it back across the bridge. Or maybe the need to play show-and-tell had been mine. Megs's borrowed dress from the previous night was strewn carelessly on the floor beside me but I was still wearing my bra and panties. That had to be a good sign, didn't it? The bile in my stomach churned as I slowly turned my head to survey the other side of my bed, praying with everything I had it would be empty. Rumpled sheets and a pillow were my only bedfellows. I slowly breathed out a sigh of relief. Whatever I did last night could be forgiven, as long as I didn't continue those mistakes in the morning. I could chalk it up to an unfortunate evening resulting from questionable judgment and move on.

"Good morning," a husky voice greeted me, my previously forgiven sins now flashing before my eyes. "I was hoping you would wake up soon."

Standing before me was Dan Evans, still wet from a shower with one of *my* towels wrapped around his hips, barely affording his modesty. Seriously, I had bigger towels; did he choose the tiniest one? Ashlyn, you are worried that he chose the tiniest towel? Seriously? Dan Freaking Evans is in your bedroom, has been in your shower, and...is. In. Your. Bedroom. *What the hell?* But damn, he looked good. All the exposed ink covered skin glistened as he moved closer to my bed. It made the colors in his tattoos more vibrant, life-like. His chest flexed as he lifted his arm to dry off his hair, thankfully with another towel and not the one wrapped precariously around his lower body. He was lean but incredibly toned, his body resembling a poster you might find in a biology lab. Each muscle clear and defined, it would be so easy to take a marker and start labeling - starting with those lower abdominal muscles no one knows the name of and what most women simply call the V.

"FUCK!" My horror overrode my libido as I realized what must have transpired.

"Now, you're talking," remarked a grinning Dan as he sat down on the bed, the mattress compressing under the weight of his body. "You know, for someone so uptight, you sure have a dirty mouth when you're drunk."

I raked my hands through my messy morning hair in frustration trying to remember how he got here, surely Dan didn't just teleport into my bedroom. Half-naked. Wet. "How? What? Where? I said goodbye to you. I remember saying goodbye to you."

"Yeah, that. That was not cool." He tossed the towel he was using for his hair onto the floor casually as the smile teased at the edges of his mouth. "Why did you kiss me and then run away?"

"Because..." The reason no longer made sense in my own head. "Because I thought I should loosen the reins a little, make out with some random guy. Megs was on my case about being normal, and you made me angry. I wanted you to stop talking."

"Way to make me shut up. You showed me." Dan's fingers slid up my arm pushing my hair out of the way. I hated to admit that him touching me didn't feel so terrible. It actually felt nice. Gah! No. I was not willing to allow myself to make the same mistake twice. I shrugged off his hand, determined to fight off any further advances. At some point I needed to get my head in the game, now would be a good time for that. I sat up, hoping my vertical positioning would prompt my smarts to kick in. Unfortunately becoming vertical also highlighted that I was in my underwear. The sheet slipped down to my waist and revealed my bra. Dan's eyes dipped down and gave me an appreciative smile before I was able to scramble and pull up the sheet to cover myself. Not that it mattered at this point; he'd seen it *all* last night no doubt. Regardless, the free show was not going to continue today.

"I know I left. Megs and I walked out of the front of the club. I know we did." I scanned my memory for an anchor - nothing.

"Yeah, you did. That's where I found you two, at the front of the club, on the floor. I don't get why girls wear such high heels. I'm all for being sexy but the ones your friend was wearing were bordering on stilts. Anyway, she twisted her ankle walking out. Fell straight onto her ass. I'm pretty sure it's just a sprain but she flat out refused to go to the ER, babbling about looking like an idiot with her folks." He shrugged, not knowing the context of Megs's refusal. Even in her inebriated state, Megs knew the minute she stepped into an ER someone would have recognized her last name and possibly connected it to her parents.

"So I called Troy and Jase and they came out the front to helped me get the two of you home. We got Megs situated with some ice and ibuprofen, incidentally repeatedly saying our last names got old, real quick." He rolled his eyes before continuing, "And then we headed out of the city to your place."

"So what? You followed me up to my apartment and took advantage of me?" I cringed knowing how low my judgment had slipped; I'd let a stranger into my apartment and let him do who knows what to me. "You are such a creep."

"Me? Oh sweetheart, last night was all you. You were all over me in the Suburban on the way home. Practically jerking me off in the back seat. I was just going to get you into your apartment and leave but you begged me to stay. Told me how much of a good girl you'd been your whole life and that you wanted to be bad." His grin widened. "It's the good girls you need to watch out for."

"No, this isn't happening. That sounds nothing like me. I don't jerk off random guys in cars and I don't have one-night stands, especially not with musicians. Hell, I've never even been to a concert." I shook my head, wishing I could go back in time, tell myself to stop drinking, tell myself not to go the VIP section, tell myself to stay home and order pizza instead.

"Whoa. Hold up a minute. You've never been to a concert? Like ever?" Dan recoiled in horror.

"No, never. That however is not relevant, what is relevant is that even when I have been drunk in the past, I have never just gone home with a guy. Someone must have slipped something into my drink. I surely must have been drugged."

That had to be the explanation. Of course, drugs. Let's go with that, except that our drinks hadn't been left unattended at any stage and there had been no opportunity for drugging to take place. Ugh! Back to square one.

"Wow, Ashlyn, You're a virgin. I'm sorry, babe. I had no idea." His voice softened as he looked on me with pity-filled eyes. His ill-directed compassion made me angrier.

"I'm not a fucking virgin, you idiot. I've had sex before."

"I was talking about a concert virgin. I kind of feel sorry for you." He eased back onto the bed unconcerned or oblivious to the telepathic mind bullets I was shooting him with.

"I just told you I think I might have been drugged and you are more concerned with the fact I've never been to a concert before. What is wrong with you?" I narrowed my eyes, wondering if this was an angle or he was just genuinely simple minded.

"Nothing is wrong with me, what is wrong with *you*? You've never been to a concert, had a one-night stand, or jerked off a guy in a car. What the hell did you *do* in college?"

"I studied, asshole. What you are *supposed* to do in college. Be a viable member of society, get a degree, try and gain a future so I wouldn't be a drain on welfare. Of course you wouldn't know about that, would you?" I spat back indignantly.

It wasn't the first time I had been questioned about my lack of college-experience. I wasn't a prude and I wasn't boring, I was a realist. I wasn't gifted with an obscene IQ and while I was far from stupid, I had to work my ass off for every single "A" I got. I literally couldn't afford to fail, knowing even if I passed every class I would still be crucified by student debt well into my thirties. Adding another semester or two because I wanted to party or make out with imbeciles who wouldn't even respect me enough to call me in the morning was not an option. I had to stay the course, knowing my pay-off would come later in life when I would be rewarded with a six-figure salary, making the sacrifice worthwhile.

"Did you have any fun? Like any at all? Your life sounds like it was a major snore." Dan yawned, punctuating his stance. His arm grazed mine as he moved. My bed wasn't huge, and his large body took up much of the space as he sat beside me.

"I had plenty of fun. I didn't have to degrade myself to do it either. Aren't you a little sick of being a crotch hound? Is that what you want on your headstone? Here lies Dan Evans, spent his life in between the legs of women."

Dan stretched his arms and folded them at the back of his neck, the colorful canvas of his breathtakingly chiseled torso flexing with his movements. He noticed my eyes dip and gave me a satisfied smile.

"I'd die happy that's for sure." He raised an eyebrow and smiled, his pleasure evident. "Can you preorder headstones? I'm thinking that would be a good one, and I don't want to forget and then someone write something lame."

"Are you ever serious? Even for like a minute?" Something told me he wasn't joking and somewhere in his mind he was leaving a mental note to commission said headstone. How this man had gotten so far in life was bewildering to me. I refused to believe that his good looks had paved his way to an easier life, that shit would just not be fair.

"Why? So I can conform to whatever fucked-up idea you have in your head? There are plenty of people who like me just the way I am. I see no point changing."

Dan grinned, edging closer to me with a complete disregard for my personal space. He invaded my safe bubble of insulation, dipping his chin so his face was inches from mine. I could feel his breath tickle my skin as he studied me with his dark brown eyes. Their warmth gave me tingles in places, *places* I'd love to see him peering up at me from. My breathing deepened as I felt my nipples harden against the fabric of my bra. What? I wasn't sure if I was angrier at my erotic thoughts or my traitorous body.

"You are making my head hurt." I pulled my knees up to my chest, affording me the slight physical distance I required to think straight, 'cause if I looked at his eyes any longer I was probably going to kiss him. I hated the lack of control I apparently seemed to exercise when I was around him. Why could I not remember? "I can't believe I slept with you. Please tell me we at least used protection?"

"You don't remember last night? Not even a little bit?" His voice sounded skeptical, almost incredulous before he barked out a laugh. "Now who is being offensive?"

"Now is not the time for me to pad your ego. No, I told you. I don't remember last night. I'm sorry if that ruins your reputation but you have at least one dissatisfied customer."

I couldn't admit that while I couldn't remember, I wasn't halfway near as pissed as I was pretending to be. It was bad enough those feelings were waging a war inside my head, battling between high fiving my drunken self for bedding one of the hottest guys I've ever seen, and the disgust I allowed myself to slip into the cliché of being another notch in his belt. Stupid girl. He's never going to respect you. How could I have given it up so easily?

"Oh you are so wrong." He leaned closer ignoring my knee barrier. "I have never left a woman dissatisfied."

I swallowed. All that skin, and he had to be naked underneath that towel. Somewhere, digging deep, I found a small pocket of bravado.

"There is a first time for everything. Don't take it too hard, I'm sure there will be someone just around the corner to scream your name and be thankful. Sorry, but you won't be finding gratitude here."

"You really have no idea, do you?" He narrowed his eyes, as if weighing my words for the first time this morning. Perhaps I should use more simplistic language, he did seem to confuse easily.

"No. I don't, so let's say goodbye and move on. Last night was an oversight. A hiccup. I can move on knowing that men like you are definitely not for me. So for that, I owe you a thank you. Now if you can kindly put on some clothes and vacate my apartment I'd appreciate it."

I turned my back to him, pulling the bed sheets around me. While he might have seen it all last night, he wasn't going to get another peepshow this morning. Besides, facing away from him was definitely the smartest decision I'd had so far. The longer I looked at him, the greater the chance I would be saying something stupid, like offering to towel off the remnants of moisture that clung to the curve of his neck…with my tongue.

"You know I didn't see it initially but you really are an evil bitch and surprisingly that kind of turns me on more." I could hear the smirk in his voice as his finger traced the line of my bare shoulder.

I felt I had no choice as I opened my mouth, and lied. "And you are still the insensitive pig I pegged you for. So now we have established this was purely one sided, please leave and allow me the courtesy of wallowing in my shame privately."

"Fine, babe, I'll leave but we both know you'll be calling me." I felt him move off the bed and heard the thud of his wet towel hitting the floor. All I had to do was turn and I would see what I had obviously been too drunk to remember. I wanted to, desperately, but refused to give him the satisfaction. *Don't turn around. Do NOT turn around!*

"I've taken the liberty of programming my number into your cell." After some rustling, I caught the telltale sound of a zipper being pulled up. "I was disappointed there wasn't even one dirty selfie on there."

I whipped my body around, too consumed by anger to worry about what I might be seeing. Thankfully while he was still naked from the waist up he was wearing jeans. "You went through my phone?"

"You didn't have a password on it." His satisfied grin danced across his smug, sexy face.

"You can't just invade my privacy like that. Who do you think you are?" I was barely able to spit out the words through my seething rage.

"Relax, babe, it's just a phone. It's not like I went through your underwear drawer." His playfully raised eyebrow did little to convince me he hadn't.

It took every ounce of self-control I owned not to launch myself off the bed and punch him right in the throat. Maybe I was wrong and he was just baiting me, he seemed to gain an inappropriate amount of joy from our exchanges. Let's not overreact just yet.

"Dan. Did you go through my underwear drawer?"

He bit back a grin, unashamedly admitting his perversion. "Okay, maybe a little, but you fell asleep so fast I got bored. Nice stuff by the way. I dig that little red thong you have tucked away."

"Get out," I shouted, grabbing a pillow and tossing it at his head wishing I had a more solid projectile within reach. I didn't even recognize the demonic voice that sprouted from my throat, it was like it was coming out of someone else.

"Okay, Okay. I'm going." He winced in the wake of my small but

HIGH STRUNG

efficient explosion, snaring his shirt and boots from the floor before stepping to the threshold of my bedroom doorway. "See ya, babe." He waved casually pulling the shirt over his head and walking out of my line of sight, not even offering a sorry. Of course he didn't, he wasn't *sorry*. In his mind, he'd done nothing wrong. I guessed as far as he was concerned, riffling through someone's panty drawer after you had just been *inside of them* was hardly a violation. From that perspective, his stupid and idiotic logic was actually somewhat rational.

As soon as the door slammed shut I grabbed my phone from my nightstand, and scrolled through my contacts. Sure enough, DAN EVANS was now listed with an attached profile photo. It wasn't a typical smiling profile however, oh no. It was of his naked torso, a display of colorful flesh that started from the bottom of his neck and stopped just before it became X-rated. It was the ultimate tease pic: no face, just sculptured, masculine skin. It was raw and unfiltered, just like him. I couldn't stop staring at it; it was possibly the most erotic image I'd even seen. My finger lingered over the glass as I enlarged the image to fill the screen, prompting an unfamiliar tug in my core. I hated him, there is no way I would be calling him and yet I couldn't bring myself to delete it. He was trouble. He was everything I had spent my life trying to avoid – reckless, dangerous and a guaranteed broken heart. He wasn't what I needed and yet I couldn't stop wanting him, even though I needed to. A part of me wished I could recall the details of the night and I wondered if it had been good; the fact he was still here in the morning had to mean it, or *I* wasn't totally bad. Damn him! I wasn't going to allow myself to be dragged down that path. I needed distance, a very cold shower and the biggest cup of coffee I could find, and then I would do whatever it took to exorcise Dan Evans from my body and my mind.

8

Dan

"SHE THREW YOUR ASS OUT, HUH?" TROY'S SMUG FUCKING FACE beamed at me as he slid into the booth and sat opposite. "I tried to tell you last night it was a bad idea dude, and here you are sitting at a Starbucks looking like a douche."

I didn't have much choice when I left Ashlyn's apartment, shit had definitely not gone to plan. I was hoping after working over that tight little body of hers with a session of morning sex, we hit up an IHOP and maybe head back to her piece-of-shit apartment and have a go at round two. Fuck knows I had been packing the biggest set of blue balls all night while I slept beside her, the only hands around my cock being my own. Each time she moaned in her sleep I had to fight the urge not to jack off. 'Cause that would be creepy, right? Does it count as creepy if I jacked off and she didn't know? Fuck there were too many rules for this shit. This broad was messing with my head.

HIGH STRUNG

Knowing I was probably going to end up loaded last night, I hadn't driven to the club. Troy, Jase and I had requested our regular driver, TJ, to chauffeur.

TJ had been our wheelman for years. Nothing fazed him; he had seen it all, especially in the early days. Back then, all the boys partook in the spoils, even James after Hannah dumped his ass. Of course, it lasted about five seconds before he went crawling back to her like a pussy and handed her his balls. They had been together forever but got into a few fights early in the piece, the label putting pressure on James to be the single front man to earn us more pussy points with the fans. Had to hand it to her, she wasn't with him for the fame or the money and she would have kept walking if he hadn't fucking begged her for another chance. James wasn't into the lifestyle; he just wanted to sing with his band and have a regular girl to come home to. We all knew they'd end up doing the walk down the aisle.

Alex Stone was another fucking story. That good-looking motherfucker had girls creaming their pants with his iceman routine. He didn't even try. He was the one I least expected to take a knee. Enter Lexi-Knockout-Reed, a feisty brunette from the Land Down Under. Done deal. And then there were three...Jase, Troy and me.

"Don't even start with me, asswhipe. If I'd known you were going to be such a whiny bitch I would have called a cab." I took another swallow of whatever it was the blonde behind the counter had recommended. Even coffee wasn't simple these days, though I had to admit, whatever it was in the cup was surprisingly delicious.

Troy shook his head. "I'm not a whiny bitch, and you know I'll come pick your ass up from wherever you call me from. You would do the same for me. I get that. What I don't get is why you have such a hard-on for this girl, when she clearly can't stand you."

Girls were a dime a dozen, especially for us. I'd never really chased anyone. Sure I'd throw a line out there and see if I'd get a nibble but I was more a numbers man, and if a girl wasn't feeling me then I wasn't about to waste time trying to convince her. To be honest, I didn't have a solid answer for him, not one that made any sense.

"You don't know that."

Troy eased back into his padded chair, the grin on his face hinted he wouldn't be letting this shit go. "Then how come you're sitting here with me instead of doing your usual morning-after pancake routine with her? I'm actually surprised she didn't come to her senses earlier, I was half expecting to get a call an hour after we dropped the two of you off."

"She pretty much collapsed once we walked in the door. We made out for about ten minutes, and I had barely got my hands on her tits when she passed out."

As much as I hated to admit it, nothing went down last night. Ashlyn had been talking a good game up until I got her front door unlocked, telling me how she'd wanted to just have one night of fun and then it was like the alcohol finally hit her. Honestly, I had been ready to see her up to her apartment and call it a night, and not because I wasn't interested. I knew she was loaded and not making rational decisions, but I wasn't about to take advantage of a girl, even if she was begging. The touching the tits happened before she passed out. Then it was either carry her to her to her room or lay her down on the tired looking couch in her living room.

Troy eyeballed me hard. "Please tell me I'm not going to have to take you outside and beat your ass for being a scumbag." I had no doubt he would take me outside and we'd have to go a few rounds if that kind of shit had gone down. None of us would ever cross that line.

"Look at me, brother. I am many things but not *that*, and I would never put my hands on a woman without her okay. No fucking way, not ever. I didn't even jerk off. I just helped her out of her dress and put her to bed."

Someone should give me a medal 'cause I can tell you it wasn't easy being next to someone that hot and not want to at least have a stroke.

"But you still spent the night? Why?"

"I don't know. I just wanted to stay. She lives in a shithole dude. Seriously, how that place isn't condemned is beyond me and she looked,

HIGH STRUNG

I don't know, vulnerable, and I didn't want to leave. So I stayed and held her for a while. It was kind of nice."

I shrugged, not really caring it made me sound like a complete pussy. Honestly, if it had been someone else, I would've probably just made something up, but it was Troy and he knew me better than anyone. We had been friends since we were kids and had been in bands together long before Power Station formed. It wasn't until we heard James and Alex were looking to form something solid, that we actually thought we'd play a genuine gig. We'd seen those two kids in the neighborhood and one day we heard them jamming in James's old man's garage. Troy knocked on the door and asked if they wanted a rhythm section, and that's how it started. Being in a band, making money doing what you love is a dream come true, and there isn't a day when I'm not thankful. But to do it with your best friend by your side, that's the motherfuckin' ultimate.

"Am I hearing right? The great Dan Evans spent the night cuddling?" Troy laughed not even trying to hide how much he was enjoying the situation.

"Whatever, asshole. I seem to remember you going home alone, and whether or not I got laid, I still went to bed with the hottest girl in the club."

I could have gone home with the two girls who had been getting hot and heavy with me earlier that night. Now I couldn't even remember their names but truthfully, after seeing Ashlyn, those two broads didn't even stand a chance.

Troy smiled, not the least bit pissed off. "I went home alone because I needed to help *you* get the *hottest girl in the club* and her crazy-ass friend, home. By the way, one of them left their purse in the Suburban. TJ found it in the backseat this morning when he took the car to the Wash and Vac."

"Well, whose was it?" I took another sip of my coffee.

"I don't know, I didn't go through it, dude. Girls have all kinds of weird shit in there, and I prefer to live in ignorance."

"Truth, right?" The man had a point. Some women were like Mary

61

Fucking Poppins with their purses; god knows what you are going to find. A man had no business going in there; some things are best not seen.

"We'll make Jase go through it, the man was in the Army. He's trained for that shit."

"I don't think they covered purse recon in basic training, Dan." Troy laughed,

"You know he was in IT, right? He wasn't actually on the front line dodging bullets. Not to take anything away from the man, 'cause straight up I am fucking thankful for his service and sacrifice, but unless you count hostile computer viruses our man wasn't in any danger."

The Army is still the Army. I don't care if you are sitting at a desk or on the front line. Those bastards are tough, and I'd rather have an IT guy who used to wear camo by my side when shit went pear-shaped, than a juiced-up security guy whose biggest claim to fame was being a mall cop.

"You wanna go through the purse?"

"Nope."

"That's what I thought. Jase it is then." I rested my case.

"So getting back to your wild night of spooning. What happened this morning? I assumed even though she isn't your biggest fan, she still would have been impressed you didn't try anything last night." Troy continued, not willing to let it go. I swear sometimes he was worse than my ma.

"Yeah, well maybe I didn't tell her that part." I'm not sure why I didn't, I know I should have told her, but I guess it pissed me off a little that she had just assumed.

"What? Why the hell not? You'd rather her think you are some asshole who takes advantage of women? No wonder you aren't getting laid." Troy chuckled. The bastard actually chuckled.

"Firstly, I can get laid any time I want. You seem to have forgotten, I scored two fine broads last night that would have more that scratched that itch. Secondly, Ashlyn had zero recollection of what went down.

HIGH STRUNG

When she woke up, she just assumed we'd done the deed. She was too busy telling me she isn't that *kind of girl* to give me a proper chance to explain. Then she found out I went through her underwear drawer and she threw me out."

I would have told her, eventually. Not to say that I wasn't hoping to rectify the no-sex thing in the morning but she completely lost her shit and told me to leave before I had a chance.

"You went through her underwear drawer? Jesus, Dan. Do you have any impulse control?"

"Oh not you, too. I was fucking bored, okay? I just looked, it's not like I sniffed it or did anything freaky with it." It was just a look, the way everyone was acting you would have thought I put it on and paraded down fucking 42nd Street. What is the big deal? It's not like she was *in* it at the time. Then, maybe you could call me a pervert.

"Well thank fuck for that. You want to wear ladies panties, knock yourself out but maybe in future get your own Victoria's Secrets."

"You are such a tool." I'd go commando before I'd pull on a pair of panties.

"Tool or not, I need to head back to the city, so if you're done crying into your caramel macchiato, let's make tracks." Troy tilted his head to my now empty cup.

"Is that what I'm drinking?" I angled the cup so I was able to read the writing on the sleeve. "It was actually pretty good." Kudos to the counter chick for her recommendation but I had to agree, it was time to eject. The small coffee shop was starting to fill with too much morning cheer for my liking. We both stood to leave. "Yeah, let's get out of here. I'm starving and there is fuck all in here to eat. No way I was chowing down on a fucking muffin." I needed food.

"What's wrong with muffins?" Troy scoffed. Poor fucker had no clue.

"It's like a poor man's cupcake. No frosting. So fucking dry. I'm putting something cake like in my mouth then I want it to be sweet and fucking tasty. Not some lame-ass muffin that has all the promise of goodness and then leaves you unsatisfied. It's like a girl who stuffs her bra to make her tits look bigger and then you get her home and boom, no big tits. I hate false advertising man, makes me angry."

I slid out of the booth and tossed my empty cup in the trash. Troy followed suit stretching out his back after standing and joined me as we strolled toward the door.

"Does it always come back to tits with you? No wonder you are sitting here with me instead of your girl. I've known you a long time, brother, but some of the shit that comes out of your mouth surprises even me."

"Tits are important, I don't know why you are fighting me on this. Cupcakes too, I love those little fuckers."

"You are so fucking weird, dude."

"Let's go, asswipe."

It was like a standoff. It eyed me from the other side of the room, taunting me. My hands fisted in agitation as I sat in the armchair across from it, watching it, wondering why something so small was giving me such a headache. I'm from the Bronx for Christ's sake, it's not like I had led a sheltered life. I've never backed away from a confrontation, not ever. And we have played some shitty dive bars in our time, especially when we first started out. Hell, some of those places we'd been lucky to walk out in one piece, and yet if someone were itching for a fight I would look them dead in the fucking eye and ask them if we had business. Now, I was getting my ass kicked by a six-inch, glittery purse that sat on my fucking coffee table. What's worse is that I'd rather take my chances with a drunk Giants fan from Jersey than crack that fucker open.

"FUCK!"

I moved to the edge of the chair wondering where the hell I'd left my balls. It was a purse, for fuck's sake, not a fucking bomb. I looked over at the half-eaten box of cupcakes sitting beside it, the lid still cracked open, reminding me I had smashed four of those bad boys on the way to my apartment. And despite Troy being an argumentative bastard and not being on the same page with my cupcake love, I let the big guy snare a couple of them too. I was a giving kind of guy. I looked away from the box, deciding I was probably already way too hyped on sugar to eat anymore, which is probably why I was jittery as fuck.

I ran my hands through my hair, frustrated, knowing I was just going to have to man up. Jase had already shot down my idea that he do it when I called him on the car ride over, laughing his ass off telling me to stop being a pussy and do it myself. What's the worst that could be in there? A tampon? It's not like I hadn't seen one of those before. Jase was right. I was being a pussy.

"Okay then, let's do this." I cracked my knuckles as I reached over and snagged it off the coffee table. I had half expected for it to shock me or something. For it to have some magical powers that meant if anyone with a dick opened it they'd get Tasered or some shit. Nothing. No sparks. No jolt of electricity passing through my body. Nada. Well thank fuck for that.

Slowly, I popped open the clasp. It looked innocent enough so I might as well dive in there and see if there was an ID or something. It had to be either Ashlyn's or Megs's and I hadn't paid enough attention to which of them had been holding this thing when they had gotten into the car. Both of them had fished out their apartment keys before we left the Suburban with Ash, who'd also pulled her phone out so she could text Megs she was home when we pulled up to her building. So that didn't yield any clues either.

I shook the contents onto the coffee table and out rolled a lipstick, a few dollar bills, and a condom. Nice, this was like CSI...piecing together a profile based on random shit.

I tossed the dollar bills to the side and I moved on to the condom. It was standard, nothing exciting. *Ribbed for her pleasure.* That shit always made me laugh. What kind of numbnuts needs a special condom to get off his woman? Straight up, if he is relying on the latex *for her pleasure* he is not doing it right. When I'm with a girl, I make her come at least once before I even stick my dick inside her. I get her nice and lubed up, soft and ready for me, so when I finally get my cock in her, she is so wound up she has no choice but to come again. I don't get the amount of girls I do solely 'cause I'm a good-looking guy. Women know when they are with me, I take care of them. I might not call them back later but while I'm fucking them, no one else exists. I was getting hard just thinking about it. Seriously, I was going to need to go jerk off soon or my dick was going to fall off. It had been hard so many times in the last twenty-four hours. I was surprised I still had the ability to fucking walk.

Next up, lipstick. I slid open the lid and rolled up the stick. Red. Like let-me-fuck-your-mouth red. I knew this color. I had washed it from my neck early this morning in Ashlyn's shower. This was hers. I'd bet my balls on it. I rolled the stick back down, imagining the color on her lips like it had been last night. That sweet, fucking mouth that talked way too much trash. Yeah, I wanted that mouth. I wanted to own every inch of those beautiful full lips, watch them stretch around the head of my cock while those sweet green eyes looked up at me.

"Get it together, asshole." I laughed out loud as I shoved the lipstick back into the purse, and had a quick look to see if there was anything else in there. Sure enough, there was a small zip sewed into the lining, and I'd figured I'd come this far, I might as well continue, right? I pulled the zipper across, the pocket it opened barely big enough for me to slide a finger or two inside. I pulled out a driver's license and an ATM card. If there were any doubts as to who the owner of the purse was before, I could put them to bed. Ashlyn's passive face looked up at me from the plastic, Boston-issued ID. She was about to turn twenty-eight, her birthday was in less than a week, and either she had never gotten around to changing her address to New York or she didn't plan on sticking around for very long. I tapped the card against my fingers hoping she wasn't planning on leaving soon. No one ever looked good with a DMV issued photo, but fuck me if she didn't look drop-dead gorgeous. She wasn't fancied up with makeup and her hair was pulled away from her face. She didn't need all that stuff to make her look good. She was beautiful without it.

"Fuck!" I closed my eyes and leaned back into my armchair. What was it about this girl that was turning my brain into a pretzel? It wasn't just the way she looked, though that sure as shit didn't hurt, but it was more than that. For the first time, I think I was actually *interested* in someone. I needed to see her again and now I had my opportunity. I would play it smart; for this girl, I was going need more than just my usual tricks.

9

Ashlyn

"MEGS!" I YELLED INTO THE PHONE WITHOUT GIVING HER THE opportunity to say hello. I needed to debrief and I needed it now. I sat on the edge of my bed, still reeling from the events of the morning.

"Ash?" Megs groaned into the phone. "My ankle is killing me. What happened last night and why aren't you here?" Her recollection was obviously just as unreliable as mine. Note to self - keep better track of how many cocktails consumed and don't go wandering around a club looking for trouble.

"So much happened last night. You fell as we were leaving *Panic*. I think we should probably go get it X-rayed. What do you remember?" I sighed knowing it was up to me to piece the riddle together.

"Did we meet Power Station last night?"

"Well I guess you could call it meeting them."

I would say what happened last night went a little beyond just an introduction, considering I woke up with one of the band members in my bed.

"The details are foggy. I think I remember hugging Troy Harris? Did

HIGH STRUNG

you make out with Dan Evans?"

I let out a long, slow breath. Megs was my best friend. Not only did I tell her everything but I also needed a sounding board. I needed her to help me make sense of this in my head, how I could have done something so out of character. "I think I did more than just make out with him."

"Ashlyn. You better start talking and fill me in with details."

"Let me get dressed and I will come to you. There is way too much to discuss over the phone. Do you need me to get you anything on my way over?"

"You don't happen to have any Percocet do you?"

"No, Megs. While I'm sure the apartment downstairs is probably a meth lab, I don't actually live in a drug store."

"Okay, then just get me the biggest coffee you can find and maybe a muffin. And hurry, I need details."

"I'll be there soon. Chill."

We said our goodbyes and ended the call. Tossing the phone onto my bed, I moved into my tiny bathroom. The fuzzy, faded bathmat was still damp from when Dan had taken his shower. He had been naked in this very spot. I tried to ignore my excitement as I stripped off my clothes. Shit. I looked around my bathroom in a moment of dread. He had seen this. A bra hanging from the towel rack, my messy vanity that was crammed with cosmetics and skin care. My wicker laundry hamper filled with dirty socks and polo shirts from the bar. The chipped paint, ugly pea-green tub with it's discolored shower curtain. The rust-covered faucet that spewed brown water for a few seconds when you ran the water for the first time in the morning. He had seen all of this. Mortified. That was probably the only apt description of what I was feeling. How he hadn't run a mile the minute he stepped inside was beyond me. I shook my head, solidifying my silent resolve to never see him again as I turned on the faucet and stepped inside the tub.

The old pipes groaned in protest through the thin plaster wall as I turned up the water to maximum capacity. It was the only way to achieve any kind of water pressure and even then it wasn't great. Still, today I had bigger problems than my ancient bathroom.

I showered and then dressed quickly, throwing on a pair of jeans and an old T-shirt before pulling on a pair of Vans. I just needed to grab my purse, my phone, and get out of here.

Now, where did I put my clutch from last night? It had my ID and my ATM card in there and while there was probably less than a hundred dollars in my savings account, the least I could do was spring for coffee this morning given Megs had paid for our night out yesterday. Hmm. Where did I leave it? I searched in the regular spots, the bedroom, and the kitchen counter - the places I would usually toss it when I walked in the apartment. Though given last night was not usual, it could be anywhere.

I ate up valuable time tearing from room to room, trying to locate the small, sequined culprit, but came up empty. I had my keys and my phone, so where was my clutch? I slumped onto my bed, willing it to reappear but sadly my *willing* did nothing but intensify the headache I was already fighting.

Giving up any hope of finding it, at least in the immediate future, I grabbed a random twenty-dollar bill I had found in my change jar and a handful of coins, and decided I would look harder when I got home. It had to be here somewhere.

"Hey." Megs greeted me at the door, hobbling while trying to balance a bag of frozen peas on her ankle. "I was getting concerned and was going to send out a search party."

"Sorry, Megs. I couldn't find my purse from last night. It had my ATM card in there. I still don't know where it is." I handed her the prized coffee before opening the paper bag that housed her muffin.

"Where did you leave it?" Megs asked, balancing her precious muffin

HIGH STRUNG

and coffee as she hopped back to the sofa where she allowed herself to fall into the large, plush cushions. Once settled, she lifted the lid from her cup to lick the whip off the top of her coffee.

"If I knew where I left it, it wouldn't be lost." I strolled out of the hallway and joined her on the sofa, pulling my cup of coffee out of the cardboard carrier and taking a sip.

Megs blew over the surface of her cup before taking a big gulp. "Okay, well you obviously got into your apartment so you must have had it on the way home…wait. How did we get home?"

"The Power Station Express," I deadpanned.

"They drove us home?" Megs's eyes widened.

"Yeah, well according to Dan, so not sure how reliable my information is." I bristled, annoyed I was at the mercy of his version of events.

"You better start telling me everything you know, Ashlyn Marie, or you are going to be wearing this coffee." Megs held up her paper cup up to verify she wasn't kidding.

"Okay, okay." I took a long breath and settled in, this story was going to take a while.

I started explaining how Dan had found us at the club's entrance, and how Megs's Louboutins were responsible for her rather undignified spill. Deciding to play hero, when clearly no one had asked him to, Dan had stepped in and with the help of Jason and Troy, bundled both of us into their car to drive us home. In reality, it could be seen as kidnap, who just takes two girls and puts them into a car? My theory was solid except obviously I hadn't been resistant to the idea and according to him, had my hands all over him on the ride home. A vague recollection of giggling in the back seat flashed into my mind as I recounted the story.

"Let me touch you." *I moved my hands down his chest as I pushed my lips against his mouth, his hand threading through my hair as our kiss deepened.*

"Fuck," *he groaned as I flattened my palm against the front of his jeans, he was hard. The denim between us was so tight it left little to the*

imagination.

"I'm such a good girl, such a good, good girl," I moaned into his mouth, sliding my hand into the front of his pants. He hissed as my fingertips made contact with his skin.

"Yeah, you're really good." He gently eased my hand away from his erection, his sexy smile making me want him more. "But unless you want me to come in your hand you are going to need to stop that, not that I have a problem with it, 'cause I don't, but I think we should probably get your friend home first."

"I want you, Dan. I want to have sex with you," I whispered into his ear, trying to be seductive but for some reason the word sex sounded so funny coming out of my mouth, it made me laugh.

Dan teased my lower lip down with his thumb. "Ashlyn, you're so drunk you have no idea what you're saying right now, babe."

It's strange, it was as if I was someone else, like I could say or do anything I wanted. I was braver, bolder, and his hand on my lips just turned me on more. I captured his thumb with my teeth, drew it into my mouth and sucked it hard. His jaw tightened. "Babe, seriously. I'm not even kidding. I'm so primed right now I'm going to blow my load in my jeans like a thirteen-year-old boy. I need you to really think about what we are doing, I'm not smart enough to be thinking for the both of us."

"It's killing me," Megs whined from the row of seats behind, reminding us she was still with us. "It's okay, Troy Harris, you can chop it off, I'll be brave."

"Megs, we're not going to chop off your foot." Troy chuckled, his voice surprisingly calm. "It looks like just a sprain. I still think we should swing by the ER and get it looked at."

"Noooooooo," Megs begged, sounding less like the twenty-nine-year-old professional she was and more like she just caught underage drinking. "They'll tell my dad. I'll be a laughing stock. We can't go to the hospital. Just get me home."

"Okay, Megs, we'll get you home." Troy tried to comfort Megs and he was being so incredibly sweet with her. "If you twist around, I can

HIGH STRUNG

elevate your foot for you. Hopefully it will help with the swelling."
As I leaned up against Dan's chest, a sense of ease flowed through me. Strangely, it was as if I didn't have to worry about Megs. She was in good hands. Whatever my thoughts had been about these guys, I was wrong. They weren't bad guys.
"Oh thank you, Troy Harris," Megs crooned, her discomfort eased by Troy's hands on her feet.
"Megs, just Troy. Seriously, just Troy." Despite it being the fiftieth time Troy had told Megs, there was no annoyance in his voice.
"I like saying your name though...it's sexy, like you, Troy Harris," Megs said sweetly.
"So you keep saying." He chuckled.
"I have to hand it to you, Dan, I was convinced tonight was going to blow but it has been rather amusing." Jason's voice floated from the front seat. I had forgotten he was with us, obviously sitting next to the mysterious driver who had barely spoken.
"Whatever, douchebag." Dan flipped him off which for some inane reason made me laugh.
"That's such a funny word." I smiled as my hands once again slithered southward.
"You girls are so wasted." Dan smirked as he gently stroked my arm.
I tilted my head to look at him saying the words I'd been dying to say all night. "Take me to bed, Dan. Stay with me tonight."
"Oh shit." I rubbed my hands across my face, Dan hadn't seduced me. I had seduced him. A fractured memory was providing more insight as to how Dan ended up in my apartment last night.

"What? What *oh shit*? Tell me I didn't make an even bigger ass of myself than it sounded like." Megs paled. While I had wanted to spare her the details, I figured it was better to be honest and tell her exactly what I remembered. Her muffin and her coffee forgotten as she carefully placed them on the side table. Obviously, the caffeine hit and nourishment was going to have to wait.

"I threw myself at him, Megs. He confronted me with it this morning and I denied it. I flat out refused to hear him out, but I remember being in the car, I remember having my hands all over him and asking him to spend the night." Sipping my coffee, not willing to forgo my caffeine injection.

"So you slept with him?" Megs's eyes widened.

"I guess I did because he was still there this morning, but I honestly can't remember." My fingers squeezed at the bridge of my nose. "Who forgets they had sex? Is that even possible to have sex and have no recollection of it at all?" I mean, surely I should have remembered something? It's not like I had sex a lot, surely it would have stood out in my brain as something noteworthy.

"There's a few times I'd rather forget but sadly they are still with me," Megs commiserated. "So you guys dropped me off and then you went to back to your place. Do you remember anything about getting home?"

I closed my eyes, trying to force the fragmented night to somehow piece itself together in temporal lobe.

"Babe, you sure this is where you live?" Dan glanced out of the tinted window of the Suburban, studying the derelict building I had directed the driver to.

"Yes, this is me. I have to grab my keys, the security light is out again and I can never find the keyhole in the dark." I fumbled in my clutch for my keys, pulling out my phone instead. *"I have to text Megs, she likes to know I get home safe. Unless I stay at her house, then she automatically knows I'm okay."* I hoped the sentence made sense to Dan, the words didn't sound right as they spilled from my mouth but there wasn't a lot I could do to steer them into anything more coherent.

Dan opened the door as I finally fished out my keys. I held them up victoriously, jingling them in my fingers as I placed my clutch on the seat beside me and unhooked my seatbelt.

Dan stepped out of the car and walked around to my side of the car. *"Let me walk you up, okay?"*

"You aren't staying? You said you would stay." I pouted as I stepped

74

onto the sidewalk, doing my best puppy dog impression and trying to not drop my keys or my phone.

Dan pulled me into a hug, his breath tickling my ear. "Babe, I don't think that's a good idea. I'm really trying not to be a piece of shit here and I have to tell you, my dick wants to kick my ass right now."

"But I want you." I wrapped my arms around his neck, ignoring the idling car waiting for his return. "Maybe I should have words with your dick, we both seem to want the same things."

"Fuck, Ashlyn." He released himself from my embrace. "Look, give me one minute."

He moved over to the car and spoke to Troy through the window. I couldn't hear what was being said but it felt like victory. I had convinced him to stay. He was going to have sex with me. It was going to be good sex too, I bet. He looked like he was built for it and I couldn't tell you the last time I actually came. Well not when a guy was present anyway. Dan Evans was going to make me orgasm.

"Okay, babe, lead the way." He put his arm around me and walked me up the stairs of my apartment building.

While I was no closer to finding out how *good* the sex had been, I was fairly sure I knew where my clutch was. Probably sitting on the backseat of the Suburban, where I had stupidly left it after grabbing my keys. I scrubbed my face with my hands. I was going to have to call him. I wasn't sure if it was excitement or dread bubbling in the pit of my stomach.

"I have to call him," I vocalized, clueing Megs into my internal thoughts.

"Well I was hoping if you'd slept with him, at the very least you were going to see each other again."

"I hadn't planned on it but I guess I don't have much choice. Unless I get him to UPS my clutch to me." I laughed, knowing how ridiculous that sounded. We were adults, sure it might be awkward, but we could move past it so that he could give me my misplaced item and I could try to salvage some self-respect.

I placed my half-empty cup on the coffee table in front of me and pulled my phone from my pocket. I scrolled down my contact list, angling my screen away from Megs so she wasn't able to see the sensual shot Dan had gifted me with this morning. My finger hovered over his name, not quite able to make that final step.

"Just call him already." Megs gently shoved my shoulder.

"Don't rush me. I'm calling." I pressed call before I had the opportunity to chicken out. My heart was beating so fast, I was positive he was going to be able to hear it.

"Yo. Talk to me." Dan's voice burst from the speaker. His New York accent seemed more pronounced on the phone.

"Dan? Is that you?" I knew it was him, so I'm not sure why I asked for confirmation. No doubt my subconscious was buying me some precious time so I could work out what I was going to say.

"Ashlyn." He said my name and all I could think about was him standing in my room, wearing only a towel. "Miss me already? I knew you'd call."

His arrogance grated on me. Had this been his plan the whole time? Knowing I would have no choice but to call? No, while Dan was cocky I didn't think he would be *that* premeditated. Still, I decided to play it safe. "Yeah well, this isn't really a social call, so don't get too excited. I need my clutch, I left it in your car."

"You left your clutch in the car? Is that some kind of riddle?" The confusion in his voice was adorable. "Isn't that where a clutch belongs?"

"Not a clutch for gears. An evening bag, a clutch." I bit back my smile as I explained, Megs watching me closely.

"Your purse?"

"Yes, my purse. I think I left it in the Suburban. Can you have your driver look for me?"

"Yeah, you left it. Troy had it with him when he came and picked me up this morning."

"Well if you had it this morning, why didn't you bring it to me?" I was slightly annoyed I had been worried about it the whole morning and

HIGH STRUNG

Dan had known the whole time.

"'Cause you were moody and I was hungry."

"Okay, so why didn't you bring it to me after you had breakfast?" I tried to remain calm despite his bogus reasoning. Five minutes. It would have taken five minutes to make the exchange and then he could have gone on to stuff his face with whatever he chose to.

"Oh we didn't eat in Brooklyn, we drove back to Manhattan. I wanted cupcakes."

I pulled the phone away from my ear and stared at it. I shook my head at Megs as I tried to follow the conversation. He wanted cupcakes? Is he for real? Or is he just pushing to see how far the dopey routine will go before I blew.

"So why didn't you call me then?"

"Um, to ask if you wanted cupcakes?"

"No! To tell me you had my purse!"

"I didn't have your number."

"How do you not have my number? You went through my phone and programed in yours."

What was it about this guy that seemed to push my buttons so hard? There was no middle ground with him. The embarrassment I had felt when I started this conversation had long been forgotten. In its place was a simmering rage that at any point could explode into something more substantial.

"I just looked at your photos, I didn't go through your contact list. Besides, stealing your number is kind of an invasion of privacy."

"Are you kidding me? You went through the photos on my phone and my underwear drawer but you drew the line at my *number*?"

Megs stared opened mouthed as she sat beside me. I possibly had forgotten to mention the fact Dan had been sniffing around in my panty drawer, my brain misfiring as the memories of the evening were coming back to me in slow bursts.

"Well...yeah. I'm not a stalker, babe."

What in the hell? His logic made no sense. None at all. Not even a little. Was he just trying to infuriate me?

"Just give me my freaking purse back," I spat out through my clenched jaw.

"Geez no need to get mad about it. It's not like I was going to keep it. I figured you'd call eventually."

He seemed so unaffected. This wasn't an act; he really just had a basic and simplistic view of things. How he had managed to get through life unscathed astounded me. Perhaps I should be impressed but it only served to remind me of the injustice in life, how not everyone had to work hard for their rewards.

"Okay, so I've called. Can I have it back please?"

"Sure, especially seeing as you said please." I sensed his smile through the phone. "I'll pick you up for lunch in an hour? That good?"

"What? No! We're not having lunch."

Did he just ask me on a date? While we were in the middle of a heated discussion? This man had zero boundaries, either that or an incredible self-assurance with no fear of failure.

"We can do dinner if you prefer, I just figured you'd want your shit back sooner."

"No, no dinner either. I just want my stuff. I'm not going out with you."

"But you have to meet me somewhere so I can give it back to you, right? I don't see the problem," he reasoned, unable to see why I was refusing his offer.

I took a deep breath while Megs tapped my arm, silently encouraging me to go. I was glad I was only going to have to recount the one side of the conversation she hadn't heard, though I'm guessing she was catching the vibe all by herself without my input. I needed to be honest. Something about him fried my brain. I didn't trust myself around him.

"The problem is that when I'm around you, I obviously exercise poor judgment. So I think it's best if you just drop off the bag and we go our separate ways. No dates."

HIGH STRUNG

"Lunch isn't a date." Dan laughed.

"Are you holding my clutch for ransom?" I half shouted into the phone, still a little hung over and too tired to deal with his circular logic. He just didn't get it.

"Why are you being so bitchy? I'm trying to be a good guy here. I have to see you anyway to give you your purse so let me buy you some lunch."

"If I'm bitchy, why would you want to buy me lunch?"

"Even bitches have to eat, don't they?" He laughed, clearly enjoying himself.

"Calling me a bitch is not endearing yourself." I narrowed my eyes, unsure of whether or not I was glad he couldn't see me right now.

"You're a bitch, I'm an asshole. Can we move on to lunch already?"

"Ugh. Fine. Buy me lunch."

"So where do you want to go?"

"Just meet me at Applebee's on West 42nd."

"You want to go to Applebee's?"

"Yes! Just meet me there in half an hour, okay? And bring my purse."

"Okay, see you then."

I ended the call and pushed my hands into my face. "He is so impossible," I groaned, annoyed he had somehow talked me into going on a date with him.

"Ash, unless you are in high school, Applebee's isn't a date." Megs laughed, pulling me into a hug. "Applebee's?" she repeated as she pulled a funny face.

"I tried to think of a place I was least likely to want to get naked around him. I clearly can't be trusted."

"Sweetie, you've already slept with him. A meal isn't going to kill you. Go have fun and then come back and tell me all of the details." Megs playfully pushed my shoulder. Of course, she was right. I could sit across a table and eat and not feel the need to sleep with him again. If anything, this would be the closure I needed. I would ask him calmly exactly what had happened last night and then say a final goodbye. I looked down at my phone's darkened screen, sitting in my lap. That goodbye would definitely be bittersweet.

10
Dan

"CAN I GET YOU SOMETHING TO DRINK WHILE YOU WAIT ON YOUR guest?" the pretty blonde waitress asked as I drummed my fingers across the table. She had to be barely twenty-one but her smile told me that if I were into it, she would be happy to show me a different kind of menu.

"No, I'm fine for now, thanks." I smiled back, not wanting to cash in on what she was offering. This was so unlike me. Ordinarily I would have taken her number and found out exactly what was hiding underneath that little black polo she was wearing.

"Okay, well let me know if you change your mind." Her hand floated down and trailed along the top of my knuckles.

So this is why Stone got so much pussy? Girls liked it when you pretended not to be interested. Well, fuck me. Wasn't that just the revelation of the century? Son of a bitch could have clued me onto this earlier though.

I gave her a smile, figuring I had to give her something, and that seemed to satisfy her. She sauntered off leaving me to sit in the booth by myself like a douche. I hadn't even bothered to check out her ass as she walked away. I must be off my game.

I had arrived at Ashlyn's choice of restaurant right on time but she still hadn't showed. I asked for a booth toward the back and let the waitress know I was expecting a guest, although why she picked this venue was a mystery. I can't remember the last time I was in one of these places. Still the location was unimportant, she had agreed to meet me and I had that tiny, sparkly purse to thank.

"Hey, sorry I'm late." Ashlyn rushed in, her face a little flushed. "I walked from Megs's apartment." She collapsed into the bench seat opposite me. "It took a little longer than I thought."

"It's okay, babe, I haven't been waiting long." I watched as she nervously picked up the menu in front of her, a few strands of unruly red hair fell across her face, the rest of her curls were pulled back away from her face and secured by a hair tie. She looked completely different, no business gear or short dress and come-fuck-me heels. Just a pair of jeans, some faded bar T-shirt, a pair of Vans kicks, and no makeup. My dick punched out in my jeans in appreciation. She was stunning.

"Here," I slid the purse across the table, feeling kind of stupid staring at her while she sat uncomfortably studying her menu. "I went through it but just to see whose it was. I wasn't doing anything shady."

She glanced up, her big green eyes looked at me and then dropped to the purse on the table. "Thank you. There wasn't much in there for you to see."

She looked awkward, nervous almost. It had seemed like such a good idea at the time, getting another opportunity to see her but now I felt like a giant dick making her sit here when she didn't want to be.

"Look, Ashlyn," I couldn't believe I was about to fucking say what I was about to, both hating myself but knowing it was the right thing to do, "you don't have to stay, you have your purse. You can take off if you want."

HIGH STRUNG

Those big green eyes nailed me as she disregarded her menu. "Dan, I'm sorry. This is just really—"

"Weird?" I finished for her. She wasn't hard to read; I felt the vibe the minute she walked in.

Strangely, I hated she felt that way and what I hated even more was that she was feeling it because of me. Maybe touching all that girl stuff from her purse did something to my balls 'cause seeing her like this was giving me feelings and shit. Next I'm gonna need a fucking box of Tampax and start blubbering while watching *The Notebook*. It's not like I hadn't cared about girls' feelings in the past, they just seemed less important than my own. Yeah, I know I'm an asshole, but I just didn't feeling like being one right now, even if the rest of my body didn't agree.

"Yeah, weird. I've never had a one-night stand before so yeah sitting across from you pretending you haven't seen me naked is…well it's awkward." She smiled and damn if that didn't make me want to reach across the table and kiss those sweet lips.

"Ashlyn, listen…about last night." My dick punched out in protest, warning me to keep my big fucking mouth shut. "I don't think you really know what went down." Her eyes widened, as she waited for me to finish. "We didn't sleep together last night. I mean we slept together, but we didn't fuck." I managed to say the word fuck just as the blonde waitress returned to take our drinks order.

"Uh…can I get you guys some drinks to start off with, maybe some appetizers?" She fumbled through her regular, obviously rehearsed speech. Thank fuck she didn't ask if we wanted to hear the specials.

"You want a soda or something?" I asked Ashlyn who continued to stare silently. I wasn't able to get a read on whether it was a surprise we-hadn't-slept-together or you're-an-asshole-I-want-to-hurt-you look. I'm going to be honest, both of them kinda blew.

She nodded, responding, "Coke."

"Make that two."

The waitress quickly left after it became obvious we were in the middle of something.

"Then we didn't do *it*?" Ashlyn leaned closer across the table. "But I remember, telling you I wanted to, in the car. You tried to talk me out of it but I..." She didn't need to finish the sentence. I remember that car ride; hardest thing I ever had to do was ask her to cool it. I wanted her so bad but I knew it was just the booze talking.

"Yeah, you said that and I have to admit, you weren't making it easy for me. We made out but that's it. You were drunk and you passed out. Nothing happened." I looked her in eye, I don't know why, but it was important to me that she knew it was the truth.

"You could have...there are guys that would have..." I hadn't seen this side of her; she'd always come across so confidently, so feisty. I wasn't sure if she was embarrassed or the realization of what could have gone down hit her.

"What? Done it anyway? Fuck, Ashlyn, no. I know you don't think very highly of me and that's fine, but if I'm going to be with a girl then she has to be able to say she wants it and she is going to damn well remember what it felt like after we're done."

"But if we didn't have sex, why did you stay?" Her green eyes sparkled with genuine curiosity.

"'Cause you asked me to." It didn't make a lot of sense to me, either. I'm not a cuddler. The whole big spoon, little spoon thing bewilders me and yet, last night, it just felt right.

"But I've been nothing but horrible to you. I don't understand." She stared me down, owning the fact she'd been bitchy.

I couldn't help laugh, all that feisty bullshit made my balls get tight. If her intention had been to turn me off, she had failed. "Yeah, you haven't been my biggest fan but you're honest and I can respect that, and the shit you said didn't really bother me."

"How? How can it not bother you? I mean honestly, doesn't it hurt when people say mean things about you?"

"Hell, no. Look at me. I am doing what I love and getting paid bank to do it. People think I'm not the smartest guy in the world but who the fuck cares? People slave away every fucking day killing themselves lining someone else's pocket with green, hating their jobs and hating their lives. I've got none of that. This is exactly what I wanted to be doing. This is exactly who I want to be. I get to travel the world and play gigs with my four best friends who happen to be some of the coolest people I know, even though sometimes they act like a bunch of douchebags."

Admittedly, I did care what *some* people thought. That group—the people I cared about—was very small however. Everyone else could take their best shot and it would slide right off me. Hell I'd be in a nuthouse if I bought into my own press. Half of the shit printed was genuine lies but I didn't care enough to set them straight.

"I just don't understand how you can be so cool about it." Ashlyn shook her head, for some reason she was having difficulty accepting my reasoning. Maybe I wasn't explaining myself clearly enough. No one had ever bothered to ask me before so it's not like I had a speech prepared.

"Easy, I'm not trying to live up to anyone's ideals, babe. I've got my own gauge. I'm fine with it."

The waitress came back with our sodas and seeing as Ashlyn had made the choice to stay, we decided to order. I was freaking starving so went with a cheeseburger and fries while she opted for a standard BLT. At least she didn't order a salad. Girls that didn't eat were always super cranky and I think Ashlyn had enough attitude without adding being mad because she was hungry to the equation.

"Wow, Dan, I feel like I owe you an apology." Ashlyn watched as the waitress left the table. I kind of wished I hadn't have left the venue up to her. The place was starting to fill with families and tourists and even though we were seated toward the back, it was getting noisy.

"For what?" We'd already placed our order so if she was having second thoughts about being here, she should have said something earlier.

She leaned in so I could hear her better over the kid that was crying two booths over 'cause he had to eat his Mac 'n' Cheese before his mom would let him have dessert. "I judged you. Assumed the stereotype was right."

"Ha, well for the most part it kind of is. James is the sensitive one - girls eat that I'm-going-to-love-you-forever bullshit. Alex is the cool one - he has the iceman routine down and it drives girls fucking crazy. Troy is like a big teddy bear – big-ass dude, but hilarious and has a really good heart so naturally he has no problem with the ladies either. Jason is the smart one – serious, but one of the most loyal dudes I know. Girls get wet knowing that he is technically an IT nerd and if the earth tilts off its axis and the band was to end tomorrow, he could go right into a job that pulls six-figures. And that just leaves me."

"The bad boy. The life of the party, sleeps around and the one ladies want to try and tame," she concluded, thinking she had me all worked out.

"Bad boy makes me sound like a jerk-off." I rolled my eyes, fucking bad boy? Made me think of eighteen-year-old punks from fucking Beverly Hills driving around in their old man's Porsches. I think not. "Let's think of something else instead."

"But that's why girls want to sleep with you - the challenge." Ashlyn smiled, no fucking doubt pleased she had hit a nerve.

"I don't know, Ash. I never really asked any of them." I rubbed the back of my neck thinking this was dangerous territory. Wasn't it fucking bad to be talking about other women with the chick you hoped to get lucky with? I'm sure Stone told me something, not that I'd ever admit he was right, but when it came to ladies, the asshole knew his stuff. "It's not like I give them a survey to fill out after."

"Might be an interesting marketing exercise."

She obviously wasn't letting it go, and it was making me confused. Were we supposed to be talking about it or not? I wish I had a phone-a-friend option 'cause I could use a lifeline right now. It was a hell of a lot easier just to get them in bed; conversation was a fucking minefield.

"Nah, I don't want to know."

"C'mon, Dan, you're not that shallow. You are sitting in an Applebee's with a girl who you haven't slept with, having a normal conversation. I think maybe there's more to you than that."

"Well, maybe that's how I am and you are just seeing me differently." I needed to change the direction of this conversation quickly. "I'm the same guy you met when you were staring at Stone's ass. This place is kind of lame though. I should've vetoed the decision and made you meet me at Hooters."

"I was not staring at Alex's ass."

The red that crept up her cheeks told me different and damn if that didn't make me jealous of that bastard.

Our server approached the table, balancing a plate in each hand. He was a pimply kid who probably had more hair on his chin than he did on his balls. Shady little shit's smile widened as he placed the plate in front of Ashlyn, making her visibly relax and sit up straighter in her chair. He looked over at me, the smug smile disappearing as I eyeballed him. He put the plate down, and wouldn't you know the kid must have been a genius 'cause he wisely kicked up the speed and took off. I wasn't about to let the Stone issue go, hell no was she getting out of it that easy.

"Ashlyn, come on. I thought we were being honest here."

She took a sip of her Coke before answering, "Fine, I'll admit it. Can we move on? Don't you dare tell him, I'll deny it and then say the reason we haven't had sex is because you couldn't get it up. Incidentally, I wouldn't have minded Hooters, I like their chicken wings."

I couldn't help myself, bursting into laughter. Wow, she was good. I backed her into a corner and she came out swinging. Fuck if that didn't just make me want her more. "No one would believe you, sweetheart. My cock has never had a problem getting it up. But don't worry your secret crush is safe with me. Oh and Ashlyn, I'd marry a plate of Hooters wings if that shit were legal."

"See, even *bad boys* want a commitment." She stole a French fry from my plate and popped it into her smirking mouth.

I could see this *bad boy* bullshit was going to give me grief. "You know, if Troy hears you calling me that he's going to be paying me out for weeks."

"It's funny, I know I met him last night but I don't remember a whole lot about him." Ashlyn turned her attention back to her own plate, picking up half her sandwich.

"Yeah, you did. He found you and your friend Megs trying to sneak into the VIP section. Maybe if you play your cards right, you might get to meet him again." I picked up my burger and took a bite. While our meeting might have started off weird, we had slipped into something else and it felt really good. I wasn't going to let this chick walk away, that's for sure.

"Why? You see us hanging out again after this? Isn't that kind of bad for your image, spending time with a girl you're not sleeping with." Ashlyn took another bite of her sandwich.

"Well maybe you should sleep with me and we can save my reputation," I suggested. Mighty fine suggestion too if you ask me, I wanted her under me so badly my balls hurt.

"No, Dan. As tempting as that offer is, I'm going to have to decline." She shot me down without even considering it. Time to work a new angle.

"Your loss then." I shrugged before adding, "Maybe you can be my exception?"

"Your exception? What do you mean?" She stopped eating and gave me her full attention. I liked it, her eyes on me, listening to what I was saying. Not just because she wanted to end up underneath me but because she honestly wanted to hear what I had to say. It had never really mattered before, having a girl's attention for reasons other than my dick. Now that I had it, I wasn't in a hurry to give it up.

"I mean, this has been surprisingly kind of nice. I don't usually just hang with girls and as long as you don't spread any bullshit rumors about me being sap or having a limp dick maybe we should do this again." I gave her a smile, knowing it would probably set her off again.

"Spread rumors about you?" She huffed from across the table. "If anyone is spreading rumors it will be you about me."

"Yeah well, we can only improve your reputation with that rumor.

Who the fuck has never been to a concert in their lives? I'm still in fucking shock." I coughed trying to suppress a laugh. I was enjoying pushing her buttons a little too much for my own good.

"I believe there were other things on that list too: a one-night stand and jerking off a guy in a car," she threw back, fighting a grin.

"Well I hate to break it to you, but the jerking off thing...you did it last night. You were pretty good for a rookie." I leaned back, my cock suddenly needing more room in my pants. The memories of last night were going to be in rotation in my spank bank for weeks.

"Oh my god. If you were a gentleman you would kindly forget that happened and not tell me any more details." Ashlyn grabbed her paper napkin and tossed it rather poorly at me.

I deflected her friendly fire with very little effort. "That's your mistake, babe, I'm no gentlemen."

11
Ashlyn

AFTER SPENDING A REALLY PLEASANT FEW HOURS WITH DAN, I, OF course, had to return to Megs's apartment and give her a very detailed debrief. I was surprised she hadn't asked me to put together a PowerPoint presentation. She made me repeat everything over and over, laughing over how funny he was and obviously how sweet he had been with me the night before, while I had displayed questionable judgment and even more questionable sobriety. I agreed with her in that perhaps my initial summary of Dan Evans being a disgusting—albeit delectable—manwhore was somewhat skewed. I still believed him to be a manwhore, and he was definitely still delectable, but something had shifted and I really liked being around him. I begrudgingly made my way back to Brooklyn.

I had my usual Saturday night shift at Garro's, the shift hardly anyone wanted to work because it was usually date night despite the guarantee of earning big tips. Granted those tips were well and truly earned and I usually had to spend most of the latter part of the evening swatting away hands from my ass. Why did men get so grabby after sinking a few

HIGH STRUNG

beers?

It had been loud and hectic at the bar. College ball had dominated the big screens with Syracuse defeating West Virginia just before the end of the final quarter. Football games always packed the venue and it generally meant my eight-hour shift seemed infinitely longer. A fight had broken out around half time when some out-of-towner wanted to start trouble with a local, but Kenny, one of the large bouncers, soon saw those two work out their issues with some choice words and a stern look. Still, game nights meant a larger crowd so when I finally dragged my ass home at three a.m. I was dead on my feet.

I peeled off my standard Garro-issued polo and stepped out of my black pants, tossing them into my neglected laundry hamper, its contents now spilling onto the floor. I was going to have to lug it down to a laundromat tomorrow, which was really just later today. I turned on the faucet, needing to wash the smell of beer and sweat out of my hair and skin and waited the obligatory few minutes until the water ran clear. I closed my eyes knowing that one day I'd be able to take a shower without this ridiculous ritual.

My stomach growled. The only food I had consumed since lunch had been a grilled cheese sandwich that Reuben the cook had whipped up in the fifteen-minute break I had taken. I was pretty sure there wasn't any food in the apartment, so growling or not, my stomach would have to wait until daylight hours.

After a quick shower, I continued to ignore my protesting stomach and crawled into bed. I closed my eyes and tried to sleep. Not happening. I tossed and turned, crawling over to the opposite side of the bed. I could still faintly smell Dan's scent on my pillow. I brought it closer to me, inhaling the rectangular feather bag like a drug addict taking a hit. Insanity. Perhaps the poison from the lead paint peeling from the walls had finally seeped into my brain? That had to be the only explanation as to why I was up at three thirty in the morning sniffing a pillow.

I punched it. The pillow. Because *that* made all kinds of sense. I groaned in frustration, annoyed that I wanted Dan laying beside me and knowing it wasn't going to happen. It couldn't happen. We were too different. I had no place in his world, how could it even work? The minute he slept with me I would turn into one of *those*. Another story to tell, another fun time. But still...I wondered if it would be worth it. I had seen another side of him today, a sweet man underneath his ever-present bravado. Was it an act?

"Ugh!" I punched the pillow again. Sadly it didn't make me feel any better than it did the first time I'd punched it, my misguided emotions still twisting through my head. I took a deep breath and reached for the phone that sat idly on my nightstand. The dark screen illuminated with a swipe of my finger. Without thinking I scrolled to his name and pressed on his photo, that erotic image teasing me from behind the glass. I could look at it for hours. Torture. Obviously that was the solution, because clearly punching a pillow hadn't worked. I brought the phone closer, the screen inches from my face, the temptation to touch it too great as I ran my finger down the image, imagining what its reality would feel like.

I continued in my silent indulgence, committing every line of his torso to memory. The sweeps of color in his tattoos burned into my brain. The light in the image shifted momentarily as I ran my finger along the glass, his name highlighted across the screen. Shit! I watched the phone dial of its own accord. My finger must have inadvertently hit call while I was stroking the image. I fumbled with the phone managing to quickly hit end before he had a chance to answer. I breathed a sign of relief silently thanking the gods the call hadn't connected.

The relief and thanks had been premature however, as my phone once again illuminated with that taunting image. Fuck. Dan was calling me.

"Hey," I answered, trying to sound casual but ended up sounding like an airhead.

"Ashyln?" Dan's voice flowed from the speaker. "Did you just call me and hang up?"

He sounded good, his voice husky from sleep. My call had obviously woken him.

"Oh. Yeah. It's my bedtime routine. I pick a random number to prank.

HIGH STRUNG

Must be your lucky night."

"Yeah, I'll say." A low chuckle filled my ear and vibrated through my body. "Are you just going to bed now?"

"Yeah, I just got home. Sorry. Honestly. I didn't mean to wake you." I pulled the phone closer, hearing the distinct sound of sheets rustling. I liked that we were both in bed, together, even though we really weren't.

"Babe, you can call me anytime. I hope you weren't terrorizing some other band in a club, 'cause I kind of thought that was *our* thing." The smile in his voice was unmistakable.

"I was working, Dan, and we don't really have a *thing*."

"So you get drunk and hassle other guys?"

"No, of course not."

"See. Just reserved for me. *Our* thing."

I sighed, surprisingly he was so easy to talk to. "Whatever, Dan, it's too late to argue with you."

"So where do you work that gets you home at this hour? Have you been holding out on me and you are really a stripper?"

"Dan, there are lots of jobs that have night shift. Most of them don't involve removing my clothes. I could be a nurse, or a gas station attendant." I pretended to sound annoyed.

"I prefer stripper." He laughed, indulging his fantasy a little longer.

"I work in a bar, Dan, serving assholes beer and nachos. Sorry, there is no pole involved."

"Why you working in a bar? Is this like Good Will Hunting where Matt Damon was working as a janitor but was a genius at night?"

"Sadly, I'm neither a genius nor doing this by choice. It's the only job I could get. Not a lot of brokerage firms were hiring commerce majors who had less than four years of experience."

"Wow, Ash, I'm sorry. That kind of sucks."

"Yeah, well it is what it is. No point bitching about, so I guess I'll just pour beers until I find something else."

"But you went for the interview with Lexi, she's bound to hire you. Why wouldn't she?"

"I don't think so. I'm not really assistant material so I don't blame her if she doesn't. I only wanted the job as a way out and I think she knows I probably won't stick around. Anyway, let's change the subject. It feels weird talking about it with you."

"It's okay, babe, you like weird with me."

"Don't flatter yourself, Dan, I never said anything about liking you."

Dan laughed, the ease in his voice warm. "So if you were slaving away all night serving assholes why didn't you collapse into bed the minute you got home?"

"I'm in bed, I just couldn't sleep."

"Hmm, so what are you wearing?"

"Dan."

"I'm sorry, babe, you want me to talk dirty while you touch yourself?"

"Um, no."

"I'll touch myself too, just so you don't feel like a pervert."

"I'm still going to decline. We're not having phone sex."

"Suit yourself, but I'm just putting it out there that I would be okay with it."

"Yeah well, I wouldn't so don't hold your breath."

My stomach picked the exact moment that neither of us were talking to break the silence with a very loud and aggressive rumble. Reminding me that in addition to the arousal I was now feeling, I still hadn't dealt with the other primal need, hunger.

"Holy shit. What was that?" His voice became more serious, obviously having heard the rumble through the phone.

"It was my stomach." I laughed, clutching it and silently willing it to shut up.

"It sounded like a fucking animal, you sure there isn't a rabid puma hiding under your bed?"

I felt my cheeks flush as I hid my face. "No, it's just me. I'm going to go now and be mortified by myself."

"Don't be mortified. It's no big deal, just eat something. I don't think that sound is normal."

"Okay. I'm going to hang up now. I'll talk to you later." I stupidly kept my face hidden even though he couldn't see me.

"Night, Ash. Eat something."

"Night, Dan."

I was equal parts horrified and elated as I placed the phone back on my nightstand. Well now I definitely wasn't going to be able to sleep. The sound of his voice was still ringing in my ear. The memory of his throaty laugh made parts of me tingle. Maybe I had been hasty in dismissing his suggestion of phone sex. Not that I had ever done it, no guy had ever asked. I'd touched myself before, lost in a fantasy while I brought myself to climax, but never with such premeditation. I chewed on my bottom lip as the frustration hummed through my body.

It had been a really long time since I'd had sex, at least seven months. Tim Reeves had been my last boyfriend, a law firm associate with a foot fetish. Of course I didn't know about the fetish until I had been dating him for a while and it seemed logical to move it to the next level. So one night after dinner and heavy make-out session in his Buick Regal, I told him to take me back to his apartment. He was smart, sexy, and had a promising career, and most of all, he seemed really into me. Problem was, he was more into my toes than the rest of me, spending a solid hour sucking and licking them before he even removed his clothes. When he finally got down to the actual sex part, he had worked himself up so much he barely got the condom on and was inside me, and it was over. I had initially chalked it up to first-time nerves so we persisted. Correction, I persisted. Six months of overpriced pedicures and bad sex. I didn't have even one orgasm that I hadn't manufactured myself. I had even tried ribbed condoms and lube. Nothing. No spark. And if the only way I was going to get satisfaction was from masturbation, I might as well cut out the middleman. It seemed like double handling, no pun intended. So I decided it was time for Tim to move on, and while he was disappointed, I let him paint my toes before I kissed him goodbye.

Dan was *nothing* like Tim. I was already wet thinking about his dark brown eyes and his sexy grin. I allowed my hand to move slowly down my stomach, settling at the waistband of my cotton pajama pants. I scrunched my eyes tight, feeling a little stupid doing this but needing something to help release some of my pent-up need. I slipped my hand a little farther down, my heartbeat kicking up as I toyed at the edge of my underwear. My nipples puckered underneath my cotton tank as I loosened the reins on my inhibitions. *Did you want me to talk dirty while you touch yourself?* Dan's words made me smile as I thought about what I was doing and how disappointed he would be if he knew he had missed it.

I was just about let my fingers slide into my underwear when I heard a thumping coming from my front door. What the hell? I sat up in bed and checked the time, four fifteen. This better be a pizza delivery boy with a prepaid order or someone trying to rob me because any other option was going to be met with grievous bodily harm. I kicked off my covers and jogged to my front door, greeted by a second round of thumping. I grabbed the baseball bat I kept in the hall closet for security and tentatively looked through the peephole.

"Dan!" I flicked open the lock and wrenched opened the door. "What the hell are you doing here at four in the morning? Have you completely lost your mind?" I stood in my doorway, the baseball bat still gripped in my hand. Honestly, I was still considering taking a swing.

"Oh easy there, slugger." Dan help up his hands in surrender, a white paper bag in this right hand. He looked just as amazing as he had earlier in the day, wearing a pair of faded blue jeans and leather jacket.

"What are you doing here?" I repeated, lowering the bat but not willing to relinquish it just yet.

"Well, you were hungry and I can always eat, so I went and snagged us a couple of hot dogs from Gray's Papaya. I figured we were both awake so..." He shook the bag in his hand. He came all this way because I was hungry? Who does that? Why was he being so nice to me when I'd been so bitchy towards him? Who was this man? What happened to the asshole I met a few days ago?

"Fine, come in." I stepped aside to allow him entry, resting the bat against the wall. "You can't just show up here at this hour, what if I had been sleeping?"

"Were you?" He didn't even try to hide the fact his eyes dipped down to my chest.

"No, not yet." I hoped to god he couldn't tell what I *had* been doing in the absence of sleep. Shit. Did I look guilty?

"So let's eat then." He strolled over to my couch and took a seat, ignoring the fact I hadn't followed him. "I'm going to start without you."

"Yes, we've already established you aren't a gentleman." I took a seat beside him and snatched the bag from his hands. "I'm starving."

"I told you to eat. I knew you wouldn't listen." He smiled, satisfied he had been right.

"It was time for bed, I wasn't going to go make something to eat." I pulled out a hot dog and took a bite. It was still hot and tasted like heaven.

"So you'd just ignore a bodily need?" He raised an eyebrow, taking back the bag and pulling out a hotdog for himself.

"No, just wait until a more decent hour," I explained in between chewing.

"That's such bullshit. If you needed to take a piss would you just wait that out too?" He shoved more hotdog into his mouth.

"God, you are disgusting. Tell me again how you charmed your way into my bed last night?" I rolled my eyes. He was so direct but despite me feigning annoyance it was actually quite refreshing.

"Sorry, let me rephrase. If you needed to *tinkle*... Better?" He smirked before continuing, "And I keep telling you, last night...all you."

"Tinkle? That was the best you could do?" I tried not to laugh. There was a strange innocence about him, he was kind of endearing.

"Says the woman who answered the door with a baseball bat. You either got lost on the way to Yankee Stadium or you were hoping to get a starring role in the next Pacino movie." He pointed to the bat still leaning up against the wall.

"Dan, just shut up and eat." I took another bite, wondering if there was another hotdog hiding in the paper bag.

"So…," he took a bite out of his hotdog, "you work a lot of nights?"

"As many as I can. Minimum wage blows and the tips are better at night." I placed the last bite into my mouth, savoring it.

"How do you get home?" Dan stopped chewing and looked at me seriously for the first time since I'd met him.

"I take the subway, sometimes a cab." I grabbed a napkin out of the now empty bag and wiped off my hands. Damn, no more hot dogs.

"Okay, how about this? You give me a call when you're working nights and I'll pick you up." He shoved the last of his dog into his mouth.

"What, you running a car service now? Don't you have important rock star shit to do? Thanks for the offer but I'm okay." I couldn't help but laugh. The thought of Dan waiting for me at the end of my shift and wondering how that would fit into his touring schedule, not to mention the scores of other women I had no doubt he attracted. I handed him a napkin.

"Ash, I'm serious. Don't take unnecessary risks. A friend of mine was hurt really badly not that long ago. Some asshole attacked her and she thought she was okay, too. I'm not saying that shit will happen, I'm just saying don't give it a chance to happen." He grabbed my arm, forcing me to look at him. "Call me. I will pick you up. I don't give a fuck what time it is, it will save you pranking me when you get home." His mouth curled slowly into a smile.

I knew what he was talking about. The *friend* in question had been Alex Stone's wife and their PR manager, Lexi Reed. It had made news when an ex-boyfriend had apparently stalked her and raped her in her Australian apartment. She had been beaten pretty badly, too, spending a lot of time in the hospital. I hadn't really given it much thought with celebrity news so far removed from my normal boring life. I guess you don't ever really see the human side to those stories, it was just more headlines. I was ashamed to admit, I had actually forgotten. Her violent attack had been relegated to old news that no longer seemed relevant.

HIGH STRUNG

Not that she would ever forget, even if the world had.

I was genuinely concerned but didn't want to make him uncomfortable by talking about it. "I'm sorry, Dan. I hope your friend is okay." I knew it was probably a no-go zone.

"She is. You going to call?" He leveled me with a stare, he wasn't kidding.

"Fine, if it will make you happy." It didn't seem like he would be letting it go unless I agreed. I knew I probably wouldn't call but it was easier to appease him than to tell him that. Strangely, it was touching he cared so much.

"It will. Are you done?" He tossed his napkin into the paper bag before angling it towards me.

"Yeah, thanks for the dog. I was actually pretty hungry." I bunched up the napkin and threw it into the bag.

"I know, I think they heard the growl of the wildebeest in Queens." He bit back a grin, instantly lightening the mood.

"Ass. I'm going to get some sleep now. Thanks again." I stood up, ready to walk him to the front door.

"Yeah sleep sounds good." He lifted himself off the coach and stretched, moving toward my bedroom door.

"Where are you going?" I grabbed his arm stopping him from going any farther.

"I'm coming to bed," he explained, clearly puzzled as to why it was a discussion.

My eyes widened from hearing his plan. "You are not coming to bed with me." He couldn't come to bed with me, could he? No. He shouldn't. I shouldn't. We should definitely not do that.

"Why, I swear I won't touch you. Even if you beg me like you did last night." He honestly seemed perplexed as to why it was an issue, like it hadn't occurred to him what might actually happen if we were in bed together. Obviously I was the only one thinking about it, and here I was thinking he was the one with the dirty mind.

"Dan, you can't just show up here and climb into my bed." I tried to rationalize, my resolve waning. I wanted him in bed with me, I did. I just didn't want to have to admit it. Not to myself and least of all not to him.

"Listen, Ash, we can argue about it for the next hour but we are both tired and I proved to you last night I'm not a scumbag. Just sleep. I promise." He wrapped his arm around my waist and pulled me down the hallway. He wasn't going to let up and I knew he probably would stand there and argue until he finally wore me down. One thing I'd learned about Dan, when he felt strongly about something he didn't budge, and I knew the only way I was going to be getting any sleep tonight would be with him beside me.

"I'm bringing the bat," I warned, though I left it safely leaning up against the wall as I allowed him to drag me into my bedroom.

"Okay, slugger, whatever gets your rocks off, but if it's a homerun you're looking for I think I'm probably better equipped."

"Do those lines ever work?" I shook my head, not believing he actually said stuff like that. I released myself from his grasp and slid into bed.

"Ninety percent of the time. You'd be surprised actually." He toed off his boots and pulled off his jacket.

"Hold on a second. What are you doing?" I sat up, watching wide-eyed as he continued his strip show, peeling off his T-shirt before moving to his socks.

"Getting undressed, I can't sleep in my clothes." His hands moved to his belt before unbuttoning his jeans, letting them fall to the floor.

I heard my voice waver as I stared at him, all that sexy inked skin on display throwing off my game. "Don't even think about taking off the boxers."

"Relax. You talk too much." He slid into bed beside me, thankfully leaving his boxers on. I couldn't help but want to see what was underneath.

I turned onto my side, knowing there was no way I was going to be able to sleep if I kept looking at him. I felt the mattress compress as he nestled beside me. His arms wrapped around me and pulled me closer.

"Dan," I whispered. "Your hand is on my ass."

"Old habits." He chuckled as his mouth pressed up against my neck. He slowly moved his hand to my hip. "Shhh. Go to sleep."

I allowed him to hold me, feeling his warmth and his scent as my eyelids started to droop. Instinctively I moved closer against him so our bodies were pressed against each other. My thoughts floated back to what I had been doing before Dan had interrupted me. The need had not gone away. If anything, with this new development, it had intensified. I tried to ignore the throbbing between my legs by squeezing my eyes shut and trying to think about something else. Anything other than the hardening length that was poking me in the ass.

I turned, knowing it was not only a bad idea but that his erection would now be poking in an entirely different area. I shouldn't have turned. What I should have done was go to sleep. But I didn't and now it was too late.

"Ash?" Dan's hooded eyes opened slightly wider as I wrapped my arms around him.

"Shhh. Go to sleep." I pressed my mouth against his, my tongue teasing the seam of his lips.

"I can't, if you keep doing that." He moved his hands back down to my ass. "Ash, what are we doing here?"

"I just want to kiss you." My lips traveled down his neck, as my hands moved along his strong, corded arms. If my body had a game plan it hadn't bothered to share it with my brain. I was winging it and had no idea on how far I was willing to let this go.

I slowly kissed my way back up to Dan's lips, and he seized the opportunity intensifying the kiss. "Ashlyn." He moaned as his tongue swirled inside my mouth. He rolled onto his back and pulled me on top of him. We continued to kiss, as frenzied hands pushed and pulled as we rocked against each other. I felt his cock lengthen as he moved me up against it. Its hardness giving me the sweet friction I craved.

Dan's hands moved to the hem on my tank top, pushing it up my body to expose my skin.

"No." My hand flung down to his, stopping the cotton from revealing more. "No sex, just kissing."

"Can't I even have a look?" Dan's wicked smile teased at the corners of this mouth.

"No." I laughed as I moved my lips back to his mouth and kissed him again. He took over, pulling at my bottom lip and dominating my mouth.

It was amazing. It was better than amazing. I had never been kissed like that. It wasn't *nice* or *sweet*; it was passionate and intense and made me feel like nothing else mattered outside of what we were doing. As if the world could stop moving and I would no longer care. In fact, who needed the earth's revolutions? The tumbling I had going on in my head was more than enough for me. Right now. At this moment. Nothing else mattered.

Dan groaned as he pushed his hardness against me, hitting me square between the legs. I gasped as he rubbed against me, the thin fabric of his boxers and my pajamas the only barrier between us. I felt something building, my body responding to his. I didn't want it to stop and I wasn't sure I should keep going. It felt so good. So very, very good. My nipples hardened under my tank top as he rubbed them against his broad chest. Our kiss deepened and he grabbed my ass underneath my shorts, guiding me as I grinded along his length. His fingers teased at the edges of my panties. His skin touching mine was electrifying. Caught somewhere between frustration and euphoria, I had never felt so alive. My heart was beating so fast and I knew I was going to come. The man was dry humping me and was about to achieve what other men hadn't while actually having sex. I arched my back and allowed the wave to take me.

"Ah." I involuntarily moaned as my body shook, the ripples of pleasure moving through me in a way I had never felt before. I should have been embarrassed, that he could do all that just by touching me, but I didn't care. I absorbed it, wanting to feel every last shudder.

"Mmmm." He groaned up against my neck. "I liked making you come." He was doing little to disguise his pride. "You know, I can make it better than that, really make it good for you."

HIGH STRUNG

"I'm sure you could." I smiled as the last echoes of pleasure moved through me, my body still entwined against him. He was still hard, the throbbing length pulsing against my clit. Without thinking, I reached for him, my hands floating down between my body and the tiny layer of cotton that encased his cock.

I lifted myself slightly off him, allowing my hand better access. I wanted to make him feel as good as he had made me feel. I wanted to touch him. My fingers breached the edges of his boxers, continuing until I wrapped them around his girth. He was big. Much bigger than I had felt before. Not only long but wide - my fingers could barely fold around him. Reading my intentions, he stretched out his body, raising his hips to meet me. He grinned. "Just letting you know, you're sober this time so I'm not going to stop you."

"Good, because I really want to do this." My fingers slowly moved up and down his shaft, squeezing as I reached the top.

"Fuck that feels amazing." His eyes closed as I continued to move faster. "Mmmm," he hummed in appreciation, as my tightly wrapped hand traveled up and down his length.

I used his verbal cues to guide me, his groans more unrestrained the harder and faster I pumped him. I loved watching his face contort in pleasure, the desperation in his hips as he rocked them against my hand. He was close; I could feel the deep throbbing between my fingers.

"Ash, I'm going to come." I felt his cock jerk in my hands as his body shook. "FUCK." He moaned as his sticky, hot load spilled onto my fingers. I continued to pump, milking every last drop, watching as he splintered beside me.

"Some kiss." Dan laughed, I felt him soften in my hand. "Fuck that felt good."

"I'll be back." I smiled as I slid out of bed and padded to the bathroom.

I turned on the faucet and washed my hand, watching as his cum slid into the sink and down the drain. I didn't do this. Take men I barely knew to bed and jerk them off. Or use their bodies as an extra large sex toy. But it had felt so good. Uninhibited. Hot. I glared at my reflection. I didn't look any different, but my actions hadn't felt like they had been my own. I didn't regret them though and strangely didn't feel embarrassed. I quickly used the bathroom, cleaning myself up before rewashing my hands. I dried them off, carrying the towel out with me into the bedroom. Dan curiously watched me as I approached.

I tossed him the towel as I climbed into bed, watching him smirk as he wiped the remaining cum from his toned stomach.

"You know, I can clean you up too if you want." His fingers swirled around my hip.

"Thanks, but I've taken care of it." I snuggled onto my side, feeling more relaxed than I had in months.

I heard the thud of the towel dropping and he curled up behind me, his hand pulling me closer to his body. "Let me know if you want another kiss," he whispered in my ear, a small chuckle traveling through his throat. I smiled in the dark, as his hands settled, resting just below my belly. He didn't go farther though and I knew he wouldn't, so I finally let my eyelids close and fell asleep.

'12
Dan

WAKING UP IN A GIRL'S BED WAS NOT NEW TO ME. I'M NOT A complete asshole. Not going to lie, I prefer to leave after the fucking has taken place but I understand that's not cool so I usually suck it up and stay. This was different. It was the second time I had woken up in Ashlyn's bed, neither time, had there been any actual fucking. The first time, I really had no business being there, but I didn't feel like leaving and if no one was going to kick me out, then I'd just as soon stay in her bed. I hadn't really done that before, actually *slept* with a woman. I mean, what was the point? But after putting her drunk ass to bed there was nowhere else I wanted to be. Last night was different. She had pocket dialed me or some shit, and hung up before I had a chance to answer. I had been home, asleep. Probably the first time in a long time I hadn't gone out on a Saturday night. Not something I planned but when Troy asked if I wanted to hang out, I told him to come over and we'd just play some poker or something. We threw a few hands and drank a few beers and it was actually a good time. Just shooting the breeze, no fucking distractions, paparazzi, or groupies. We called it a night around midnight with Troy giving me some fucking weird-ass look like I'd fucked his sister when I'd said I was heading to bed. So that's where I was when I heard my cell. When I saw the missed call I was pissed. Not that Ashlyn had woken me, but because I didn't get a chance to talk to her. Did she need something? She hadn't even left me a voicemail. I didn't even think about it, I just called her back.

I could have spoken to her for hours, the subject of conversation meant nothing and everything at the same time. So after hearing her stomach making a noise like a dying fucking bear, I jumped in the car, grabbed some food and took the drive over the bridge. Gray's was open twenty-four/seven and who didn't like hot dogs. I didn't even think about it, I just did it. I didn't even consider the fact she might not want to see me or that she wouldn't let me in. To me it was simple. I wanted to bring her something to eat, so I did.

When she opened the door holding a baseball bat and wearing more fucking attitude than actual clothes, I wanted to laugh my ass off. There was no way I was just dropping off the food and leaving, and I wasn't even thinking with my dick. There was something about this girl and I couldn't get enough. She wasn't like the ones I usually met, she didn't give a shit about me being Dan Evans and she sure as hell wasn't shy about telling me. I don't know why I felt the way I did but I just didn't want to go.

The kiss had been something else. I ain't going lie, the minute we were in bed and her body moved up against me, I got hard. I couldn't help that though, I was in bed with a sexy woman; my dick was just doing what he had been trained to do. I wasn't going to do anything about it though. Fine, I touched her ass but that was a reflex, like breathing. I mean, how could I not touch it? It was so fucking perfect. The point is, even though I was packing a hard-on that could have drilled through metal and I had briefly touched her ass, I fully intended to just

HIGH STRUNG

curl up beside her and go to sleep. I guess she had other plans. Plans I was happy to get on the same page with.

Kissing her was intense. Like being kicked in the balls intense. You can't think straight, you can't breath and all you can do is concentrate on what is happening right then. I could tell she was turned on. The little noises she made when I moved my tongue in and out of her mouth, the way her body moved up against me. It was killing me not to take off those fucking pajama pants and get inside of her but this wasn't about me. I wanted to get her off, to hear her pant and know it was because of what I had done to her. I had pulled her on top of me, positioned her so that my cock could hit her right where she needed it and made sure I didn't stop until her eyes rolled back and her legs shook. It was fucking beautiful and if I hadn't jerked off a few hours before, I would have spewed my load the minute her pussy came anywhere near my junk. The hand job had been unexpected. Who'd have thought I would get so fucking excited dry humping and getting jacked off by Ashlyn over actual sex? She had skills too, seemed like all that time pulling beers meant she was more than conditioned to handle me. I held out for as long as I could but when she looked at me with her hand wrapped tightly around my cock, it was game over.

I didn't want to wake her this morning but there was no way I was leaving without saying goodbye. She had this adorable dopey, sleep face and mumbled it was too early, while I explained I had to go but I would call her later. There was nothing I wanted to do more than to stay in the bed with her, having her tucked up tightly against me, but there was something I needed to do.

So without giving it too much thought, I jumped into my Benz and hightailed it back into the city. I didn't even stop for breakfast. I was focused on what I needed to do and I didn't want anyone talking me out of it, least of all not Ashlyn. Actually it was better if she didn't find out at all. It's not like it would make a difference; it was just useless information.

I hit the buzzer on the external door. There was no getting in unless you had a pass or were escorted in. Security was tight but I understood the why of it.

"Yeah," DarNell's voice boomed from the box fixed to the front outside wall.

"Yo, D. It's Dan. Let me up."

"A little early for you isn't it, sunshine? Your latest conquest turn into a pumpkin or she sober up and kick you out?"

"Yeah, something like that. Open up, will you. I'm starting to freeze my balls off."

The door hummed and then clicked, allowing me to open the gate and getting me into the building. Getting up to the Penthouse was another story. D would meet in the foyer, which was our usual drill unless he was in a mood and then he'd make me sweat it out. Lucky for me today he wasn't on his period and we can go about our business.

"Dan." Darnell gave me a once over, stepped out of the elevator and into the foyer.

"Hey D, we good to go up?" I stepped toward the big bastard and put out my hand. Six foot seven and as big as a linebacker from the NFL, he was pushing at least two hundred sixty pounds of pure muscle, with a big-ass bald head, and a stare that was as intimidating as fuck. I missed DarNell. Sure he used to ride my ass but he had been part of our security detail for years until last year, when he moved on to a private job. I understood things were different now and he had other responsibilities, but still, it was good to see him.

"Yeah, you're clear to go up but next time, maybe call ahead. You hear me?" And there was that stare that usually made the uninitiated piss their pants.

"I hear you. You need me to take a piss test or you relaxing the security measures?" I laughed as we walked side by side into the elevator, D inserting a key and hitting the access to the Penthouse.

"Keep your dick in your pants. I've seen enough of it to last me a lifetime, thanks buddy. As for security measures, you know why they are in place. Let's just get this over with. I'm imagining this is not a social

HIGH STRUNG

call and pretty sure whatever is about to happen, while it might be highly amusing for me, is probably going to suck for you." His big-ass grin widened, showing his pearly white grill. He always was such a wise-ass.

"Yeah, no doubt," I agreed, knowing he was probably right, not that it was going to change my mind. It wasn't the first time I'd been torn a new asshole at the hands of Lexi Reed.

The elevator doors opened into the large entranceway of the Stone Penthouse. This place was mint, huge by regular standards, but in Manhattan real estate terms, it was a fucking palace.

Alex was waiting at the door, wearing a stupid grin on his face like he usually did when he was around his hot fucking wife. "Dan, to what do we owe this unexpected pleasure?"

"Not here for you, asswipe, here for your Mrs." I gave him a friendly punch in the shoulder.

"Really?" Alex's shit-eating grin got wider as we walked inside the apartment. "Oh, I'm going to enjoy this."

"Yeah, yeah. You and D knock yourselves out with your merriment. Where's your wife?" I looked around the room noticing Lexi wasn't around. It was ten a.m. on a Sunday, so surely she wasn't too far.

"She's feeding Grace. You're going to have to wait." Alex pointed at the couch, clueing me in he wanted me to take a seat. I wasn't in the mood to sit and wait.

"I can talk while she's feeding Grace. I'll watch my mouth with the cussing. Where is she?"

"You'll wait, Dan." Alex leveled me with a stare. It seemed he and D had been spending too much time together; Stone had the don't-fuck-with-me look down pat. "Lexi's breastfeeding, there is not even a shadow of a chance you are getting anywhere near my wife. So sit your ass down and wait." He pushed me down on the couch. Touchy motherfucker. He had become so fucking territorial lately. Still, looking at what he had to come home to, I can't say I blamed him.

"So is that kind of hot?" It's not like I hadn't seen a woman pull out a tit and feed her kid before but I had to wonder if it was your own woman, if maybe that didn't turn you on. And don't think I hadn't noticed Lexi's tits had gotten bigger since being knocked up and having the baby. That shit right there was proof god was a dude.

"You did not just ask me that right now." Alex shook his head as he took a seat beside me. I couldn't believe the bastard was holding out on me.

"C'mon, dude. She can't hear us." I have to admit, I was kind of curious. "Tell it to me straight. Have you tasted it?"

"Tasted what?" Lexi walked in, her hand tapping little Grace's back who happened to be perched up on her shoulder.

"Nothing," Stone and I both answered in stereo. Good to know he was smart enough not to repeat it.

"Hey, Lex." I walked over to Lexi and kissed Grace's forehead. "How's my number one girl?" Man, that kid was something else. I think they must put some kind of crack in baby powder or something 'cause whenever I saw that little face, she could ask me for the pink slip of my car and I'd sign it over.

"She had a bad night. None of us got much sleep." Lexi continued to pat Grace's back as she took a seat in the armchair opposite us. "She's got a good set of lungs on her that's for sure."

"Well, looks like daddy's going to have to teach her guitar to back up those pipes." I couldn't help but grin as I sunk back into my seat. With her mother's looks and attitude and her father's talent, Grace Stone would be unstoppable. Of course she'd have her Uncle Dan's advice too so she wouldn't sell out and sing bullshit manufactured pop crap. She'd write her own stuff for sure.

"So, Dan." Lexi wasted no time cutting to the chase. Good to see not much has changed. "I didn't see any photos of you last night nor did I have any calls about your questionable behavior. Being that it was a Saturday night that can only mean two things. You were either in jail or you were laying in a ditch somewhere. Both are going to be a headache for me so you might as well come clean now."

"Geez, Lexi. I wasn't in jail or a ditch last night. I was home, I didn't

HIGH STRUNG

go out." Really, this was just like old times. Lexi always assumed the worst, so it made me a little sentimental. At least I knew she cared.

"You were home? On a Saturday night? Are you feeling okay?" She stopped patting baby Grace and gave me a funny look.

"Yes, I'm feeling okay. I just didn't feel like going out. Troy came over we had a few beers and played a few hands of poker. That was my night."

Alex and Lexi looked at each other then back to me like I'd grown another head. Was it so hard to believe that I hadn't gone out? Sure I usually was at a club most nights during the week, especially on the weekends, but it's not like I had never spent the night at home. Shit. When *was* the last Saturday night I had spent at home?

"Look last night isn't important. I was home, that's all that matters. Why I'm here is I need a favor." I moved around in my seat, this crap was making me uncomfortable.

"What kind of favor? Dan, this better not be about Sydney. She's not interested," Lexi warned. Yeah I knew where Sydney stood on the dating issue, she'd made herself clear. Truth is, now, *I* was no longer interested.

"It's not about Sydney. I know she isn't interested. I'm fine with that. I've moved on."

"Well, good." Lexi looked relieved but unconvinced. "So what is it that you need?"

"I need you to hire Ashlyn Murphy as your assistant. Please."

"Ashlyn Murphy? The broker? Dan, while she's probably capable, she's not exactly suitable. She has no industry experience, she has never worked as a PA, and would probably hand in her resignation as soon as she got offered a job on Wall Street. I need someone qualified and reliable. I have three potentials and Ashlyn didn't even make my short list. Why are you asking?"

"I met her. I know she can do the job and she will stick around. In case you haven't noticed, there aren't a lot of jobs going on Wall Street right now."

"You've met her? You had an altercation with her in my reception area and from that one interaction you have surmised she is the correct person for the job? Is she threatening a harassment lawsuit? Did you promise her the job if she blew you or something?"

"Fuck, Lexi, why does it always have to be something shady? No, I did not ask her to blow me in exchange for a job and there is no lawsuit. Look, it's a long story but I got to know a little bit about her and I know she *needs* this job."

"Do you see *Goodwill* painted on the front of my door? I can appreciate she might need a job but so do lots of other people, people who are more qualified, Dan. I'm running a business not a fucking charity."

"God, you are being such a bitch right now. You know James took a fucking chance on *you*, didn't he? Why can't you give her the same chance?"

"Dan. You have taken it way too far this time." Stone was in my face before I even had time to register he had moved off the couch. For a tall bastard, he was pretty quick.

Grace let out a cry, the commotion upsetting her. Fuck. This was not going well.

"It's okay, sweetheart." Lexi cradled Grace in her arms trying to stop her from crying. Alex ignored me and walked over to where his girls were.

"I'm sorry, sweetie, daddy didn't mean to yell." He kissed the top of Grace's head and with the sound of his voice she started to calm down.

"Alex, calm down. I've got this." Lexi held up her hand to calm Alex who was shooting me dirty looks. He took Grace from Lexi's arms and continued to settle her.

Lexi lowered her voice, which made me edgy. "Okay, what the fuck is going on because this is not about some job. And Dan, don't you *ever* insinuate I got this job on anything other than merit. I had years in public relations and events. I worked my way up from a shitty assistant to running million dollar campaigns so I was *more* than qualified to handle the tour James hired me for. Me, running the band's PR now, having my

HIGH STRUNG

own business, is because of all the hard work I put in over all that time. So watch your fucking mouth. I didn't get, nor have I ever had, a free ride."

"All right. You made your point." I shook off the murderous vibe that was currently being shot in my direction. "And I didn't mean it that way. Look, I know you are qualified and I know sometimes we don't see eye to eye but you do an amazing job and I'm glad it's you who's watching out for us and not someone else." I swallowed before continuing. "I know I'm a pain in your ass. I know you get sick of my shit. The girls, the pictures, and everything. I'm sorry if I have made your job difficult but I need you to do this and if you do it, I swear I'll never ask for anything ever again."

"Dan, you are starting to scare me now. Tell me what's going on. You better not be dying or I'll kill you myself."

"I'm not dying, but it's good to know that if I was, you'd end it for me early. Nice. Thanks for that." I couldn't help but smile. There was no doubt if I was ever in need of being put out of my misery, Lexi Reed would be the person I'd turn to. She was not only tough but she didn't flinch, not even a bit.

She returned the smile. "That's how you know I care. I wouldn't want you to suffer. That's the special kind of love I have for you."

"So you saw us argue. Ashlyn and me. At your office. Well later that night she ended up at the same club we were at. I was getting busy with a couple of girls when Troy found her trying to sneak into the VIP section."

"Classy, Dan. Two girls. Really?" Lexi asked, but she didn't sound surprised. It wasn't the first time. I chose to ignore her and continued.

"Anyway, she was pretty drunk and Troy found her poking around the VIP section and he thought it would be funny to bring her in because she was pissed at me. Apparently I had *offended* her." I rolled my eyes remembering that nothing I had said was offensive, if anything, she had been the one who had been rude.

"Cue my lack of surprise." Lexi smirked. I once again chose to ignore her. Seriously, did she want to hear this story or not?

"So yeah, she yelled at me for a while and then left." I didn't bother mentioning the bit about her making out with me before walking out, though no doubt Troy or Jase would flap their gums at some point and they'd both find out.

"So she piqued my interest. She is kind of a loud mouth like you, but not as aggressive. No offense." I held up my hands, not wanting to piss her off at this point.

"None taken. Go on." Thankfully Lexi didn't seem pissed.

"I found her and her friend at the front of the club. Her friend had twisted her ankle so we got them home safely," I explained, remembering finding Ashlyn trying to help Megs off the ground, her ankle already starting to blow up. I don't think I'll ever understand girls and their fucking shoes.

"Did you sleep with her, Dan?" Lexi looked me square in the eye.

"No, not like that. Honest, Lexi. I swear, I didn't do shit but spend the night at her place to make sure she was okay."

"But wasn't her *friend* the one who was hurt?" Lexi narrowed her eyes. I couldn't tell if she didn't believe me or was trying to slip me up. She always had a knack of making me confused and then I'd end up saying shit I didn't mean.

"Yes. What does it matter? I stayed." I pushed my hands through my hair. She was really enjoying raking me over the coals on this.

"So the next day we got talking and I got to really know her. No one will hire her even though she is super smart and amazing. She is working in a bar, Lexi. She spent all that time in college and now only works in a bar. She lives in a shithole apartment in the bad part of Brooklyn. Can you do this for me? Please?"

"Holy shit. You are really serious. You have feelings for this girl." Lexi's eyes widened.

"What? I just met her. I don't have feelings. I'm just trying to be a decent guy and I can tell she is doing it tough. So will you do it?" I didn't want to talk about the way I felt about Ashlyn, not with these two anyway. I didn't know what I felt. I knew I wanted to make her smile and try and make things easier for her. I knew I liked spending time around her and I hated she was working a job she hated, dealing with dickwads, and coming home late at night. I was just being a concerned citizen who was looking out for someone who was down on their luck. It didn't have to be about *feelings.*

"Dan, I can't just give her a job. While I think what you are doing is admirable and I love seeing this compassionate side to you, I can't afford to gamble on this. It's a big risk." I started to interrupt, wanting to argue if money was the issue, I would happily pay her salary when Lexi stopped me. "Wait. Let me finish. I'm still on maternity leave. I'm hardly in the office other than a few important meetings so I need someone who is not only going to be able to step in but step up. I need to hire someone who can do that, and while I don't think Ashlyn is suited to the role, I can tell she would be an asset to the right company." Lexi reached out and rubbed my arm. "Let me make a few calls. I think I might be able to find her something more suitable."

"Thanks, Lex." I nodded, the gratitude making me feel kind of emotional.

"Look, no promises. I'll get her in the door, a meeting with someone, but she is going to have to do the rest herself. It will be up to them if they hire her, I need you to understand that," Lexi continued, making it clear it wasn't a done deal.

"I got it. No promises." All she needed was a start. She would wow them. I had no doubt she had the goods to get a job if she was just put in the right place at the right time.

"Dan, if you really like her, make sure you play this straight, okay?" Lexi moved out of her chair, snagging her iPhone off the coffee table.

"Lexi, just make your calls. Not everyone has to end up with a SUV with a baby on board sticker on the back." I couldn't help myself; I knew that shit pissed her off.

"I do not have a baby on board sticker on my car," she spat out defensively.

"Let me do my thing. I know what I'm doing."

At least I thought I did, and if I didn't, I wasn't about to front to it now.

13
Ashlyn

I WOKE UP ALONE AND THAT DISAPPOINTED ME. WHAT DISappointed me even more was I cared I was alone. Make sense? No, I didn't think so. In fact, none of it made sense. I had woken up alone more times than not, and I had never lived with a guy, so why I was feeling this way was a real mystery. The last few days had effectively scrambled my brain and I wasn't thinking clearly. How had I gone from disliking this crude, obnoxious rock star with questionable social skills to wanting to see him when I woke up? It was a slippery slope being with Dan, and I was free-falling.

Perhaps this is my version of rebellion, being with a man I knew I could have no future with. I knew whatever we were would be fleeting, a bump in my road. I could never assimilate into his world any more than he could to mine. He was a fantasy, a pot of gold at the end of the rainbow. You could run and run in an attempt to reach it but it never got any closer. But that didn't mean I didn't want to follow the rainbow a little longer, see my days through the magic of its colors. It would be okay as long as I kept my reality in check. I couldn't afford to lose sight of who either of us really were. Wow. This was all very deep. Too deep. Especially at this time of the morning.

Dan had woken me before he left, saying he had to *get some shit done*. I shouldn't have expected him to stay. It would have been weird. I had rubbed myself against him, climaxing before giving him a hand job. Sure, that wasn't awkward. What do you say to someone who you actually *haven't* had sex with? It was for the best. Him leaving, I mean. The no sex thing? The jury was still out. If Dan was able to give me the best orgasm I've ever had without actual penetration, I could only imagine what it be like if we actually *did* it. I really needed to stop. I was getting dizzy just thinking about it.

New plan. One that did not involve me moping around in my apartment analyzing all things Dan Evans. I scrounged through my kitchen cupboard and found a box of Cinnamon Toast Crunch. Things were looking up. So after devouring a bowl of cereal and my usual morning get-ready ritual, I headed out of my apartment to enjoy the sunshine. It was October, which meant that soon the warmth would be replaced by the icy chill. Just another thing I didn't want to think about it.

I don't know why I ended up at Columbus Circle. Today wasn't a day for making sense so I just went with it. It was liberating, not having a road map. Just walking around aimlessly like a tourist. I stopped for a coffee and sat on the grass. Everything I was doing was pointless and yet it felt great doing it.

I had just made it back to my neighborhood when my phone burst into life shaking me from my daydream. Nearby, pedestrians turned around at the commotion. I quickly grabbed it from my purse. The old George Michael song, "I Want Your Sex" spewed loudly from the speaker, the screen filled by Dan's photo. I can't believe he had changed my ringtone.

"Dan," I half-yelled into the phone, my finger swiping to accept the call as fast as I could. Really? I want your sex? Could he be any more obvious?

"Wow you answered fast." Dan chuckled. "Are you missing me,

babe? That's so fucking sweet." I didn't have to see his face to know he was smiling. Smug. Confident. Sexy. I couldn't help but smile back. I almost jogged back to my apartment not wanting to be distracted by the outside noise.

"I'm not missing you, ass, I just didn't want the rest of the neighborhood to be subjected to my ringtone. Speaking of which, do you have any boundaries at all?" I tried my best to sound annoyed but as much as I tried, I was coming up short in the convincing department. I had become desensitized, his charm winning me over.

"What did I tell you about putting a password lock on your phone? Relax. It's just a ringtone. Besides, it's what we both know you're thinking when you see that pic." His low voice vibrated through the phone sending a shiver through my core. I would never admit it, but he was right.

"Could you be any more conceited?" I asked, glad he couldn't see how flustered he made me. I cleared my throat doing my best to sound like I had my shit together. "Does this call have a purpose, Dan, or do you just want to harass me?"

"I was thinking about you," he purred into the phone. He was too good at this. The seduction. The man needed a warning from the surgeon general.

I climbed up the stairs of my apartment building, juggling the phone while trying to open my front door.

"Okay, I really didn't need the update, but thanks." I tried to sound bored as I chewed on my bottom lip. Why did it excite me so much he had been thinking of me? This is what he'd reduced me to. Elated yet annoyed. I was my own contradiction. I collapsed onto my couch, no longer able to stay upright.

"Were you thinking about me?" His voice swirled around each word. I was going to need to sit down. Hell, I was already sitting down. Maybe I needed to stand up. Get the blood moving, hopefully enough to where my brain kicked into gear.

"No, I've had lots on my mind today, so sorry, you didn't feature," I deadpanned.

"You are such a liar." Dan laughed. "Was I doing dirty things? Whatever you are imagining isn't even close to how good it can be."

Yep, Standing up now. I think I could probably run a marathon at this point and it still wouldn't shake my train of thought.

"Well I guess I will happily live in ignorance, because you know *that* isn't going to happen." I wasn't really sure whose benefit I was saying it for.

"I think it will, but you keep living in denial."

"Look, last night..." I swallowed, my eyes closing slowly before I continued. "Just don't read too much into it. I had an itch and you helped me scratch it. That's all." Yep, that's right. That's all it was. At least that is what I needed to tell myself. I had a need, and he was able to appease it. Nothing more. Certainly nothing romantic. Dan was right. I was a bad liar.

"Is that what it was? Huh." A gentle chuckle vibrated through the phone. "I think you will find if you ask my dick, he would tell you different."

"Well then your dick is just as clueless as you are." I smiled into the phone like an idiot.

Dan let out a loud, throaty laugh. "It's been called a lot of things - huge, magnificent, amazing, outstanding, oh-my-god-don't-stop, but never clueless. If there is one part of me that knows what it's doing, it's *that* part."

"Okay, hanging up now." Before I said something stupid. Or *more* stupid, as the case may be.

"Wait. What are you doing later? I want to see you." His voice turned serious, not allowing me to end the call.

"Dan..." I blew a long breath into the phone. "Why?" Was I a game? The thrill of the chase? Was I just another name to add to his long list of conquests?

"'Cause I like you and despite you saying different, I think you like me, too."

His honesty startled me. Why couldn't he just say what I had expected him to say, that he wanted to sleep with me. That I could handle. The fact he liked me—whatever that meant—just complicated everything. He was supposed to say he wanted sex. I couldn't go down that road with him. A relationship? No, Dan probably wasn't even capable of that.

"Dan, we would never work. You know that I'm right. I want a lot of things, and dating a musician who can't keep it in his pants isn't on that list."

"That's cool, Ashlyn, 'cause I have a list, too. See my girlfriend has to have huge porno tits and be seriously good at blowjobs, so sadly, you don't really fit the bill either. Great news about that is, we don't have to worry about impressing each other or pretending we're each other's soul mates. We can just hang out."

I blinked. He hadn't missed a beat, throwing off my protest like water off a duck's back. He should have been offended. Hell, I should have been offended but his whole rebuttal was so comical and sincere it just made him more endearing. His way of making it okay for us. And damn him if at that moment, Dan Evans had weaseled himself into a tiny corner of my heart. He was going to be the death of me.

"You're crazy, you know that, right?" I giggled. "I'm going to give you a little hint, if you want a girl you probably shouldn't tell her where her deficiencies are."

"Just being honest, babe. Figured you've probably had enough douchebags lie to you to get you in bed. I'm never going to lie to you."

"So big tits and blowjobs, huh? She sounds like she is going to be such a catch." I smiled.

"Oh, hell yeah. The tits I *might* be able to overlook, as long as they are at least adequate, but the blowjobs, they are non-negotiable."

"This is all very informative, I'll let you know if I see anyone who meets the criteria." I continued with his ruse. He made it so easy.

"Aw, Ash, you are kind of making me hard."

"You are impossible, you know that?" I sighed, letting my head fall against the back of the couch.

"Yeah I know. Impossible to resist. So when can I see you?" he persisted. I repeated in my head my earlier sentiment. Death. Of. Me.

"I have to work tonight, Dan. Maybe some other time." I was more than just a little disappointed. I wanted to see him. I wanted that and so much more.

"Wait. You're working tonight? When were you going to tell me? I thought we agreed I would be taking you home." Something in his voice shifted, an edge I hadn't heard before.

"It's okay, Dan, I know you're just trying to be nice and it was a sweet thing to offer but I'm not going to hold you to it. I'll promise to be safe. I'll catch a cab."

"Babe, I'm not nice or sweet, and I offered 'cause I wanted to. Besides *you* already agreed to it so you can't take it back now. It's a done deal. So you can forget taking a cab. Tell me what time and where to pick you up." His tone darkened. Wow. He really wasn't playing around.

"Dan, this is really—" I didn't get a chance to say *unnecessary* before he interrupted me.

"I said where and when, babe." His voice softened, the edge was still there but I could hear he was trying to rein it in. "If you want to make something harder than it has to be, I've got something between my legs that would love the attention. If not, then tell me what I need to know."

I wasn't going to argue. Dan had a way of talking until he got his own way and I was having enough trouble keeping check of my own emotions. If he wanted to drive me home, then fine, he could drive me home. But that's where it would end. I would be sleeping alone tonight. As for his *something special between his legs*, he would be tending to that himself as well. I wasn't a doormat, no matter how well intentioned he might have been.

"Fine. Two a.m. Garro's. It's a sports bar in Lower East Side. Don't expect me to be friendly or give any part of you any attention."

"Yeah, I know. I'm not your type. Got it. See you then."

I ended the call more confused than when it had started. I had never

HIGH STRUNG

met a man who pushed all of my buttons like he did, *all* of my buttons. He infuriated me and yet excited me. Gah! I was a hot mess and I didn't know if Dan Evans or I was to blame.

It was another busy night at the bar. My arms were getting a work out from the numerous pitchers of beer I was putting up on the bar. It was easy to forget my earlier annoyance, getting lost in the noise of the crowd. They commiserated, consoling each other after a Giants loss, the replay from the earlier game being piped through the big screens adding insult to injury. This only fueled the alcohol consumption.

"Another, sweetheart," Mack slurred, his crumpled fiver extending over the bar. Mack and his crew were regulars. Hardcore New Yorkers and sports fanatics, they had been coming to Garro's since the day it opened.

"Going to have to cut you off, Mack. Why don't you let me buy you and the boys a round of soda instead?" I smiled knowing while they were loud and rowdy they weren't the kind of guys to start trouble. Still, rules were rules and they were all on the other side of sober.

Mack swayed unsteadily on his feet. "My boys let me down tonight, Ash. A man needs to drown his sorrows."

"I know, but if I serve you another beer we are probably going to end up sharing a cell together and as exciting as that sounds, Rosie would probably have my hide." I shot him a quick wink.

Rosie was not only the love of his life, but a tough-as-nails housewife from Long Island. I wouldn't want to be on her wrong side or have to make the call that her husband had been hauled off on a public intoxication charge.

"You're lucky I'm not younger." Mack smiled, his light blue eyes twinkled hinting at the trouble I knew he must have caused in his youth.

"She's a handful, buddy. Lot's of trouble." Dan's smug face beamed as he took a seat at the bar. I did my best to ignore him, turning my attention to polishing wine glasses. I clearly needed the distraction, because these glasses were rarely used, no one ever drank wine. It had just turned midnight; I hadn't expected to see Dan for at least another hour.

"The best ones usually are." Mack nodded in agreement. "She your girl?"

"Nah, she's too smart for that. I'm just her ride for the night. My name's Dan." Dan stood and held out his hand. He looked good. Too good. His leather jacket was unzipped revealing a Black Flag T-shirt underneath, finishing his look with a pair of faded blue jeans.

"Mack." He clasped Dan's hand firmly. "Good to see someone is looking out for her." Mack turned to look at me, grinning approvingly.

"Doing what I can, but she isn't making it easy." Dan eased into his seat, doing little to hide the fact his response had been directed at me rather than Mack.

"Okay you two. I'm right here." I tossed the dishrag aside. They both now had my attention.

"Well if you aren't going to serve us any more beer, might be time for me and the fellas to call it a night." Mack shot me a wink. "Think I'm about done. Nice meeting you, Dan." He tipped his head to Dan before strolling off.

"Likewise, Mack." Dan nodded, watching Mack shuffle away. He waited until Mack was out of earshot before leaving across the bar. "You flirting with the customers to make me jealous?"

"Come on, Dan, Mack is like sixty." I rolled my eyes wondering if he was serious.

"Makes no difference to me. Do I need to lay him out?" I watched the smile spread across his face. He had such an amazing smile, why had I never noticed? I needed to concentrate on the fact I was still mad.

"You are such a tool. I'm still mad at you by the way. Don't think you can come in here and be all charming."

"I'd rather you be mad at me and know you're safe than the alternative." He didn't offer me an apology or explanation.

"I'm not the kind of girl who needs a man to tell her what to do." I planted my hands on my hips. If he was going to be standing here then he might as well know how I felt. I didn't need a hero.

"Look, Ash. I'm sorry I snapped at you but this is not something I'm going to back down from. I'm not trying to own you or order you around. If you want me to go wait in the car, I will, but you have no chance of me letting you go home alone tonight." His voice softened but was still resolute. His dark smoldering eyes didn't break contact with mine. There was something else I saw within those dark expressive pools. He wasn't trying to be possessive but protective.

"It was Lexi, right? Your friend." I felt myself relent. He was trying to be kind and while his execution wasn't great, his motives were sound. It was the *why* of the motives that still confused me.

"That's not my story to tell, Ash. Sorry." He reached across, his hand grazing my knuckles. The sincerity was not missed, nor was the sweetness in his tone. There was no way I could stay angry.

"Maybe I overreacted." I gave him a slight smile before warning him. "Don't start any fights with the patrons and you don't have to wait in the car."

"I won't start any fights if you stop flirting with other men." He gave me a cheeky sideways glance. It was our way of calling a truce.

"I don't know, Dan. That old-timer in the corner has been giving me the eye all night and I have to admit I'm kind of tempted." I fanned myself, biting my lip to suppress my smile.

"Just point him out to me, babe, and I'll set him straight."

'14

Dan

THE BAR WAS DESERTED EXCEPT FOR A FEW OTHER STAFF MEMBERS and the security. The doors had been shut half an hour ago but they had let me wait inside as I was driving Ash home and it didn't hurt the bouncer was a fan of the band. I signed the back of his security shirt and handed him a guitar pick I had stashed away in one of my pockets, and he was grinning like a kid who'd just touched boobs for the first time.

Despite this being a bullshit job I knew that she hated, she refused to cut corners and she worked her ass off making sure the place was immaculate before she punched off the clock. I watched Ash move around the bar, the boring, shapeless uniform she was wearing trying to hide the smokin' body she had underneath. Fuck, she was beautiful. Not just in the I-wanted-to-get-her-under-me sense, but also in I-could-look-at-her-all-day. I watched as her perfect ass swayed toward the staff locker room, the thought of taking her to the shithole apartment she lived

HIGH STRUNG

in made me want to break shit.

"I'm good to go." Ashlyn pulled on her coat, her purse in her hand.

"Let's roll then." I waved to the bouncer as I guided her out toward the door. Yeah, there was a lot on my mind right now. Sleeping alone was not one of them. I didn't even care if she didn't want sex, not that my throbbing dick would listen to reason, but I needed her tucked up beside me.

We walked outside, our feet hitting the sidewalk as the blast of the night air licked us in the face. It was October and the chill was starting to move in. She shivered as we made our way up the street to where I'd parked my ride.

I moved in close and pulled my arm around her waist. The feel of her body hitting me harder than any fucking breeze ever could. "Cold?"

"No." Her body shook in my arms as we rounded the corner, my car parked at the curb.

"So why are you shivering?" I moved my other hand around her waist, gently pushing her body against the hood of my car.

"I'm just tired." She sighed. I wasn't convinced and the thought I made her edgy made me all kinds of uncomfortable.

"You're not nervous around me, are you?" I tilted her chin toward me, hoping like hell I didn't, or worse, that she would lie about it.

"Don't flatter yourself, Dan. It's been a long day and I just need to get to bed." She yawned, relaxing in my arms.

I moved in closer, wanting to kiss her. "Well I'm all about getting you into bed."

"You know I'm not going to have sex with you, right?" She didn't pull back so I moved in closer. My body up against hers, there was no way she couldn't feel the hard-on I had going on.

"I know, but I still want to sleep with you. Come home with me, Ashlyn. I won't put the moves on, I swear." I took her face in my hands my thumb playing with her bottom lip. Even tired, sweaty, and smelling like stale beer, she was the sexiest girl I'd ever seen.

"You like torturing yourself, don't you?" She gave me a weary smile.

"I haven't got anything to sleep in."

This was not a legitimate problem. In fact, if anything, I saw it as one hell of a positive. "So sleep naked, I won't mind."

"Nice try, but no."

"So I'll give you a T-shirt to sleep in. Come home with me."

I had never had to beg a girl to come home with me and I wasn't about to now. Still, if there was one I would get on my knees for, it would be the one standing right in front of me. Mind you, I could think of something else I'd rather get on my knees for and the begging would be coming from her, telling me not to stop.

"I'm wearing a T-shirt and a pair of your boxers and there is going to be no sex." She gave me a look that meant she wasn't kidding. I didn't care what look she was giving. It looked like victory to me.

"Yeah, yeah. Whatever you want. Can we go now?" I smirked, wondering how fast I could get from here to my apartment. Thank fuck it was at some bullshit hour in the morning and the traffic was light.

"Okay we can go." She nodded as I fought the urge to fist pump. Not only did it mean I got another night by her side but also that I had the home field advantage.

I hit the keyless entry and opened the car door. She slid into the passenger seat, her legs stretching out in front of her. I closed the door, trying not to imagine those legs around my hips. Ash was right about one thing - tonight was going to be torture.

"This isn't what I thought you'd drive." She smiled as I slipped into the driver's seat.

"Hey, pick on me all you want, babe, but leave my ride out of it." I hit the ignition and pulled out on the street.

"No, that's not what I meant." She giggled and man, if that sound didn't make me feel warm inside. "I mean, I thought you would drive something more pretentious, like a Porsche."

"I don't need to compensate. I like style and comfort."

I had always owned an American car and when we got our first big check I went and bought myself a sweet Corvette. I still had it, it was

HIGH STRUNG

kicking around in my mom's garage but it just didn't feel right to me. The Mercedes SLK 55 AMG spoke to me. I drove up to the dealer and saw this baby parked on the lot. Looking all badass with the top down with all those sexy curves, I just knew this was the car I needed to be driving.

"You just continue to surprise me." Ashlyn nestled into the soft leather seat and I swear I heard her purr.

We drove the rest of the way in silence. It wasn't forced or awkward, just an easy ride with no need for dialogue. I saw her eyelids droop, fighting against her long blinks as we pulled into my undercover parking garage. I needed to get her out of this car and into my bed ASAP.

I flicked off my seat belt and ejected myself from the car. She sat unmoving until I popped open the passenger side door, the noise startling her awake.

"Shit. I must have drifted off." She blinked under the bright halogen lights.

"Let's get you into bed." I leaned inside the cabin, wrapping my arms around her and pulling her out.

"I can walk, Dan. You don't have to carry me," she protested, wriggling till her feet hit the floor.

"Okay, babe. Let's walk then." My hands found their way around her hips and guided her toward the elevator.

She mumbled something I didn't quite make out, leaning into me as we climbed up the belly of the building till we reached my floor. It was the top level, which only housed two apartments. Mine, with the other belonging to my brother, Troy. Having your best friend as your neighbor had been the coolest feature of this place so when the two penthouse apartments opened up, we didn't even think twice about signing on the dotted line.

We slid out of the elevator and made it to my front door, her hot little body molded to my side. I managed to open the door, while holding Ashlyn in my arms, kicking the door closed behind us the minute we'd stepped through it. Last thing I needed was for Troy to take an interest and poke his head outside his door.

"I need the bathroom. I can't sleep unless I wash this bar smell off me." Ashlyn stirred awake.

"Mmmm, you're going to need help washing your back." My dick punched out against my jeans in appreciation.

"No. By myself." Ashlyn struggled to keep her eyes open. "I mean it, Dan. I'm locking the bathroom door."

"Okay. Okay. I promise I won't look but leave the door unlocked. If you fall and crack your head on the tub, I want to be able to get to you." She could barely stand straight; I'm not sure how the whole showering herself was going to work.

Still, I knew I had to pick my battles and this one wasn't one I had my heart set on winning. She was obviously trying to prove a point and I would let her do that. End result would be the same. Her. Me. In my bed. I half-carried her to my bedroom, stepping into the large en-suite and flicking on the overhead lights.

"Here are some towels." I placed them on the tub beside her. "You sure you don't want me to stick around?" I gave her one last chance to think it through.

"No, I'm good. I'll only be a few minutes." She yawned, leaning up against the bathroom sink. "Go!" She pointed to the door, slightly more awake than when we had walked in. Well at least now she wouldn't drown.

I begrudgingly walked out of the bathroom, closing the door behind me. I heard the spray of the water hitting the tiles of the bathroom stall as I made my way back into my bedroom. I laid out a pair of clean boxer shorts and my Ramones T-shirt on the chair in the sitting room between my bedroom and my closet. I figured she would work it out, having no other way to walk to get to the bed. I wasn't going to risk pissing her off by barging in on her.

I pulled off my clothes and shoes, leaving them in a pile in the corner. It had been a long-ass day for me, too, my sheets felt fucking amazing as I slid between them. My body relaxed between the layers of Egyptian cotton. No shit, as douchey as it sounded, you really *could* tell the difference between thread counts. I thought for sure the sales lady at Bed, Bath and Beyond was just flirting with me when she fed me that line.

No crashing sound came from the bathroom, so I assumed Ashlyn was doing okay. I closed my eyes and tried to not think about the fact she was naked and wet not more than ten feet away. Fuck. I squeezed the bridge of my nose. This was not going well for me. The water shut off and I rolled to my side, figuring it was probably better she didn't see the massive hard-on I was packing. I would keep my promise and not touch her but I couldn't stop biology from happening.

After what seemed to take forever, Ashlyn walked in, toweling off her hair. My Ramones shirt looked huge on her tiny little body. I rolled onto my back to watch her. Fucking mesmerized by her.

"Thanks for the clothes." She shot me a smile that hit me square in the balls.

"Don't mention it." No really, don't mention it 'cause the more I think about her skin touching my stuff the more I was likely to combust.

"They smell of you." She slid into the bed beside me, her hair still wet. Her leg brushed up against me and I tried to remember to fucking breathe.

"Is that a good thing? I promise they're clean."

"Yeah, it's a good thing. I like the way you smell." She moved her face close to me on the pillow. I was struggling not to kiss her.

A kiss should be okay though, 'cause I only promised no sex. Kissing was definitely allowed. I leaned and lightly touched her lips, my hand moving up her leg. The edge of the boxer shorts she was wearing hitting my fingertips as I moved up her thigh.

"I like that your pussy is currently sitting where my junk used to be. Please tell me you aren't wearing panties." I couldn't help grin. That thought alone almost made me come, hotter than imagining her in sexy lingerie.

"Dan." She smacked me across the chest. "You always have to take it that step too far."

"Ashlyn, I'm fucking dying here. I know you said no sex and I'm going to respect that, but you're fucking beautiful. As far as my balls are concerned, I'm not taking it far enough." I kissed her neck, slowly. I didn't want to scare her off but there was no way I could not touch her, even if it was just with my lips.

"You know, there are other things we can do other than sex." She gave me a slow smile.

My heart fucking stopped beating as I looked down at her, those gorgeous green eyes boring into me. "Yes, whatever it is, yes."

"You haven't even heard what it is yet." She giggled, scrunching up her nose. She had the tiniest freckles just below the bridge and fuck if that didn't make her more adorable. I wanted her in whatever way she would let me have her.

"I don't care. Whatever you are suggesting I'm down for." The realization of what I was saying hit me square in the nuts. I'd never wanted a woman enough to just have her any way she'd let me. Fuck, most of the time if the girl wasn't down for what I was suggesting, there would be ten others waiting in line to take her place. But with Ash it was different, and apparently now I was different.

"Dan, I meant just holding. Maybe some kissing." She turned in my arms, her back flush against my front. This was not what I had in mind.

My hands wandered down her body, moving across her hips before cupping her ass. It was so pert and perfect just like the rest of her. "Can I touch your ass when I hold you?" I nipped at her ear.

"Yes." She sighed or was it a moan? It was all kinds of fucking sexy and wrapped up in the same kind of need that I had going on. I don't know why she was fighting this. I wanted her and I know she wanted me.

"Babe, you have an itch tonight? 'Cause I'm more than happy to help you scratch it." I licked her neck, pulling her ass tight into my groin.

"Dan." I loved the way she said my name. She could ask me for anything right now and I'd probably agree. "Can I be honest with you?"

"Babe, my erection is poking you in the ass. Please, by all means be fucking honest." I tried not to laugh because it really *wasn't* funny. No

HIGH STRUNG

girl had ever gotten under my skin like this one.

"I like you but this is moving way too fast. I'm not like those other girls, I don't just want to be a lay for you." She turned to face me, her eyes wide.

"Ashlyn, you could *never* just be a lay to me." My fingers tipped her chin toward me. "Or to any other guy for that matter. You're different." I was lost right now. The thought of her with someone else made me want to punch something.

"Are you just saying that because you want to sleep with me?" She wasn't convinced. I could hear the vulnerability in her voice. This was her, no bullshit, no attitude, just her. It twisted me in knots so tight my chest hurt.

I knew how to get a girl into bed. I knew how to make her feel good and come so hard she forgets where she is, but I had no idea how to convince a girl, *this* girl, that she meant more to me than that.

"No. I mean yes. I mean, I want to sleep with you but that's not the reason I'm saying it. Honestly, babe, I have no idea what I am doing here. I have no fucking clue but I know I would rather have no sex and sleep beside you all night than be screwing a whole bunch of random girls. I know it's not romantic but it's all I've really got."

"Dan, that was plenty romantic." She pressed her lips against my mouth, her sweetness fucking destroying me.

"Sooo does that mean we're going to have sex?" I bit back a grin, the throbbing between my legs unrelenting.

"No, not tonight. Just hold me." She flung her arms around my neck and nestled up against my chest.

I groaned as her thigh moved up my body, snaking around my leg. My balls were so tightly drawn up I'm surprised I wasn't gargling them.

"Okay, babe. But I'm probably going to have to go jerk off first." I squeezed her hip. "Unless, you want to do it?"

She smiled before closing her eyes. "You go handle it yourself this time. I need to sleep."

I choked back a laugh. The feel and smell of her on me meant it wouldn't take very long. I was so hard it hurt, and I wanted inside her in the worst way. Hell, at this point, I wouldn't even have to jerk off. Just thinking about her would probably be enough.

I woke up in a panic, like some really bad shit was going down. I couldn't work out if it was a dream or something else was going on, like some kind of alarm had sounded. I pushed myself up in bed, trying to work out what the fuck was going on and noticed Ashlyn was gone. I fumbled for my phone to check for a message. I had about ten unread texts but nothing from her, and it was six a.m. I kicked off the covers, my heart beating so hard in my chest I thought it would crash through my ribs. Where had she gone? Why was she not with me? The reasons *why* taking a backseat to finding her. I flung open my bedroom door and jogged out to the living room. The glow of the TV hit me as I entered the room. The sound had been muted. Ashlyn was sleeping soundly curled in an armchair, the remote control tucked up under her chin.

"Hey." I knelt down beside her, brushing the hair away from her face. It's like someone put my internal organs in a blender. I was so fucking relieved she hadn't left. "Ashlyn." I traced her chin with my fingers, wondering why she had left my bed.

"Hmm." She slowly opened an eye, mumbling something that made no sense.

"What are you doing out here?" I pulled the remote from her hand; the stupid buttons had made indentations on her face. I wanted to pitch it against a wall for trying to mess with the perfection.

"I woke up and I couldn't sleep." She yawned, stretching out in the chair. "I didn't want to wake you so I came out to watch TV."

"I don't care if you wake me." She didn't fight me as I lifted her into my arms and pulled her off the chair. "Just don't go leaving my bed in the middle of the night." As strange as it sounded, I hated the thought of

HIGH STRUNG

her being out in the living room alone. It pissed me off, which made no fucking sense. Feelings are just plain weird. "I'm taking you back to bed."

The remote was still in my hand so I hit the power button and tossed it on the now vacant chair. Ashlyn's body was limp in my arms, allowing me to pull her closer to my body.

"Dan," she mumbled into my bare chest, the vibrations from her words kind of tickled as her head rested against me.

"Yeah?" I carried her from the living room back into my bedroom.

"I had an itch while you were sleeping." She had a dopey grin on her face as her sleepy eyelids closed.

My dick jumped in my boxer shorts, all of sudden very interested in the conversation we were having. Yeah, you and me both buddy.

"Fuck, babe, now I'm really pissed you didn't wake me."

"It's okay. I scratched *it* myself." She laughed to herself as I gently laid her on the bed. Well that sure as hell got my attention. The thought of her touching herself made me both hard and jealous. Jealous I had missed out on seeing it.

I slid into the bed beside her, pulling her body back onto mine. "That's kind of hot. Did you think of me?" Hoping like hell she did, 'cause if it were any other fucker I would be hunting him down and ripping off his balls. No shit. I would tear his sack right off.

"Oh yeah. I came hard, too." She mumbled against my chest as I hooked her leg up on my hip.

"Ashlyn." I swallowed, imagining her hot, wet pussy being teased by her fingertips, her body shaking with pleasure, as she got closer to climax. I'd only seen her come once and it killed me to know I missed it. Fuck, it killed me to know I wasn't the one who was making her come. The only consolation was that she'd had me in her head while she was doing it.

"Yeah." She opened one eye slightly, the slash of bright green searing me.

"If you won't wake me can you at least film it for me next time?"

"Maybe. You'll have to wait and find out."

15
Ashlyn

"SO YOU GUYS ARE DATING?" MEGS HOBBLED OVER TO HER refrigerator. "I need more peas for this foot. The Physiotherapist said I'm so lucky I didn't tear anything. I can't believe I needed to take a sick day." She barely took a breath as she hopped back to the couch.

Megs rarely took a personal day and when she did, she was usually dying. Not literally, but really sick. So when I called her this morning and she told me she wasn't going to work, I thought it was the perfect time to spend the day with her. Monday was my usual day off and the only plans I had was more fruitless job searching on the Internet. Which was depressing. Plus, I needed to tell someone what the hell was going on.

"I guess we're dating. It's so weird, we didn't really talk about it. I swear I lose IQ points when I'm around that man. I can't think straight."

Only I would be stuck in a situation where I wasn't exactly sure whether or not we were actually dating. I mean, we hadn't agreed on anything and he hadn't exactly asked me out, he was just there. All the time. I had spent the last three nights with him. And I was seeing him again tonight. And despite him being a manwhore, he hadn't slept with me yet and was still interested. If I was compiling a case, the evidence surely pointed to the beginnings of a relationship.

"Just go with the flow, Ash, have some fun with him. No one said you have to marry him. I for one, think this is amazing news. Dan Evans. He really is hot." Megs piled the peas on her bandaged foot. Those shoes had a lot to answer for.

"Yeah, well don't go patting me on the back just yet. I'm probably just a phase for him or something. By next week he'll be interested in someone else. I'm not getting ahead of myself just yet."

By his own omission I wasn't his type - big tits and blowjobs. Big tits I didn't have and as he hadn't experienced my blowjobs, the jury was still out. I think I was okay. I hadn't exactly had a lot of practice, but of the guys I *had* blown, none had ever complained. I needed to keep perspective. Like working at the bar, it's for now not for always.

"So enjoy it while it lasts." Megs was constantly chasing that silver lining. She leaned forward to whisper despite us being the only two people in her apartment. "Is he...as good as they say?"

"I don't know." I shrugged. "I haven't slept with him yet but I've seen it and felt it and it's huge and I'm not sure how the hell it's going to fit."

By *it*, I meant his penis. I had taken a peek on the second night while I was giving him a hand job. Not that I'd seen it in its entirety, more like I surmised what it would be like from the sum of all parts. It was long and thick. It was definitely a two hander. Far from average. I could only imagine how spectacular it would be in the flesh. Flesh. An appropriate word based on what I was thinking.

"It will fit. I'm sure it will be fun working out the logistics." Megs laughed.

Sure, it was funny for her; she wasn't the one who would be attempting to insert *that* into her vagina. Although, I really wasn't sure I would be either. Now, there was this heavy expectation around the sex. What if it sucked for him? And I don't mean in the oral sex kind of suck,

HIGH STRUNG

I mean just really average sex kind of suck. It was all too hard. No pun intended.

"I guess I'll find out. Eventually." Or at least I hoped. Maybe I didn't. Gah! I was impossible. Things were easier when he was just some sexy, cocky musician I'd never sleep with.

"Hey, you should invite him to your birthday party on the weekend." Megs sat up, prompting the bag of peas to spill off her foot. She was wearing her up-to-no-good face, the one that could only mean trouble. No doubt the trouble would be meant for me.

"Megs, I don't think that's such a good idea. I mean, I just met him," I said, trying to rationalize.

I need to gain control of the runaway train that was playing out in Megs's head. Oh I know I didn't know what she was thinking, unfortunately I did not possess mind-reading abilities, but I knew where this was heading. The trouble that I spoke of. Right here. Alive and well in Megan Winters.

"Not sure I want to subject him to something as personal as a birthday party. Besides it's hardly a party, just a couple of our friends getting together for drinks. Introductions to the friends is a pretty serious step. He will think I'm trying to show him off and it will make his ego bigger than it already is, or think I'm pushing the relationship issue." Solid argument. She could hardly argue with that logic.

As much as I wanted to celebrate my special day with Dan, it just didn't seem likely. Firstly, I'd known him for less than a week. It was too soon even if I was dating a regular guy—assuming what we were actually doing was dating—and secondly, it's Dan freaking Evans. The last thing he probably wanted to do was hang out with a bunch of my friends.

The other thing was the whole pressure of the occasion. I didn't want him to feel obligated to do anything. Best solution was to let it go. Just not mention it and if we were together next year…yeah like that would happen. Welcome to Delusionville, population one. Let's face it - we wouldn't have to *deal* with it next year.

"Well I still think you should ask him. So you've only known him a few days, big deal. He made you come without putting his cock in you, that alone deserves an invite." Megs was not buying my *solid* argument. While Megs liked to banter around idealism, I preferred realism. As in, I am really not going to embarrass myself by asking him and being turned down or worse, him saying yes and being bored. Nope. No chance. End of story. There would be no sexy Power Station bass player helping me ring in my special day.

"Nope." I folded my arms defiantly across my chest. "I'm not asking and neither are you. Besides, I assume that because they aren't touring right now means they are probably recording, so I'm sure he has better things to do."

"Fine. Kill joy." Megs pouted. "You know it wasn't just for your benefit you know. You could have invited that sexy best friend of his too so I had some entertainment. Has Troy Harris mentioned me?"

"I haven't seen Troy. Like I said. We haven't really done anything much other than be in bed together."

"Sounds like a fling to me. Minus the no sex part. In that department you are letting yourself down."

"You're impossible, you know that? This didn't start out as a fling. I'm not sure what it started out as, all I know is I'm now in it and still none the wiser as to what *it* actually is." Saying it out loud didn't actually clarify it either. Hell, was I going to have to ask Dan?

"So, you seeing him tonight?" Megs was fishing. Not that she really had to, I would happily volunteer everything I knew. Which we had already established wasn't a lot.

"Probably. He knows I have the night off. I told him I might see him around." I tried to sound casual but in fact I was an internal mess. I wanted to see him but that would mean I had seen him every night since I met him. I'm sure that wasn't smart. Better to leave it as a possibility. Maintain some control over this situation.

"Might see him around? What are you planning a date or a drive by?"

I had been at Megs's most of the day. Well, all of the day. The subject of Dan had featured heavily in the conversation, as had the consumption of Ben and Jerry's Half Baked. We had moved on to Chunky Monkey, and I was glad I was wearing my old jeans and Bruins jersey. That kind of indulgence was bound to end up on my ass. The ice cream I meant, though I'm sure if Dan had the chance he'd take a shot at my ass as well.

"You are supposed to be supportive. What happened to being on my side?" I took a spoonful and shoved it into my mouth.

"I'm supportive of you getting some. Stop playing it safe. Just turn up. Surprise him." Megs dug in with her spoon. We should probably stop before we finished another pint. *Should* was a word I seemed to be having a problem with these days.

"His apartment has a heap of security. I need like a retinal scan just to get in the door."

I was exaggerating. I had no idea what I needed to do to get in his building but I assumed I wouldn't be able to just walk in off the street.

"So surprise him at the door. Turn up." Megs stopped eating. She was serious. Like I could just turn up on his doorstep unannounced.

"What if he is doing something, or someone else?" Even though we hadn't explored the boundaries of what we were doing, I was hoping this wasn't a possibility. He had said things last night, things I hoped just weren't for my benefit. There was still I had a tiny bit of doubt. Okay, more than a tiny bit.

"Ash, he wouldn't."

"Do I know that?"

"Well, one way to find out. Go there and see for yourself." Megs pushed her spoon into the half-eaten pint, hopping to her feet. "Go, then report back." She yanked on my arm.

"I can't just go. I need to change or something." I glanced down at Jersey and jeans. I wasn't even wearing makeup.

"Ash, he won't care what you're wearing. Stop making excuses and go." She tugged on my arm again.

"I'm going, I'm going." I rolled my eyes, lifting myself from the couch. "Sit back down and elevate the foot. I can see myself out."

"'Bye. Call me," Megs called out from behind me. I knew she would start burning up the phone if she didn't hear within an hour.

"'Bye." I grabbed my purse and phone and headed out the door.

Megs was right. I needed answers or at the very least some kind of definition as to what we had going on.

I paced in the front of Dan's building; the wind tunneled through the high-rises and it was freezing. I needed a strategy. I had been partially right about the security. While no retinal scan was required, you did actually need to be a resident. Though the whole element of surprise would be gone if I called him and told him I was here. If he had anyone up there then she could easily be shoved out a back entry. Think Ashlyn, think. I paced. My Vans padded softly against the concrete. It came to me. Brilliance. Pizza.

I called a local pizza delivery and gave them Dan's address, paying for it on my sad and overused credit card. It's not like the pizza charge was going to make a huge difference in the big scheme of things, I was already skating on the poverty line. Besides, it would be worth it for my peace of mind.

I waited, hoping my brilliant plan would work. See, I'm sure I wasn't the only girl who had thought up the whole order-a-pizza-and-get-into-meet-the-band idea but my version had a twist. While ordering said pizza and making payment, I tipped them an extra ten bucks to deliver it with a message. I wanted credit for the pizza so when the delivery guy showed up he would tell Dan I had sent it as a gift. Which of course he would accept because, it's not like I was going to send him flowers. Then the second part of my plan would spring into action but this was largely dependent on the delivery driver. This was one time I was hoping for a bored stoner who didn't care about job integrity.

I waited. And waited. Finally after thirty agonizing minutes, a car

HIGH STRUNG

with a pizza box mounted on the roof came into view. Thankfully no one had called the cops to report the redheaded loiterer who was talking to herself in the street.

I raced to the door just as the delivery guy was buzzing the intercom. I put my head down, pretending to fish for my keys in my purse.

"Yeah." Dan's unmistakable voice burst through the speaker.

"Hey dude, I have a pizza delivery for Dan Evans." The driver was not only bored but also clearly not interested. I hit the jackpot of slackers. Score.

"Um, I didn't order any pizza. Wait, what kind is it?" Dan's confused voice made me smile. He sounded adorable, knowing he didn't order pizza but still interested in the possibility of pizza.

I continued digging around in my purse, not that I needed to bother with my theatrical display. Delivery guy didn't even glance at me, let alone care I was there.

"It's peperoni with extra cheese but it's already been paid for. Some girl called Ashlee Murphy sent it to you." Delivery Dumbass read off his provided receipt. I wanted to choke him. How fucking hard is it you say Ashlyn? My parents had a lot to answer for - I'd never had my name on a lunch box growing up.

"Dude, do you mean Ashlyn?" I breathed a sigh of relief thankful Dan pieced it together.

"Dude, I didn't take the call, I'm just the driver. Do you want this pie or not?" Dumbass barked into the intercom. So much for service with a smile.

"Yeah, sure. Let me buzz you up. I'll code you into the elevator. Just hit P."

I pretended to insert my key as the lock popped open, walking through casually to the elevator. Dumbass followed close behind me, giving me a sideways glance as we both reached for the P on the button.

"You going to the Penthouse?" I raised my brow at him, pretending to act surprised.

"Yeah, I've got a delivery." He tapped his padded delivery bag like I was an idiot and couldn't see he was holding a pizza. Visual reinforcement was obviously important because the uniform he was wearing wouldn't be a big enough tip off.

"I didn't order pizza." I acted annoyed, giving him the stare down, holding the door open to stop the elevator's assent.

"Look, lady. It's for some guy called Dan." Dumbass was getting annoyed or impatient. I didn't care for either of his moods.

"Dan is my neighbor. He is also a shitty tipper and an asshole. He should know better than to let unauthorized people into this building. You could be a murderer or a thief. Give me your stinking pizza and I will deliver it myself to him, where I will give him a piece of my mind." I held the door open, unrelenting.

"Here." He tore open the Velcro flap and shoved the box in my hand. "I don't get paid enough for this shit." He stalked from the elevator and back out toward the door.

I smiled at myself, pleased with my ingenuity. I now had access and the pizza. It was a win-win. I let the metal doors close, my silent victory bubbling from the inside.

My heart pounded as I moved up the floors, I wasn't sure if it was from excitement or from nerves. Dan had asked me to come by later. Technically we hadn't discussed time, so this was later. He had also randomly shown up at my door so precedence had been set. Yes? Yes!

The elevator doors parted, opening out to the Penthouse floor, Dan's door only a few feet away.

I knocked loudly on the door, wondering if Dan had video surveillance. Pizza in hand. Feeling a little vulnerable.

A stunning brunette opened the door, her beautiful brown eyes shining brightly. My phone buzzed from inside the pocket of my jeans. I decided that what was in front of me deserved more attention. Her long legs clad in designer jeans, her ample boobs strained against her fitted cotton top.

"Hey, thanks!" She handed over a five-dollar bill and accepted the box from my hands.

HIGH STRUNG

I blinked, dumbfounded. Did I trip and hit my head on the way up here? My mind couldn't register what my eyes were seeing.

"Umm..." I looked at the money in my palm, which had taken the spot of the pizza box.

"Oh Sorry. That's just the tip. Dan said the pizza was paid for by some girl. Is that right?"

"Yeah." That's right, *some girl*. The very girl who is standing in front of you. What an ass. Not only was he with someone else but they were going to be enjoying the pizza I had paid for. I secretly hoped they both choked on it.

"Mommy," squealed a little boy as he ran to the door and hugged his mother's legs, aka the women standing in front of me; he must have been no older than three. What? I lost all muscle control of my face as my mouth dropped open and my eyes almost popped right out of my skull. There was no mistaking the resemblance, Dan's dark hair and eyes in a tiny little boy package. What the actual fuck? He had a fucking kid? I felt like I was going to throw up.

Unable to speak and quite impressed I still had the ability to move, I slowly turned to walk away. I should have known better. What was I thinking? He was a player. What did I expect? The kid had definitely thrown me; I couldn't believe that clown was responsible for another human being.

Blindly I rounded the corner, desperate to get back into the elevator and as far away from here as possible. Whatever we had been doing was over. Dan wasn't going to get the opportunity to explain, I believe it was all fairly self-explanatory. There was no way in hell I was going to stoop and make a scene, why should I bother? I was worth more than that. Granted, we hadn't spoken about being exclusive and technically we weren't even dating, but I would be no one man's alternative. My phone buzzed again from my pocket. Once again, bigger fish to fry.

I didn't see the body I collided with. My face mashed rather spectacularly into a warm and muscular chest. It was hard to breathe but he smelled good. Nice. Death by pectorals would be a cool way to die.

"Ashlyn?" Troy's throaty voice pulled me from destiny with suffocation. Great. The scenario would be so much more enjoyable with an audience. Not.

"Oh, hey." I casually righted myself, trying to keep my expression neutral. No doubt he had been covering for his bestie. Even though inside I felt like a bunch of explosives just had a party with a box of matches, I wasn't giving either of them the satisfaction. Yep, nothing to see here, folks. "I was just leaving."

"Leaving? Dan called and mentioned you and pizza." Troy looked confused. I wondered if woman and child in Dan's apartment would have the same level of confusion. Perhaps they needed a diagram. See here, people, this circle of crazy is you and *this* is Ashlyn, walking away. Dumbass. I wasn't sure if that insult was directed at Dan or myself. Either one was a viable option.

"Ashlyn. What the fuck?" Dan's unmistakable voice boomed from behind me. He actually had the nerve to sound surprised and irate. Seriously, the balls on this guy.

My mind conjured up which slow and painful death would be most satisfying. "I really underestimated you, Dan Evans. Well done. Worst judgment call of my life." I fought the urge to applaud. This for me was a new kind of low.

"Me?" He narrowed his eyes as they raked over my body. "I'm not the one who turned up to your apartment and disrespected you. Troy, so help me, if this is your fucking doing, I'm going to punch you right in the nuts."

"Dude, ease up. I get you're upset but it's not the end of the world. Now kick it down a notch or me and you are going to be having words." Troy glared at Dan.

"Troy had nothing to do with this. Your friend stayed loyal to the end." I had no idea why I was defending Troy; right now I couldn't stand the sight of either of them. A huge bonfire with all things Power Station sounded like a good idea, possibly followed by a Dan voodoo doll I would castrate. "And as far as disrespecting goes, you are in a class all onto yourself. Take a good look, Dan, 'cause I'm out of here."

"Fuck." Dan grabbed my arm and blew out a slow defeated breath. "Look, maybe we can work through this. I should have told you. It just didn't come up."

Was I hearing him correctly? Was this man actually that delusional? I didn't know whether to laugh or cry as I shook off his grasp. "Didn't come up? What is wrong with you? How can you be with me in any capacity and not have fucking told me, Dan? I shouldn't have to walk up here and find out like this. What if I hadn't been here today? Would you have ever come clean?"

"Of course, eventually. I didn't think it was going to be an issue. You know you are partly to blame here, too, Ash. You should have said something." He folded his arms in front of his chest looking disappointed. *He* was playing the victim card? No words. Okay maybe I had just a few left.

"Oh my god. You have the nerve to blame me? Excuse me while I call the men in the white coats, Dan, because you are even crazier than I thought."

"Hey guys, maybe lets move out of the hallway. I think you both need to calm down. Yeah?" Troy tried to play the diplomat. Delsuionville had another resident it seemed. Calming down was not on my agenda. Along with ever seeing or speaking to either of them again.

"I cannot believe you're asking me to calm down. Troy, I'm appalled." And disgusted and most of all hurt, I finished the sentence in my head.

"Ash, I know he sounds like a lunatic but Dan's just passionate. Honestly, let's sit this down and see if it's something you guys can work through. You came all the way down here. With a pizza." Troy smiled as he continued to mediate.

"Which was straight up one of the sexiest things any girl has ever done. Until you show up..." Dan waved his arms wildly in front of me, "like that."

"There is nothing to work out. I'm not sorry I showed up. At least now I know the truth. The only thing I *am* sorry is that I wasted any of my time on you." My voice sounded strangled, a mixture of anger and betrayal. I was trying to maintain control but my body was not cooperating.

Dan blinked as if seeing my hurt for the first time. His unexplained anger slightly receded. He had to know this was the end. There could be no coming back from here. He hissed out through his clenched jaw. "I hate the motherfucking Bruins!"

"What?" My brain went into free fall and I wondered if I had missed a part of the conversation somewhere. The part where that comment actually made sense.

"You," he paused running his hands impatiently through his hair, "are wearing a Bruins jersey." I glanced down the hockey jersey I was wearing. The same one my father had given me when I turned twenty-one. He had played hooky from the bar and taken me to a game. He rarely took time off but for each of our twenty- firsts he made the time. It was just the two of us. We had heckled the visiting side and eaten pretzels. He bought me a beer and told me that even though I was all grown up, I'd always be his little girl. It was one of the greatest gifts he'd ever given me. Every time I wore this jersey, it reminded me of my dad and how much he loved me.

"I hate them, Ash. I mean, at least you're not supporting a Canadian side but, Jesus Christ. The fucking Bruins?" Dan screwed up his face with such distaste.

"What?" I repeated, hearing what he had said but not understanding any of it. How did the Bruins have anything to do with the fact he had a child and possibly a girlfriend? Both of which he hadn't told me about. The fact we supported opposing teams was not an issue here, the fact he was a lying, cheating low life was.

"I said," he slowly repeated. "The Bruins—"

"I heard you, moron. How does that change the fact you have a son?" I planted my hands on my hips defiantly.

"What the hell?" Dan's eyes widened. "I don't have a kid!"

HIGH STRUNG

"Dan, I saw the girl in your apartment. That little boy looks just like you." I couldn't believe he was going to continue to deny it. There was nothing wrong with my eyesight, and I know what I saw.

"Ash, that's my sister Kim. The little boy is my nephew Sam. I guess he kind of looks like me, half the kid's luck if he does." He smirked before the smile slowly slid from his face. "Wait a second, you thought that he was *my* kid?"

"Well, what was I supposed to think?" His nephew. Well that would explain the resemblance. Still, it was an easy mix up. Dan wouldn't have been the first rock star to have a love child.

"I thought you were pissed at me 'cause I didn't welcome you with open arms wearing *that* jersey. Holy shit, you weren't even going to ask me? You were just going to walk?" The realization hit him. He moved closer, leaving little room between us. The tension was palpable.

"What about you? You can't get over the fact I'm a Bruins fan," I shot back. At least my reason, albeit misguided, was valid.

"Ash, that's a big fucking deal. You show up here on my turf, wearing the enemy's colors. What did you think was going to happen?" He stared down at my jersey with such disgust.

"Enemy's colors? You are seriously deranged."

"Children. Play nice." Troy stood between us, pushing our bodies apart. "Obviously there has been a misunderstanding here. Everyone needs to take a fucking breath and chill."

"Hey, Dan." The mysterious brunette who had now been identified as Dan's sister emerged into the hallway. "Looks like you're busy. We'll see you another time." Her eyes darted toward me. Great. She had heard everything. Not that there was any danger of her *not* hearing, neither of us had been using our inside voices. Could this get any worse?

"You don't have to go," Dan and I both echoed over each other, adding to the awkwardness. Apparently it could. Get worse, that is.

"It's getting late and I wanted to get Sam home before dark." She wrestled with the dark haired little boy in her arms.

"No wanna go home."

"Heya, buddy." Dan temporarily diffused the awkwardness, and gave his nephew his full attention. "Don't give your mama a hard time, okay? Your daddy is going to be getting home soon and will want to see you before you need to go to sleep. Don't forget what I taught you." He ruffled the little boy's hair.

"I wanna wock!" Sam proudly held his fist in the air.

"That's it, Sammy. You're making Uncle Dan so proud." The beaming smile was a dead giveaway.

"Stop being a bad influence." Kim rolled her eyes at Dan before turning to me. "Ashlyn, hopefully we'll see you again."

"Sure." I nodded politely. Not like I could say, *actually I'm hoping the earth beneath my feet will open up and swallow me whole so chances of us crossing paths are remote.* My silent prayer remained unanswered, Kim giving me an amused smile before ushering Sam into the waiting elevator.

And then there were three.

"We still need a Ref here or are you good?" Troy didn't even try to hide his amusement.

Dan and I stared at each other, neither one of us wanting to be the first one to cave.

"You are both nutjobs," Troy volunteered, trying to coax one of us out of the imposed game of verbal chicken we had going on.

"Dude, it's the fucking Bruins." Dan cracked first. Silently I celebrated. Victories were still victories no matter how small. Pretty sure I read that on a fortune cookie somewhere.

"She's from Boston, you moron. They don't have a lot of love for the Rangers over there. I can guarantee you that associating with her is not going to affect our chances of winning."

"I give up. I can't keep it a secret anymore." I couldn't help it; the situation was just too absurd.

"What?" Dan's eyes narrowed as he moved closer to me. "What secret?"

"The whole career thing on Wall Street was just a cover. I was really

HIGH STRUNG

sent here by my city to infiltrate New York and send information back. I've been watching training camps and practices of all of your teams." I leaned in and whispered, "The end is near."

"I fucking knew it."

"Dan, she's joking." Troy shook his head, biting back his grin. "Ash, listen. He isn't the sharpest knife in the drawer but I assure you, he's no woman's baby daddy. And, Dan, there is no sporting espionage going on here. You are both acting like tools and on that note, I'm out!" Troy strolled past us and into Dan's apartment. He emerged a few moments later carrying the pizza box. "Neither of you deserve this, I'm taking this baby where she is appreciated." He shoved a slice into his mouth and walked into his apartment, shutting the door behind him.

"Well that was just fucking rude." Dan scratched his head. "So this is all kinds of messed up, huh?"

It was so hard not to smile at how adorable he was. "So you don't have any secret girlfriends or children?"

Might as well get it out there. I mean we were already knee-deep in craziness, what's an extra inch or two.

"Ash, I never have unprotected sex. Not ever. Unless I have some magic power that can get a chick pregnant through a rubber, there is no chance."

"You didn't answer about the girlfriend."

"I haven't had a girlfriend in three years and that's the truth. I don't really date. You know, being on the road, fans and stuff. Gets kinda hard to maintain a relationship." He rubbed the back of his neck and shrugged.

"Oh. Of course. Yep that makes sense." I swallowed.

Well, that answered *that* question. He doesn't date. My heart sank. I know this was the first time I was asking the question, I mean *seriously* asking the question, but I was still a little disappointed. He hadn't led me on and at no point did he tell me this was anything more than what it was. Which was nothing. I had to at least admire his honesty. Right? Why wasn't it making me feel any better?

"Ash, you wanna go inside? I don't think Troy is going to share so I'll

151

order another pizza. We can hang out." Dan nudged my arm with a playful grin teasing the corners of his mouth. He had no idea how his honesty had punctured my heart. I had wanted to know and yet not been prepared for the truth, and upon hearing it, my heart retreated back behind its guarded wall.

"Sure." I pushed aside my feelings of rejection, plastering a fake smile across my face as I made my way to the door.

"Ash, can you take off the Jersey before we go in." Dan grabbed my arm stopping me from entering. "Please."

"Dan," I dug deep, finding the sweetest voice I had, "of course. That is no problem at all."

There were so many reasons for me to just turn around and head home. Or go back to Megs's and devour the pint of Clusterfluff she had tucked away in her icebox. Yet, I didn't. Instead, I found myself wanting to stay. Perhaps even make Dan suffer a little. Oh, I know it was juvenile but I shouldn't be the only one who felt the pain. No, I should share it. That would be the polite thing to do.

I peeled off my jersey reveling the cute, pale pink bra I had on underneath. After neatly folding my prized top and storing it in my purse, I found my real smile.

"Holy shit." Dan's eyes widened, unable to pull his gaze from my breasts. This really was just a little too easy.

I sauntered past Dan and into his apartment. Maybe now I knew where I stood, things would be easier. No more questions and I could stop second-guessing myself. Maybe I should just break the rules and have a one-night stand. If there were ever going to be time to do it, this would be it. Dan was sexy and interested in me. What could be the harm? I was willing to play the night out and see where it took me and if I ended up naked, underneath Dan Evans, rock star, I knew I wouldn't regret it. At least, I hoped I wouldn't.

16
Dan

I DIDN'T KNOW IF THIS WAS SOME BULLSHIT TEST OR SOMETHING, but there was no way I was *not* going to look at the pair of perky tits that Ash had on display. Who fucking knew that when I asked her to take off her top, she would actually do it? Of course, that hadn't been my plan when I'd asked. I just couldn't stand the thought of that fucking jersey being paraded around in my house. Shit, it took everything in me not to tear that monstrosity from her perfect, tiny body. It was like watching your enemy sleep with the girl you wanted and I was not going to let the fucking Bruins screw with me like that, not with her.

"Stop staring, Dan."

I couldn't pull my eyes away. She could dress herself up in a million cute little pink bras and it still would be like throwing gasoline on a fire. Fuck, it just made me want her more. Wondering what was underneath, feeling those perfect tits in my mouth, in my hand, surrounding my cock.

Ash snapped her fingers in front of my face, like that was going to be enough to hinder my view. "Dan. You're acting creepy."

"Ash, I'm not making apologies and I'm not looking away. You're fucking beautiful."

"So you're going to sit there and stare all night? I thought we were going to order pizza and *hang*?" She slid her hand down to her waist, popping her hip to the side, with a raised eyebrow. Daring me. Well, I didn't back away from a dare.

I grabbed her waist and pulled her up against my body, my lips going to work on her mouth. I wanted in her in every fucking way. My hard-on punched out against my jeans as her body rubbed against mine, the friction making me harder. She whimpered in surprise but she didn't fight me and just as well 'cause stopping was going to take an act of god.

I attacked her mouth, needing to kiss her more than I needed air. She let out a gentle moan as she rolled her hips against me. I didn't stand a chance. I was so far gone right now she could probably ask me to wear the fucking jersey myself and I would, if it meant I could be inside of her.

"Dan, slow down." She pulled her lips away, her mouth all puffy and swollen. "You aren't going to fuck me in your doorway."

"Ash, I'm not trying to be an asshole right now, but I told you I would be honest, so I am." I tipped her chin so she was looking at me in the eyes. "If we aren't going to get naked in the next five minutes and have sex then we're going to have to call this a night. My balls are so tight, I'm surprised they haven't crawled up inside me and become fucking ovaries. Now, if you want to cuddle, you're going to have to give me at least a solid hour in the bathroom to jerk off 'cause this," I rubbed my hard cock against her, "ain't going away by itself."

I watched her eyes roll back as I hit the sweet spot between her legs. Her hips tilted to meet each roll of mine.

"Dan," she panted, pulling away from me.

"Ashlyn, you need to tell me, babe. You need to tell me right now if you don't want this. I'm not playing tonight."

I stopped, giving her a minute to consider, my cock throbbing so hard I could feel its heartbeat in my ears.

"Yes." Her hands flew around my neck, dragging me back down to her.

"Yes, what?" My lips sucked against the soft skin of her neck. It was probably going to leave a mark but I couldn't make myself care. In fact, it excited me she would have a reminder, of me. Of this.

"Yes, I want this."

Conversation was obsolete. The green light was all I needed as I grabbed her ass and hauled her onto me. She wrapped her legs around me as I continued to grind against her and everything else just fell away. It was like my skin was burning and the only way I could stop the pain was by being inside her. It went beyond just a fuck; this wasn't about me getting my rocks off. This was some deep-seated need I had no explanation for.

I carried her through my apartment, my mouth locked on hers as my hands palmed her ass. This was not going to be a quickie on the floor, oh hell no. For whatever reason she was finally saying yes, and I was not going to give her an opportunity to regret it. Not even a little.

She moaned against my mouth as I threw her on my bed. Clawing at her body as I tried to rip off her fucking jeans. I wasn't trying to be rough but the time for easy had long past. She responded by yanking up my shirt, her fingernail grazing against my torso as she stripped it off. It was so fucking hot.

I lifted off her, pulling off her Vans before peeling away her jeans, tossing them onto the floor. Her hands latched onto the front of my pants, stroking me through the denim while I tried to rid myself of them. It was torture, sweet fucking torture.

"Let me get them off, babe." It killed me to pry her hands away from my crotch. No seriously, I died a little inside, but if I didn't get out of my jeans soon, I would probably be filling them with my load, and that was not an option.

"Get them off or get me off?" Her raised eyebrow and smirk almost did me in.

I kicked off my shoes, socks, and jeans like they were on fire, tearing off my boxers so that nothing was between us. Ash glanced up at me as I moved back onto the bed, her smile clueing me into that she liked what she saw. Her eyes widened when they moved down to my cock, I stroked it for her so she could get the full effect.

"That's never going to fit."

I suppressed a laugh seeing genuine panic cross those sweet green eyes. "It will fit just fine, babe, trust me." I moved my hands to her back and flicked off her bra. Fuck me if it didn't feel like I was unwrapping a present on Christmas morning.

"No seriously, Dan, that thing is huge. It's going to tear me in half."

I pulled the bra away letting her gorgeous tits spill onto her soft, warm skin. They looked even better than I'd imagined. Sure, they weren't huge but my hand fit around them perfectly, the pink tight nipples standing to attention under the roll of my thumb.

"I'll only give you what you can take, Ash, just relax." I lowered myself down onto the mattress, taking her with me.

"Let me make this good for you." My hand moved down her belly to the edge of her panties, deliberating whether or not tearing them off would be a good move. I toyed with the pink lace that matched her bra, not that I gave a shit. It would be so easy to make them disintegrate in my hand. Just one tug would be all it took.

Her own hands joined mine, skirting off her panties before I was able to give their removal any more thought. My fingers roamed in between her legs to feel her bare and wet pussy.

"Hmm, wet already." My fingers circled her core as my mouth lowered onto hers. "Let's see how much wetter I can make you."

I plunged a finger inside her, making her gasp at the invasion. It felt so tight and hot, better than I could have ever imagined. Her wide eyes softened as I slowly stroked her from the inside, my thumb getting busy across her clit. Her back arched, melting into me as I slid in another finger, stretching her as I fucked her with my hand.

"Dan," she moaned. Just hearing her saying my name was getting me off, my swollen cock begging for attention.

"That's it, baby. Let me feel you." I moved in and out of her slick, hot pussy, applying a little more pressure with each thrust. Her wetness coated my fingers in appreciation.

"Ah." She rocked her hips against me, her pussy tightening around my hand.

"You going to come, babe? 'Cause I want to taste you before you do."

"Oh, Dan."

"Not yet, Ash." I shifted down the bed unable to stand it any longer. My fingers slid out of her soaking wet pussy so I could part her thighs. She was fucking beautiful.

"Dan." She grabbed at me with desperation but I wasn't about to be steered off course, my tongue traveling her belly until it reached the top of her pussy. I could smell the sex rolling off her. She wasn't going to last much longer.

My mouth covered her opening, my tongue darting inside and tasting her. Her thighs wrapped around my head in a vice-like grip as I continued to eat her out. I was merciless, plunging my tongue deeper and deeper into her while my thumb continued to circle her clit. I heard her muffled scream as she grabbed a pillow and bit into it. Her body shook as it got closer to its release. She was wound so fucking tight. I could feel the explosion building.

She was dripping—I felt it run down my mouth and onto the mattress—and bucking against me like a woman possessed. It had obviously been a while since a man had done this right, especially if those ribbed condoms were anything to go by. It made me fucking smile listening to the strangled noises she was making, hearing the girl who was usually so in control unraveling around my mouth. Her eyes were tightly shut as I watched her squirm. She was so close.

"Ash. Let go," I demanded, lifting my mouth away from her for only a second. I thrust my tongue inside her one last time, feeling her tighten around it, pulsing as she came hard. Her screams muted by the pillow that covered her face.

"That's it, babe, let it take you." My fingers replaced my mouth, as I gently continued to pump her, working every last inch of the orgasm through her body.

"Fuck, Dan." Ashlyn pulled the pillow from her face as she relaxed onto the bed. "I've never…it's never been like that." Her sleepy pre-orgasmic grin lit up her eyes.

"I'm not done yet, babe, that was just the preshow. If that impressed you, just wait for the headliner." And fuck me if it didn't make me puff up my chest like a fucking superhero.

My fingers continued to play as she rolled onto her side. I had to momentarily let go as I moved up beside her, pressing my cock against the crease of her ass. The image was so fucking hot, I wanted to burn it into my brain. I reached across her, digging into the top drawer of my nightstand and pulling out a condom. My cock was so hard it hurt.

She turned, sitting up in bed, and watched as I tore open the packet and rolled the latex down my shaft, licking her lips as I stroked my dick a couple of times. I wanted to fuck that sweet little mouth of hers as well, but right now it was her pussy that I wanted.

"Dan—" I could hear the hesitation in her voice.

"Shhh." I moved my lips to her throat, kissing her skin. "Trust me, I'm not going to hurt you."

She nodded and relaxed back onto the bed, letting me take the lead. Her nipples were tight as my tongue flicked them, teasing the opening of her pussy with the head of my cock.

Ashlyn moaned as I alternated circling her entrance and her clit, and watched me as I stroked my shaft. I could feel her relax, tilting her hips up to me as I continued to tease her. I smiled, knowing that while it was driving me all kinds of crazy, she was riding that train along with me. Her tits bobbing up and down as she sucked in air.

"Dan," she moaned, her hand flying around my cock and pulling it closer toward her, "I want to feel you."

"Here I am, babe." I guided her hand up and down my shaft as I pushed the head of my cock into her.

"Fuck, you're tight." I breathed, feeling the walls of her pussy clamp around my dick. It took everything I had not to blow my load right there.

"Relax, Ash. You put the death grip on me, this is going to be over before either of us wants it to." My dick jerked in protest as I slid out of her. "Just going to give you a little more."

She nodded as I circled her clit with my thumb, watching me push in a little farther this time, her pussy stretching to accommodate me. God, she felt so good. I pulsed slowly, pushing in a little bit farther each time while I kept working her clit. The little noises she was making were driving me fucking insane.

"Oh!" Her mouth formed an "O" as I entered her a little more deeply, her hands bracing against my chest as I arched into her, finally getting most of my dick inside.

"That's it, babe, almost there." I slid in deeper. "You feel so fucking amazing." My hands moved to her hips to steady her as she bucked against me. She was so tight and wet, even with a condom I could feel everything. I imagined if there was fucking in heaven, this is what it would feel like. She stilled as I slide the last inch in, her pussy pulsing around my cock.

"Babe?" I stopped, wanting to be sure she was cool before I continued. Right now a squeeze of her pussy was probably going to set me off anyway, so the break served a dual purpose. She looked so beautiful, her red hair floating around her face like some kind of wild bush fire, her eyes wide.

"OH," Ashlyn moaned as she started to move again. "Holy shit, that feels so good." She rocked against me, grinding her pussy along my shaft.

It was all the reassurance I needed, as I started to pick up the pace. With my hands wrapped around her hips, I started really getting some momentum, sliding the whole length of my cock in and out of her hungry pussy. Her wetness coated me like a badge of honor as I hammered into her a little faster.

"That's it, babe, you got all of me now." I bowed my head down and sucked her neck, tasting the saltiness of sex and sweat. My heavy sack slapped against her ass as I pounded harder.

"Fuck!" I looked down at my cock sliding in and out of her, wanting it to last forever but I knew if I kept watching it was going to be over soon. Me fucking Ashlyn was hotter than any porno.

I slid my hands down her thighs and lifted her legs, resting them over my shoulders. She tilted her hips, her ass rising off the mattress as I got a deeper angle. So fucking tight.

"Dan. Oh. Yes. Yes," Ash moaned, her hands kneading her tits as my cock moved faster.

I could die right now, balls deep inside this girl and I would die with the biggest fucking grin on my face. I'd had a lot of sex over the years, been with a lot of different girls and fucked them every way imaginable, and nothing even came close to the way Ashlyn was making me feel. Fuck, I'd live inside her if I could.

I felt her clamp around my cock and her legs start to waver and I knew she was close. I wanted to make her come more than I wanted my next breath. "That's it, Ash, come for me." I lifted her hips and I drove in deep.

"YES," she screamed, her voice bouncing of the walls. "Yes. Yes." Her body shook as she came hard around me. Her pussy milking my cock sent me into oblivion. Not even Superman and his balls of fucking steel would have been able to fight the urge to come.

"Fuck." I groaned as I exploded into her, my load squirting so hard against the condom it almost hurt. I couldn't stop, riding out the rest of the orgasm while my dick continued to pulse inside her. I let her legs slide off my shoulders and lay either side of me. Her body was limp as I collapsed on top of her. I didn't want to move and hoped like hell I wasn't smothering her as I breathed heavily against her neck.

Ashlyn fisted a handful of my hair, forcing me to lift my head. "Dan." My brain rattled around in my skull as some of the blood that had been in my cock traveled back toward my head.

"Yeah?" I pushed her tangled hair away from her face. She was absolute perfection. I wasn't just thinking that on account having just blown my load either, she was just insanely beautiful in every way imaginable.

"I've never had sex like that. Come like that. I mean, I know it's no big deal for you, but I think you have pretty much ruined me for all other men." Her palm rested against my face.

The thought of her being with another dude made my blood run cold. Some other guy touching her, kissing her, being inside her? Hell, no. It made me want to kick someone's ass just on the possibility it could happen. I would do whatever I needed to do to make sure that shit didn't go down.

"I can assure you, that was a big fucking deal for me, too. And I'm going to keep making you feel good for as long as you'll let me. So you don't need to worry about anyone else, you just bask in the afterglow." 'Cause if I had anything to do with it, she would be too busy screaming my name to worry about finding anyone else.

"Oh, Dan, you are such a romantic." Ashlyn laughed, running her nails up my back and fuck if it didn't make my cock twitch. Which conveniently, was still buried inside her.

"Give me a minute to lose the condom." I kissed her forehead and lifted off her, wanting to take care of business quickly so I could get back to bed. I wasn't usually a cuddler, preferring to get some sleep once the sex was done, what else was there? But having spent the last few nights with my arms wrapped around Ash, it's exactly how I wanted it to be while I waited for the sandman.

I kicked off the damp sheets and slid off the mattress, moving to my connecting bathroom and hitting the light on the way in. I pulled off the rubber, knotting the end and tossing it into the wastepaper basket beside my toilet. I gripped the sink, looking at myself in the mirror while I turned on the water to wash my hands.

"Staring at yourself now? I guess your fascination with me had to end eventually." Ash's sheet-wrapped body leaned against the doorframe.

"Just making sure I didn't break out in some crazy rash after sleeping with a Bruins fan. It's a legit concern." I cut off the water and turned around. Even with her lips puffy and her hair a mess she was still a knockout. It was the first time I'd ever felt I was out of my depth with a girl, and that feeling made me edgy.

"Ass!" Ashlyn punched me in the arm, her tiny fist barely making a dent. "If you're done priming yourself, I need to use the bathroom."

"So, use it." I smirked, not having anywhere better to be.

"Dan, I need to pee."

"Do you want me to put the seat down for you?"

"No, I need you to leave. I'm not going to pee in front of you."

"Babe, we just had sex and you're embarrassed to take a piss in front of me?"

"It's not the same thing and I'm not embarrassed. Bathroom stuff is private. I don't want an audience."

"Just go, what's the big deal? I don't have any issue taking a piss in front of you."

"Dan, I'd doubt you'd have an issue taking a piss in front of anyone. I, on the other hand, would rather keep some mystery about me. Thanks."

I didn't move, instead I settled up against the wall holding my arms across my chest and enjoying the show.

She stomped her foot impatiently. Seriously, it was too fucking adorable. "Dan, seriously. I need to go."

"Ash, you are way too uptight. Stop overthinking shit." I wrapped my hands around her arms and moved her to the front of the toilet. "Sit down and take a goddamn piss and don't care what anyone is going to think about it, least of all not me."

"I hate that you are making me do this right now." She lifted the sheet wrapped around her body, and sat on the toilet seat. "I can't even believe I'm doing this."

"Performance anxiety?"

"Stop it. Turn the water on or something. It's bad enough you're watching, I don't want you to hear it as well."

"Fine, fine." I turned the water back on, the free-flowing tap drowning out any other tinkling sound.

She obviously finished, grabbing some toilet paper and wiping before standing up and flushing. Honestly, the whole process was kind of fascinating. A lot more involved than just pulling it out and taking a leak.

"Better?" I stepped aside so she could wash her hands, I couldn't hide my shit-eating grin.

"Yes and I still hate you." Ash pushed me out of the way as the soapy water went down the drain, grabbing a hand towel and drying off. "We can never speak of this again."

"Nah, it was magic. The mystery is all gone and I still want to sleep with you. We're going to be friends for life."

17
Ashlyn

I woke up, tangled around Dan's arms and legs, my cell impatiently ringing on the floor from the pocket of my jeans. It was morning but I had no idea what time it was, the light streaming through the gap in the curtain leading me to believe it wasn't as early as I first thought.

I reached down and retrieved my phone, fishing it out of the pocket and answering it before it went to voice mail.

"Hello." My voice sounded croaky and hoarse. I didn't have sexy morning voice, not even a little. Dan stirred beside me but didn't bother waking up. Ass. He just rolled over and went back to sleep.

"Ashlyn? It's Lexi Reed. Is now a good time?" Her bright voice burst through the phone. Her unmistakable twang, immediately identifying her as Australian. I totally loved her accent, not that I would ever tell her. That would just sound so condescending.

"Oh. Hey. Yes. It's me. Sorry. Just woke up." A jumble of disjointed words tried to form a sentence in my mouth. My brain not having the courtesy to connect the dots before it ejected them.

"Great. Ashlyn, I wanted to tell you how impressed I was with your interview. I think you presented well and you were obviously prepared..."

I knew a brush off when I heard one and this particular gem was the thank-you-but-no-thank-you where I was told my application had been unsuccessful. I was half expecting it, knowing my chances hadn't been great but hoping that maybe I had skated in. It was another disappointment, you would think after twenty or thirty rejections I would be used to it. Sadly, it still stung.

"Thanks, Ms. Reed. I'm guessing I was unsuccessful." I thought it would be better just to get it over with. No point dragging it out. It wasn't her fault I was completely unsuitable for the position.

"Ashlyn, I'm sorry. Not this time." At least she had the decency to sound regretful. Some prospective employers had sounded down right chirpy while dashing my hopes and dreams. *Congratulations, you suck* doesn't sound any better with a smile in your voice.

"What I wanted to tell you is that though you weren't successful for my assistant's position, I have a contact who needs a financial analyst. Now I can't promise you a job but he would love to interview you if you are interested."

"Oh my god! Are you serious? Yes, yes. Of course I'm interested." It was like someone just plugged an IV of Red Bull into me and I was instantly awake.

"Great, I'll get my colleague, Matt Burns, to email you the details and I will pass on your resume to Simon Jennings. He'll be in touch so you can work out a time convenient for you to meet."

"Thank you so much, Ms. Reed. You have no idea how badly I need this job."

"I know, Ashlyn, and please call me Lexi. All I'm doing is getting someone with an impressive resume a job interview in an appropriate field. The rest is up to you."

"Thanks, Lexi. Goodbye."

"'Bye, Ashlyn, and good luck."

I ended the call and squealed. Unashamedly squealed like a little girl. This was my turning point. My lucky break. Things were finally going to start improving and who knew where it could lead.

"What the fuck, Ash?" Dan groggily turned to face me, his dopey sleep face making him more adorable. "NSync getting back together? You know it will only work if Justin comes back, I don't like boy bands but that kid from Tennessee has talent."

"No, you moron." I swatted his arm. "How did you know I used to be an NSync fan?" Granted it had been a while, but I had loved their catchy tunes and stylized dance moves. So non-offensive and easy to listen to. Not bad to look at either.

"Lucky guess." Dan grinned folding his hands behind his head. "Can you pretend to listen to one of our albums, I don't even care if you like it. Just fucking lie to me."

"I'll listen to one of your albums if you get Alex to sign it for me. He's got such dreamy eyes."

"I thought it was his ass you were interested in, not his eyes."

"Ass, eyes. I'll take whatever's on offer. Has he mentioned me?"

"Don't even joke like that, Ashlyn. I can't tell if you are serious."

"I'm kidding, Dan. I'm not interested in Alex. Now stop being an ass and let me tell you my good news."

"What's your news? Can you pull down the sheet a little? I think we both will benefit from hearing your good news while you're naked. It's all in the telling."

"Be serious. I got an interview. A real interview for a job that I could actually be happy doing."

"Wow, Ash, that's awesome. Congratulations. I'm happy for you, babe."

"Thanks. I'm so excited. This is a big deal. I just needed someone to see my potential and take a chance. Can you believe Lexi Reed recommended me? Damn, I owe her huge for this."

"Yeah, she's good people when she isn't chewing us out. You must have really impressed her."

"Dan." I wrapped my arms around him and kissed him hard. Really kissed him. It was probably me getting caught up in the moment but it seemed like for the first time in a long time, things were actually going in my favor. Ordinarily I would have jumped on the phone and Megs and I would have screamed for a few minutes before deciding where we were going for a fancy celebratory dinner, but being in Dan's bed, having had one of the most amazing nights of my life, it just seemed right to share this with him.

"Well, good morning." His smile widened as he grabbed my ass. "I like seeing you happy, it makes me horny."

"You're always horny, but yes, I'm really happy."

"And I'm really horny. We should celebrate with lots of sex and then pancakes. Then maybe more sex."

"I'm not spending the day having sex with you. I've got important stuff to do, like get this interview locked down and research the company who is offering the position."

"You can do all of that *after* sex. I might be willing to let the pancakes slide, but feel this?" He grabbed my hand and placed it on his very hard erection. "This needs some special attention."

"Wow, that does need some attention." I slowly rubbed up and down the shaft of his cock before releasing it. "YOU should probably take care of that."

"See that's what I thought too, but I was talking with my cock earlier and he kinda has a hard-on for you. I tried to tell him it was a bad idea being you're moody and really anal, but fuck me if talking about your ass just didn't make him want you more."

I couldn't help but smile. Only Dan Evans could make being so crude so endearing. "You have problems, you know that? You and your cock."

"Babe, say what you want about me but you're going to hurt his feelings by saying shit like that out loud. He can't help himself. He sees a beautiful girl and he needs to show his appreciation. Think of it as a standing ovation."

"I'm not sure how I'm supposed to feel about that but I apologize to your penis if I hurt his feelings."

"It's okay, babe, he forgives you, but if you really want to make things right he says you should kiss him better."

"Creative way of angling for a blow job, Dan. I have to admit, I'm slightly impressed."

"Aw, Ash, I've impressed you. We all knew it was bound to happen sooner or later. You can try and resist all you want but in the end, my cock and I, we're just too damn charming."

Well damn him and his cock, because he was right, and I had been utterly charmed by the both of them.

So I caved. While my intention was to get up and head back to my apartment to prepare for my job interview, I ended up spending at least another hour in bed with Dan. In the end, it just wasn't his cock that was doing the convincing, his mouth and fingers had come into play as well and not even I was strong enough to resist him. He wasn't kidding about being amazing in bed. He actually had the goods to back up that big mouth of his.

I had never had sex like that. Not ever. Not even if you added up the sum total of my entire sexual experiences could you compare them to what one night with Dan was like. He was raw and primal but most of all, intense. He didn't poke and prod aimlessly hoping to get me off. No, every action was calculated and deliberate for maximum impact. I didn't know it could ever be like that. That I could come while actually *having* sex. And oh, how I'd come. It was explosive and addictive and more amazing than anything I'd ever felt. He hadn't stopped at one orgasm, oh no, the man was a show off. Not that I was complaining. He could demonstrate his talent all he wanted to, and continue to make me shatter into a million euphoric pieces. After all, what's the point of a fling if you can't indulge in mind-blowing sex?

HIGH STRUNG

My body ached in places that had long been forgotten, and while I was probably going to need an icepack and a good dose of Tylenol, I was happy. Happy. It's such a funny word, with such a wide range of meanings, but for me, it was a place of contentment and calm, and that's what I felt while I was with Dan. I know it was going to be short-lived and it probably meant a lot more to me than it did to him, but I didn't want to stop feeling this way until I absolutely had to. I would deal with that when the day eventually came. He was so unfiltered but real, which is not what I expected from a rock star. Sure his ego was huge and the things that came out of his mouth were unpredictable and dripping in innuendo, but he was so genuine I couldn't help fall for him. Therein lies the danger. The falling part. A little was to be expected. He was larger than life, ridiculously attractive, funny, and unsurpassed in the bedroom, but too much would mean heartbreak.

I wasn't sure if what I was feeling was infatuation or love. To be honest, I didn't really have anything to compare it to, but I couldn't deny I had actual feelings for him. I just needed to keep them in check and not get caught up in the fantasy. Dan Evans didn't date, he said so himself. I was never going to be his girlfriend.

"I Want Your Sex" blared obnoxiously from my cell, I didn't have the heart to change it and honestly, he was right, it was what I was thinking.

"Couldn't live without me, huh?" I smiled as I pressed the phone to my ear. "Really, Dan, we're going to have to get this dependency problem under control. I'm going to have a real job soon and not have time to listen to your heavy breathing and jerking off."

"Why must you say such hateful things? My heavy breathing and jerking off should be prioritized, woman. I expected you to carve out at least twenty minutes of your day for it. If you won't participate you can at least be my audience. Masturbation is important."

I giggled into the phone, this man was all kinds of wrong but I really, really liked him. "So did you call for a purpose or just to remind me how vain you are?"

"I was actually calling to make plans with you. I was thinking we should do something Saturday. Celebrate you landing this big shot job offer."

"Dan, I've only got an interview, there is no guarantee they'll offer me the job. Let's not get ahead of ourselves."

"Please, we both know you've got this in the bag. They are going to love you. You're going to roll in there being all badass with your fancy degree, wow them with S&P indices, and they will probably offer the job on the spot."

"Dan, are you trying out your big boy words again? Where did you hear about S&P indices?"

"Wall Street Journal and for your information, that paper sucks. There are no pictures of girls in it at all, just a bunch of crusty old men. Lame if you ask me. I can't believe you have to pay money for this shit."

"Aw, you're reading the Wall Street Journal for me. Be still my heart."

"Well when it's done being *still* can we make plans for Saturday? I'll even let you pick the place."

My heart fell. Saturday was my birthday and I had already committed to going out with Megs and a few of our friends for drinks. It wasn't going to be a huge event but because I worked most weekends, I rarely got to spend any time with them, and I would hate to cancel. I didn't want to be *that* girl, the one who blew off her friends just because the sexy rock star she happens to be sleeping with snaps his fingers. No, I had to honor my commitments. That's who I was. Dependable and reliable. God, I sounded like a Toyota. In any case, the only option would be to invite Dan but I had already discussed it with Megs and ruled that out. It was too much, too soon. I didn't want to rock the boat. Not now when things were going so well.

"Dan, I'm sorry but I can't. I've got plans already." I shook my head knowing I was probably going to regret it. "Maybe we can do something another day?"

"What plans do you have Saturday? Lifetime channel tele-movies don't count, Ash."

HIGH STRUNG

"I'm not staying at home and watching TV, you moron," I laughed. "I'm meeting up with a few friends. It's nothing important but it's been planned for a while and I just can't cancel. I'm sorry, Dan. I really would love to come out with you."

"Okay. Yeah. No biggie. We can do whatever, some other time."

"Of course, any other day."

"Okay, well I'll let you get back to your boring shit. I'm going to go hang with Troy. Later."

"'Bye."

Had he actually sounded disappointed by my inability to meet him Saturday or was I projecting? I'm sure it was more likely he couldn't believe I would actually say no, as I doubt he heard the word very much. Yes, that was it. He was probably annoyed he had wanted me to do something and I wasn't available. I'm sure his ego would recover by noon. Dan wasn't the type of guy who let disappointment sit with him for long. I wondered if he would ever ask again or if I'd blown my chance. Not that it had been a date. At no point did he imply it was going to be a date, he was just trying to be nice. Still, I'd really liked him asking me out. More than I cared to admit.

I sighed, walking over to my beat-up desk and sat in the recycled office chair that had come with the apartment. Well, came with the apartment in the sense that it was placed next to the outside dumpster. Either way, it was functional and unwanted so I hauled it back up the three flights of stairs and it became mine. I fired up my outdated laptop waiting for the operating system to kick in, it was just one of the many things that needed to be replaced and had been added to the when-I-have-the-money list.

My email menu flagged unread messages and I scouted through the endless irrelevant crap that seemed to fill my inbox to find the one from Matthew Burns, Lexi Reed's senior PR manager. He gave me a basic run down on Simon Jennings. He was a New York born and bred real estate broker who had made some wise investments just before the housing bubble burst in 2007. A self-made millionaire, whose office was located in the financial district, was looking for an analyst for a twelve-month contract with scope for ongoing employment. Standard. It sounded perfect.

I also had an email from Simon Jennings, asking me to call his office to make a time for an interview. My heart thumped loudly in my chest as I picked up my phone and dialed the numbers. I hoped Mr. Jennings didn't have crazy sensitive hearing and assumed I had a heart condition.

"Good afternoon JenCorp, Joanna speaking."

"Hello Joanna, my name is Ashlyn Murphy. I received an email requesting I call so we could set up an interview time."

"Ah, Yes. Ashlyn, we've been expecting your call. I have your resume in front of me. Mr. Jennings requested I set up a time for you."

"Sure, I'm flexible with my schedule so I can almost do any time." I hoped I didn't sound too desperate. I was flexible because I was mainly working nights in a bar. Not that they needed to know that. Selective resume listing I called it.

"How about tomorrow at eleven?"

Crap. Not a lot of time to prepare but I could run with it. It would mean I would be up all night but if I could land this job it would be worth it.

"Tomorrow at eleven sounds perfect."

"Wonderful, I will forward you a confirmation of your appointment. It will include directions to our offices and any additional information we may require."

"Thanks, I'll see you then."

"Goodbye."

My stomach flipped. I felt sick. I was so nervous I couldn't stand it. Job interviews were hard enough for me to get through; they always put me on edge. But an interview for a job I wanted? That was hard-core pressure. I squeezed my eyes shut. Concentrating on my breathing. It was my time. I could do this.

18
Dan

"DUDE, SIT YOUR ASS DOWN. YOU ARE GOING TO WEAR A HOLE through the floor." Troy tapped out some rhythm with a pair of sticks onto a chair. We were about to head out to rehearsal; Alex and James had some new material they wanted to test run.

"She flat-out lied to me, dude. She totally dissed me on her birthday. What the fuck is up with that?" The more shit rotated in my head the more it pissed me off. I never gave the whys of the situation much stock, but now…now it was all kinds of important.

"Dan, you going to give me some context or am I supposed to just fill in the fucking blanks? What are you talking about?" He lifted the sticks, twirling one in his hand as he stared at me, grinning like an asshole. Of course this would be amusing for him. He wasn't the one being dodged.

"It's Ashlyn's birthday Saturday. When she left her purse in the Suburban, I checked it for ID and I saw her date of birth." I don't know why it bothered me so much. It sure as hell wasn't the first time a girl had lied to me, but this time it really bugged me. It was also turning me into a whiny bitch. If it had been anyone but Troy I'd have shut my mouth and pretended it was business as usual, but with the big guy, I didn't have to fake it. He always seemed to know when I was ate up about something anyway, so I was just saving time by coming clean.

"I wanted to take her out for her birthday. Thought we could go out to dinner or something. She said she had plans." I pushed my ass into the couch beside him. He was right; I was going to wear a hole through my carpet. Besides if we were going to get all Dr. Phil with this, I might as well be comfortable.

"So? It's not like the girl didn't have a social life before she met you, numbnuts. It's short notice, of course she is going to have plans for her birthday."

Fucking Troy, trying to be Captain Fucking Obvious. Of course I knew this. Hell, of course she had a life before we'd met, no doubt, with a steady line of douchebags trying to crawl into her panties. A fact I was trying to get out of my head before I put my fist through a wall.

"So why didn't she just say she was going out for her birthday? She made up some bullshit about it being no big deal, and that she was going out for drinks with friends but couldn't cancel. If it's no big deal why the fuck can't I go?"

Was she going to try and hook up with some other motherfucker or was it that she didn't want me around? Both of these scenarios pissed me off, the first more so than the second, and I was cool with neither. I pushed my hands through my hair wishing I had some way of knowing what was going down in her head. Mind-reading powers would be good about now.

"Dude, you are starting to freak me out. If you are going to start menstruating we are going to have serious problems." Troy laughed, slapping me hard on the back. Clearly he was enjoying the situation.

"Fuck you, asshole. I'm serious. This shit is messed up." I punched him in the arm. This was no laughing matter. I wasn't spilling my guts for Troy's enjoyment.

"Have you fucking asked her?" He relaxed into his chair, putting the sticks down and clocking me with a look. "Or is this just you pulling shit out of your ass?"

I waved him off as it was bad enough I was talking about it with him. I wasn't about to lay it out on the line with her. "I'm not going to ask her, numbnuts. A man has his pride."

"Can I ask you where you left your fucking balls and who the fuck is this dude standing in front of me? 'Cause I've got to tell you, Dan Evans has never given two fucks about what a girl did or didn't do and he sure as shit didn't care what she thought."

"Don't fucking start." I pushed out a breath, leveling him with a stare. "I don't know why but I fucking care and it pisses me the hell off." Shit, I'd gone this far I might as well just let it fly. "I fucking want to be with her all the time, dude. It's like a sickness. It's not just about the fucking. It's about her. She doesn't take my shit but she doesn't try and change me either. She's cool, dude. We can just hang and she isn't trying to score free shit or be on the cover of some bullshit magazine." She was the first girl I had been with in a long time who hadn't tried to selfie and tag herself while she was with me. Hadn't even hit me up for tickets or a backstage pass. Hell she hadn't asked for anything.

"Sounds like to me you've got yourself a girl."

"Asswipe, it's not like that. She's got some weird ten-year plan or some shit. She's not interested in dating, made that quite clear early on. We're just chilling."

"So is it just fucking?"

It pissed me off that Troy would talk about her like she was just some groupie. "Dude, don't talk about her like that. She's not that kind of girl."

"Dan, newsflash. If you are so ate up about this chick and it's more than just fucking, then I hate to break it you, but you have yourself a girlfriend."

"Asshole, did you hear what I just said? She isn't interested in dating."

"Dan, brother. You know I fucking love you but you are seriously fucking dense sometimes. If you two are doing stuff, other than just fucking, you already *are* dating."

"Are you sure, man? I'm thinking there needs to be some kind of agreement or some shit. People don't just start dating."

"If she is spending time with you of her own free will, then she is agreeing. I'm telling you. You're dating, man."

"How the fuck did I start dating and not know?"

"'Cause you're a dipshit with emotional issues? How the fuck should I know? What I do know is you need to get some sack and sort that shit out."

"You're right, dude. I think I have feelings and stuff. I haven't even thought about another girl since meeting her, not even to jerk off." I scrubbed my face with my hands.

"Sounds pretty serious. I can't remember the last time you were with just one girl." Troy surprisingly wasn't being an asshole about it. "I think it's a good thing. James and Han have been happy for years and Alex and Lexi still dig each other. Maybe it's time. I know I'm getting sick of groupies and band whores. Ash seems like she has a good head on her shoulders. I can't see her being in it for the money or the fame. Fuck, if she has to put up with your sorry ass, I say she deserves a pay out."

"Yeah, I think I want to try, man. I know I'm probably going to screw this up, but the thought of her being with another dude makes me want to gut him like a fish. No seriously, I want to grab a knife and fillet the motherfucker and I haven't even met him yet."

"Easy there, Hannibal Lector. Just concentrate on your game plan, the rest will take care of itself."

"True. We should probably make tracks. I want to try and catch Lexi before we start jamming."

"You solid? You need a hug or something? We can swing past the drug store and grab you some Tampax if you still need it."

"Whatever, man. Just grab your stuff. We'll take my car."

HIGH STRUNG

The drive out to James and Hannah's was always a great ride. We got to leave the traffic and noise behind and hit the open road. The afternoon sun was pooling on the dash and even though the weather was starting to turn, we still had a couple more weeks of fall before shit got nasty.

James had this estate just outside of the city. When he'd bought it I thought it was kind of douchey, but now it made sense. Big house with a massive yard, tucked away from the world, plus James had a state of the art studio built into his basement. We could rehearse or lay down tracks whenever we wanted without having to worry about booking studio time. It was actually pretty sweet. Han was awesome, too. She didn't come down there and bitch and moan, she let us do our thing and most times kept us supplied with snacks and beer. James knew what he was doing when he brought her into the fold.

We pulled up the drive and parked up front. Alex's Escalade was already there, which meant he had his ladies in tow, with Jase's 'Stang parked beside it. Looked like we were the last ones here. Not that it mattered, they were all probably shooting the shit; it had been a while since we had all been together.

Troy gave me a shit-eating grin as he opened the door and ejected from the car. I knew him well enough to know he would probably be riding me about the Ashlyn thing for the rest of the day. Not that I gave a shit, 'cause even just thinking about her gave me a case of the warm and fuzzies. Fuck. Maybe I was getting a period? Screw it. Whatever the reason, I was bear-hugging the hell out of it, because letting it go wasn't an option. I pushed open the door and joined Troy at James's front door.

"Hey!" Hannah pulled open the door before we had a chance to ring the buzzer. "I was wondering when you were going to make it? Everyone's already here." Her face lit up as we stepped through the doorway.

"Hey, Han." I gave her a hug, "We ran into traffic. How's the little dude? When's Noah going to pick up the mic and give his old man a run for his money?"

Hannah smiled. "Noah is playing with Grace. Everyone is out in the living room."

She led us through the hallway to where everyone was gathered. Alex and James were on the floor playing with the kids while Jase was sitting on the armrest of the couch deep in a conversation with Lexi.

"Is Noah macking on my girl?" I walked over to where the boys were sitting, our entrance getting their attention.

"Might have some competition there, buddy. Noah's pretty sweet on Grace." James laughed, lifting himself off the floor.

I gave James a thump on the back. "Lucky for him he got his looks from his momma so he stands a fighting chance."

"No man is ever going to get close to my daughter so you're both SOL." Alex brushed off his ass as he stood, Grace stretching out her little arms wanting to be picked up. No denying that little sweetheart was daddy's girl.

Lexi alternated hugs and hellos with Troy and me as Jase lifted his beer in acknowledgement.

I cleared my throat, hoping not to make an ass out of myself as I moved over to the side of the room for some privacy. "Hey Lexi, can I have a minute?"

Truth was, when Lexi came into our lives I was more than skeptical. Being who we are and doing what we do, you meet a lot of people. People who want to get their claws into you for what they can gain out of it. No point bitching about it, it comes with the territory, but Lexi had been different. Not to say I wouldn't have jumped at the chance at fucking her, she was all kinds of sexy, but I was glad the way things had ended up. She had more than earned her place with us, she was kickass handling our shit and you could always count on her.

"This is a little cloak and dagger, Dan." She smiled as she joined me. "What did you need?" She might be a ball-buster but man, whenever I asked for something, even if it was for shit she didn't want to do, she always came through.

"Yeah, I just wanted to thank you for hooking up that job interview for Ashlyn. I was with her when she got your call and she was seriously stoked. I know you went out on a limb and I just wanted to say thanks." I scratched the back of my neck feeling like a douchebag. I don't know why I bothered to try and do this privately, the way Hannah and the boys were eyeballing us, I knew I was going to get twenty questions the minute we were done.

"Wow, Dan, look at you with manners and everything. You've really got it bad for this girl." Lexi gave me a big shit-eating grin, no doubt pleased she was making me feel like I'd just put my nuts on a chopping block. Did I mention what a ball-buster she was?

"Not you, too, Troy's already giving me shit." I didn't expect anything less, Lexi and the rest of them would probably ride my ass, but I didn't care. Ashlyn was worth it.

Lexi grinned, she was clearly enjoying this. "I think it's great. Really I do. Just wondering if strip clubs are going to survive without your business."

"Yeah, have your fun. I don't give a shit. I like her and I'm not hiding it. Not saying we're going to run to Vegas and get legal or anything but yeah, I'm going to be with her." They could make fun of it all they wanted. I'd take it. Being with Ashlyn was important to me and if all I had to do was listen to these dickheads joke about it, then I'd do that, happily.

Lexi smiled. "Devil must be pissed that Hell just froze over."

"Thought he would've been used to it after *your* marriage to Stone." I reminded her of how quickly she'd waltzed down the aisle even though she swore ever since she met us that she wasn't the marrying type. Firstly with their impromptu Miami wedding, and then again on Alex's birthday. "Two times no less." Probably not wise to poke the bear but I was on a roll.

"Well, well. Manners *and* quick off the mark. Impressive." Surprisingly she didn't seem annoyed. "But it's not me who you should be thanking. Sydney organized the interview. Her father is a close friend of Simon's. Apparently he's been looking for someone for a while but hasn't found the right candidate. He was excited by Ashyln's resume and we had a quick chat over the phone, but it was Syd who put it all into play."

Wow Sydney had gone to bat for me? I mean we were friends and she had been working her ass off with Lexi, but she didn't owe me anything. Syd and I had fucked and unlike most girls, she hadn't gotten all weirded-out after. In the beginning it kinda made me want her more. I even asked her out a few times, but she just said that we'd had our fun and it was time to move on. She didn't avoid me or anything. Ain't going to lie, she was pretty badass.

"Well I guess I'll give her a call. I know she didn't have to do it."

"No, she didn't, but she's awesome, and quite frankly, she was as surprised as I was you cared so much. She was happy to help." Lexi rubbed my arm and damn if this whole exchange wasn't making me a feel a little emotional. Maybe Troy was right; perhaps I was turning into a girl.

"Dan, you done monopolizing Lexi? I thought we were actually going to play?" Jason tossed a pillow at us, the stupid grin on his face evidence he'd heard at least some of the conversation. Not that I gave a shit, hell they were bound to find out sooner or later, so might as well word them up now.

"All right, assholes, let's go make some magic. But before we do I have an announcement to make. I don't give a rat's ass what you think, or what trash-talk you are going to throw my way. I'm dating Ashyln and that's how it's going to be."

"Good one, numbnuts." Troy twirled a stick in his hand. "Maybe tell her first though next time."

'19
Ashlyn

SPENDING A NIGHT AWAY FROM DAN HAD BEEN HARDER THAN I thought. The idea was to use the time away to focus and prepare for my interview without the sexy distraction that he was, but when I finally went to bed I couldn't sleep. I spent most of the night tossing and turning. It was strange that on some level having him beside me calmed me. I didn't understand it because the man was more hyper than a child who had OD'd on too much sugar. If I were honest with myself, I'd admit that just his physical proximity made me sleep better. It was nice. Actually, it was better than nice. Lying with him in bed was amazing. Not even thinking about the sex, which had surpassed every expectation I'd had and more. It was how being in his arms made me feel while I slept. It did things to me, things that both confused and elated me. On paper, Dan and I made no sense, but being with him, felt right. God. I needed more coffee and a lobotomy.

  The interview itself had been flawless. Well flawless if I you don't count the dry heaving in the bathroom thirty minutes before I walked into the boardroom. After I'd gotten over my mental and physical freak out, I was able to pull it together to actually present a rather intelligent and well-rounded front. I didn't even seem to be the slightest bit nervous which even surprised myself. I wasn't delusional enough to think I had it in the bag but I knew I had performed well and would be a serious contender. It pleased me to know I could actually have a shot at this. To get off the treadmill I had been on for months and start making progress in my life. It was as if things were finally falling into place. Like somehow, I had paid my dues and now I could start reaping the rewards. Who says karma is a bitch? Sometimes, it's just plain wonderful.

"I Want Your Sex", Dan's ringtone blared from my purse, making me smile. I really should change the ringtone but for some reason I didn't. I would get around to it one of these days.

"Hello, Dan." I couldn't help purring into the phone. Just knowing I was going to be hearing his voice excited me. Yeah, I know. I had issues.

"Well hello, babe. What are you wearing?" His words rumbled in my ear.

Dan was so unapologetically sexual and sleeping with him only reinforced it. It wasn't just a case of big ego. Well he had a *huge* ego, but with Dan, what you saw was what you got and what you got was high-octane sex. If you weren't careful the fumes alone were enough to make you dizzy.

"A latex bustier and crotchless panties." I bit my lip to stop myself from laughing.

"FUCK! Where are you? I'll be there in five minutes," Dan hissed and I heard the telltale jangling of keys. He was so easily baited and it thrilled me to know that on the flip of a dime, I could get a reaction out of him.

"Relax, Dan, I was kidding. I just got home from my interview. I'm still in my corporate gear." I slid out of my jacket and surveyed the rest of my boring and unsexy get-up. This was not what dirty dreams were made of - that's for sure.

"That's just hurtful, Ash. I got hard instantly on that image alone. To find out you were joking, well I'm actually wounded." The disappointment in his voice was real; I could hear it in his tone.

"Oh poor, baby. Do you need a hug?" I kicked off my heels half wishing I could do just that. Hug him. What was wrong with me? Wanting sex from Dan was one thing, but wanting hugs? That was dangerous territory and I needed out of it. Now.

"By *hug* do you mean my dick in your pussy? 'Cause those are the hugs I prefer." I didn't need to see his face to know he was grinning. Predictable Dan, any concerns I had of things between us being anything more than sexual was clarified. There was no gray area as far as he was concerned; *dick in your pussy* was pretty black and white.

"You are such a charmer. How I manage to leave your bed at all with lines like those is a mystery to me." I undid the zipper of my skirt letting it fall to the floor.

"Well you know, if you didn't have anything on for the next few hours we could test that theory." He wasn't joking. Dan rarely joked about sex and he would think nothing of spending hours in bed. I wish I could be so flippant, pushing aside responsibility to take care of the primal need that seemed to ache between my legs. One that intensified the longer I considered it. In truth, I'd never found a lover who I *wanted* to spend time with in bed. Dan took that idea and turned it on its ass. He made up for everything I'd ever missed and possibly what I'd never have with anyone else.

"As tempting as the offer is, I need to get ready for work." *Because if I go to bed with you right now, feeling the way I do, I will probably tell you how much I need you. How much I don't want to let you go and how much I want to be more than just a fling to you.* My mouth thankfully clamped shut after saying the word *work* so I didn't embarrass myself by spilling what was tossing around in my head.

Deep. That's how far I'd tumbled. No matter what I cared to admit to myself, to Megs or to Dan, I wanted more. I craved more. I wasn't wired for the fun-time-no-strings-attached rendezvous. There was a very real possibility I could fall in love with Dan. Okay, maybe I had already started. I cringed at the world of hurt I knew would be in my future if I pursued this path. It was like waiting in line for a rollercoaster. I was going to end up a mess by the end but I wanted to ride it anyway.

"You working late tonight?" Dan broke the silence and thankfully, derailed my train of thought. The one where he would tell me he felt the same way about me.

"Yeah, but Megs is picking me up so I don't need a ride." I lied. Flat-out lied. It's not that I didn't want to see him. I craved that more than anything. But not tonight. Things were finally starting to go right for me and I didn't want to screw it up. Not with him. I felt needy and I needed space. As pathetic as it sounded I still wanted him, even in the limited capacity in which he was available. That meant regrouping and a serious pep talk. And somehow flushing these crazy ideas from my mind.

"Why is Megs giving you a ride? I thought we were going to hang out tonight. We can even stay at your place if you prefer, though I have to tell you, your place is kind of a dive."

"There is nothing wrong with my place and it's within my budget. I just thought I'd come home and sleep tonight. You must have something else to do." Distance. That's exactly what I needed. Distance and someone to beat some sense into me.

"Other than you? Nope, nothing. But if you really want to sleep, I can be a good boy." Dan refused to make it easy for me. I wasn't expecting him to be insistent.

"Dan, you want to come over and cuddle? We both know that is not what you want." I said it more for my own benefit, to reinforce how stupid I was being for considering more.

"Can we cuddle naked? I like feeling my cock against your ass." Dan's voice dipped seductively. I tingled like someone just hit the hot button to my girlie parts.

"Um that's not cuddling, Dan," I clarified, unable to stop the grin spreading across my face.

"Listen, you might be smarter than me but unless I'm sliding it in, it's still only a cuddle."

"Sounds like to me there's a lot of scope in your kind of cuddles." I slowly undid the buttons of my blouse. Undressing and talking to Dan was a bad idea. The cool air hitting my skin gave me goosebumps reinforcing that notion. Why was I avoiding the mind-blowing sex I knew he was going to give me? Oh, that's right. 'Cause I was dumb enough to start having feelings for the man. I only had myself to blame. I felt my libido glaring at me all judgey. Ass. I wasn't sure if that was directed at me, or my libido.

"See, you aren't the only one who's smart." Dan apparently was not buying my let's-spend-the-night-alone suggestion. "So let's just stop arguing about it. What time you get off?"

"Is that a trick question?" I responded a little too quickly, wondering if I'd accidently moaned or something, tipping him off to my current state. Confused and aroused. I was such a catch.

"Ah, babe. Did you just think dirty thoughts?" His laugh was sexy and husky. Yep, totally not helping this situation.

"Clearly I've been spending too much time with you. Anyway, as much as I would love to sit here and talk dirty to you, I need to put some clothes on." I shivered, the rusty old radiator in my apartment not even coming close to warming the room.

"Sooo does that mean you are currently undressed?"

Why did I have to open my big mouth? "Not for long, I'm about to get dressed for work."

"Hold on a second. When did you get naked?"

"Dan, I've been getting undressed while talking to you. I told you, I needed to get ready for my shift at the bar." I looked at the pile of discarded clothes on my bed.

"You start undressing, you need to tell me. In fact, let's make it a rule and it supersedes anything else in the conversation."

"What if I start touching myself?" I breathed heavily into the phone. It really was just too easy to tease him. "Do you still want to know about the naked thing first?"

"Fuck, Ash. You start touching yourself you lead with that." His breathing deepened and followed by the noise of a zipper being lowered.

"By the way, now *I'm* touching myself."

"Dan, I actually wasn't. I was just playing." I swallowed hard as my heart thumped loudly in my chest.

"Play all you want, babe. I encourage playing of all kinds." He half-moaned into the phone.

"Dan. I'm not." At least not yet. Should I start? I'd never had phone sex before. Not that I was against it but if I was going to be making myself come, what was the point of trying to maintain a conversation. Clearly, I'd be missing out.

Dan's lowered voice reverberated against my ear, "Suit yourself, babe, doesn't mean I'm going to stop."

"Okay. I finish at two a.m. You can spend the night." The words leapt out of my mouth. All on their own. I had no control over any of my body parts it seemed, as I squeezed my thighs together. Traitorous body. Obviously seeking revenge for the earlier name-calling. This was clearly my libido's doing.

"Glad you saw it my way. So what color were your panties?"

"Goodbye, Dan. I'll see you later."

That night had been like every night that week. I stopped fighting it. I was too far gone anyway, so I might as well surrender myself to it. It was more than just wanting him, more than just sex, more than just an infatuation. Whether I tried to distance myself or not it was too late. I'd been infected. Like a test lab monkey with some rare communicable disease, it was already in my blood. It was already in my heart.

He came into the bar about an hour before the end of my shift and waited through last call. Most people had no idea who he was; it's not the kind of place we got celebrities, so they would assume he was just a random good-looking guy. The whole hiding-in-plain-sight thing was not as stupid as it sounded. He watched as I closed the bar, paying close attention to my ass as I loaded the under-the-counter dishwasher. We'd walk out to his Benz and he would drive me home. Well, his home. He'd complain about not wanting to go to mine and honestly, his place was a hell of a lot nicer. I'd make him work for it though, just because despite me being desperate (yep, that was the word I was using these days) to be with him I wasn't about to let him in on it. He was an excellent negotiator. The things he could do with his tongue… Well, needless to say we both got what we wanted.

Part of me felt like I was holding my breath, waiting for the most epic crumble of all time, and another part felt like the only time I could breathe was when I was with him. Make sense? No, of course not. None of it did. And yet, every night I found myself in the same place, my hands tearing at his sheets as he owned my body and then wrapping my arms around him as I drifted off to sleep.

The closer it got to the end of the week, the more antsy I got. Firstly, I still hadn't heard from the job interview and that was making me seven different shades of nervous. I know it hadn't even been a week yet but still, put me out of my misery already and let me know. I had convinced myself I had rocked the interview, so not even getting a call back for a second interview was seriously messing with my head. Not like I wasn't already on a permanent vacation to Crazyville, but still. The other issue that was causing me anxiety-inducing, mental dry-heaving was my birthday. Sure, I had told Dan I had plans on Saturday but I had been more than a little evasive about the occasion. Not much I could do about it though, an invite at this late stage would be insulting, not to mention raise questions as to why I'd lied about it in the beginning. No, stay the course. Celebrate my birthday, move on, and forget it ever happened. It was going to be a totally low fanfare event anyway. Technically so insignificant, it wasn't worth the mention. That's what I was telling myself. Jury was still out on how good a liar I was.

My phone buzzed early Thursday morning. I say early, but it was actually nine forty-five. However considering my shifts didn't finish until the early hours of the morning, and then there was my nightly sextivites with Dan, it would be five or six in the morning before I'd enter la-la land. I untangled my body from Dan's heated core—he was literally hot like a furnace…yeah I didn't understand it either—and reached across to answer my phone, mentally taking a roll call of any potentials who could be on the other end of the line. Most of whom I'd yell at and demand they call at a more reasonable hour. Like lunch time. With promises of coffee and pastries. Certainly not now.

"Hello," I mumbled, not offering anything more intelligible in greeting. It was surprising the word *hello* could still be identified as English. Small victories, and in the mornings, I'd take what I could get.

"Ms. Murphy?" the voice on the line questioned, "Ms. Ashlyn Murphy?" Huh, maybe high-fiving my linguistic skills had been premature? I tried not to smirk thinking about what Dan would say about the word *linguistic*. I-do-have-a-college-degree, I-do-have-a-college-degree, I silently chanted as my mind played in the gutter.

"Yes, this is she." This is she? Was I on the set of some turn of the century drama? Had I mistakenly swallowed the spirit of Jane Austin? This is what happens when you try and live rock star hours without actually *being* a rock star. I should not be allowed to interact with the world until I had ingested my first coffee. It was for their protection as much as mine.

"I'm sorry, Ms. Murphy, I didn't recognize your voice. This is Joanna Miles, from JenCorp. Have I caught you at a bad time?"

"No." I shot out of bed like a kid who inhaled a fistful of pixie sticks, earning me a disgruntled groan from a still sleeping Dan. "This is a perfect time. Sorry, I'm a little under the weather." I tried to shake the remnants of *Ms. Pride and Prejudice* from my psyche or at the very least from my vocab.

"Sorry to hear that, Ms. Murphy. Hopefully it's nothing too serious. I was just calling regarding the position you interviewed for here at JenCorp." And here it was, the part where Joanna told me I'd been unsuccessful. Another thanks-but-no-thanks, good-luck-with-your-future let down. I had been so sure I had been in with a chance. My chest

HIGH STRUNG

tightened as I slumped onto the edge of the mattress.

"It's okay," I found myself whispering. "Thanks for the opportunity." I couldn't hear it again, deciding it was better to anticipate the pain rather than hearing the words, *you're not good enough*.

"Um, Ms. Murphy? I'm actually calling to let you know Mr. Jennings would like to offer you the position. He just needs you to come back in so you can negotiate the terms of your employment."

"Huh?" I wasn't sure if I'd actually said it out loud or if I was just thinking it. What was all that about a college education? Yeah, I'm thinking I was going to need a refund.

"Yes, sorry it's taken me a few days to get back to you, but Mr. Jennings has been out of town. However, he was incredibly impressed with your presentation and interview and is very enthusiastic about welcoming you to the team." Joanna was polite to ignore my momentary inability to talk. Other than random sounds that served more to embarrass me than contribute to the conversation.

"Oh my god. YES. Yes. Thank you. Thank you." All composure and control evaporated as I listened to Joanna's words. They wanted me. I was done tending bar. This was it, what I had been waiting for. My plan was finally coming together. I felt dizzy.

"Well I'm glad you feel that way, Ms. Murphy." Joanna giggled, her professionalism cracking slightly. Not that I could blame her. "If you would like to stop by tomorrow at ten, Mr. Jennings will be able to work through your offer and you can counter with any terms or conditions you may have. Does this suit?"

"Yes. Thank you. See you tomorrow." I nodded into the phone. The reality that she couldn't see the nod was lost on me. I didn't care. If I could've conveyed it telepathically I would.

"Goodbye, Ms. Murphy. Welcome to the JenCorp." Her friendly voice ended the call.

Dan slowly raised an eyelid. "Babe, I thought you told me you weren't into phone sex? Kinda rude to do it right in front of me though. At the very least you could hit the speaker and let me join in." I couldn't be sure he wasn't serious. He was smiling, so either way, not annoyed.

"Like I would have phone sex with an audience." I crawled back over to where he was positioned on the bed, his arms folded behind his head. His flexed muscles highlighted his intricate tattoos, and that smirk, which meant trouble, was plastered all over his face. He undid me. Each and every single time.

"It was a job offer." I scooped up my tattered thoughts enough to start forming sentences. "They offered it to me. A real job. As an analyst. No more working at the bar. I get to play with the big boys now."

"Of course they offered it to you. I knew you had it in the bag." He unfolded his arms and pulled me onto his chest. "Best you learn now, babe, I'm always right. And as for playing with the *big boys*, pretty sure I already took care of that."

"Could your ego get any bigger? Is there even a shred of humility that lives within you?" I nestled into the crook of his arm, falling into my own little happy place. My distaste was purely superficial. His self-assurance didn't bother me as much as it usually did. Desensitization and all that. His attitude was sexy.

"It's not my ego that is getting bigger babe, that's my cock," he whispered into my ear.

I tried to resist laughing. Honestly. I even bit my lip, but it was futile. Between floating on clouding freaking nine from the amazing news I had received and Dan's predictable but well-delivered response, I didn't stand a chance. Instead I dissolved into a fit of laughter, wrapping myself around his firm, warm body like a vine.

"I'm really happy for you, Ash." Dan's finger traced the edge of my jaw. "I love it when you laugh."

It was official. My long-term plan was going to need modification. I was too deliriously happy to walk away from Dan. Whenever that kick in the gut came, I would take it. I would accept whatever misery came after this. The days I would spend in my PJs crying into a pint of Ben and Jerry's after he had eventually broken my heart. It will have all been worth it, just for this. This moment, right now.

20
Ashlyn

"YOU KNOW, I'M NOT FEELING WELL. WHY DON'T WE GRAB THE check and I'll head home." I swiped the screen on my phone. It was nine thirty and as far as birthdays went, this one kind of blew. I wanted to go. Find an excuse to ditch my friends and go see Dan. I knew it was wrong and one night apart wasn't going to kill me, but it was my birthday so surely I should be able to do what I wanted to do.

It was almost impossible to get a booking at The Mexican Cantina, the wait unusually extending months. They had the best Mexican food in the city and how Megs had been able to secure us a table on such short notice was still a mystery. Maybe her dad had called in a favor or something? The food was amazing. I almost died when I saw the prices, but the atmosphere was fantastic and the margaritas delicious. Still, I was dreading the bill.

"Ash, there is nothing wrong with you, unless you count being a bad actress. You are going to go straight to Dan's." Megs took a sip from her frozen margarita. "And if you check your phone one more time, I'm going to have to confiscate it. Seriously, I've seen people waiting for kidney transplants less anxious."

"Oh, ha-ha, Dr. Winters." I twilled the stem of my still full margarita glass. I wasn't feeling it. Not even a little. Pathetic.

"C'mon, Ash. Give us one night, you can see him tomorrow." Kyla waved over a waitress. "Besides, when are we going to meet your new guy? I can't remember the last guy you dated."

"He's not really *my* guy. It's complicated." My hand moved from the stem of my glass to the napkin in my lap, anything to help distract me from these questions. Complicated was an understatement.

Megs knew the full story but Kyla and Brianne had no idea. As far as they knew, I'd met some guy at a job interview—not a lie—and we were kind of seeing each other. They also knew his name was Dan, and they had assumed he was a businessman of some sort—also technically not a lie. Being that I hadn't dated anyone recently or shown any interest in dating, they were more than a little excited to meet this mystery man. The idea made me nauseous. How would I even introduce Dan? While I was happy with our *arrangement*—that was the best word I could think of to describe it—I didn't want to complicate this situation with labels or lack-there-of.

"Not fair trying to keep him all to yourself." Brianne pouted. "Boyfriends need to be vetted. It's girl code."

"Guys, I already told you. He's not my boyfriend. We're just trying to keep it casual right now, which I'm fine with. He travels a lot. For business," I qualified, hoping my lame explanation would stop the questions about Dan. Questions I didn't want to answer.

Megs rolled her eyes at my poor attempt. Secretly, I think she was enjoying it. "Well, it's obvious Ash isn't going to play nice. I say we hit a club and dance until we can't stand up."

"Yay." "Yes," Brianne and Kyla both chimed in enthusiastically. My opportunity to escape slipped further away. I was going to have to remember to kill Megs and her bright ideas when I got her alone.

"I don't know. I'm tired and I start my new job on Monday. I should probably get an early night so I can spend the rest of tomorrow pre-

HIGH STRUNG

paring." I threw out my last ditch effort to derail Megs's plans. Plans that had not been discussed nor agreed upon. She knew I hated surprises.

"Yes of course. The fancy-schmancy new job." Brianne's brow lifted suggestively. "Does Dan work there too?"

"No." I shook my head, knowing it was going to take a lot to get them to let this go. Another reason why tonight had been a bad idea. "I've been offered a twelve-month contract with JenCorp as an analyst. Of course, Mr. Jennings explained they have room on their staff if they are happy with my performance but he's pretty conservative which I completely understand."

The twelve-month timeframe had initially disappointed me, but I understood why a company would take that route. It made smart business sense, and the package I was offered was more than generous. No, seriously. I hadn't even dreamed of the kind of cash they were throwing at me. Not to mention a company credit card for expenses and use of the company car service. It was like a fantastic fairy tale come to life, but better because it was real.

I knew that within the year I would be able to prove my worth and secure a more permanent position and during our follow-up meeting yesterday, Mr. Jennings had made it clear he was pleased with what I was bringing to the table. While our interaction had been very formal—he'd sat behind his desk the entire time and didn't crack a smile once—he didn't seem cold, just cautious. I could deal with cautious. Hell my middle name was cautious. Well, at least it used to be. Ashlyn Cautious Marie Murphy had been a bit wordy, so I guess my middle name was now back to being plain old Marie. Not sure if the relinquishing of the title was a good thing. Time would tell.

"You have all of tomorrow to get responsible," Megs unhelpfully added. "It's your birthday and your last weekend of freedom before you become a slave to the corporate machine. You owe this to yourself. Besides, *Dan* would want you to have a good time."

"Okay." I let out a long dramatic sigh. I wasn't going to get out of this easily so I might as well use it to my advantage. "I'll agree to get incredibly drunk and go to whatever club you all want to go to on one condition. We don't talk about Dan. No one can mention him or ask anymore questions about him?"

The waitress who Kyla had waved over a while ago finally made her way to the table and brought the check. Not that we'd asked, and given we still hadn't finished our cocktails, it was kind of rude.

"Here." She placed the leather folder containing our bill on the table before disappearing.

"What a bitch. She is totally getting minimum tip." Kyla seethed as she opened up the folder and surveyed the damage. It was a fancy place but we'd been sucking down cocktails for a couple of hours. It was bound to be brutal.

"She is probably having a bad night. It's busy. Don't be too hard on her." I couldn't help but feel an affinity with that poor girl. I'd been there too many times myself.

"But what's the point in getting you drunk if we can't get you to divulge juicy information?" Brianne completely avoided the situation with the waitress, preferring to obsess further about Dan and me, and the possibility of finding out more. Not likely.

"Those are my terms, ladies. Take it or leave it." I was serious, too. If I couldn't be doing what I wanted on my birthday I would at least have some level of control over it. "So am I getting in a cab and heading home or we going to drink overpriced shots and fend off unwanted advances?"

Brianne drained what was left in her glass. "Fine. He's probably boring and wears a sweater vest."

Megs spluttered loudly as she bit back her smile from across the table. I knew what she was thinking. Dan and boring didn't even belong in the same hemisphere let alone in the same sentence. I coughed, taking the opportunity to finish my drink. Just thinking of Dan in a sweater vest was hilarious. I should totally buy him one for Christmas. Assuming we are still seeing each other.

Megs pulled out some cash and waved the waitress over. It was a lot of cash. Enough to cover the entire check, and a sizeable tip. Two problems with this: one, there was no way I was allowing her to foot the bill for my birthday dinner and two, Megs rarely carried cash.

"What are you doing?" I asked pointing to the leather folder.

"Ash, it's your birthday. I've got it covered." She waved me off like it she hadn't just put a stack full of fifties into the folder.

Kyla gave Megs a pointed look. "We'll sort it out later." I knew that at the very least both the girls would be covering their share. Money wasn't an issue for Megs. We all knew it, but no one was about to take advantage of her generosity.

"Yeah, yeah. We'll work it out." Megs pushed out her chair doing little to convince me she was going to be accepting any money from anyone. "Let's get out of here. I'm nowhere near drunk enough and I have our names on a door."

"Oooo name on the door. I like it. Megs is in charge of my birthday party next July. Just sayin'." Brianne smiled as we left our table and made our way to the door.

I had no idea where we were heading and to be honest I didn't really care. It might have been my birthday but Megs was running the show, and for whatever reason, this seemed important to her. Maybe it was to show me I would be okay post-Dan, maybe it was to show me I could still have a good time with my friends, or maybe she was just being a good friend and making sure I had a happy birthday. Any of those reasons would do. What we needed now was to start drinking. Let go and enjoy the night. Without Dan.

"You took us to a bar?" Kyla looked horrified as the cab pulled up to a plain looking brown and red building on Lower East Side. "I thought you had an in at a club?"

"Oh stop being so snobby. This place is great. I've heard good things." Megs smiled as she pulled out even more cash and paid the driver. What was with all the cash?

"I don't know, Megs." I looked at the large arched windows. This was not the kind of place I imagined spending my evening avoiding thoughts of Dan. It didn't look like the kind of place I'd spend my time, period. At all. Ever.

"You getting out?" The driver opened the window divider, his engine still running.

"Yes, of course." Megs popped open the door and all but pushed me onto the sidewalk. "Give it an hour. You hate it and we'll go somewhere else. Okay?"

"Sure. Okay. Whatever." I didn't even try and hide the fact I wasn't onboard with her choice in venue. What the hell was this place and would I need a Hep C shot after leaving?

Brianne and Kyla followed us toward the bar/pub/dive/whatever. As we got closer to the front of doorway, I saw a bright red sign with the word *Tommy's* on the front. The name of this fine establishment I assumed. There was a long line, not that Megs seemed too deterred. She smiled as we walked to the front of the line. She'd already told us that she'd organized our names at the door so I guessed she wasn't worried about the people who were eyeing us off as we walked past them.

Megs gave the door guy our names and he immediately let us through, shooting us an overly familiar smile. I'm sure in his head he was mocking us. While most people were dressed in denim and leather, the four of us were wearing short skirts and heels. Sure there were other women whose barely there outfits rivaled our skirt lengths, but they were on a different spectrum. A trashier one. Only calling it like I see it.

"Sixty minutes and counting," I tried to scream over the music, hoping Megs heard. A wall of bass hit us square in the face as we walked into the venue. It was loud and gritty. Some DJ was playing some music I'd never heard, and god willing wouldn't have to hear again after tonight. Realistically I wasn't going to need fifty-nine of those minutes, I had already decided. We were out of here the minute the counter expired and the clock was ticking.

"Let's get closer to the stage." Megs moved us deeper into the throng, her hand wrapped around mine giving me no way out. Fifty-seven minutes. Brianne and Kyla were looking just as horrified as I was. Good, so it's not just me.

"I hope you know this is the worst place ever," I all but yelled into Megs's ear. "Is this punishment for not talking to Troy about you?" I was joking of course. At least I think I was. She couldn't honestly be mad at me for that. It's not like Troy and I were friends. I barely counted Dan as a friend, and I was sleeping with him.

"This isn't a punishment. So self-absorbed." Megs laughed back. "One might question the company you are keeping." Her smirk widened.

Oh smart. She hadn't exactly mentioned Dan so therefore technically not broken any rules but the implication was there. Not that the other girls picked up on it. They were too busy looking around with wide-eyed expressions. We looked like tourists and we weren't fooling anyone.

"Hello Manhattan." The music had stopped and a voice pierced through the blackness on the stage. That voice. I knew that voice. I swallowed, trying to place it. Think, Ash. The stage remained dark, forcing me to play more mental guessing games.

"I was wondering if it would be okay if we hijacked the stage for a while," the voice continued, the toned dipping slightly, teasing the audience seductively.

The crowd around us seemed to have clued in and had started screaming and yelling excitedly. I was assuming it was their way of saying yes, they didn't mind. Either way, I was glad the mysterious voice meant DJ whoever had quit spinning whatever crap he'd been spinning at ear-bleeding decibels. I guess there was a silver lining. Crap. How much longer did we have left?

"I'm going to take that as a yes." The voice chuckled sending the crowd into an even bigger frenzy.

A spotlight fired across the stage, lighting up the area to reveal five men standing ready to play. My heart stopped. I think I forgot how to breathe as well as the room around me started to spin. My eyelids peeled back so far away from my eyes I'm surprised my eyeballs didn't fall right out of my head. Holy shit. Is it really? Yes, it is. It is Power Station, standing four feet in front of me.

Dan stared right at me, shrugging before attempting to give me an innocent-looking smile. Not even close, buddy. I knew this was more than just some freaky coincidence.

James—the now identified owner of the voice—smiled, dazzling the crowd as their screams got louder. Their suspicions were clearly confirmed as to who had been taunting them from the dark. He had a nice smile. James, I meant. I could see why girls loved him.

"Our bass player has a few words. Have you guys met Dan Evans?"

The screams got louder as Dan stepped into the center of the stage. His smile grew bigger the more the crowd hollered, his ego no doubt expanding as well. He was clearly enjoying himself. He looked down at me, as James handed him the microphone and he brought it to his mouth.

"Hello Manhattan."

The crowd erupted.

"Wow, it's Power Station. Dan is fucking hot." Kyla grabbed my arm and shook me. You know, in case I wasn't sure of who was standing in front of me. She had no idea.

"So you see, ladies and gentlemen, I have a problem. I have talked it over with my brothers and they agree with me that this shit cannot stand. So we're going to need your help here tonight." I take back what I said about James's voice being seductive. It was nothing compared to what was coming through the speakers now. Raw, hot, and demanding attention. I couldn't stop watching him if I'd tried and there was no way I was going to try and stop. Not even for a minute.

"I met this girl." Dan grinned as he looked directly at me. I had no idea what he was about to say. None. Not a clue. I needed to remember to breathe.

"And while she was fucking drop-dead beautiful and smart and has an attitude like no other, I couldn't date her."

My heart stopped. Again. No this time I was serious. I think I was actually dying. Was Dan seriously and very publicly telling me I was not his girlfriend? Did he have a soul? The disruption to my cardiac rhythm was short-lived. I unfortunately wasn't going to die. Not from a heart attack at least. If ever there were a case of someone dying of embarrassment, I would probably be it. I was mortified.

"You see, for all her fucking perfection, she has never been to a concert. How does that even happen? I mean, I can't be with someone who hasn't been to a concert. Troy, can you believe that shit?"

Dan smirked as he continued, looking back toward the drum kit. Troy seemed amused as he glanced back, shaking his head. I couldn't understand whether this was some bad, bad joke or a bad dream. Neither seemed plausible and both seemed horrible.

"So because it's her birthday and because I'm not willing to walk away from her, we are going to rectify that situation tonight."

What? What did he say? My head whipped around to Megs who was grinning, obviously in on whatever the fuck was going on. All of which was still unclear right now other than the fact that Dan Evans was standing on a stage talking about me.

"I need you to be loud, and I need you to rock this joint off its foundations so my girl can see what she's missed."

Did he just call me his girl? The crowd roared, giving Dan exactly what he wanted. Loud. Fevered. Crazy. I, on the other hand, stood stupefied. Wondering if I'd actually heard him correctly. Now would be a good time for that intelligence he spoke of to kick in.

"Ashlyn Murphy." Oh fuck he said my name. Kyla and Brianne whipped their heads toward me, reflecting the shocked, bewildered look I was wearing. At least now I wasn't the only one who had no idea. That was a positive surely, no longer alone in oblivion.

"Ash," he repeated in case anyone had missed it the first time. "You have no idea how much it turns me on to be your first, and trust me, babe, I'm going to pop your cherry like it's never been popped. Happy birthday." His voice rumbled low through the microphone as he eyed me with intent. Intent to blow my mind and ravage my body. Although probably in the reverse order. And while I was still clueless as to what was happening, I was almost one hundred percent sure if he touched me right now I'd orgasm on the spot.

The noise around me was insane, the crowd engulfing us as Dan handed the microphone back to James and they launched into the first song.

The people around us started jumping in unison with the beat. Bodies pushed and pressed up against us as they carried us closer to the stage. I looked around at Megs, Brianne, and Kyla and their expressions matched those around them. They had experienced this before. They knew what awaited them. The anticipation of greatness was written all over their faces. I was the one who didn't know what this would be like. To have them with me as I experienced this made it that little bit sweeter. That and having one hell of a live band be your first.

It was amazing. The sounds of the instruments and the vocals meshed seamlessly. It was uncanny. Flawless. It was exciting. It was thrilling and it was more emotional than I could have ever anticipated. I didn't know what I felt just that I was feeling. Excited, elated, exhausted and they were just the E emotions. I totally got it now. What the appeal was. Why people lost their minds. Why people would line up for hours in those hopes of being this close to the band. It all made sense, and I took back whatever I may have thought or said about Power Station. They were amazing. Each of them worked their asses off. They moved through the set, each song pulling just a little bit more from the crowd. The crowd seemed to know every word, they sung it back to the band with so much passion, their arms outstretched hoping one of the band members would reach out and touch them. Girls dissolved into a puddled mess if Alex, James, Jason or Dan made contact. Troy was even able to evoke the same crazed reaction with just a look and smile, being hidden behind a drum kit not hindering his contribution to the mayhem. The temperature of the room and the excitement rose to a maddening level. I was awed.

The music stopped and the lights dimmed, plunging us back into darkness. The band left the stage but the noise continued to ring in my ears, disorientating me for a few minutes. I had no idea what I was doing or where I was. If asked, I would have been lucky to remember my own name.

"Ash." Dan wrapped his arms around me materializing from the rowdy crowd. Wow. It was like magic but cooler, and with no cheesy bikini-clad assistant. His body, saturated from sweat, coated my skin as he embraced me. I loved it. He was so raw. I want to rip his clothes off and fuck him. The fact we had an audience didn't even bother me. I just wanted him and I didn't want to wait.

"Dan," I moaned as I attacked his mouth with my own. I kissed him. Hard. I settled for my tongue doing the fucking for now. At least I could have that immediately.

"Whoa, Ash." Dan's hand's reached down to my ass and pulled me up, grinding me against his cock. He was hard and obviously just as turned on as I was.

"So I take it from that reaction you enjoyed the show?" He smirked, squeezing my ass as he pulled away from me slightly. "Hey, Megs. I was beginning to think you weren't going to show up."

"Well your *girlfriend* was being difficult and wanted to go home. Like a spoilsport. On her birthday. I had my work cut out for me." The word girlfriend rattled me to my core. Her choice of words or his? Megs had been in on the plan from the beginning. The fact that this whole night had been orchestrated was slowly coming together.

"How? What? When?" I waded through random thoughts unable to make my mouth function properly. How did Dan know it was my birthday? I hadn't mentioned it. Did Megs go behind my back? I know she had good intentions but I couldn't see her deliberately telling Dan when we had discussed not telling him.

"Hi, I'm Dan." Dan peeled one of his hands from my ass and shifted me to his side so he could greet my friends.

"Kyla."

"Brianne."

They took turns in answering, still playing catch up as to what was going on.

"Nice to meet you, ladies. Thanks for coming out for the show. I swore Megs to secrecy." Dan winked at Megs before dazzling the girls with his smile. He was charming them. It wasn't hard.

Brianne nodded, unwilling or unable to speak.

"So the *Dan* you are seeing is Dan Evans?" Kyla pieced together, the penny finally dropping.

"Ah, she mentioned me. Be honest, did she tell you I'm the best sex she's ever had?" Dan couldn't help himself. Not sure if he was trying to embarrass me or he got some wild kick out of it, but there was no way we were going to be talking about our sex life with my friends. In a public bar. On my birthday.

"Actually I believe the words that were used were boring and sweater vests. Sorry, Dan." I tried to steer the conversation away from anything sexual. And I was in fact telling him the truth. Granted they hadn't been my words to describe him but they had been used while we had discussed him.

"Don't make me fuck you in front of your friends to prove a point, Ashlyn. You know I'll do it." He wasn't joking. I think we had established that when it came to sex, Dan didn't ever joke and if given the chance he probably would have sex with me in front of all these people. Hell, I'd considered it not even twenty minutes ago.

"You crazy, crazy man." I kissed him, knowing it was the only way I was going to shut him up. And because I wanted to kiss him, *really* wanted to kiss him.

"I don't understand. You guys look like you are together. Who's the guy you aren't *really* dating?" Brianne found her voice finally in time to make things awkward again. I guess it was better just to get things out in the open.

"We aren't dating? I'm kind of crushed, babe. I hope you haven't been seeing someone else." Dan pouted holding his hand to his chest, but I wasn't sure if he was playing it off like it was no big deal or it actually was no big deal. It's not like I had this thing worked out and deliberately tried to complicate things, and by the sound of it, he had no idea either.

"No, of course I'm not seeing someone else. You said you didn't do girlfriends and I didn't want to assume..." It had actually tormented me. He had put the idea in my head that what we had wasn't a relationship. I had wanted it to be but I'd figured he'd made himself clear and I wasn't about to beg. No matter how much I cared for him. No matter how much I was falling in love with him.

"Well just so there is no confusion. We're dating. You are my girlfriend. This is a done deal." He gestured between us. Well I guess it was. There was no way I wanted to fight it. It's what I had wanted him to say. I just never believed he'd actually say it. Those words sent me even further into an emotional tailspin. Elation replaced the uncertainty I had been feeling. Every cell in my body tingled with excitement as he held my hand. We were dating, and I never thought I could feel so relieved.

People had started to surround us and while I hadn't noticed before, it was painfully obvious now. Sharing this private conversation with my friends, while not ideal, was one thing. Sharing the conversation with a bunch of random people with camera phones, that was something entirely different.

"Hey, let's get you ladies backstage." Dan seemed to come to the same conclusion as I had. "You can meet the rest of the band."

Everyone agreed, especially Megs who hoped to speak to Troy. I don't know why she didn't just go ahead and ask him. Actually I know why. The same reason why I hadn't asked Dan for clarification on what *we* were. The promise of maybe was better than the disappointment of no.

Dan walked ahead through the crowd, leading us to the edge of the stage where they had played. A security guard let us through the minute he saw Dan. He didn't ask any questions. I guess he just assumed Dan had hit the groupie lottery. Either that or he'd been sent off to hunt and gather for the rest of the band. I hated someone might think of me in that way, like I could be disposable. I pushed it from my mind not willing to let someone's possible perceptions of me ruin a good thing.

We walked along the narrow, dark hallway until we got to a room hidden in the back. Dan didn't bother knocking, instead swinging the door open wide to reveal the rest of the band. It was surreal. Seeing them all there. Together. Sweaty and spent. In front of me.

"Hey, Ash. Happy Birthday." Troy was the first to come over and greet us. He gave me a hug and a warm smile. I heard Megs's breath hitch beside me. No doubt she was hoping the hugging would extend to her.

"Hey boys, this is Ashlyn." Dan pulled me close against his side. In case they hadn't got the memo we were together. "These are her friends: Megs, Brianne and Kyla." He held out his hand pausing and gesturing to each of the women as he introduced them. The girls each stood silently, managing a slight wave at the mention of their name.

"And this is the band, Troy, Alex, James, and Jason." Dan pointed around the room to the corresponding band member.

Alex Stone strolled over and smiled, all six foot four of rock god sexiness. "I believe we've already met. Nice to see you again. Happy Birthday."

"Thank you. It's a pleasure to see you again." While I still thought he was a good-looking guy, I wasn't tongue-tied like I had been the first time I'd met him. Nor was the compulsion to lick him pulsing through my veins.

"Back off, Stone. You can stop being so charming, she's not interested." Dan playfully punched Alex in the arm.

Alex's smile twitched. "Stand down, Dan. I'm just saying hi. Not trying to be charming."

"Well whatever you're doing, do less of it." Dan gripped my waist possessively. He was jealous, which was absurd but kind of cute.

Alex moved on and introduced himself properly to my friends, each of them struggling with saying hello. All except Megs, who was ignoring Alex entirely and making flirty eyes at Troy.

"Hi, I'm Jason. We met at the club a while back. Not sure if you remember. You were a little lit up." Jason laughed as he offered his hand.

HIGH STRUNG

It's not like I could have forgotten that night if I'd tried. The night that had started this adventure. It was also the first night I'd spent with Dan. Not that I'd been conscious enough to know at the time and not that anything sexual had happened, but he had spent the entire night by my side. I was a little mad at myself I hadn't seen how sweet it had been at the time. Hindsight is twenty-twenty.

"Yeah. Not my finest moment." I shook his hand. Mentally shaking myself.

"Are you kidding? That night was spectacular," Troy chimed from the other side of the room.

"It truly was." Jason agreed. "Happy Birthday by the way."

"Thanks." I shuffled a little awkwardly. This was so weird. Being around the band and pretending they were just regular people. I hope I wasn't giving anyone any crazy looks and at least I was still able to string sentences together.

"And I'm James. Happy Birthday." The charismatic lead singer moved closer, his smile even more dazzling up close.

"Thank you." I felt like I was repeating myself, unable to think of anything else. Lame.

"So how was it?" James cracked open a bottle of water Alex had tossed him.

"Huh?" I stared at him blankly. Oh please. At least repeating *thank you* was better than random sounds. I swear I'm not a moron. Not that I was doing a good job of proving it.

"The show." James paused and took a large swallow of water before continuing. "Dan tells us it was your first time seeing a live act. Did you enjoy it?"

"Yes. It was great. Really good." I avoided tacking on a *thanks* to the end.

James smiled politely, ignoring the fact I didn't contribute much more to the conversation.

"I saw you watching me while I played." Dan kissed the base of my neck and I had to stop myself from moaning loudly.

Unable to stop myself, I turned into him, my body seeking even more contact. "You like girls watching you play with yourself, don't you?" I mumbled against his skin. It felt so good and yet so strange. The public display of affection. We were outside of our bubble.

"I'd rather watch you," he answered predictably, moving me to a more secluded area of the room. Not that there was any privacy. This was as good as we were going to get for right now. It sort of disappointed me.

"Are you thinking about touching yourself?" Dan smirked when I didn't answer right away.

"No." I rolled my eyes, shaking my head.

"Thinking about touching me?" He didn't even try and hide his excitement.

"I was just taking stock." I answered benignly not really able to make much sense of the mess of thoughts inside my head. Was I really his girlfriend?

"Snore." Dan faked a yawn. "Did you enjoy dinner?"

"Um, yes. It was great." Had Megs told Dan our dinner plans? "Actually we went to this Mexican place. I think you'd really like it." I leaned against the back wall needing some physical support.

"Who do you think chose it, babe?" Dan licked the shell of my ear. That was not helping.

I stopped. Dan had chosen the venue? "How much of this was you?" I sucked in a breath and held it. How had he known?

"The whole thing." Dan pushed me up against the wall. "I saw your ID when you left your purse in the car that first night so I knew it was your birthday. I don't know why you didn't tell me, but I decided I was done being a whiny bitch and sitting on the sidelines. It seemed I hadn't made myself clear."

"I thought you weren't interested in me. In that way." I reached up and touched his face. The room around us dissolved. For all I knew, and cared, we were alone.

"Oh, babe. I'm interested in you in every way." Dan pressed up against me. "So I called your friend Megs, got her to help me hook this up. Just so you know she flat-out denied shit for a solid twenty minutes, and it was only after I called bullshit and told her I saw your ID that she bent a little."

I was silently relieved. Glad she hadn't just rolled over on account it was Dan who was asking. Of course had he enlisted Troy, she probably would have given my social security, bank account details, and blood type. Thankfully it seemed like it had been a Dan solo mission. "Megs is good people. Loyal. She's more like family than a friend."

"Yeah, she's great." He rolled his eyes, hinting there was more to the story. "I had to fight her for this, you know. She wanted to plan your birthday. Take you to dinner and all of that, but I argued she'd had you all those other birthdays and this was my first one. I wanted to make it perfect even if I didn't get to spend all of it with you."

My heartbeat thumped out of control as the gravity of his words hit me. This was my first birthday with him and he wanted to make it memorable. Most of all, it hinted to the fact he wanted there to be others, that we weren't as temporary as I had initially thought. "I thought you said you weren't romantic." Okay, maybe not in the traditional way but organizing all of this? For me to be so important he would go out of his way? It was better than any romantic gesture I'd ever received. "So you paid for it all too I supposed." The truth was slowly coming out.

"No... Maybe..." He was such a bad liar. "Would you be mad if I said yes?"

"When I saw the roll of fifties Megs was packing I knew something was fishy. She doesn't carry cash. That was a major flaw in your plan." I wasn't the slightest bit pissed. It had been sweet and I was glad Dan had bankrolled the evening and not some unknown criminal activity that would explain the cash.

"She wouldn't take hundreds, said it was too obvious." He shrugged, not comprehending that most people didn't kick around with hundred dollar bills in their pockets. It definitely would have tipped me off sooner. "I have to give her a pair of Troy's sticks as well. Fuck if I know what she's going to do with them. I got them signed in case she want to throw them on eBay."

There was no way those sticks were going on eBay or anywhere else outside Ms. Megan Winters's possession.

"Thanks for an amazing birthday, Dan, and thanks so much for the show. I loved it. Every second of it." It was so much more than I had anticipated. The dinner. The concert. Our official *coupling*. That was by far the standout.

"The night ain't over yet, sweetheart." His eyes darkened as he licked my neck. "Not even by a long shot."

21

Dan

I DON'T KNOW WHEN I TURNED INTO A BIG FUCKING SAP, BUT I HAD decided there was no way I was going to miss Ashlyn's birthday, regardless of whether she told me or not.

Talking over with Troy had put things into perspective. We were seeing each other and there was no one else. At least not on my part, and Ash didn't seem like the kind of girl who'd juggle two guys. Not by a long shot. So there was absolutely no reason why we shouldn't just bite the bullet and get with the program. The one where she was my girl and I didn't have to pretend that spending nights away from her didn't gnaw at my brain. I slept better with her tucked up beside me and I loved waking up and finding her ready and wet. It's a wonder I'd let her leave.

I'd tossed it around in my head for days and came up with the same conclusion. Fuck the reasons we shouldn't be together, fuck her ten-year plan and fuck the fact we are different. She made me happy and as far as

I could tell, I made her happy too, so that's all that should matter.

The concert idea seemed cheesier than a hallmark commercial but when I suggested it to the band they had been eager to get onboard. We didn't get the opportunity to play smaller venues anymore. Not that I was complaining, but there was something magical about playing a bar and having the audience right in front of you.

James jumped on the phone and made it happen. We kept it tightly under wraps so the place wouldn't be swarmed beyond capacity and we agreed we would only play one set. Tommy Zampelli, the owner, was one of the guys who had let us play in his bar when we were starting out. He'd retired and his kid Ritchie was running the show, but they were happy to have us and jacked up security for the night just to make sure it ran smoothly.

Getting Megs onboard had been a challenge but hadn't been impossible. I flat out told her there was no way I was going to let my girlfriend celebrate her birthday without me. The word had just kind of fallen out of my mouth without even thinking about, but the more I thought about it, the more it fit, and I wasn't about to take it back. Hell, no. So it hung there for a while, like a pair of big hairy balls, and when Megs saw I wasn't about to drop or forget it, she agreed. Only took thirty minutes of sweet-talking and the promise of a pair of sticks from the big guy. What the fuck she wanted to do with those was beyond me but I couldn't give a rat's ass. The important thing was she would take her to the place I had originally wanted to take Ash—before she blew me off— and bring her to me when they were done. The whole money thing was another fucking headache. Seriously, I could see why her and Ash were such good friends. They were both fucking stubborn. The fact she was a shrink made me edgy though. They start pulling that lateral thinking bullshit on you, and before you know it, you agree to something maybe you shouldn't have. In any case, I stayed on course and stood my ground. Megs finally agreed.

Waiting for her to show had been a whole other hell. Megs had texted me a few times saying Ash had been trying to make excuses to bail and it was making me fucking antsy. The whole point of this show was for Ash to see it, and for us to be the first live act she saw. The fact we were even dealing with this still baffled me. It was like finding a unicorn in Queens. That shit just didn't happen.

When she finally walked in looking all kinds of miserable, it was like being clocked in the nuts. I hated it and I hoped this little stunt didn't blow up in my face. Either way, we were locked on for target so it was too late to abort now. I had manned up and whatever the outcome was, I'd deal.

I never expected to see the look on her face when she saw me. Fuck. Her smile made me feel like Superman and I'd challenge anyone who didn't think I could've outrun a train. Playing for Ash rocked my world. Watching her move to our songs, reckless and unrestrained, I knew she had it in her. She didn't know any of the words, which was amusing 'cause everyone around her did. But damn, seeing her covered in sweat, having a good time at my show was better than any porno I'd ever seen. I had a killer fucking hard-on to prove it.

I couldn't get off the stage quick enough. I bypassed the backstage area and jumped off the front of the stage and into the crowd like a fucking rookie. Some girl grabbed my ass but I was able to get free of her pretty quick, just as well I did 'cause it's hard to make a play for one girl when you have another trying to get into your pants. I know this first hand. It gets ugly.

So I grabbed Ash, pulling her from the crowd in the dark. Her face was priceless. And after some appreciated mouth action and our dance floor confessional, it seemed like we were finally on the same page. I'd taken the girls backstage to meet the rest of the band which hopefully would mean we could call it a wrap, and I could get my girl back to my place.

Troy, Jase, and TJ had made sure Ash's friends got home; all of them too liquored up to drive and thankfully smart enough to cab it in. They loaded up into the Suburban and hit the road. Alex and James said their goodbyes and went home to their wives and kids. They didn't hang around much these days, not that I blamed them. Why bother when you have a sweet deal waiting for you at home?

"Where's your car?" Ashlyn giggled as we walked along the sideway.

I insisted Ash do a few shots before leaving the bar. Tequila on your birthday is mandatory, and I'm a stickler for tradition.

"Just in the parking garage up the street, babe. Just a little bit farther." I wrapped my arms around her tight little body. She shivered despite me giving her my jacket to wear. I liked it on her. The leather dwarfed her tiny frame.

"Dan," Ashlyn purred as she nuzzled into my side, my dick responding by punching out against my jeans.

"Yeah, babe." I kept my feet moving, taking her along with me. Stopping wasn't an option. Not unless she was planning on spending the rest of her birthday in lock-up for a public indecency charge.

"Am I really your girl?" She looked up at me. Her eyes were full of fucking need and want as she breathed on my neck. She undid me.

"You sure are." I tried to concentrate on the words coming out of my mouth instead of the pain in my balls. My body was not on the same page as my brain, arguing whether or not we were going to have to wait until I got her home to my apartment. A few more steps till we reached the car. A few more steps too fucking far.

"I like that." Ashlyn ran her hand down my back so that it rested on my ass. Yep, I was probably getting a speeding ticket on the way home. I didn't even give a shit. I just needed to get inside of her. Like five minutes ago.

We rounded the corner into the multilevel garage and I handed the valet my ticket. The kid looked about twenty, he didn't even try to hide his shit-eating grin when he saw Ash all sweet and relaxed, no doubt a result of the tequila. Yeah, a little less time checking out my girlfriend and a little more getting my ride, asswipe.

He took the hint the way it was intended and didn't waste any time flapping his gums making small talk. Good thing too, 'cause I wasn't interested in the "how-are-yous," just wanted my keys and my Benz so I could get the fuck out of here.

"Dan," Ashlyn mumbled into my chest, her hand slowly traveling down the front of my shirt. And fuck if I wasn't torn between asking her to stop and begging her to keep going. How the hell long does it take to get a car? Where did he park it? Vermont?

"Hang in there, almost home." I don't know if I was saying that for her benefit or for mine. Hoping my balls would get the memo and yank on the brakes.

The douche who'd been ogling my girl finally pulled up in my wheels and not a second too soon. I peeled off a twenty as I took back my keys. His tip had been decreased when I caught him checking out my girl's ass. Not cool, dude. Not even close.

I slid into the driver's seat and made sure Ash was buckled in tight, my hard-on dictating we get home and get busy ASAP. Time to see what the 5.5 Liter, twin turbo V8 under the hood could do. I revved the engine and tore out of the parking garage like a bat out of hell. Ashlyn laughed as I pulled onto the secluded side street surprisingly not running her mouth about my driving. That had to be a first.

"Dan, pull over." Ashlyn grabbed my arm before we had a chance to get onto the main road.

"You going to be sick?" I looked over at her as I slammed on the brakes. God, I hoped she wasn't going to puke all over my car; that would really kill the mood. Not that it would stop me from fucking her. There wasn't much that could right now.

The sudden stop punched us both back into our seats, Ashlyn breathing heavily as she fumbled with her seatbelt. Yep, she was going to be sick. Probably could have skipped the last few shots. I put the car into park and engaged the emergency brake, just in case she needed me to hold her hair back or something.

The belt restraint flung back and she wrangled herself out of her seat, but instead of opening the car door, she flung herself at me.

"Whoa," was the only response I managed as her lips covered my mouth. The taste of salt and tequila was still fresh on her tongue as she swirled it around in my mouth. It tasted like heaven. Well, if heaven had a bar, I bet it would taste just like that.

I reached down and unhooked my seatbelt and eased back the driver's seat, keeping my mouth firmly locked on hers. I needed more room but there was no way I was stopping this. Not a fucking chance.

Ash climbed over the console and into my lap, my hands finding their way onto her ass. She straddled me, her short dress creeping up her thighs and flashing me a peek at the black satin panties she was wearing.

"Fuck," I groaned, sliding my hand underneath her dress as she rocked up against my cock. The car might have gotten from zero to a hundred in four-point-eight seconds but I just got there in under three.

"Dan, fuck me," Ashlyn moaned in between kisses, my brain misfiring on the fucking words coming out of her mouth. Was there even a possibility I wouldn't? Was she meaning now? In the car? On the fucking street?

"Babe, I want nothing more than to have sex with you but you sure you want to do it here?" I looked around at the deserted street, knowing this wasn't her. Maybe it was the booze talking.

"Isn't this what you used to do?" She giggled into my ear as she reached down in between my thighs. "Have sex in your car?" She unzipped my jeans as I struggled to hear the words she was actually saying.

"Not really. Maybe the Escalade or the Suburban but never in my car." My brain was able to get my mouth to come to the party and answer her. My dick wondering why the fuck we were still talking.

"Well then, it's going to be a first for both of us then." She threw her head back and laughed, hitting it on the windshield.

"Fuck, are you okay?" I rubbed the back of her head, Ashlyn still laughing despite bashing her melon on the glass. Alcohol is a great pain neutralizer. Been there myself.

"I'm fine. But I'm horny and I want to have sex with you." She moved forward, leaning against my throat. "Here. In your car. Knowing you haven't done that with any other girl and I haven't done it with any other guy. You said you were going to pop my cherry." She teased, clocking me with her fuck-me eyes.

Well you weren't going to have to tell me twice, if she wanted this then I was all about it. After all, it was her birthday and I'm sure there's some law or some shit about not disappointing a girl on her birthday.

I pulled her onto me, wrapping a hand around her neck and threading it through her hair. I kissed her hard, and she gave me as good as she got. She was so wild. Crazy. Out of control, and I loved it. I grabbed the top of her dress, the stretchy fabric was no match for my fist as I pulled it down, her tits spilling out of the top. No bra. What do you fucking know? Not only is it her birthday but must be fucking Christmas as well.

My mouth moved to the tip of her tit, flicking it with my tongue before swirling it around her nipple. She moaned as she let me lick her, her pussy rubbing up against my crotch sending me into overdrive. I wasn't going to last long.

"I need to be in you, Ash. This is going to be fast." I reached down to her panties and tore them straight from her body. There was no way I was going to wait for her to slide them off. Fuck that. We were on a schedule, one that was dictated by my dick.

She yelped as the cool air hit her ass, my hand moving from her neck, down across her tits and over her belly. She was so hot I couldn't stand it. She proved what a team player she was by pulling out my dick and jerking me off. I bunched up her dress around her waist giving me unrestricted access, just the way I wanted it. I slid a finger inside of her while my thumb played with her clit. She was already wet.

"Fuck, Ash. You are so wet. How long have you been thinking about fucking me?" I pushed in another finger, and damn if my dick wasn't getting all kinds of jealous of my hand.

"Since I saw you on stage." She groaned as I fingered her, my hand fucking coated in her wetness.

"Ash, I'm usually all about the foreplay but if I don't fuck you right now I'm going to blow my load like a fucking teenager who just watched his first porno. I promise I will take care of you later." I pulled her hand from my dick knowing a few more pulls was going to make me come.

"Fuck me, Dan. Fuck me." She moaned as I continued working her with my hand, her pussy riding up against me.

"Babe, I need to get a condom." This was one of those times where it honestly sucked only having two hands. I know I had a condom in my back pocket, but that meant moving and stopping what I was doing. Neither of these options made me happy. I slid my hand out of her, both of us cursing under our breath.

"Dan," she moaned as she rubbed her pussy up against my shaft, bracing herself against my seat as she traveled up and down the length of my cock.

"Ash," I groaned. Her hot, wet pussy teased the head of my cock as I lifted my ass off the seat, hoping Ash might be able to reach the condom and we wouldn't have to stop. The inside of the car proving not as *spacious* as the douchebag car salesman had claimed. "Can you reach into my pocket, babe? Left side, grab my wal—" I wasn't able to finish my sentence as I accidently slid inside her.

"Fuck," I groaned, as I couldn't stop myself from pushing in deeper. Holy shit, this felt amazing. Her hot pussy wrapped around my bare cock. I'd never had unprotected sex. Too fucking scared I'd get some disease that would make my dick fall off or I'd end up being someone's dad. No fucking way. But feeling how good it felt, I completely understood why a man would roll that dice. Right now we could play Russian roulette, and you could pull the trigger of that loaded gun as long as I got to keep sliding inside of the tight pussy.

"Ash." I pumped harder, waiting for her to tell me to stop. One of us needed to think straight and I didn't think it was going to be me.

"I'm clean. Don't stop. I trust you." She pushed down hard against me, giving me the green light.

I wanted to tell her I was clean. To reassure her I wasn't putting her at risk, but I couldn't fucking talk. What I needed to do was fuck. Hard. I palmed her ass, guiding her up and down as I pushed inside her. My dick so fucking hard I impaled her with each thrust. She screamed as she rode

HIGH STRUNG

me, her fucking pussy fisted me like a vice then milked my dick as she came. I pumped into her as she shook, those pussy pulses sending me over the edge as I shot my load into her. We collapsed against each other, our breathing out of control like freight train barreling down the tracks.

It was one of the most intense experiences of my life. It was like every single part of me shot out through my cock. It was amazing.

Oh, Shit. I just came inside of her. The reality of the situation started to poke its ugly fucking mug, as soon as the high from the awesome sex started to fade. I had meant to pull out. What the hell was I thinking?

"Fuck, Ash!" I pulled her close against my chest. "Please tell me you are on the pill or something." I had already been an asshole by jacking into her like a fucking nympho so I guess a little slide further down the dickwad scale wasn't that big a deal.

"A bit late now." She half-laughed as she kissed my neck. "You think you may have implanted the seed for a little Dan in there?"

I couldn't laugh. This was not funny. I tried to swallow but it got stuck in my throat. The thought that I could have made her pregnant was as serious as shit got. It had been stupid. I'd been thinking with my dick and not my head. Whatever happened though, I was going to be a man about it. I would not be one of those deadbeats who cut and run, no fucking way. I would take care of my business.

Ashlyn pulled away from me, studying me when I didn't speak. "Oh my god. You should see your face. Of course I'm on the pill. I'm not ready to be a mom." She gently shook my shoulders.

The near miss still rattled me a little. I'd never been so careless. "Babe, I should have asked first. If shit went down," I swallowed, "I would have still stuck around."

I wasn't sure exactly what I should say but I knew I had to say something. I hadn't even pulled out of her yet. My fucking cum started spilling out of her onto my jeans. As far as romantic got, this wasn't it. Still, I wouldn't have traded it for anything. Feeling her like that.

"I know, Dan." She smiled sweetly, like I hadn't just fucked her brains out. Her voice mellowed as she moved in to kiss me. "I think I'm in love with you."

I'd heard girls tell me they loved me all the time. Usually while I was either fucking them or while I was on stage. To me it was a throwaway line, it didn't hold much weight. No one really meant it and hearing it did little for me. It was sweet they felt that way, but it wasn't going to change anything. People fall in and out of love all the time. Hearing it from Ashlyn though was a whole new ball game. It was like a punch in the gut, knocking the wind right out of me.

I blinked, dumbfounded. This five-foot-six, hundred-thirty pound redhead just knocked me on my ass. I'd just fucked her. In my car. The windows still fogged up from our heavy breathing. Her dress still hiked up around her waist. My semi-hard cock still inside her. There was nothing romantic or gentle about it, and she told me she loved me? This was not how I ever imagined this moment would go down if it ever happened for real. I'd never felt like a bigger asshole than I did at that moment.

"You don't have to say it back." She moved her mouth on me before I had a chance to answer. "I just wanted you to know."

"Ash." I closed my eyes and rested them against the headrest. "I love you, too."

"Please don't say it just because I did." Ash grabbed my chin forcing my face forward. "I'd rather you didn't say it, than say it just because you *think* you should."

My eyes flung open. She had no idea. No clue as to how far gone I was, and whether I said it or not it wouldn't change the fact I'd do anything for this girl. I'd walk through fire for her, and it wasn't 'cause she said three words to me. It was 'cause of what was going on in the blood-pumping organ in my chest. I guess I hadn't looped it back to the whole love thing, not in a serious way. I've been in love before. Or at least I thought I had. But it never felt like this. Nothing like this.

I pulled her head closer, resting her forehead against mine. "I'm not saying it because you did. I'm saying it because it's what I feel. I do love you, Ash. I fucking love you."

HIGH STRUNG

"Then let's do this. I mean seriously do this." She wrapped her arms around the back of my neck.

"You're mine, babe, and I'm yours. It's already done."

The street outside was dark. Not a fucking a car or person insight. The inside of the car was another story; it was a mess. Bodily fluids spilling all over the place and I just handed this woman my fucking balls. And, I regretted neither of them.

22

Ashlyn

FIRST DAYS USUALLY BROUGHT A JUMBLE OF NERVES, BUT I WAS more excited than anything else. Exciting to be starting this amazing new chapter.

I had just had the most amazing weekend. My twenty-eighth birthday had been so much more than I could have ever hoped for. Ever since I'd left Boston, I'd dreaded birthdays, celebrating them more for everyone else's benefit than my own. It's not that I didn't enjoy the occasion but I missed my family. We spoke on the phone, emailed, Skyped, you name it, but it wasn't the same. It wasn't the same as having your workaholic dad take the time to hug you, wish you happy birthday, and tell you were always going to be his little girl. I'd never really thought about how much I had missed home, not wanting to derail my plan, but I guess if I was honest, I missed it a lot. And Dan and his crazy surprise concert reminded me of that. Of pushing everything aside for a few moments to wish someone you loved a happy birthday. He had orchestrated the whole thing, dinner, Megs, the show. All for me. Then he told the world I was his girlfriend. Not just the room, literally the world. Dan's little speech had already been uploaded to twitter and YouTube and the number of hits just kept climbing. Then we'd had unprotected sex in his car and I'd told him I loved him. I'm not sure why I picked that moment. I guess I got caught up in the fact I truly trusted him. Letting myself be completely bare with him. Literally and figuratively. Not that I planned it that way. He had accidently slid in. Into my vagina and into my life. That, or I'd been moved by the totally hot car sex. In any case, the road map for my plan just got a reroute. I was now happily part of a pair.

"Your first day?" A smiling good-looking stranger watched as I wrestled with the swipe pass I had been given only a few hours before. He was wearing the typical suit. His hair just a little longer than unspoken corporate regulation. Clearly a rebel.

It *was* my first day. My first day as an analyst at JenCorp. Starting a new chapter in my life with a kick-ass boyfriend and kick-ass new job.

"That obvious?" I laughed, as I pressed the errant plastic card against the white scanner. Maybe they haven't activated it yet?

"The trick is a light touch." He gently removed the card from my hand. "May I?" He looked at me for permission.

There was a look I hadn't seen in the work place in a long time. I almost had to grab a wall to stop myself from fainting. Someone who actually wanted to help me? And not holler at me for a beer, or try to touch my ass? Wow. I had the best life. No, I wasn't being dramatic; these little things rocked my world.

"Please." I nodded my head to the scanner that refused to *scan* me.

"See if you just tap it like that," he gently touched my pass to the wall and it lit up green, "it works first time." He handed my swipe pass, a pleased grin on his face.

"Thanks for the tip." I held out my hand, wondering what else was an appropriate form of greeting. Handshakes seemed a little out dated and honestly I felt kind of lame but yeah. I was still going with it. "I'm Ashlyn Murphy and you already know it's my first day."

"Rob Sawyer. The new analyst?" He took my hand without hesitation. If he was thinking I was a loser he wasn't showing it. Maybe he was too polite or he wore a killer poker face.

"Yes. Am I wearing a sign?" I was only half-joking, wondering if it was written all over my face I was fresh meat. It usually only took a day or two until I found my feet in a new job but I would hate to think I looked like I didn't belong. Not after it took me so long to get here. This is exactly where I should be.

"No. I am going to be working with you." Rob laughed. "I was told you were starting today. I had meetings this morning so I missed your induction, but by all accounts you had no issues." He had a nice smile and seemed genuine but I was cautious. Was he fishing? Or just being friendly?

The corporate world could be brutal; it had spat me out the first time without a second thought. If Rob was sizing me up as competition, I wasn't going to make it easy for him. "It was a lot to take in, but nothing I can't handle."

"Good, then you'll do well here." He was so collected and well put together. It wasn't just the way he looked it was his whole vibe. This was his world and he was comfortable in it. It was like the Discovery channel. He was a tiger in his native environment, just wearing a different kind of striped suit. I wanted to be that majestic.

"That's the plan."

I figured I'd probably filled my quota for awkward conversations for the day so best move on. Besides, I should probably head back to my office. That's right. I had an office. I was still pinching myself this was real and if it wasn't, I didn't ever want to wake up.

"Well, I better get back. Thanks again." I waved my swipe card over the sensor lightly and it immediately flicked green. I actually stepped through the doorway this time. "I'm sure I'll be seeing you soon."

"You sure will be." Rob smiled as the automatic door closed between us.

Was he hitting on me? No. What was I thinking? This wasn't a bar where people just hit on some random person they just met. This was a work place. I was just out of practice and reading way more into his kindness. Right? Right. Geez I'm beginning to think being with Dan was giving me his ego as well. It's not like every man who sees me wants to sleep with me. It sounded so conceited in my head; thank god I wasn't repeating it to anyone else. I laughed at myself as I walked to the elevator and pressed the button for my floor. The metal doors opened immediately and I stepped inside. It was empty, giving me the opportunity to take a few extra moments to collect myself and get my head out of my ass.

My phone vibrated silently in my purse. I said a silent prayer of thanks I had switched off the volume when I saw who was calling. I didn't need explicit lyrics announcing my arrival.

I didn't answer. I wanted to, but taking personal calls on company time was the easiest way to get fired. It killed me to let it go to voice mail, but the last thing I needed was Dan getting me into a hot mess. He did that often and usually I liked it but now wasn't the time. Which kind of sucked. We would make up for it no doubt tonight. I sure as hell was going to need it.

I had spent the morning in the conference room with Mitch, my new supervisor, getting the run down. It was typical, very dry, but necessary. There was no easing into the position, it was very much a sink or swim kind of deal. They didn't have time to handhold and I hated to be micromanaged so it seemed like a perfect situation, albeit intense. The afternoon was an overload of information. Account names, departments, and clientele listings. It was made marginally easier by the fact I had my own office, something I hadn't had in very long time. It had a door too, it wasn't just a cubbyhole or cubical. It was a real office. Little things obviously excited me, and this was one.

I had tried to contain my excitement when Mitch had showed me where I would be working. Breaking into over enthusiastic squealing seemed so inappropriate. So I squealed on the inside and gave a reserved nod instead in response. It was a compromise.

Rob's office was right next to mine so it seemed I would be seeing him quite a bit. Seeing as there was only the two of us in the department we would be working closely together. Mitch, our boss and the CFO's right-hand man, made it clear they expected me to hit the ground running and I wasn't going to give them an opportunity to be disappointed.

I was mentally exhausted by the end of day. Parts of my brain I hadn't used in months had to limber up and get back into the game. It was scary and exhilarating all at the same time and five o'clock didn't come a moment too soon.

The minute I stepped out from the revolving glass doorway of JenCorp and onto the sidewalk, I saw Dan's Mercedes. We'd never discussed him giving me a ride home, but I was glad I wasn't going to have to brave the subway in peak hour. I couldn't help smiling knowing he had cared enough to come. The whole relationship was so new; the fact he seemed as invested as I was, floored me.

He was out of the car the minute he saw me, wrapping his arms around my waist and pulling me up against his body while his mouth attacked mine. There was nothing sweet about his kiss, it was desperate and heated, and obviously I'd been missed.

"Dan, not on the street." I half-heartedly pulled away not wanting anyone I worked with catching me making out in front of the building.

"You seemed to have no problems with public displays of affection on the street last Saturday." His satisfied grin leaving no doubt he was remembering my birthday celebrations. His hand snaked around behind me and opened the car door.

"True but there wasn't the possibility of my boss seeing me either. Keep it in your pants long enough to get me back to my apartment and I'll make it worth your while." I unwrapped myself from Dan's grasp and slid into the car. He didn't miss a beat as he stalked around the driver's side and jumped in. The car roared to life as we pulled away from curb.

I laughed like a five-year-old, throwing my head back against the headrest as Dan tore onto the street. He then had to jam on the brakes not soon after when he realized we were in downtown Manhattan and not the interstate.

HIGH STRUNG

"You want me to pull over so we can reminisce?" Dan shot me a grin that did crazy things to my body. The tingling parts thought pulling over was a good idea.

"Just keep your eyes on the road and get me home in one piece." I reached over and squeezed his thigh. I had never been this into a guy. It was intoxicating. Made me dizzy. I loved it.

"I wanted to talk to you about that." Dan grabbed my hand in his lap and gave it a little squeeze. "I had a key cut for you today. Figured it makes more sense for you to stay at my place 'cause it's closer to your work. Plus, your place. Well, it ain't great."

"Dan Evans, you are such a diva. My place not flashy enough for you?" I laughed. Not that I blamed him. Given the choice; I wouldn't want to stay at my place either.

"Babe, if the only thing wrong with it was *no flash*, we wouldn't be having this conversation. I'm pretty sure I saw a rat running across the kitchen floor. Son of a bitch even had the nerve to stare me down."

"I'll call the Super and get an exterminator organized." Rats happened from time to time. I wasn't proud of it, but the drainage in the building probably predated Christianity, so rats unfortunately found their way into apartment.

"Ash, you don't need an exterminator, you need an exorcist for that place."

"You sure you aren't a girl? One little rat and you want to run back to your penthouse?" I enjoyed teasing him. I loved we could do this. Play. With Dan, I didn't have to think. I could just say what I thought. It was like riding around without a seatbelt. Dangerous, but thrilling.

"Don't even start with that shit. It wasn't a *little* rat. The fucker was huge, even had a tattoo."

"Fine, let's stay at your place then. You're lucky I'm in an incredibly giving mood." It wasn't a hard sell. His place was nicer. It was also larger, more luxurious, and, as he rightly advertised, was closer to work than mine. Not to mention it didn't need to be bug-bombed bi-monthly.

His smile tugged at the corner of his mouth. "You think the goodwill could extend a little further and you can maybe unbutton that coat? Your tits look sensational in those tight little business shirts."

"Dan. It's a business shirt. It's not supposed to be sexy."

"Well then their marketing team failed 'cause just thinking about you in that shirt makes me want to jerk off." His hand moved to the top of my coat and flipped open a button. The man had a sickness. Sadly, I think I too was infected.

"You say that about everything I wear, Dan. I'm surprised you don't have RSI."

Dan let out a huge laugh. "Babe, for you it would be worth it."

Things fell into a rhythm as the weeks wore on. While I hadn't moved in with Dan, more and more of my stuff seemed to find its way into his apartment. I was surprised how easy it all was. There had been no real discussion; it just kind of evolved. I had always assumed that when I made that leap into cohabitation there would be a strategy meeting. Pros and cons would be weighed, parameters drawn up, expectations and even personal requirements exchanged. After all, living with someone was a big deal. You don't just start living with them. Or do you?

Work was amazing. I was on a steep learning curve but I loved the challenge. Rob was great, too. He was friendly and easygoing. Rob had mentioned Dan a few days in. It seemed our sidewalk displays hadn't gone unnoticed. I cringed hoping no one else had seen.

Streaks of gray clouds stretched across the sky, their wispy latitude hiding the sun. The thin sheet of rain hit the glass of the office window before tumbling onto the busy street below, and yet none of it bothered me. My smile widened as my thoughts of the day turned to Dan. I leaned back against the leather chair absorbing it, as the case study I should have been reading sat open on the boardroom table in front of me.

"So the guy with the AMG, he's your boyfriend?" Rob glanced up from the file that had our attention. We were working in the conference room, trying to see if there was any value in acquiring a small flagging company in Reno. My gut told me no, that absorbing it under the JenCorp banner would actually have a negative effect on the market share but we were being thorough.

"AMG? Is that an acronym for something?" I tried to work out what the letters might stand for. Nope. Coming up with nothing.

"It's the type of Mercedes. Very nice car I might add. Sorry. I was walking out behind you yesterday, I saw the two of you." Rob looked down at his papers and shuffled them.

"Oh?" I hadn't seen anyone behind me as I'd left the building but then again, I had been too fixated on Dan to notice anyone else. My lips tingled just thinking about the kiss. His kiss. "Oh." While I hadn't wanted to be give my co-workers a show, Dan it seemed, had other ideas.

"He's the guitarist from the band, Power Station, right?"

"The bass player. But yeah, he's in Power Station."

"That must be difficult for you. Having a boyfriend with such a high profile. I'm a little bit surprised; you seem so down to earth and normal. Nothing like what I imagine those people to be."

I'm sure he was saying what a lot of other people didn't have the courtesy to say to my face; I didn't look like I belonged in his world anymore than he belonged in mine. I'd had the same thoughts initially but for whatever reason, the two of us fit. Strip away all the hype and Dan was still just a man. Well, not just *a* man. *My* man.

"They are just regular people, Rob. Just like you and me. Sure they work different hours and wear different clothes, but they aren't that much different than us. James and Alex get most of the media attention, so overall, we get left alone, but occasionally there is someone sniffing around. It's not as bad as you think."

I wasn't annoyed. I was glad he had asked rather than just assuming. Or gossiping. That would be worse. Besides over the last couple of days, we have talked about all different things. Family. School. Friends. I had told him I was in a relationship but didn't elaborate further. It was bound to come up sooner or later, and no one was forcing me to answer his questions. They weren't even overly personal, he just seemed curious.

"I'm sorry, I shouldn't have said anything. I didn't mean to offend you. It's none of my business." He reached out and gently ran his thumb over the back of my hand.

"You didn't offend me. If I didn't want to answer, I wouldn't." I smiled. It was forced but I didn't want him to feel bad, especially when he'd done nothing wrong.

"So do rock bands still have groupies or is that no longer a thing?" He winced. I guess he had been working up to that one - the inevitable question about women throwing themselves at my boyfriend. Women who didn't care what his relationship status was.

"Unfortunately, yeah, they do. I hate it, but it isn't going to change anytime soon. Short of carrying around a big stick and beating anyone who looks at him longer than five seconds there isn't a lot I can do to dissuade anyone." I tried to laugh it off. I imagined eventually Dan would go on tour and that whole scenario would get very real. It's not like I could pack up and leave, follow him around the world like some obedient poodle. I pushed the notion out of my head. What was the saying about borrowing trouble? Leave that shit for another day.

"That must be hard. Seeing someone you care about being pursued by other women."

The last bit stung. I hadn't really seen it. Not yet anyway, but I guess I should be prepared for it. It would come. Inevitably. Like the winter that was sneaking in, every day a little colder than the last. Burying my head in the sand wasn't going to make it any less a fact.

"I try not to think about it. I trust Dan." I tried to sound convincing. More for my own benefit. Like hearing the words would reinforce them. I did trust Dan. It was everyone else I had a problem with.

"Of course you do. I'm sure he loves you very much. I should probably shut up."

"He does. It's fine, really. I'm fine." I shifted uncomfortably in my seat. I guess I was going to have to get used to this. People assuming because of who he was, he would screw around. He wouldn't. Why would he ask me to be his girlfriend and then turn around and be unfaithful? It didn't make sense. Dan meant what he said. I was his and he was mine. No one else's.

"Sorry. I was out of line." He raked his hand through his hair, for the first time giving me a glimpse he didn't have it all together. "Ashlyn. I was insensitive and I really am sorry. You shouldn't have to defend your relationship, least of all to someone you barely know. The curiosity got the better of me. It won't happen again."

Rob spent the rest of the afternoon apologizing and overall being very sweet. True to his word, he didn't mention groupies or the trappings of being a celebrity again. Even later in the week, whenever the subject of Dan did come up, he was always respectful and let me set the tone. He didn't have a girlfriend, so I paid him the same courtesy in not asking too many questions as to why a good-looking, smart, and successful guy was still single. None of my business.

Dan hated Rob of course. He was convinced that Rob had ulterior motives, which I thought was ironic. I didn't give it airtime. JenCorp had a predominately male workforce. So I was either going to be friendly with men or I was going to be enjoying a very lonely existence at work. Not an option.

Secretly it made me a little relieved Dan was jealous. Not that I wanted him to throw down for me or anything like that, but at least I felt like I wasn't a forgone conclusion. I guess we both had a few insecurities. It just meant we were human and made what we had more real.

23
Dan

ASHLYN WORKING FULL TIME SUCKED BALLS. I WAS GLAD SHE wasn't at the bar any more dealing with douchebags who no doubt wanted to fuck her, but I hated she was gone so much. I had convinced her to spend most of her nights at my apartment. It made sense seeing as it was closer to her work than traveling in from Brooklyn, plus it meant we got to spend the nights together. I gave her a key to my place so she didn't have to worry about getting in if I wasn't home, and I was hoping we could make the shacking up arrangement more permanent, but I wasn't going to push it. She didn't say as much but I could tell how much this new job was taking it out of her. She had to be up at five a.m. What kind of lame-ass time is that? Of course, I made the sacrifice and would wake up early too, making sure there was no need for her alarm. A Dan wake-up was so much better. Rather than being pulled from sleep by some random piece-of-shit noise coming from her iPhone, she woke up

HIGH STRUNG

with me between her thighs. Personally, I can't think of a better start to the day than morning sex and I couldn't start my day properly until I'd heard her scream my name while she came beneath me. It was the breakfast of champions.

The whole sex without a condom thing was fucking mind-blowing. It took sex to a whole other level. It had never been this good with any of those other girls. I didn't know if it was the skin on skin that made it seem like more, or whether it was because I was in so deep with this girl, I couldn't see straight. But I knew there would be a cold day in hell before I would be walking away from this. I totally got the whole monogamy thing now. When you find that one person who is perfect in every way, it's not that you *can't* fuck someone else, it's that you don't *want* to fuck anyone else. I used to think those poor assholes had to make this huge sacrifice to keep their women, but it had been us poor losers who didn't know what we had been missing who had been doing the sacrificing, and I wasn't willing to anymore. Not a chance.

Sure it wasn't all morning sex and rainbows. Ash was tired when she got home, and sometimes the band would have a late session which meant I'd miss picking her up from work, but they were just teething issues as far as I was concerned. Ash was happy and I fucking loved seeing her smile.

Of course there was this dickwad she worked with who I was convinced was trying to put the moves on her. Rob. While he seemed like a nice guy, I didn't trust him, and there was no way I'd be letting my guard down around him. I knew his type. I'd seen it play out a million times. Hell, my sister had even tangled with one of those sons-o-bitches, and Troy and I had broken his fucking nose. His name was Brad. Same-same as far as I was concerned. Girls think those douches are their best fucking friends and then boom, one night when they are feeling vulnerable, good old Rob has his pants down around his ankles and asks her to suck his dick. I might not have been a choirboy, but I never played women like that. Fuckers like Rob were predators, some just more patient than others.

Ash thought I was just being jealous, so I didn't push the issue. I sure as shit didn't want to rock the boat seeing as everything had been perfect the last couple of weeks. So I kept it on the down low, knowing if that asshole even breathed on her in the wrong way, I'd fuck him up. Some things were worth jail time, if you know what I mean.

The knock at the door pulled my head back to where it needed to be, away from thinking about shit going wrong between Ash and me. I knew who it was, a conversation that needed to happen, and I was going to man up and have it.

I opened the door and saw Sydney standing out in the hall. It felt like an eternity ago since we'd been together. I had to remind myself it actually happened.

"Dan." Sydney walked through the doorway and into my pad.

"Hey, Syd." I gave her a hug. We hadn't had a proper conversation in god knows how long. It's funny how I'd always thought it would be weird between us after the sex, but it just wasn't. I liked that about Sydney; she didn't say one thing and mean another. She was a genuine kick-ass chick, and I had a lot of time for her even if from here on out, it was going to be solidly in friend-zone.

"Let's take a seat in the lounge room." I didn't want to have this conversation in the fucking hallway. I was probably going to need to sit down anyway.

"So what's got your kickers in such a twist that you couldn't talk to me over the phone?" She took off her coat as she followed me through to the main living area of my apartment, her heels clicking on the polished floorboards.

"Shit I needed to say wasn't for the phone, Syd. I wanted to speak to you face to face and I didn't want to bug you at work. I know Lexi still hasn't found a new assistant yet." I gestured for her to take a seat on the couch. Syd draped her coat over the arm of the chair before settling in.

"Well thanks for the consideration. I'm sure Lexi thanks you, too. Not that it ever really stopped you from bothering me before."

"Yeah well, sometimes I just can't help myself." I shrugged.

HIGH STRUNG

"So what is so important? I know we're not here to talk my work schedule." Sydney was smart. Not much got by her, it's one of the reasons I respected her so much. I think that is why her and Lexi were so tight and probably one of the reasons I was attracted to them both at one stage. Clearly I have a thing for mouthy women.

"No, we're not." I grinned, taking the armchair opposite her. "I wanted to thank you for hooking up Ashlyn with the job. She needed a break, and it really made a difference. I know thank you doesn't cut it but, yeah I wanted to thank you."

"Do my ears deceive me? The great Dan Evans being all sweet and thankful. My, my, I'm not entirely sure what to do with the gratitude."

"Take it for what it's worth. A thanks. You know, I really didn't expect that. You, helping me. Helping her. I mean it's not like you owe me anything."

"Why wouldn't I help you if I had the opportunity? If I have the means to assist a friend, I'll happily lend a hand. And before you make some innuendo about hand jobs, you know I don't mean that."

"Wouldn't take it even if you offered. I got myself a girl now, and she's the only one whose hands are getting on me. But all jokes aside, I'm glad you see me as a friend."

"Well of course I see you as a friend. I'm not in the habit of sleeping with people I can't stand. You know we both went into *that* with our eyes open. I never expected anything more from you than that night, and at the risk of inflating your already ridiculously large ego, it was probably the best sex I'd ever had. I don't regret it. Still, I never thought I'd see the day where you would be happily off the market. I have to say, I'm half expecting an asteroid to come hurtling toward Earth, taking us to our deaths. At least I can say I've seen it all."

She always was a wise-ass, but I was glad she was cool about the whole thing. Not all the women I'd slept with shared Syd's carefree philosophy. I never promised them more, but some assumed what was only a fuck would turn into a *beautiful* relationship. I had probably been a bigger dick than I needed to be, but I never really cared enough not to be. Guess it didn't really matter now. That shit was well and truly in my rearview.

"Yeah, have your fun, Syd. I've been getting it from Troy for weeks now. Jase too. I'll take whatever you guys got."

"I think it's marvelous you've found a lady. It's obvious she's captured your heart. Now, just don't do something stupid and cock it up." Syd smiled as she moved off the couch. "Come on then, let's do this properly." She held out her arms in front of her.

I laughed as I lifted my ass off the chair. I wrapped my arms around her and gave her a hug, "Thanks, Syd. You're pretty awesome."

My eye caught the reflection of the door. Ash was standing there. Her coat still on, like she'd just walked in. "Hey, babe. I didn't hear you come in. This is Sydney, she—" I didn't get a chance to finish to explain before Ash cut me off.

"We've already met. At my interview with Lexi." She seemed annoyed. I guess she had seen me with Sydney and had gotten the wrong idea. Sort of like when Ash had come to my apartment and my sister and nephew had been there. We would probably laugh about it like we did then. I mean, as if I would cheat on her. That would never happen.

"I was just on my way out. Nice to see you again, Ashlyn." Sydney smiled but Ash didn't respond. Syd shot me a concerned look, "Dan, good seeing you."

It wasn't looking good. I was probably going to have to do a lot of groveling. Although, I was confident that once I explained Sydney was just a friend, Ash would come around. She could sometimes fly off the handle but she wasn't unreasonable. And we were finally in a good place.

"No probs, Syd. 'Bye." I walked her to the door while Ashlyn stood simmering in the hallway, her arms locked across her chest. Not sure how much she heard but whatever it was, she was pissed.

"Listen, Ash." I had no idea what I was going to say other than whatever she was thinking, she had it wrong. I felt like I had to say sorry, but I had no idea what I was supposed to be apologizing for.

HIGH STRUNG

"Don't," she whimpered. "Please, just don't." She didn't take off her coat or put down her purse. She just stood there. I fucking hated it. Seeing that look on her face and knowing that it was because of something so stupid. There was nothing going on.

"Ash. I'm not sure why you are mad but, whatever it is, you have the wrong idea. Sydney and I are just friends."

"Just friends? Really?"

Fuck. Well, I guess this was going to be harder than I thought. Granted, I had my arms around Syd but it's not like I was grabbing her ass.

"Ash."

"What, Dan? I knew you had a past, but it's a little different when it is flaunted in front of me. Are you telling me you haven't had sex with her?" She dared me to deny it, probably guessing I couldn't. How could I? I *had* slept with Sydney.

"Babe, I'm not going to lie to you. I did sleep with Sydney. But, it was before I knew you, and it was only one time." How could something I did before I met Ashlyn come back and bite me?

"Only one time?" she repeated, her eyes were filled with hurt. I hated knowing the *hurt* was because of me,

"It was insignificant, Ash." I took a step toward her. "It didn't mean anything. It was just sex."

"How could you say that? *It was just sex.* Goddamn it, Dan, is there anyone you haven't slept with?" Despite being angry, she didn't yell.

"What do you want me to say? I can't take it back." I couldn't change my past. I couldn't un-fuck all those women. Even if I could, it wouldn't make me love her any more than I already did. It was in the past. Ash was my future.

"Why?" Just one word, but the way she said it made it sound so much worse.

"Why, what?" I wanted to go and touch her but her arms across her chest made it clear that was a no-go. I knew that if I could put my arms around her, I could show her how much she meant to me.

"Why did you sleep with her if it she didn't mean anything?" Her voice was almost a whisper.

"I don't know. It just happened. I wasn't trying to sleep with her." I moved closer and she stepped back. I blinked. Did she just move away from me?

"So I should feel better about the fact you had sex with her even though you weren't *trying* to?"

"No. I'm just saying. I don't know what I'm saying but I can't feel bad about something I did before I even knew you." I needed to get through to her. So she could understand how much this shit didn't matter. Why wouldn't she fucking see this wasn't important?

"I knew there had been lots of women, but I didn't think I would have to see them, that they would still be in your life. Is that what will happen to me? When we're done?"

"Ash, I swear to you on my mother's life, it's not like that with us. Do you think I'm just going to be done with you?"

"Then why was she here and why were you hugging her if it was just one night that meant nothing?"

"Ash, she was telling me she was happy for us."

"Please, stop." Ash held out her hand. "I need to know. I need to know the truth. Why. Was. She. Here?" She paused between each word. I could see the torment on her face, second-guessing what we were. She still hadn't moved. Her body radiated an invisible force field of don't-fucking-touch-me.

Part of me wanted to go over and drag her into the living room and make her listen to reason. Prove to her this was all fucking bullshit. She would never be just another fuck to me, and as for the situation with Syd, she was looking for something that wasn't there.

"I was thanking her, okay? That's all. There was nothing shady going on. Do you honestly think if I was going to go behind your back I'd do it where you'd find out? I know you have a key. C'mon, Ash. Don't let these doubts ruin shit for us. I can't change the fact I slept with her. I am not denying it, but I am telling you that is in my past and I would never

hurt you."
"What did she do for you?"
"What do you mean?"
"Why did you need to thank her?"
"She just worked something out for me. Trust me, Ash, just let it go." This was another can of fucking worms I was not ready to open. I knew if she found out about the job she would take it the wrong way. She just needed to let it go.
"You're asking me to trust but you won't tell me what she did. What are you hiding?"
"Nothing. I'm not hiding anything."
"Dan, I know you aren't being honest with me. If you care half as much as you say you do, you will just tell me."
Hearing her say I didn't care, fucking lit a fuse. I didn't mean to yell but I couldn't believe she would think I would lie to her, cheat on her, and fucking throw what we had away.
"She gave Simon Jennings your resume. She set up the interview for JenCorp. That's it. I was thanking her for that."
"You asked a girl you used to fuck to get me a job?" She looked disgusted and no matter how bad it had been, it was so much fucking worse now.
"No. Look, it wasn't like that. I know you are mad, and probably a little hurt, but Sydney isn't just some girl I've fucked." Syd wasn't just some groupie, and she had done nothing wrong here. If anyone was an asshole, it was me, and I wouldn't let someone who had been a friend take the fall.
"I thought you said she didn't mean anything? You can't have it both ways. I thought Lexi recommended me for this job?"
It was just getting worse. It was like a runaway train I couldn't stop from derailing. My mouth just saying anything to try and make it better
"The sex didn't mean anything, but that doesn't mean Sydney isn't a good person. She's a friend. I'm sorry you had to find out this way. I went to Lexi because I wanted her to hire you. When she said you didn't

make the cut, she agreed to help find something else." The minute I'd said it I realized how bad it sounded. I couldn't find a way to make her understand the way I had seen it in my head. It wasn't supposed to hurt her.

"You did *what*? You went to Lexi and asked her to hire me? Holy shit, Dan. Did you have any faith in my ability? So this whole job has been a big pity fuck?"

Her eyes watered and I could tell she was trying not to cry. I fucking hated seeing her like this, and knew I was the cause. I would do anything to make it better for her. I hated this distance. Standing in the same place in the hallway.

"I was trying to help. You wouldn't let me help any other way. Lexi asked Sydney and she just passed on the resume. I figured if I could do this, help you find something else, then you would be happy." It was starting to break me, too. Maybe my execution was shit but my intentions weren't. It was supposed to make it better. Why had it turned into a big ball of shit?

"I knew when I started having feelings for you that it was going to be hard. Reconciling myself with all the women. Wondering if I measured up. I wanted to believe that I was different. That you loved me *because* I was different. What I never thought I would have to doubt is whether or not I was good enough. *You* didn't even have faith in me to find a job. You can't just change people's lives, Dan. I should have known from the start I didn't fit. We didn't fit. I don't belong in your world. I was happy before I met you. I was happy with my shitty apartment, in my shitty job with my shitty life because as shitty as everything was, it was real. And right now, I have no idea what is real anymore."

She didn't mean that. I know she couldn't mean that. I got that she was hurting, and I would jump through whatever fucking hoops I needed to put shit back together, but what we had was the realest thing I'd ever had. I knew this wasn't one sided.

"This is real, Ash. What we have, it's not a lie. The other stuff, Sydney may have set up the interview but *you* got that job on your own."

I moved closer and she stepped away again. Every single time she did that I wanted to put my fist through a wall. That *I* was what she was trying to get away from.

"Tell me one thing, Dan, and I want you to tell me the truth." She had wrapped her arms so tightly around her body if I hadn't clued in that she didn't want me to touch her, I was fucking getting the hint now. She was losing the battle with the waterworks, too. Her eyes were red and she was blinking really fast, trying to stop them from spilling over.

"Ash, I know this is fucked up and I know I kept things from you, but you can't doubt what we have." I looked at her right in the eye. She had to believe me. I'll be the first person to put my hand up and say I may have omitted some details and maybe I fucked up. Okay, so I *definitely* fucked up, but I've never lied to her. I would never hurt her.

"That day...in Lexi's office." She swallowed hard as the first tear dropped from the corner of her eye. She tried to wipe it away before I could see. "When I met you the first time. Why were you there?"

She looked like she was in so much pain. I couldn't make it worse. Why couldn't we let go of that shit and concentrate on what we had. On what we had built. Nothing else mattered.

"I was with Alex, he had to see Lexi."

I remembered that day like it was burned into my brain. We had been rehearsing at James's. Hannah had been looking after Grace, and Noah had helped keep her entertained while her daddy played rock star with her uncles. We had wrapped and Alex had said he was going to stop by and see Lexi. I thought it would have been the perfect opportunity to see Sydney, maybe ask her out. It wasn't supposed to be a big deal. She would shoot me down like she always did and I'd move on. It was almost like a game. I never expected to find something else there that day. *Someone* else. Someone like Ash.

"Dan, from the little I know of Alex, I know he does not need a babysitter to see his wife. Why were *you* there that day?"

I couldn't lie to her. I promised I wouldn't. I wasn't sure if this was some sick fucking test I had to pass or what, but whatever happened from here on out was going to be the fucking truth.

"I was there to see Sydney."

It was as if the words had smacked her hard in the face. Her hand flew to her mouth as she let out a gasp.

"Why?" she barely choked out.

"I was going to ask her out." The truth, no matter what happened she was going to get the truth.

"So I was the consolation prize?" The pain in her eyes tore through me. I'd swallow broken glass before I had to see it again.

"No. Ash. No. I swear to you." Fuck the consequences. I needed to hold her. To put her in my arms and for her to feel it. To feel us. I moved to her, toe to toe. We needed to make sense of this and the only way I knew how was to touch her.

"I can't." She pushed me away, her hand hitting me square in the chest. "This is too much. I can't."

"Ash, don't fucking leave. Do not walk away from this." I grabbed her hand. Did she want me to beg? Whatever the fuck she needed, she just had to say the word.

She held my stare, her green eyes annihilating me as I watched her fight against the tears. "I need to be enough, and I can't be that with you. The girls, the job, being your second choice? It's too much. We never belonged together, Dan. We were a mistake that just went on too long. Neither of us was going to admit it, but you and me, it was destined to fail. We are just too different, and I can't be anyone else anymore than you can. Goodbye, Dan."

She didn't yell and somehow that was so much worse. It fucking scared the hell out of me. I wanted her to scream, to slap me and tell me what an asshole I was, but she didn't. Instead, she turned around and walked out. She didn't even slam the door. Nothing. She was just gone. I kept staring at the door. Hoping it would open and it was all a big mistake. Like what just happened, didn't actually happen. But it didn't. Nothing changed and I was left standing there with the biggest pain in my chest I'd ever known. All that shit about feeling like your heart was tearing in two was a lie. That didn't even come close to the pain I was feeling. It felt so much worse. Like having your heart ripped from your chest, tossed on the floor, and forced to watch it helplessly while you slowly die. That's what it felt like. It felt like dying.

24

Ashlyn

MEGS KEPT ASKING ME HOW I FELT AND I DIDN'T KNOW WHAT TO say. Hurt. Sad. Angry. Tired. Sad. Hurt. It was everything wrapped up in a huge indescribable fuck-you emotion. I felt betrayed. I felt stupid but most of all I felt an overwhelming sense of pain and loss that compared to nothing I'd ever experienced before. I'd experienced break-ups before. Nothing even came close to this. This was some kind of medieval type pain. Epic. Sustained.

It was like a hole had been torn through me, letting the cold seep in and I could never warm up. My body shivered. I felt empty. I felt lost. I felt so incredibly sad I couldn't stand it.

"Ash. I've never seen you like this. Sweetie, I don't know what to do to make this better." It's a sad sorry state of affairs when one of my best friends, who happened to be a psychologist, didn't know what to say. That's where I had ended up. Pushing the boundaries of even professional help. Go hard or go home, right?

"Nothing, there's nothing." I was curled up on my couch in my pjs. It was the weekend so therefore it was my go-to attire. I wasn't leaving the apartment. Not unless I had to. Like if the place was on fire or something like that, and even then I'd probably seriously evaluate the size of the flames before actually leaving.

It had been exactly one week and one day since I'd walked out of Dan's apartment. He had been calling me relentlessly. I didn't answer. Letting every single one of those calls go to voice mail, and deleting them before I had a moment of weakness and listened. I couldn't. I couldn't go back. It had hurt too much.

I had made it through in a daze. Faking it through the days when I had to see people, going to work and pretending it hadn't happened, but allowing myself the luxury to fall apart at night when I was alone. It had been three days before I'd finally confessed what had happened to Megs. I had a feeling she already knew, maybe through Troy, or maybe even Dan trying to gain an ally, but she didn't say a word. She just held me and let me cry on her bedroom floor.

I wanted to pull myself together. To stop it. But it was something I just couldn't manage. Part of me didn't want to. Like finally letting go of the pain would be letting go of that last piece of Dan. How stupid was that? That even after all of this, I still loved him. I was insane.

"Ash, maybe you should talk to him. Even if it's just for closure." Megs sat beside me. She was grasping. Looking for anything to pull me out of it.

"No, I have all the closure I need." I didn't even look at her. My eyes fixed on the television screen in front of me. Not that it was actually playing anything. Staring at the black focal point just helped me not to cry.

"Ashlyn Marie Murphy, you are full of shit. You aren't anywhere close to closure." Megs pulled on my arm, forcing me to look at her. We both knew she was right. One of us was just not ready to deal with what she was suggesting.

"I'm not calling him, I don't want to hear his voice. It will hurt too much."

"Ash. I get that you are hurting right now, and I'm not going to pretend I know what you are going through, but anyone can see you are still in love with him. Maybe there is a way you can work through this."

I loved Megs, and usually her optimism was welcomed, but today I wanted to ask her *what the hell was she thinking?* She had to be kidding, trying to get me out of my funk with shock treatment. Like delivered pulses into my brain by electrodes, this was her mental equivalent.

"Megs." Where to even start? "He made a play for me while interested in another woman. Then he went to Lexi, a potential employer, and asked her to give me a job, obviously not having any faith in my own ability and making me look desperate. Then failing that, he went to a girl who he'd had a one-night stand with and got her to pull some strings. The same girl he had been trying to win over when he met me. See where I'm going with this? My pride is about all I have right now." The words come out in a jumbled rush. I barely took a breath before continuing, "What's worse is that I don't even know if the job is still mine. Like if now the gig is up, will JenCorp pull the pin? After all, they don't need to do me any more favors now I'm no longer screwing Dan. The whole week I've been waiting for someone to come into my office and hand me my walking papers. My world has dropped out from under me. None of it was real. It had just been an illusion."

"Ash, take a breath. I don't care how or who got you that interview at JenCorp, you earned that position. You are more than qualified, and you are doing an outstanding job. Even assuming they hired you as a favor, which they didn't, but assuming they did, they wouldn't keep you if you sucked. It's a business, Ash; you look at their bottom line every day. Do you think they going to sink money into you as a charity case? Even you have to admit that regardless of how you got there, you have more than proven your worth."

If I gave it some proper consideration, what Megs said was logical. JenCorp had thrived on ruthless business decisions. Simon Jennings wouldn't think twice about firing me if I didn't perform. That man was only interested in what I could do to expand his net worth, rather than who my boyfriend was. Not that it mattered now. I had no boyfriend.

HIGH STRUNG

"Even if I could find a way to work through it, he didn't believe in my ability to get a job on my own. I'm not sure if I could somehow find peace about possibly running into one of his past and numerous conquests. Or even, believing that if we had met under different circumstances, he still would have wanted to be with me, it doesn't change anything. All those problems did, was highlight one major flaw. We didn't belong together. We were too different."

"Ash, you were happy. I saw it. I know that those feelings you had for him were real. He was a manwhore and he had slept with a lot of women, but that was before he met you. He wasn't with anyone while you were together, right?"

I pulled my knees to my chest and wrapped my arms around my legs. "I don't think... I hope he didn't." In my heart, I believed he had been faithful even if my head, the jury was still out. I hated that either way, I just wasn't sure.

Megs rubbed my arm as she continued her dissection of our break-up. "The job thing, perhaps his methods weren't great, but I think his heart was in the right place. We've already established you got the job legitimately; all he did was get your foot in the door."

"I know it doesn't seem like a big deal, but I need to know that I'm good enough on my own."

"Oh sweetie, you are. He was just trying to help. He wanted you to be happy because he loves you."

"It doesn't matter. Whether he loved me or not, nothing changes. I mean really, what the fuck was I thinking? A rock star, Megs. A fucking rock star. What kind of future was I going to have with him? Maybe we'd date for a few months, a year at most? Then, what? We move onto *friends* like he did with Sydney? Is there some special club of girlfriends past, where we all gather and commiserate? I can't do that. It would hurt too much. He was larger than life, and I got caught up in the madness. When I met him, I knew that it wasn't going to be forever. I just stupidly forgot, and then went and did something dumb like falling in love with him."

It felt like the room had become suddenly larger, or I was smaller in it. The overwhelming hurt hung in the air above us. It had consumed me, and I knew there was no going back. I wasn't that strong.

"Please think about this. Please, talk to him," Megs begged, pulling me closer into a hug.

"You are supposed to be my friend. Please don't try and make me feel worse than I already do." I couldn't understand why she wouldn't let this go. My heart was broken into a million tiny pieces and I wasn't even sure whom to blame.

"I'm not. I promise. Ash, I really believe he loves you. I know he is hurting just as much as you are. I'm trying to help."

"Well if you want to help, stop trying to convince me that I've made a mistake. Help me get over him, and help me move on." Help me to forget how much I love him. I couldn't say that last part. Not out loud. Not ever again.

"Okay. If that's what you want." Megs sighed. Her expression was sad but resigned, like she was finally going to let it go.

I closed my eyes and let out a long, slow breath. I didn't want to feel like this, I didn't want to hurt. I'm not sure what part cut me the most, maybe it was because I had felt like a consolation prize. He had admitted he didn't do long-term, and perhaps he wasn't wired for that. Either way, even if I still loved him, and he me, I needed to look after my heart.

"It's what I need."

25

Dan

"DUDE, GET YOUR HEAD IN THE GAME. I'M PLAYING A C SHARP major, and you aren't even in the same scale. What the hell key *are* you in? Did you forget how to play? Did you tune at all?" Alex flung a guitar pick at me as I looked up from my bass. I actually had no recollection of what I played, and we'd gone over this progression at least six times.

"I'm fine, asshole. Just making sure you're paying attention. You just worry about making sure your part is tight. I can handle mine." I stretched out my fingers before flipping him off. Fucking Stone and his perfect-ass playing.

"Hey, why don't we take five?" James put his mic back on the stand and walked toward me. If there was a mediator in this band, that guy sure as hell fit the bill. Sure, he was a tough business guy and when it came to music, he knew that shit inside and out, but he was too smart to let that go to his head. Whenever things got hairy, James was always the first one to step up and take control.

"What's going on, brother? I've never seen you this edgy before a show." James clapped his hand around my shoulder. Now I felt bad about letting him down. Another heaping spoonful of disappointment.

"The show isn't the problem. I can play this shit sideways. Just got some other stuff clouding up my gray matter."

Ashlyn still wouldn't take my calls. I had left maybe forty voice messages, and I was half expecting the sheriff to show up and issue me with a restraining order.

"We can cancel the gig, dude. It's no big deal." Troy rested his sticks on his snare and popped out his in-ear monitors. "It's just an exhibition show. No tickets have been sold. No harm, no foul."

If anyone knew what private hell I'd been living with for the last two weeks, it was the man sitting across from me. He had found my sorry ass, a bottle and half of bourbon later, on the floor of my fucking apartment where Ash had left me. He didn't even say anything, just parked his ass on the floor beside me and helped me finish the other half of the bottle.

I'd fucked up. I got that. I should have told Ash right off the bat about the job. But I knew if I did, she would take it the wrong way, which she did anyway. The whole Sydney thing was a kick in the nuts. I had gone back and forth a million times and still didn't know what else I could have done differently. I came up blank each and every time. I had slept with Syd, but that shit was in the past, and the minute I fucking laid eyes on Ash, Sydney wasn't even on my radar. Ash was never a consolation prize. She was the fucking jackpot. She was The World Series and Superbowl rolled into one and no girl had even come close. The fact she didn't get what a big deal she was made me feel like I'd had my dick slammed in a car door.

"Ash and I aren't together anymore, but I'm fine. We're doing the show."

"Dude, I'm sorry. I didn't mean to blow up at you like that. I was a complete dick." Alex put down his ax and walked over. He looked all

HIGH STRUNG

regretful and shit. "Why didn't you say something?"

"Nothing to say." I shrugged. There really wasn't. 'Cause talking about it just made it harder, and it was bad enough running through it in my head. It was a car crash, and yet I couldn't stop the fucking loop.

"We're here for you, brother. Whatever you need." Jase joined the improv therapy session.

Jase already knew. He had joined Troy and I in one of my post-break up drinking sessions and listened to me in my misery, but like the stand-up guy he was, had kept his trap shut and didn't tell James and Alex. It's not that I didn't want them to know, I just didn't want to have to say the words. Like maybe some miracle would happen and she would come back. But all the hoping in the world didn't do jack.

I was not willing to let down my brothers. It was bad enough I'd let down the only woman I'd ever loved. Yeah. There was that. I fucking loved her. Still did. The fact she'd bailed did nothing to change up that sitch.

So, I guess I knew. Knew what it felt like to have your heart broken, and knew what it felt like to live with the fact that the only person you want to be with didn't want you. It was a kind of suck that you couldn't even begin to understand, or explain. Unimaginable pain.

"I'm going to need a minute." I pulled the strap from my chest and rested the bass on the stand. I needed some air.

The guys looked at each other before looking back at me. I didn't need to be a mind reader to know what was going on in their heads. They were wondering how long I was going to be able to keep my shit together. I couldn't even clue them in, 'cause the truth was, I had no fucking idea.

I walked out of James's studio and into his backyard. It was the tail end of fall and the chill factor was getting good and cozy with the day. I wasn't wearing a jacket but I didn't give a shit. I welcomed the cold air hitting my skin like an ice bath. Gave me something else to concentrate on other than this pit of emptiness I was dealing with.

I pulled out my phone and flicked through my contacts. I stopped at her name; my finger hovering over it like it did every single time. I didn't call. Not this time at least. I reserved the calling for when I got good and worn down. Usually late at night or the early hours of the morning, hoping her automatic reflexes would kick in and she'd just pick up. But she didn't. It always diverted to voice mail where I'd get to live a different type of hell and listen to her sweet pre-recorded voice tell me *she can't come to the phone right now*. I fucking hated it, but it was my only connection to her, and like a fucking junkie, I wasn't willing to go cold turkey. For those few precious seconds, with her voice in my ear, I could pretend that she was still mine and that was I going to hold her again soon.

I scrolled down the names in my phone a little farther, and before I could stop myself, I hit call. It was the other number my brain liked to wrestle with before hitting dial; today I was all out of fight.

"Hey, Dan. You really need to stop calling me. It feels wrong going behind her back." I knew it was only a matter of time before she said it, and today those words had finally come.

"I know, Megs. I'm sorry. I just miss her and I need to know she's okay."

I closed my eyes and tried to reconcile with the fact this was probably the last time Megs would take my call. Not that I blamed her. Her loyalties were with Ash, and I was thankful she'd been so patient up to this point. A lesser person would have told me to fuck off the first time I'd called. We'd both been surprised. Me, for the fact I'd actually let the call connect, and Megs that I'd kept the number after planning Ash's birthday celebration.

Maybe it was 'cause she was a shrink, or maybe 'cause she was just a decent person, but she listened to what I had to say with no judgment. She let me spill my guts and lay myself bare with no need to censor. Her advice was sound and she was kinder than I fucking deserved, but I lived for those rare fucking moments where she'd let down her guard and tell me about my girl. Anything. Even if it was just to know she'd finally slept. I wanted to know. I needed to know.

HIGH STRUNG

"Dan, I've tried to be impartial, but this whole situation is really fucked up. You are both in so much fucking pain. It's horrendous. Maybe it's for the best if you let her go."

"I wish it was that easy." I swallowed, cursing the fucking lump forming in my throat. "She's always going to be with me, Megs. I love her. She's deep in me now, and even if I never see her again, I'm always going to love her."

"Fuck, Dan, you're making me cry." Megs's voice cracked and I heard her breath hitch as she tried to hide the tiny sobs.

"I'm sorry, Megs. Seems like making girls cry is all I'm good for these days." I balled my fist up against my eyes. "I know I've got no right to ask, but I'm going to need you to do me one more thing."

"What is it?" Megs hiccupped, having lost her battle with the waterworks.

"Take care of my girl for me, will you?" I tried to pull it together so I could finish what I needed to say, my body fighting a losing battle with my fucking emotions. "You or she ever need anything, I don't care what it is or when, you call. No strings. She doesn't even have to know it's from me. I don't ever want her without."

Megs cried into the phone and shit got real quiet on my end while I tried to absorb the pain. I listened. Listened to Megs's tears and let the misery wash over me. If she could do this for me, then I'd give her a blank check for whatever she wanted. She could call on favors for the rest of her days, and I'd shut my mouth and pay up with a fucking smile. I couldn't let go and I'd never stop loving her, but if I knew someone was looking out for her, I was willing to step away. She deserved a chance at being happy, and I'd obviously fucked that up. It wasn't about me, or what I wanted anymore, and I'd give my last fucking breath to make sure she was happy. Even if that meant saying goodbye.

26
Ashlyn

IT'S FUNNY HOW I NOW MEASURED TIME. IT WASN'T DECEMBER tenth. It was three weeks post Dan. It was cold, brutal and unrelenting. The gray sky fought for slivers of sunshine, not usually successfully. And it had already started to snow.

Dan had stopped calling and I didn't know what was worse. Knowing he'd finally given up, or realizing I wish he hadn't. Not that it was his fault. He stuck it out a lot longer than I thought he would. I just had been too scared to give it another chance. The gamble. Not knowing if he had loved me as deeply as I had loved him, or if it had been an illusion.

I had stopped crying, too. Well mostly. There was still a night here or there when I'd slip from the wagon, but overall I was doing better. Work kept me busy which helped, hard to be sad when you're neck deep in property analysis. I was still cautious online, avoiding any website that could potentially spill gossip, and I ran past newsstands like they contained a life threatening disease. I was okay, but I just couldn't see it yet. Dan with other women. Even though I knew I had no right to think it, I just couldn't stand the thought of him with someone else. He would

HIGH STRUNG

have moved on by now. Found someone else, perhaps more than one. Maybe one for every day of the week? I don't know why I tortured myself.

If it weren't so tragic, it would be funny. That I had been the one to end it, and yet here I was, obsessed over whether I'd been replaced. I really needed a hobby. I'd heard knitting had suddenly become cool; maybe I'd knit myself a scarf. Or I could cut out the lead-time and just become a crazy cat woman now. Except that I hated cats and wool made me itchy.

"Ash, we're heading out for lunch. You want to join us?" Celeste from marketing knocked at my door. I'd tried to make friends around the office, thought it would help. But it didn't. It just added new names to the list of people I had to fake it for. So much for intelligence. I was clearly a dumbass.

"Thanks, but I think I'm going to work through. I have a vicious deadline," I lied, not wanting lunch or the company.

"Maybe some other time."

"Yeah, another time." Like when I stopped being a downer. I forced a smile back.

She was kind enough to leave without pushing it further. It wasn't the first decline she had received from me. Honestly, I'm surprised she kept asking. Maybe she was going for sainthood. Or, I just looked really pathetic.

I turned my head back to my monitor, the sound of her heels heading down the hall marking the end of the conversation. What was I doing again? That's right, reworking this email for the hundredth time, and hopefully making it seem like someone who was college educated wrote it.

"Hey." Rob rapped his knuckled against the doorframe. Not sure if it was a knock or a call to attention, but it got me to stop shooting daggers at the computer screen for the minute.

"Thought you might be hungry." He held up the plastic bag of nondescript containers. "Got some lunch. You want to share?"

My stomach growled on cue, shooting down the anticipated *I'm-not-hungry* my mouth was working on. Both of them, my stomach and my mouth, were assholes.

"I'll take that as a yes." Rob grinned, strolling into my office. The bag of takeaway waved like a victory flag. "I hope you like Chinese. There's enough here to feed an army."

"Thanks," I conceded. Busy or not, I had to eat. My body was only going to tolerate the lack of fuel for so long before it turned on me. My stomach's vocal protest proof it had already started the revolt. "Chinese is great," my asshole mouth offered. It sounded like a shitty tagline. Something a second rate advertising manager would come up with. Thank god I was in the numbers business instead of words.

Rob pulled up a chair, seating himself opposite my desk and started unpacking the takeaway bag. "Sooo." It began. The small talk. I should have known the Chinese would come with a side of conversation. Hadn't we already established that words were not my friends?

"I'm not trying to pry," Rob held up his hands in mock surrender, "but it's hard not to notice how sad you've been." While he was still oozing sympathy, his hands moved to a more important task, like spooning out the General Tso chicken.

"I'm okay." I shrugged. It wasn't complete bullshit. I was definitely better, and at least I hadn't said *I'm good*, which would have been a total lie.

"I liked it better when you weren't just *okay*." He handed me some chopsticks, the look on his face telling me he wasn't buying it - that I wasn't anything other than miserable.

"Dan and I broke up." I might as well tell him. He probably already knew. The absence of Dan and his fancy car would have been the first tip off. Followed closely by recent overtime and my reluctance to go home.

"I figured as much. I'm sorry." He looked genuinely sorry for me, which I couldn't decide if that made him a nice guy or me pathetic.

"It was for the best." Sure, it's been a while since we've tried this explanation on. Let's walk around in it and see how it fits this time

HIGH STRUNG

around. "We were just too different." Nope, it still didn't feel right, even though it was the truth.

"Ash, if there is anything I can do… ," Rob paused like he was shifting through what he was about to say, "I know it can't be easy to lose someone you care about."

No it wasn't. It was the opposite of easy, and I didn't just care about him, I loved him. Which made it even harder. Which got me wondering if Rob was talking from experience, or just commiserating.

I knew he dated, I'd seen the odd female friend stop by the office, although never the same one twice, and I had ruled out him being gay. He didn't seem like a player, but he'd never spoken about a significant other, and from what I could see he didn't have any major flaws. He was polite, well spoken, and good-looking. A winning combo. And assuming he was earning at very least what I was, although probably more, he ticked the box for steady job and good income. Rob being single didn't make sense. Unless he was rocking some deep, dark secret? Or he had a tiny penis.

"What about you?" I heard myself say it before my brain had a chance to back out. "No girlfriend?" I stuffed a spoonful of fried rice in my mouth before I could do anymore damage. I guess it was only fair, he knew about my love life.

"Not recently. In the past, sure. Some I even thought maybe could be the one. But none of them really filled the criteria, and as conceited as it may sound. I just didn't want to settle."

"I used to have criteria, too." I had to smile as I remembered my old list of requirements. "Before Dan. He blew it all out of the water though."

"Do you think maybe that's why it didn't work out? That even if your heart wanted something your head knew better?"

"Is that the way it was for you?" I stopped eating, suddenly interested in his response.

"Yeah. I know this sounds a little messed up but, what the hell, right?" His easy laugh was a nice sound and I realized that I was having a conversation, and wasn't thinking about running away. Or crying. Or wanting to cause someone or myself physical harm. He took a deep breath. "I have it all planned out."

There were no sparks between us, Rob and me, but we were so similar it was impossible to ignore we would make an amazing team. After our lunchtime confessional, he'd asked if I'd consider going out with him. I wanted to say no, that there was no way, but I agreed anyway. Better to move on and move forward right? I had no reason not to, unless you counted that I was still in love with someone else. There was a perfect guy, with the perfect criteria right in front of me, and we were both single. I should at the very least give it a chance. See if maybe something can grow. Make me happy. Six months ago I wouldn't have even had this debate. I would have been giving thanks to the relationship gods and high-fiving my good fortune. Sadly, it wasn't six months ago.

Megs was trying to be supportive, but her lack of encouragement told me otherwise. She hadn't spoken about Dan or suggested I call him, but I think deep down she thought we'd get back together. We weren't though, so sitting around and avoiding men didn't make sense. Even if things didn't work out with Rob, at least it would get me back in the game.

"So where's he taking you?" Megs sat on the edge of my tub and watched me get ready.

"A play. Off Broadway." I applied a layer of mascara. I was supposed to be excited. Why wasn't I excited?

"Wow. Could he be any more pretentious? Off Broadway? Why doesn't he just take you to a jazz club and call it a day." She yawned. She wasn't tired, and I knew sarcasm when I saw it.

"Megs, give him a chance. He's a nice guy." I moved the mascara wand to the other eye. I wonder if he's going to try and kiss me. I really hope he doesn't.

HIGH STRUNG

"Nice and boring. Come on, Ash. You don't even like productions." Megs's support had come to an impasse.

I wasn't sure if she was anti-Rob, or if she'd have reservations about anyone I would be dating. Strangely, I would have assumed she would have welcomed this. A return to my old self now my course had been corrected.

"Well if I recall, it was you who said I should try new things. This is new. Besides, it's what grown-ups do. He's exactly the kind of guy I should be with."

"Ash, he's the perfect guy, except that he is all wrong for you." Megs took my face in her hands. Forcing me to stop applying another layer of mascara. Probably just as well. I didn't want to look like a hooker.

"He won't make me cry." This was the only reason I could offer.

"Ash," she wrapped her arms around me, "I love you." She hugged me closer and I tried not to get emotional because a, we had talked about me *not* crying and, b, I had just applied mascara.

"I'm going to go to this boring-ass play, and I'm going to learn to like it. There are worse things in life."

I think we both knew I was no longer talking about the play. I was happily resigned. Accepting that while I had gone slightly off the rails, I was done with that chapter. The one where I made out with guys I barely knew in nightclubs, and let them hold me all night, the one where I got into relationships I didn't understand and had crazy unrestrained sex, and the one where I fell in love with a larger-than-life rock star, who turned my world upside down. Yes, done with that.

27

Dan

"DAN."

Troy yelled over the noise, as I passed the waitress another fifty. She'd been a sweetheart and kept our glasses full. Not that I'd been doing much drinking tonight. I was still nursing the same Jack and Coke I had palmed an hour ago.

"What's up?" I handed him a fresh beer as he closed the gap between us.

"How long we going to keep doing this?" He took a swig of his long neck.

"What you mean? This is what we do." I was wondering if the music wasn't fucking with his head. The DJ was spinning this bullshit techno shit, and it was making me seriously angry. I could understand the big guy wanting to bail.

"Dan, you want to feed yourself those bullshit lines 'cause it makes you feel better, go right ahead, but this is *not* what we do. We haven't done this shit in a long time." Oh, we were back to that again.

The asshole was trying to get his Dr. Phil on, and start dissecting the whys or the whats. What he didn't understand is right now, I had a huge case of the I-don't-cares, and just wanted to feel good. I wanted to feel something, even though I knew it wouldn't be a hundredth of what I had with Ashlyn.

"Fuck, Troy. Stop being a whiny bitch already. You want to go home, go home. No one is keeping you here, but I'm staying and getting laid."

Or so was the plan, not sure my balls had got the memo though. It seemed I'd had the ghost of limp-dick past wave its wand over my crotch and no amount of tits or ass was getting me hard. Even jerking off had become a chore. I wasn't entirely sure I wasn't permanently fucked up. I should've probably been more worried about it, and yet, I couldn't find the motivation to give two fucks. Pun entirely intended.

"Like last night? Or the night before? Or what about the night before that? Those times all good for you? Funny, 'cause my recollection is you ending up going home alone." Fucking Troy pointing out the obvious.

Maybe we *had* been beating this dead horse, a little too much. We'd been out every night since Tuesday. Different clubs, different parts of town. The end result always the same.

"I'm just biding my time. Just waiting for the right girl." More like trying to forget her.

"Well then, you are in the wrong place, 'cause the right girl is in a piece-of-shit apartment in Brooklyn, not trying to score in some shady club." Troy had to go there and state the fucking obvious. Again. It wasn't enough how much it killed me to try and forget her, like that was even a possibility, but he had to fucking bring her up too. Throw a bit more salt in the fucking wound. 'Cause I got to tell you, it hurt plenty without the reminder.

"You really going to come at me with that? What the fuck, dude? She doesn't want me. It's finished. Done. Don't be playing like I didn't fucking try."

If she had even given me the slightest hint of a chance, I would have toughed it out. But all I seemed to do was make her cry, and she made it clear she wanted nothing to do with me. Short of embracing my new stalker status, and getting cozy with an orange jump suit, I had no choice but to let it go.

"Dan, seriously, what are we doing here? We both know if you wanted to fuck someone, you would have done it already. This shit was never my scene, so you can't be telling me this is for my benefit."

"I don't know what I'm doing, but I have to do something. Something that will hopefully get me back to where I don't feel like beating the living shit out of everything, and everyone. This is what I know. This is what I should be doing."

I couldn't think of anything else to do. At least nothing that made sense.

"So do it. If you think that going back to what you were doing before is going to make shit all fine and dandy, then why are you sitting around with me, drinking watered down bourbon and Coke, instead of getting your dick sucked. You like redheads right, there's one right over there." Troy pointed to a chick that'd been trying to catch our attention all night. She'd been pushing up her tits and playing with her hair for hours. Her efforts wasted. I almost felt sorry for her.

"Watch it, Troy. I'm giving you a pass right now on account you've gone above and beyond for me in the last couple of weeks, but don't think that if you keep running your mouth, that you and me ain't going to have problems." I stood up and got in his face. The fucking reality of the situation at breaking point.

Troy didn't back down, instead meeting me toe to toe.

"You wanna take a swing at me, brother, be my fucking guest. At least it's a fucking reaction. Something. You've been on the cruise control for too long. I'll take you mad any day of the week, rather than indifferent."

"Troy, I know what you are doing, and you know I love you for it. But I'm fine."

HIGH STRUNG

"Fine you say?" He eyeballed me hard. "You still have her number?"

"Nope. Deleted it." I tipped my chin toward him. I had deleted it, a safeguard to stop me from trying to call her. Only issue was, I'd dialed the number so many times the digits were permanently burned into my brain.

"How many times you drive by her place?" He tilted his head, testing me.

"I don't, she could have moved, and I wouldn't know." Well if she'd moved anytime *after* Monday, then I'd have been oblivious. Just another reason for our repetitive, late night excursions, it stopped me from getting my car, and cruising by her neighborhood.

I know all this shit was making me sound like a contender for creeper of the year, but I was worried that she was going to throw in the towel at JenCorp, and go back to the bar. While I couldn't give a rat's ass where she worked as long as she was happy, the thought of her coming home late at night, by herself, was enough of an incentive for me to get familiar with her nocturnal activities. Thank fucking Christ, she liked her job more than she hated me. I figured if she hadn't left by now, she probably wasn't going to, so I relaxed the after-dark tail.

"So you don't know anything?" Troy gave me a cocky look, like he knew something that maybe I should.

"What should I fucking know, Troy?" I looked him dead in the eye, this wasn't playtime, and if she is in any kind of danger or trouble, I didn't give a fuck what promises I'd made about staying clear of her. All bets were off.

"Just thought it was interesting that she'd recently start seeing someone, and you hadn't mentioned it."

It's like someone pulled the fucking pin on a grenade. Even though I hadn't been drunk, I was immediately sober, my reflexes razor sharp. I couldn't even hear the music anymore, the backdrop of the club completely off my grid.

"How recently?"

"Two days ago. I have it on a good authority that your girl is fucking miserable. And about to make a mistake with an asshole, 'cause for some messed-up reason, she doesn't think she has a choice."

Seemed like pretty specific intel for a dude who played drums for a fucking rock band. So, unless Troy had been moonlighting as the new *Gossip Girl* of the Upper East Side, he had been swapping late night whispers with one Megan Winters.

"You've been talking to Megs?" The fucking smile on his face was enough of a yes. "Please tell me it's not that motherfucker she works with."

"Bingo. Give the boy a prize."

"Troy, don't fuck with me. What did Megs say, and do not paraphrase for my benefit. I want you to be real clear about it."

My heartbeat had jazzed up to double what it had been clocking before. The thought of Ash unhappy made the blood ring in my ears.

"She's given up, Dan. Lost the fight in her. Decided she'll settle for mediocre, and that douchebag she's dating, she doesn't even like him let alone love him."

That's all I needed to hear. Shit was already in motion, and I couldn't stop it if I tried. "You know where she is?"

"I do, but before I give you that information I need to know what you plan on doing with it."

I fished my phone out of my pocket and texted TJ to bring the car around. We were out of here.

"There's no plan about it. I love her and I'm getting her back."

28
Ashlyn

"I'M REALLY GLAD YOU SAID YES." ROB GAVE ME A SATIS-fied smile and gentle hug as he walked me to his car.

Megs had given him the stare down at the door, not even pretending to try and like him and given me the eye roll when he showed up with a single red rose. It was cliché and maybe a little boring but still sweet nonetheless.

I nodded, not able to think of anything to say in response. *"I'm really glad I said yes, too,"* wasn't coming out of my mouth. I was with him and I was smiling and that was about as *glad* as I was going to get tonight. Though I really hoped this production we were heading to didn't bore me to tears. I never did fake enthusiasm well.

"This is me." The lights flashed on a navy Chevrolet Impala. It had just been cleaned. The fact I noticed shiny chrome on the car, but couldn't tell you what my date was wearing was already a red flag. Damn Dan Evans. No man would ever compare.

"Great." My smile tightened as I mentally kicked my own ass. I'd gone exactly ten minutes without thinking about my ex-boyfriend. We were already off to such a stellar start.

Rob opened the car door and I ducked inside, trying to calculate how many dates it would take to convince myself this was fun. Maybe I need to reward myself with chocolate, build up some learned psychological response. Go on a date with Rob, treat myself a box of Godiva. My mood improved just thinking about the promise of the gold box, so maybe it was a viable option.

The drive was quiet and slightly awkward. He didn't seem nervous at all, which annoyed me a little. He didn't have to be so cocky. I hadn't agreed to sleep with him yet, and that sure as hell wouldn't be happening tonight.

"Are you hungry? We can grab a bite to eat before the show."

"Sure."

What I meant to say was, no, I've changed my mind. I don't think this is going to work out, so let's get me that box of chocolate and I'll get back to my solitude. Maybe I could wait until intermission, and fake a headache. That was about as cliché as the rose he'd brought me, but I figured we were reading from the same playbook, so not entirely unexpected. I still got chocolate though, right? Half dates most definitely counted.

Dinner didn't yield any surprises. A quaint little café near the theater. Trendy and overpriced. Nuevo French cuisine. It helped me learn about myself that I really didn't like French food. Who knew? Well at least the date hadn't been a total loss - the lesson in self-discovery and the promise of Godiva rewards.

The conversation was just as contrived as the meal I hadn't been able to finish. Rob asked about college, family, and my hometown, but it felt more like a survey than actual interest. I reciprocated, even nodded and smiled in all the right places. Proof the performance had started well and truly before the scheduled show. I was so fucking bored.

A short walk later and we were standing in front of a small playhouse theater, and I was looking for a sharp object I could stab myself with. Even the allure of Godiva wasn't cutting it. My planned headache

HIGH STRUNG

replaced by a mid-performance bathroom dash, where I'd-obviously-eaten-something-bad-and-needed-to-go-home. It's not like it couldn't happen. People got food poisoning all the time.

Rob put his arm around my waist as he walked through the doorway and suddenly the idea of being sick wasn't so much of a hypothetical. My stomach gurgled uncomfortably. There was a lot to be said for psychosomatic. Megs could totally do a case study on me.

"Hey, babe, I think you're lost," a voice whispered into my ear. "Unless you are looking for douchebags, and then you've totally come to the right place."

"Dan?" I turned around to see him standing behind me.

He looked good. A little more tired than usual, like maybe he hadn't sleep, but other than that, he was perfect. He was wearing a pair of jeans, heavy boots and Black Flag T-shirt, his inked arms on display. My mind barely registered the fact he wasn't wearing a jacket. I was too overwhelmed to be standing before him. He didn't even flinch at the attention he was attracting, not sure if it was because he looked out of place, or if the crowd had guessed who he was. He didn't even acknowledge them as he moved in closer, getting so close to me I could feel my skin tingle. My stomach doing some Olympic-inspired flip as he refused to take his eyes off me.

"Listen, Dan. Let's not make scene." Rob tried to step in. *Oh, he was still here?* "Ashlyn doesn't need the drama right now. Why don't you give her some space?"

"See, hearing stuff like that convinces me even more what an asshole you are." Dan turned to Rob. "You know nothing about her, and you know even less about what she needs. So how about you don't embarrass yourself any further, and you let me make shit right with my girl."

Hearing him call me *his girl* knocked the air right out of my lungs. I wanted to be mad at him. I wanted to yell at him and tell how much he hurt me. But I also wanted to wrap myself around him, and lose myself in his kisses, until nothing else existed. If it was a vote, the last option was most definitely winning.

"Dan." I found that I could actually open my mouth, and words showed up to the party.

"I'm not..." There was no way I could finish that sentence, not convincingly anyway. "Maybe we..." Nope, that wasn't going to work either. "What are you doing here?"

"Doing what I should have done weeks ago." He threaded his arm around my waist, pulling me closer, and my body of its own volition moved against him. It was like I had no control of it. I wanted to stop but I just couldn't. It. Felt. So. Good. We ignored the crowd and moved outside the theater. I left Rob open-mouthed and red-faced in the lobby. A better person would have been more concerned about him—my date—but I wasn't that person. Not today.

I followed Dan silently into the alley that separated the old brick buildings. I thought if I spoke this would evaporate, so I kept my mouth shut, needing to see where he would lead me. The Suburban's flashing lights marked the end of the alley. Troy was leaning against the doorframe of the truck until he saw us, and then he disappeared into the dark cabin, leaving us relatively alone.

"I'm sorry, Ashlyn. I'm sorry I was an asshole, and I didn't tell you the whole truth. I should never have kept shit from you. You deserved better than that but I don't regret helping you. I don't regret giving you an opportunity to be happy, even if it meant I would lose you."

"Dan—"

I wanted to speak but I wasn't sure what I wanted to say. Whether I would ask him to keep going or ask him to stop. But he took that choice out of my hands.

"No, wait. Let me get this out." He held his hand gently over my mouth. "You don't want to be with me, I'll hate it but I'll accept it. What I won't fucking accept is you settling for anything less than perfect. Being with *him* 'cause you think you should, 'cause it conforms to this idea in your head, this plan? It's bullshit and I won't let you do it yourself."

"Dan—"

HIGH STRUNG

"Ash, I'm not done." He cradled my face with his hands. "I don't deserve you. I never did. I've fucked a lot of women, some I didn't even know their names. It was something to do, a distraction, and I never really thought about the consequences. I can't change what I did, or who I was back then, but I can only tell you that now, that man no longer exists. I never thought in a million years I'd meet someone whom I wanted to be with forever, so I never cared enough about what I was bringing to the table. I never cared enough to stop myself from giving it away. There's only one piece of me that all those girls I've slept with have never had. And that's my heart. Only you, and whatever happens now, that shit is not going to change. I know I can't quit loving you even if I tried. I've been trying, and I'm not even close to being able to stop.

"I love you. I am in love with you, and I'm going to love you until the end of time. We're not done. We'll never be done. There isn't anything in this world that will convince me otherwise, and I'll do whatever I need to do to make this right. 'Cause now that I've got you in my arms, I ain't never letting you go."

He brushed his finger gently along my jaw. Being that close to him, having him touch me, and to be intoxicated by his delicious scent, it overwhelmed me. I knew I was fighting a losing battle, my body had stopped fighting the minute I had heard his sexy voice. Looking into his beautiful eyes, seeing how much this had hurt him and how much he still loved me, tore away at any of my remaining defenses.

"Shut up and kiss me already." I had barely got the words out before he sealed my lips with his. The world fell away beneath me. Nothing else existed. Just us in that perfect moment where the man I couldn't live without, couldn't live without me. And I loved him. So much. So whatever we needed to work through, we would get past, because being apart wasn't an option. We'd tried it. We both failed. We belonged together.

I had spent my life up until this point planning for perfection, avoiding the extraordinary, and playing it safe. I thought it would make me happy and give me a good life. What I couldn't have planned for, was meeting a man who was so exceptional it would redefine my expectations.

Life isn't about the perfect plan. It's about the perfect storm that engulfs you when you're busy living it.

ACKNOWLEDGEMENTS

THE THANK YOU PART IS ALWAYS THE HARDEST BECAUSE I'm always worried I'm going to leave someone out. I am lucky to be surrounded by an amazing support team, one that makes all of this worthwhile. There aren't enough words to express my gratitude. I love you fiercely, and without limits, and here is my humble attempt in acknowledging how you changed my world.

To **Gep**, **Jenna**, **Liam** and **Woodley** - I could never overstate how much you mean to me. Thank you for allowing me to follow my dream, and sticking with me while I jump off the cliff into the unknown. I'm nothing without my wolf pack.

To my amazing friends who keep me laughing, listen to my crazy rants, humor my insane ideas and who love me unconditionally. **Sam**, **Mini**, **Juzzie**, **Golf**, **Nat**, **Shell**, **Kylie**, **Jo**, **Grace**, **Bec** and **Kirsty** – you are the best cheerleaders ever, a million thanks.

To my outstanding Beta readers who read my raw work, laugh at my typos, and give me valuable feedback. **Sam**, **Kelly** and **Amy**. Nipples could have still worked in place of Nibbles - as Dan would say, it's all in the telling. It is without a doubt that you made this a better book. Thank you x

Thank you to the amazing authors who have welcomed me into their world, or more accurately, just not ejected me when I crashed in, uninvited. **KM Golland, TJ Hamilton, JB Hartnett, Rachel Brookes, Lili Saint Germain, Lilliana Anderson, CJ Duggan, Skyla Madi, JD Nixon, Kylie Scott, Joanna Wylde** and **Kim Karr**. I believe I owe few of you pie, feel free to collect anytime. Thank you for supporting me and accepting me into the sisterhood. You are all stuck with me now. *insert maniacal laugh here*

Thank you to the amazing **Hang Le**, who makes scorching hot teasers and design pretties for me. You nail it each and every time.

Thank you my brother **Gian** for his repeated design prowess on my covers. You are the man. I'm so glad you decided to become a designer instead of a chef, although those almond biscotti were pretty bad-ass.

Thank you to **Angelique Ehlers** for cover photography.

Thank you to the bloggers and blogs who have supported me and continue to support me. **Helen S**- Kinky Book Klub, **Kelly O**- Kelly's Kindle Konfessions, **Marie M**- Surrender to Books, **Jodie O**- Fab Fun and Tantalizing Reads, **Rebecca** and **Nicole** – Author Groupies, **Tammy M**- A Slice of Fiction, The Book Nuts and The SubClub, **Francessca W** – Francessca's Romance Reviews, **Rose** and **Tash** (even though Tash is gone) Forever Me Romance, **Mel L**– Sassy Mum book Blog, **Debbie O**- Hard Rock Romance, **Tash D**- Book Lit Love, **Stephanie G** – The Lemon Review, **Kristine B**- Glass Paper Ink Bookblog, **Karen H**- A Thousand Lives Book Blog, and sorry to anyone I have forgotten. I love you all.

Thank you to my outstanding **T Gephart Entourage** girls. I love your enthusiasm, naughty pictures and fights over my characters. If ever I'm having a down day, our little group is the perfect shot I need.

Thanks to the Fictionally Yours, Melbourne 2015 crew- **Penny**, **Mel** and **Simone**. #WordWizard

Thank you to my editor, **Marion Archer**, for making sure my manuscript is perfect. I'm not the easiest person to edit and I appreciate your effort and patience even if you kill my five hundred exclamation marks!!!!!!!!!!!! (← Here are some of their grieving cousins.) PS. I used brackets as well.

Thank you to **Max Henry** from Max Effect for formatting and making my pages beautiful.

Lastly, thank you to the readers who have welcomed my words and characters into their lives and into their imagination. Your love for these guys floors me, each and every time. I love meeting and interacting with you and I will never take you for granted. Thank you so much. In my book, you are all rock stars!

ABOUT THE AUTHOR

T GEPHART is an indie author from Melbourne, Australia.

T's approach to life has been somewhat unconventional. Rather than going to University, she jumped on a plane to Los Angeles, USA in search of adventure. While this first trip left her somewhat underwhelmed and largely depleted of funds it fueled her appetite for travel and life experience.

With a rather eclectic resume, which reads more like the fiction she writes than an actual employment history, T struggled to find her niche in the world.

While on a subsequent trip the United States in 1999, T met and married her husband. Their whirlwind courtship and interesting impromptu convenience store wedding set the tone for their life together, which is anything but ordinary. They have lived in Louisiana, Guam and Australia and have traveled extensively throughout the US. T has two beautiful young children and one four legged child, Woodley, the wonder dog.

An avid reader, T became increasingly frustrated by the lack of strong female characters in the books she was reading. She wanted to read about a woman she could identify with, someone strong, independent and confident and who didn't lack femininity. Out of this need, she decided to pen her first book, A Twist of Fate. T set herself the challenge to write something that was interesting, compelling and yet easy enough to read that was still enjoyable. Pulling from her own past "colorful" experiences and the amazing personalities she has surrounded herself with, she had no shortage of inspiration. With a strong slant on erotic fiction, her core characters are empowered women who don't have to sacrifice their femininity. She enjoyed the process so much that when it was over she couldn't let it go.

T loves to travel, laugh and surround herself with colorful characters.

This inevitably spills into her writing and makes for an interesting journey - she is well and truly enjoying the ride!

Based on her life experiences, T has plenty of material for her books and has a wealth of ideas to keep you all enthralled.

CONNECT WITH T

Webpage
http://tgephart.com/bio/4579459512

Facebook
https://www.facebook.com/pages/T-Gephart/412456528830732

Goodreads
https://www.goodreads.com/author/show/7243737.T_Gephart

Twitter
@tinagephart

BOOKS BY THIS AUTHOR

THE LEXI SERIES
Lexi
A Twist of Fate
Twisted Views: Fate's Companion
A Leap of Faith
A Time for Hope

THE POWER STATION SERIES
High Strung
Crash Ride (Coming Soon)
Back Stage (2015)

Made in the USA
Charleston, SC
31 May 2016